KT-198-289

04572178

An Unravelling

An Unravelling

Elske Rahill

LILLIPUT

First published in the UK in 2019 by Head of Zeus Ltd

9 7 5 3 1 2 4 6 8

A catalogue record for this book is available from the British Library.

ISBN (HB): 9781786691002
ISBN (XTPB): 9781786691019
ISBN (E): 9781786690999

Typeset by Adrian McLaughlin

Printed and bound in Great Britain by
CPI Group (UK) Ltd, Croydon CR0 4YY

Head of Zeus Ltd
First Floor East
5–8 Hardwick Street
London EC1R 4RG

WWW.HEADOFZEUS.COM

For Bomama

PART 1

1

UP HERE THE AIR is weighted with the mulchy tang of slow-drying laundry.

With careful steps – the baby is sleeping in the room below – Cara moves across the low-ceilinged attic and sets the cafetière on the floor by her desk. It's an architect's desk; a wide thing of hollow metal, its drafting board covered in a faint grid. The desk was designed to support clean, calculated marks, but she has defied it with clusters of stones, leaves, shells, photographs of tiny animals enlarged to grotesque detail.

She lifts the sheet off yesterday's work and positions her pages in sequence – the burrow scene with its filigree of roots, then the rabbit emerging into the moonlit undergrowth... Oh but, no. No. The ears are wrong, and the whiskers too. How did she go on working yesterday without seeing it?

The morning brims up at the rain-sprinkled skylight, turning shapes of freckled white across her drawings, a sudden heat on her face. It's later than she thought. The kids will be up soon. She pulls down the blind and switches on the lamp, filling the space with merciless light.

She gathers the three pages into a pile, spreads them out again and squeezes her eyes shut before looking at them afresh – all wrong. Page after page, the rabbit's ears are cutesy, limp things; the idea of a bunny and nothing rabbit about it at all. She thought she was on a roll yesterday, but she was just being sloppy. She's even committed one of them to ink. Stupid girl. She'll have to scrap it all and start again.

Coffee first. Squatting by the cafetière she presses too hurriedly on the plunger, sending a quick little splurt out the spout, and peers under the desk for something to drink from. She has allowed the mugs to collect again – mugs and jam jars and ceramic yoghurt pots, silt rings glazed into their floors. Pat is right; they'd have enough mugs if she just kept on top of the housework. She selects the cleanest one – a tin camping mug bought on honeymoon in Italy – and returns to the desk for sugar. She keeps a stock of it beside her ink pots – chunks of blonde crystals filling a small cork jug that once belonged to her grandad.

She pops a piece into the mug and pours, uses the wrong end of a paintbrush to stir.

She blows at the coffee, and sips – the relief of caffeine, calories, heat; a promise that this headache will lift.

Look at that mawkish snout! It's like a greeting card. She will have to rethink this project. Dürer's *Young Hare* – she needs to go back to that; that life inside the stillness, the distillation of a moment. Her grandfather had the print hanging in his studio. A reminder, he said, not to get lost in the page, to stay with the subject. It was the ears she liked best –

cool envelopes of sound and each fleck of fur alive to the passing light.

With a pen from her dressing-gown pocket she blacks over yesterday's ears. She marks the hump where they should sprout from the narrow skull; a sensitive spot, maybe, for a rabbit. Whiskers too – she makes thick sweeps above the eyes and muzzle. It will all be in the whiskers and the ears – that's where Little Luke Rabbit's personality will lie. The ruined page can be her guide. There must be no stasis; no overworking; just action – trembling, bristling, swivelling, sniffing—

Cara's pen stops. She listens – the ugly clacking of magpies far down the garden, the groan of the boiler rumbling through the house, but there's someone here. Her daughter – Cara can feel it on her skin and down into her glands – the animal signals of her child; a softening of the muscles, warmth surging to her breasts. Megan is there at the foot of the stairs, her breath moistening the air. Then the whine:

'Mammeeeya?'

Cara holds her breath. There is a chance Megan will give up and go in search of breakfast.

The child lurches up the steps on all fours, hands slap slapping, the thud of one slippered foot, the drag of the other.

'Mammmeeeeya? Maaaaaa – meeeeeee!'

'Mammy's working, darling.'

'Mammeeya no but Mammy don't work. I want you.'

'Go and cuddle Daddy. Say good morning to Daddy, baby. Tell him your mammy is working.'

'But Mammy no I want you. I want to give you a twiss.'

'Come and give me a quick kiss then, Megan.'

When she reaches the top the child scuttles speedily at her, clambers onto her knee, face alight with a victorious grin.

'Good morning, Megan my lovely.'

'My mammy.'

Megan's cheeks are very red, her nosetip glazed with dried snot. Cara touches her mouth to the dark, sweat-slicked hair, nuzzles in behind her daughter's ear, cheek pressed to burning cheek; breathing her in.

'Dood mowning Mammy.' Megan raises her chin to receive the kisses, nosing her mother like a purring cat. She draws back and plants a sticky palm on either side of Cara's face, kissing one cheek, then the other, then her nose; puts her face into her mother's throat, a hand under the lapel of her robe, and sighs. Cara lifts Megan's hand away from her breast, and kisses her fingers. She puts the lid on her pen, pulls the sheet back over her work.

'Are your sisters awake?'

Megan nods against her chest. 'DenDen is be doing Lego.'

'Baby Peggy?'

'Nope. Baby Peggy is being in her cot. Her be sleeping maybe.' She shakes her head, and adds an exaggerated, studied shrug – hands turned out, one shoulder hitched to her ear, mouth twisting, nose wrinkled. The idea of maybe is new to her. 'Maybe,' she says again, holding the pose, 'Baby Peggy be sleeping *maybe*.' Then, as an afterthought, 'Or needs a feed maybe. Boobies.'

The little fingers slip in under her robe again; cold. Cara pulls

Megan's hand out and makes a pocket around it with both of her palms, blows on it.

'Where's your dressing gown? Is Daddy up?'

'I hate Daddy.'

'You don't hate Daddy.'

'Do.'

'Come on, I need you to help me find something quickly. Then we'll have some breakfast.'

'You smell horwible, Mammy. You need to wash you.'

'Come on, off you get. Help me. We need to find a picture of a bunny rabbit. It's somewhere in here, I think. So, I'm going to lift down the books one by one and you keep looking and when you see a picture of a bunny you say *BUNNY!* Okay?'

There's a stack of mess against the wall – old specs from projects that never happened, her grandfather's illustrated encyclopaedias with strips of paper and twists of yarn stuck in as bookmarks. The hare is in there somewhere, crouched in one of the books, staring with that mute blend of disgruntlement and terror at the blank weight of leather-bound volumes.

Megan hooks her arms around her mother's neck. Cara can feel the saliva on her breath. 'Otay. But Mammy... Hello?'

'Okay but Megan hello.'

'I'm hungry.'

'You're hungry.'

'Yep and my froat hurts.'

'Your throat hurts?'

'Yep.'

The bang of the front door sends a gentle rattle up through the house, and Grandma's voice whoops from the hallway – 'Cooookoooo! Lazy girls!'

'Mimi, Mimi Mimi!' Megan jiggles on her mother's lap and leans back, pulling with all her weight.

'Ouch, Megan! Gentle, baby, stop hanging out of me.'

It's with a mixture of relief and rage that Cara carries the child down the attic steps – she'll have to start this project all over again. Today was a write-off from the start. Dribs and drabs are no good – it will take a few hours just to get on track. It will have to be Monday, when the girls are at Montessori…

'Mammy?' Megan's fingers are on Cara's chin now, her lips up close enough to speak into her nose. She whispers, 'Mammy tell Mimi I am hungry otay?' and nods for confirmation, her eyes open round.

Cara inhales her daughter's stewy breath. 'Okay, my love.'

'And tell her I have a sore froat.'

'Yes, okay, I'll tell her. You go on down, Megan.' She lowers the child onto the landing carpet, prying the arms from her neck.

'I'm just going to wash my face.'

'Caaaaara!'

'Coming, Grandma! Just a second.'

Cara soaps her cheeks quickly, swishes mouthwash around her teeth.

Her grandmother has set a big wicker basket on the kitchen table. Megan is jumping up and down like an excited pup.

'Mimi Mimi Mimi, I'm hungry!'

'Poor chicken, has your mammy been neglecting you?'

Cara kisses her grandmother on the cheek. 'Hi, Grandma.'

'Well Cara, wouldn't you be ashamed! Are you not dressed, darling? And what a day! It rained last night and, oh this morning when I went out to feed the birds I looked at the grass there, bright wet and I thought, you know Cara, what could be more beautiful than a sunny morning after a night of rain? Well, and the birds came—'

'Mimi I have a sore froat. Tell her, Mammy!'

'She's fine.'

Megan frowns at this betrayal, a ferocious bulldog frown, black brows eclipsing her wolf-pale eyes, fists bunched tight at her sides.

'She has a bit of a sore throat...'

Grandma cups Megan's head and gestures towards the kitchen table, where Cara's eldest is kneeling, hands on her knees, peering into the basket.

'Denise opened the door all by herself!'

Denise nods. 'I got a chair.'

'Well,' says Cara, smiling guiltily at her eldest daughter – how long has she been down here all by herself, no slippers on her feet? – 'she's a big girl now, aren't you, Denise?'

'Yep. I'm *so* much. Mimi, guess what number I am?'

'How old are you, darling? Let me think… two, is it?'

Denise shakes her head, a broad, lipless smile pulling a variety of dimples up into her cheeks.

'Oh. Okay, I know – three?'

The child scooches to the edge of the table and stands upright on the wobbly kitchen bench. She is pot-bellied, her knuckle chin plumping into her neck and a ruff of softer chins beneath. Some trick of genetics has given Denise her Aunt Freya's white-blonde fuzz for hair and a complexion that can range from rose-white to the colour of crushed berries in a matter of seconds. Now her cheeks flush fever-pink with pride, and she pushes a splayed hand up at her great-grandmother.

'This much, Mimi. Five.'

'Five? Well Janey Mack, Dennie, aren't you a great big girl?'

Grandma removes her coat. She is wearing her summer blouse; shoulder pads, short sleeves, yellow flowers on swathes of blues and flecks of green. She hands her coat to Cara and works hurriedly at the headscarf knotted beneath her chin. Even on a sunny day like today, she won't leave the house without a scarf over her head to protect her perm from the wind.

'Well now my little waifs, your great old grandma has brought you pancakes. She's still of some use after all!'

Lifting a foil-covered plate from the basket, she looks at Cara and nods towards the hallway.

'Your sister is just changing for work. She needs you to mind Jem.'

'What? Why?'

'She's working all day. Poor chicken. She has three gigs, one after the other. Get the tea on, Cara, good girl. She's in a rush.'

While Cara fills the kettle, her sister Freya jangles into the kitchen, dressed up as a genie in billowing indigo-coloured pants, a gold-sequined waistcoat and many cheap bracelets. Her hair flops at the top of her head in a great flossy mess. There is a clatter of foil coins strung across her forehead, giving an exotic look to her wide, sleepy eyes. Her five-year-old son, Jem, is holding her hand.

'There he is, my darling boy!' says Grandma.

'You don't mind if Jem stays here for a bit Cara, do you?' says Freya, kissing her cheek. 'I have three gigs today, and it's too much for Grandma.'

'Yeah, fine.' Cara hunkers down to Jem. 'What do you think, Jem? The girls are making a birdhouse, are you going to help?'

He gives a small smile, then looks up at his mother for sanction. Freya nods. 'That sounds fun doesn't it? Cara, is the kettle on?'

'Yep.'

'I'll have a quick cup and then I better go.'

Grandma peels the aluminium off a stack of pancakes, releasing the buttery swelter, and steadily unpacks an ice-cream tub of lemon wedges, a jam jar of demerara sugar, a pint of squeezed oranges in a glass passata bottle – on its label three tomatoes, washed yellow.

'No pancakes for Megan,' says Cara, 'she's allergic.'

Grandma rolls her eyes. 'Allergic,' she says. 'Poor chicken, doesn't your mammy talk such nonsense? What could be healthier than an egg? Get me some plates and glasses, will you, Cara? Jem helped to squeeze the oranges – didn't you, my little man? For his cousins.'

Jem nods delightedly, climbs onto the bench and waits for his breakfast, hands on his lap, legs swinging, mild little smile and great brown bush-baby eyes. A yellow light filters in through the wide kitchen window behind him, dances along the contours of his cheek, catching on the tiny hairs and illuminating the tips of his ears.

Grandma nods at Jem – 'Such a blessing, that child' – before turning to the little girl at her knees.

'Now, Megan, you can have bread if your mammy is going to be funny about the pancakes. I made some nice soda bread just for you. It might sting your throat a bit, chicken, but drink up some juice and you'll be all better in no time. They are lovely ripe oranges. I got them from a lady on Moore Street – a whole box so ripe you could smell them from the other end of the street.'

Cara watches the sun on her nephew's face – the different colours it makes of the gristly little ears, the padded curve of his jaw. She stroked a rabbit once – a friend from school had one. It shrank down, trembling. When she moved a hand over it, the fur shifted a little, loose over the tight muscle and bone. Its head and body were warm, but she can remember the alarming cold at the tips of its ears. If the sun shone from behind Little Luke Rabbit, it would make the fibrous streaks of his ears wine-red and turn the veins to snaking black. But not the moonlight. That's what she's been forgetting – how should the moonlight work on his ears and his wet snout?

She lays a pile of plates and a tower of plastic cups on the table. 'Where are you working, Freya?'

'Oh God, I have a birthday party at one o'clock and then a christening – both for Southside mummies. Then a nine-year-old's birthday… Oh, before I forget, I need to plug in the phone…'

'So you'll be back around what – seven?'

'Around that, yeah.'

Grandma is busy pouring orange juice and rolling pancakes. 'There's soda bread in the basket,' she says, 'and I brought chicken broth for your tea, Cara – go and get it out of the boot. Freya will help you.'

It takes both of them to carry in the huge pot; the gelatinous heave of cold bone broth. 'There's two chickens-worth in that,' says Grandma, as they lower it unsteadily onto the table, a quiet gloop as it settles. Freya stands for a minute with her fingertips touching the table edge. She looks at Cara, and then at her feet – gold-glittered pumps over hot-pink tights.

'What is it, Freya?'

'Cara, can I borrow your car actually?'

'What's wrong with your car?'

Freya won't meet her eye. She has made a beautiful job of the 'magical genie' makeup: turquoise eye-shadow shimmering on her big lids and tiny sequins twinkling along her cheekbones. 'I don't know, it was pissing petrol out the bottom – I had to leave it at the garage. It needs a new part.'

'Freya, that means I can't take them to the park or anything…'

Freya glances quickly at their grandmother, who is slicing Denise's pancake into bite-size swirls, pretending not to listen.

'Oh come on you weren't going to take them to the park. They can run around the garden. Or, the other thing we could do is you drop Grandma home and I could take her car?'

'Grandma needs her car. It's fine.'

'So you don't mind?'

'It's fine, take the car.'

Thick-knuckled hands curled around the arms of the big kitchen chair, lips pursed: Grandma surveys her granddaughters.

'Well, don't you look a funny one, Cara? Why aren't you dressed darling? What does your husband think of all this?'

Cara bends her hands around the mug. The tea tastes wrong after the mouthwash.

'He's asleep.'

'You'll keep him some pancakes, won't you? A man like that, working hard all week. They need to feel looked after, darling, you know.'

'I look after him, Grandma. He's asleep. I'm up. I'm up with the kids. I was hoping to get some work done this morning—'

'Pass me my handbag, Freya.'

Freya's jewellery tinkles as she scrambles under the bench and pulls up a heavy leather handbag, navy with silver buckles and a plaited handle, and passes it to Grandma. Grandma sets the bag on her lap. She takes out her glasses and puts them on, then pulls some knitting out – a child's sock. She lifts it by the nest of needles, and arranges the wool on her lap.

'You can put my bag away there, Freya. Zip it up, will you?'

Freya does as she is told. 'I better go,' she says. 'Grandma, I'll be home late – eightish. We'll eat here with Cara. I have a break between gigs, do you want me to do the shop?'

'No darling, you have enough to do. I'll do the shopping. I owe a visit to my deli.'

'K. Right, I better go.'

She kisses Grandma, kneads her shoulder, then kisses her again before turning to her son.

'Bye bye, baby, be good for your Aunty Cara, have fun with your cousins. Bye girls, have a nice day, see you later...'

She wiggles her fingers at Cara. 'Thanks Cara, see you later – oh, can you help me move my stuff actually?'

On the way out the door, she stops – 'Shit, my phone!'

Cara helps her heave a botched polka-dotted suitcase from Grandma's four-by-four into the boot of her own little hatchback.

Grandma is sitting where she left her, but the ball of wool has rolled under the chair, and she is out of breath, picking hurriedly at some dropped stitches with the end of a needle.

'What have you been up to, Grandma?'

Grandma peers up at her playfully. 'Oh, me? Oh no, nothing ma'am!' and winks at the children. The girls clamp their hands over their mouths, but Jem climbs down off the bench and pulls at the cord of Cara's robe.

'What is it, Jem?'

Fist drawn up to his cheek, prodding the air with one finger and his eyebrows bouncing, he points at the sink. It's steaming with soapy water. There is a row of washed plates on the draining board.

'Grandma, don't do the washing up!'

'Oh no, no I won't, ma'am, it's a little robin did that,' says Grandma, biting her cheek and winking again at the girls – Cara's children begin to giggle into their sugar-grubby fingers, but Jem frowns at the lie.

Making an exaggeratedly straight face at Cara, Grandma says, 'You know me. I'm just knitting darling. An old lady knitting.'

As she approaches the table, Cara spots a plastic bag of laundry under Grandma's chair. Grandma regularly steals washloads from the utility room. Then she sends Freya over with a cardboard box of clean clothes – all of it washed and dried and ironed – even the kids' tracksuit bottoms. Torn knees come back expertly patched, moth holes darned. Pretty lingerie is replaced with enormous cotton knickers. Cara makes a mental note not to let Grandma leave with the bag.

'You need a dishwasher, darling.'

'We're grand, Grandma.'

'Be sensible, Cara – there are such wonderful things nowadays. Why don't you have a dishwasher, Cara? Are you short?'

'No, no, Grandma, we're fine.'

'Don't be short, now.'

'No.'

'I got a bank statement yesterday in the door – well, Cara, disgusting amounts of money now, you know, from the estate. I can't take it with me, you know. It's the tax man will be taking it after, so don't be short, darling. Don't be a martyr. You know I can't stand a martyr.'

'No.'

'But how can you have time for it all? You need a dishwasher. You're still doing your scribblings are you?'

'Yes, Grandma.'

Grandma straightens her back, chin tucked into her porridge-loose neck – she has picked up the dropped stitches and hardly glances at her hands now as the yarn spins round and round beneath the double pointed needles.

'Well, ladies!' Pat appears at the door in his boxer shorts and slippers. The sight of him makes a little leap in Cara's belly. His arms and chest are still all brawny contours, but his belly has collapsed into a soft little paunch.

Grandma blushes girlishly. 'Well Pat, you are not very decent!'

'Hi, Molly!' he says. Denise has jumped up onto his hip and he holds her with one arm as he bends to kiss Grandma's cheek. 'I smelled the pancakes. I should have known you'd be behind all this.'

'Get dressed, Pat,' says Molly, 'and your wife will prepare a plate for you.'

Pat kisses Cara's head, pulls her face into his belly and strokes her earlobe between his thumb and forefinger. 'I thought you were working.'

'I tried.'

'Go on up. Go on up now. I can take over here.'

'No, it's fine. It's not going well anyway.'

Grandma wags a needle at her. 'You have to go on, Cara, you

have to go on with that, darling. You have a talent, you know that, don't you? Your grandad always said it – he said, "That little girl has talent."'

'I'm working away, Grandma, I've a commission I'm working on now. A children's book. Lots of rabbits. But it's a little tricky. It hasn't come right yet…'

'Oh, you'll do it, darling, don't you worry. You always had something special, you know – an eye. Oh, it made your grandad laugh – you remember, don't you? That time in the Shelbourne. We were there, the four of us. The Shelbourne is beautiful.' Grandma brings the tip of her thumb and her index finger together, leans forward in her chair and pinches the air. 'Classy,' she says.

Pat throws Cara a closed smile, mouths, 'Getting dressed,' and quietly leaves the room.

'The Shelbourne is classy. There we were, all the waitresses in the most beautiful outfits – clean black dresses and white collars! Well, beautiful. Classy, Cara, classy is the only word for it. Starched like you don't see anymore. It was a red-haired girl with very refined manners brought a beautiful silver pot of cocoa for you and Freya – well, you were delighted with yourselves! Big smiles on you. There you were – sitting there with big smiles. And on the wall there was this painting – the kind of nonsense that people had started going in for at that time – some streaks on a page, you know, as if someone threw the palette at it – and there you were, a little thing of eight "Oh," you said. "That's like something Freya would do!"'

Grandma rests her hands on her lap, rocks her head back

and gives a laugh that makes her lungs sound deep and healthy. 'Well, we laughed and laughed! Because you were right! It was like something a little child would do…'

Cara smiles. This story always makes her uneasy. The day was so nice – the warm hotel with the delicate little tea cups, music playing low, Grandad calm, Grandma smiling and smiling, pink-cheeked. Cara was bewildered when Grandad chuckled so much that his face coloured like a bruise and he began to splutter and thump his sternum. It was a small painting with green and blue against warm white, pink stuttering on the surface. It was like the sort of thing her little sister did with Grandad's leftover paints; and she liked the way the small canvas could shift space and colour, change everything around itself.

Cara puts her hands around the tepid mug of tea.

'Will I make more tea, Grandma? Is your tea cold? Mine is.'

But Grandma's face is suddenly serious, her mouth slack with fear, her voice comes low and spittle-quick: 'Stupid old woman!'

'What's wrong, Grandma?'

Grandma drops the knitting and shakes her head disgustedly, then snatches it up again. 'Stupid goose. Stupid, stupid old eejit.'

'Grandma, what?'

She holds the bundle out to Cara, palms up: 'I forgot the turn. Look at this now… I'll have to pull it all out, right down to the heel flap.'

'Oh – you were distracted.'

'No.' Grandma shakes her head and lowers the knitting into her lap, gives an exasperated sigh. 'No, darling, you don't understand. It was last night I did it Cara. I wasn't distracted. I sat in my chair with the television off – nothing but nonsense on the television – and I worked the garter flap and then didn't I go straight on without turning the heel. I've never done a thing like that before. Not since I was six years old.'

She pulls angrily at the wool, making the sock spiral shorter and shorter; a hill of crimped yarn on her lap.

'Hang on, Grandma, let's wind it up properly—'

At the other end of the table, a cup tumbles to the floor, spewing orange juice as it bounces noisily to a halt.

'Oops. Sorwy Mammy…' Megan's hands fly up to her cheeks. Cara stands to get a cloth, but Grandma fixes her with a stern gaze. 'Sit down.'

She sits. Grandma's eyes are bright with urgency. 'I don't want to be a halfwit, Cara. I don't want to go loop-the-loop, and you all there humouring me.'

'You're not, Grandma – I do stuff like that all the time.'

'Yes, well I don't. I can rely on you, can't I, Cara? If I start to go loolaa you'll give me a tablet won't you? To finish it.'

'Grandma—'

'Now don't tell Freya about the sock, will you?' She holds up a thick, trembling finger, wags it. 'Not a word.'

2

Tongue-point clinging to her upper lip, Molly backs carefully into her driveway. She likes to park with the car's nose facing out. She takes her time. No rush. Checking all the mirrors, though it strains her neck to turn like this; a crunch like ground glass between the tendons.

Pleased with her parking, she turns off the engine, lets down a breath with the sigh of the car, and sits for a moment.

Tired today.

She takes her headscarf from the passenger seat, smooths it into a triangle along its crease, loops it over her head and ties it under her chin. Then she hauls her big handbag onto her lap and feels for her housekeys. The one for the front door has a bit of blue yarn wound around the top. It was Dinny's idea to do that. No more fussing to find the right key. She points it snugly between thumb and forefinger, then zips her handbag closed and opens the car door, easing herself around carefully, slowly – no rush – shuffling on her behind.

The neighbours had a dog that used to wipe its bottom on the carpet, pulling itself along. Disgusting.

She steps down from the car – one foot, then the other. No

rush. Her home: the friendly diamonds of the leaded window-panes, the shaggy pelt of ivy over its brick face. Does she have everything? Her bag and her key and her coat hanging neatly over her forearm. Oh, the messages – there's a whole bootful to take in, meat and vegetables and the whole lot.

Next door's car is there, flashy wasp of a thing. Molly saw it as she pulled in. They might notice her and come out to help…

Queer enough fish, the new neighbours – never a peep out of the man, and the wife a working mother. An airs-and-graces sort of a name, long, with roundy letters in it… Decent girl, but a miserable job she's done on that house – tearing down the honeysuckle and knocking the cladding off the front.

Very quick it happened, the whole thing. It was Freya spotted it one morning through the upstairs window. 'Grandma, look the Breretons' has sold!' Molly couldn't see from there, but just the thought of it made her gasp as though something had stung her… She went down to look and there it was – 'SOLD' pasted over the 'For Sale' sign. And the very next morning in comes a skip – huge clang of a thing – emergency yellow and cold pewter where the paint was lifted off it – plonked there just like that with a corner of it jamming into the flower beds. Molly didn't have to be snooping to know how those poor daffodils had their stalks crushed and the heads snapped off, and them just ready to open. Last spring it was, was it? Just as the apple blossoms were pearling. Weeks and weeks that skip sat there, filling up with all the things the new people thought useless – floral-papered plasterboard, an avocado-green handsink and slices of that cladding; stone humps bulging from the level cement like the backs of bathing hippos. The scene made Molly think of faraway places where there are earthquakes.

But she's alright, the new girl next door, lovely manners, helping Molly in with the shopping sometimes, and always asking before she has the partition hedge pruned. A soft-spoken girl, but loud makeup on always, a thin neck and mumpsy cheeks – tapping at the door all meek, like maybe there could be a baby sleeping. 'Mrs Kearney, I wonder would you mind if Gavin gave the hedge a little trim?' Had Molly been a bit gruff that time, opening the door with a bull face on her? To make up for it, she said, 'Oh, you can call me Molly,' but the girl still calls her 'Mrs Kearney'. Molly appreciates that.

The thing is, the Breretons were Molly's neighbours nearly fifty years. There was a time, when the children were small, that she and Jackie Brereton were a great help to one another. They had their tea together every morning, nearly. So it wasn't nice to watch her get that way – stooped and shaky suddenly. It was a miserable thing, and cruel. Pain twisting up her lovely open face, and she nearly seven years younger than Molly. And then Mr Brereton had a fall and their son moved the both of them off to a 'granny flat' out the back of his house away in Rathgar or somewhere. A big sly article, the son. A bit of a galoot, Molly always thought. 'They're packing us away in the garage to die,' – that's what Jackie said before she left. She chuckled then, but it was like a sendup of her usual big laugh, a drowning-inside sound that Molly never thought she'd hear from the likes of Jackie Brereton. It was a sad cup of tea they had that time. The last time Molly saw her alive, was it?

She was hardly cold when the 'For Sale' sign went up, then the red banner saying 'SOLD' across it, the skip and the smashed daffodil buds, and poor Mr Brereton still in shock, hardly a notion what was happening. Ugly business. Illness, death, property.

Molly takes a good breath of the pollen-thick outdoors. She leans on the car while she heaves the driver's door shut. Her knees hurt but they hold her there a minute – one hand flat on the glossy, warm metal, her bag stuffed under her arm, her key ready in her hand – just a minute so she can gather herself up. Tired today. All that cooking this morning. Oh, she's glad though, the children will have some good fatty broth for their supper. Cara exaggerates with all her healthy things sometimes; wheat-free this and sugar-free that. No cups of tea for the children either, on account of the caffeine. Poor chicklings.

Well, what a day – the sun warming the brick drive to a lovely rust, the air soft, a bright, open day with a sky high and aloof. Molly moves around to the boot. Nice weather for the children to play in the garden. Little Megan was looking pale today. The same look Cara can get sometimes; over washed, her top lip thinning off to a greyish blue. Bone broth will sort her out. Bone broth is good for everything. Oh, but a pig's head is good too. She might phone the butcher on Monday, see if he can get her a pig's head to boil; if she was to make a pea soup with the water, the children would drink it up, even the baby. Split peas and fresh peas mixed – deep and sweet, and it would do little Megan the world of good; put the colour back. She could tear a bit of meat into it too, from the cheeks. Tiring though, all that.

She will sit with a cup of coffee now when she gets the shopping in. Then she'll sort out her knitting. It'll take her an hour, only, to put it right. She'd no cause to get so upset about that this morning. Mistakes happen.

By pressing a cushiony button on the car keys, she can make the boot yawn slowly open, and there's a button to make it close again all by itself. Marvellous things they have nowadays. It was her daughter Sinéad who organised that for her, after her neck that time...

She surveys the contents of the boot – she's bought more than she planned to. The vegetable man brought it all out for her in a cardboard box, but she won't be able to lift it into the house. She forgets sometimes that things like this aren't as easy as they once were.

She'll start with that little bag of laundry – if she puts it in the machine now, it might even be dried and ironed by the morning. But she won't manage that big box... Molly glances over the neat hedge. Fair play to those daffodils; the way they multiply quietly in the hard winter soil, emerging each year with more and more of themselves. No stopping daffodils, once they're down. She hopes Mr Brereton doesn't know about the new people pulling down that cladding – Mother of God, it took him so many months to put it up that summer – and then a van of men came and hacked it off just like that.

There's no sign of the new girl coming out to help with the shopping. Molly could ring the bell and ask... Oh, but that house is vicious looking now, stripped back to the cold bricks and the door painted the squeaky grey of a mushroom.

3

STOPPED AT THE LIGHTS, the car's tinny floor jittering, Freya pulls an old copybook from her bag, opens it on the passenger seat and hurries through the pages. There it is – *SAT/March 4/1pm/GENIE FULL PACKAGE* scratched across the top in the waxy skids of a blunt, splintered colouring pencil. Beneath this, she has written *Trí Mian*, and, boxed in with red streaks, the phrases *GIRLY GIRL, 6 Precocious???* and *right at + rds.*

She scans the page for some landmark to type into her phone. Then she remembers – she rolls her eyes and smacks the wheel, whispers 'Fuck,' and sighs out the window as though to blame the concrete footpath and the quiet row of shopfronts. She was supposed to come up here in advance to check out where the house is. It's that snooty client who wouldn't give a proper address, *We certainly won't be in the sat nav I'm afraid, the postman just knows who we are, you know, it's that sort of area…*

The courtesy call took over an hour. Freya even had an urgent piss during it, her thumb pressing the mouthpiece mute.

'Fuckfuckfuck!' How did she forget to do it?

She's hungry already. She should have eaten a pancake at Cara's. She opens the glove box of her sister's car, unleashing a clatter of ancient cassette tapes just as the traffic lights flash green. Shit, she's to take a right here. The car staggers into gear, sending the contents of the glove box sliding out over the passenger seat and onto the floor. Steering with one hand up a steep country road, she uses the other to sift the mess for something to eat. What she needs is instant sugar – a chocolate bar with nougat and nuts in it – but apart from the cassettes, all she can find is a half-full packet of crayons, a cream-coloured spray bottle saying 'All Natural Crystal Deodorant' and a pair of grey oat biscuits covered in cellophane.

The house is somewhere up here on the left. She's drawn a wobbly oval on the page, scribbles of grass beneath it – *The name of our property is carved on a granite rock at the entrance* – Trí Mian – *it means three wishes. For our three little treasures…*

Head low to the wheel, Freya peers either side at the stone walls, white sun on the scrawny trees. She looks at the page for another clue. She has drawn a balloon with a little cartoon face on it, rolling eyes and its tongue sticking out.

Still no granite rock. Only the scabbed road and rain-filled potholes. Now and then a small, rusty gate, a dreary pebble-dash house clinging to the hillside. How long should she keep driving before she calls the client? Did she give no other directions at all? She turns the page – only the details for the christening party.

Then she spots it – a pink balloon bopping against a road sign. Great, a balloon trail! She loves when they do this. Up and up she drives, and the balloons grow more frequent – a burst one frittering on a telegraph pole, a big purple one buoying softly on the wall, the string flexing and rumpling in the low wind. She must be on the right track now – there could only be one 'Girly girl' party up in the Dublin mountains today... And there it is! Five minutes before schedule. A big driveway winding up to a stolid white house with little turrets at each corner. By the gate, a great silvery hunk of rock says, *Trí Mian*. There are three helium balloons sprouting from it – one pink and two blue.

Freya takes a breath and puts on her big party smile as the car crunches up the gravel drive.

The mum is waiting on the portico entrance, flanked by miniature fluted columns with bunches of balloons tied to each of them. She sounded taller on the phone, and better groomed. She has an unhealthily thick throat and lank, no-colour hair smeared back off a protruding forehead. She watches Freya's approach with a small, hopeful smile, hands clasped before her. When Freya steps out of the car, the smile opens – one of those desperate, down-turning smiles more like a grimace now. 'Hello!!!!' A hand waving wildly beside her face. 'Hello, Genie Gilly!'

Little girls in Disney-inspired party dresses are already emerging as Freya hauls the big polka-dot suitcase from the boot. Clutching it with two fists, she struggles to the portico and plonks it onto the mossy wooden slats.

'Hello!' Freya says, smiling and reproducing the client's manic wave. 'Hello! Excuse me for disturbing you, but my name is Genie Gilly and I have been searching and searching all day long for a very special birthday girl called Lottie! Does anyone know a birthday girl called Lottie? Waldo the Wizard told me that there is a very special girl called Lottie who is SIX today, and I have been searching up and down the Dublin mountains...'

The children grin, and disperse like startled birds. In the moment this makes, the mum shakes Freya's hand, her face all anxious gratitude, her head bent. 'Hi Gilly,' she says, 'I'm glad you found us alright.' The hand is dry and cool. 'What do you need to start?'

'Just a plug socket for the speakers—'

'Oh yes, you told me that. I have the conservatory all organised...'

'... and a table and some water for the facepainting – and just leave the rest to me!'

The mum doesn't release her grip. Instead she lays her other hand over Freya's. 'There are more than I expected,' she says, her voice lower now, confiding. 'I said RSVP on the invitation, but...'

Freya has time to flash her a reassuring smile before the children rush back out. A reluctant little girl is pushed towards her by an older boy (her brother – Eamon? Aaron?).

'Lottie,' he says. The boy bends level with her face, his hands between his knees, and nods. 'Say hello, Lottie.'

Freya gives a great big gasp. 'Is THIS Lottie?'

There is a crowd of little girls around them now, and they all giggle, wide-eyed, and nod. The birthday girl crosses her arms and raises a softly cleft chin at Freya. Freya likes the look of her – a bony-faced child with freckles and vague, peach-coloured eyebrows stretching the width of her forehead. Her hair is in two painfully tight French braids, darker than her pale orange fringe, as though plaited when wet. She is wearing denim shorts over black leggings, and a vest. She has bony shoulders, wiry arms slick with muscle.

'Oh my goodness, Lottie, I am so excited to meet you! I heard that you are SIX today, is that true?'

Lottie blinks at her and looks up at the balloons bobbing against the Grecian columns. They are tied on with generous lengths of foil ribbon, their silver ringlets tangling in the breeze.

'Well, I just LOVE birthdays,' continues Freya, 'and because it's your birthday I think we should do some magical, fun birthday things. What do you think, Lottie?'

Lottie shrugs and slides her jaw from side to side. She plunges her fists deep into the pockets of her shorts and looks at her feet.

'*I* hear... that you like dancing! Is that right?'

The child's brow crimps and pinkens.

'*I* like dancing!' cries a small girl in fairy wings, an island of pink polish on each scrappy nail. She stands very close to Freya, stroking the tasselled fringe of her waistcoat, and dips her head to catch Lottie's downward gaze. 'Do you like dancing Lottie?'

Lottie sucks her lip. Freya stretches up on her toes and calls,

'Hands up who likes birthdays?' She raises her own hand in the air and cries, 'Me!' and the party guests copy her. 'Meeeee me me me!'

'Hands up who likes facepainting? Meeeee! Hands up who likes magic tricks? Meeeee! Hands up who likes dancing? Meeeee! Yeahhh! Well come on then – let's get started!'

Freya rolls her suitcase down the hallway carpet, over the loud marble floor of the kitchen and out into the hot glare of a new-smelling conservatory. She plugs in the speakers, her mic and the company-issue iPod. Smiling brightly, she selects her playlist – 'Girls age 5–8' – and unpacks her facepaints to the opening verse of 'Girls just wanna have fu-hun' – beaming and nodding around her at the princesses and snot-nosed fairies that maul at her earrings and paw her hair: 'Genie Gilly, I want to be a butterfly'; 'Genie Gilly, can I be a crocodile?'; 'Genie Gilly, I like your sparkly shoes...'

The birthday girl is watching from a distance, leaning against the glass wall.

When her facepainting station has been set up, Freya gives a blast of the bubble machine, sending a shoal of bubbles across the room. The children jump after them, and Freya takes the mic. 'Hands up who wants their face painted!'

'Meeee!' the little girls shriek, heads and hands bopping.

'Well... who do you think should go first? I think it's the... birthday girl! Come on up Lottie and let's make you an extra special sparkly birthday girl!'

Shoulders curled, the child is nudged along by her mum – 'Come on Lottie, come on my little lambkin.' Freya sits by the facepaints and takes the child's lean fingers in hers – cold hands, like the mother.

'Now Lottie, sit down here for me. What would you like to be?'

Lottie shrugs and sits down, arms wilting into her lap.

'Well let's see, you could be… a butterfly?'

Lottie shakes her head.

'A sparkly princess?'

'No.'

'A goldfish?'

'What's that like?'

'Well, it's all orange and scaly with big fishy lips, and I can paint goggly fish eyes on your eyelids so when you blink everyone will get a fright!'

Lottie gives a narrow grin. She nods.

The mum is standing behind her.

'What's she going to be? What are you going to be Lottie?'

'A goldfish,' says Freya, sliding a wink at the child.

'Oh. Would you not be a pretty princess Lottie? Lottie? Would you not be a princess or a butterfly? I saw on the entertainer's website, you know, the butterfly is really lovely. You would look lovely Lottie, with your lovely plaits…'

Lottie stares ahead, and swallows.

'Wipe that sourpuss off your face,' says the mother, her cheeks muscling and a bite in her voice so sudden and penetrating that it makes Freya flinch. 'After I went to all the hassle of organising an entertainer and everything; you sit there with a puss on your face like nothing's good enough for Little Miss Lottie…'

Lottie stares ahead, grinding her back teeth. Freya recognises that feeling – like a hand clamping the back of your neck, like drowning in your own breath.

'Oh the goldfish is super-duper cool!' Freya says. 'It's extra special, a very unusual choice.'

The mother speaks through stiff lips, her voice low and jagged. 'I don't know what's wrong with you, Lottie. You know, you could be quite pretty, but you're dog-ugly when you scowl.'

A gulp forces itself into Freya's throat, her chest; an ache spreading down her limbs. There is something of her own mother about this woman; she could see it straight off – the over-enthusiasm, the whole performance on the portico. Freya's own skin cools and tightens. 'The Lily' is what she and Cara call their mother, the definite article separating her from them.

Lottie's mother turns to Freya and shakes her head fondly, but there is a violence in the tendon tensing up her neck. Her cheeks are the colour of coral. 'That's my Lottie,' she says. 'Always has to be different. Very much an individual.'

The child is hunched in her chair. Her face glows the same colour as her mother's.

'Come on, chicken,' Freya says, swiping her makeup sponge in a disc of orange facepaint, 'let's make you a goldfish.'

The mother shoots a quick frown at her daughter before turning to Freya with a smile. 'Kids,' she says. 'It's all ahead of you.'

'Oh, no, I…'

She was nineteen when Jem was born; she was young, and they made her feel it – the midwives, the other mothers – as if her maternity was something she had stolen. But Freya is twenty-four now. Why doesn't it occur to other women that she could be a mother too?

The doorbell rings and the mum flurries off. 'More guests! It did say RSVP on the invitations…' Freya can feel Lottie releasing a little breath. There are goose bumps prickling down the skinny white arms.

'Are you cold, chicken?'

Lottie shakes her head. 'No. I'm just a bit sad.'

Freya has sponged orange paint all over Lottie's face. She loads a fan-brush with yellow, and then dips the tip in red. She uses it like a stamp to press two-tone scales all over the cheeks. Her face is close to the child's. 'You're a very lovely girl, Lottie,' she says. 'Don't you mind anyone telling you mean things. You just remember you are a very lovely girl.'

Freya can feel tears of embarrassment wash up from her throat – what's wrong with her? Talking shite like that to a little girl she doesn't even know. She dips her finger in a pot of glitter and dabs a sparkly fingerprint on each fish scale.

'Don't you mind.'

Until Jem was born, Freya was all frustration and bewilderment, yearning for her mother's love, but then she started seeing it differently. There was simply a glitch in The Lily, she decided – some cog that didn't catch its groove. Something had gone wrong with her. It was nobody's fault.

Lottie's mother marches back into the room.

'I got her from the Polly's Parties agency – they're great, really professional. Great reviews. She's going to do dancing and magic tricks and everything in a minute.'

She is followed by a low-set lady wearing many scarves and bulky pieces of jewellery. Freya ignores them but there's that hot-cold clench up the back of her neck again.

A couple of years ago, Freya clicked her way to a support site for 'Daughters of Narcissistic Mothers' and was delighted to see her mother dismantled there into a checklist of traits. For a moment, she felt victorious and safe. But she encountered herself there too – many versions of her – women who held tenaciously to childhood slights, who topped each other's stories and denigrated their mothers with a rage so jealous and insistent it made Freya hate herself.

She is using a pale blue to paint fish eyes, but since her mother has returned, Lottie's lids keep trembling. By one eye, a plump vein twitches helplessly under the young skin.

'It's alright, chicken,' says Freya. 'Are you alright?'

The fishy lips now – she mustn't make the paint too wet. Leaning in close, she builds them like the lips of a geisha, swirling her brush to make two circles balancing on a bigger one. Then she uses a metallic paint to draw lines for the creases.

The child has fine, narrow lips, clean breath.

Her sister thinks she was too young when it all happened, but Freya can remember. Watching from the door as their mother beat her own arm with a rolling pin, the silence pulling tight across her lips and her eyes steady. Standing before the pretty *bán Garda,* her mother's fingers digging into her shoulders, *Tell them, Freya, tell them what Cara did...* She can remember, back before Lily finally sent Cara away, being dragged about to strange houses – the smell of sandalwood and patchouli, her mother's voice always changing to match the person she spoke to; she had that amazing ability to adapt everything – her accent, her tone, her beliefs, her history – *I need help with my eldest, Cara*— then her voice lowering, threatening – *a dark soul.*

She knew her share. And wasn't it Freya who was abandoned, really? In the end, it was because of the social worker that The Lily left her with their grandparents; they never came for her. And did Cara ever wonder what they were like, those months all alone in that house, trying, trying all alone to dance for their mother's love?

'Oh, Lottie! Look at you, isn't that brilliant!' The mother shrieks, slapping her hands onto her own cheeks. 'That's my Lottie,' she says, turning to her friend. 'That's my Lottie – a real *individual.*'

4

MOLLY WARMS HER HANDS around the cup, pulling some of the steadiness into her bones. She likes her coffee very hot. Dinny used to pour his tea into the saucer to take the heat out. He'd lift it very carefully and slurp from it, while the rest cooled in the cup.

Oh, she's tired now.

She's brought in the ham from the deli, and a brick of real butter – lovely stuff with a sour tang, wrapped in greaseproof paper – then the chicken and lamb chops from the butcher's, and the milk. It took her a few journeys just to do that much; just the stuff for the fridge. She's left the rest for Freya to get in the morning.

Maybe she should have waited until Monday for the messages. Or she could have sent Freya, of course, but Freya would have insisted on spending her own money, and Molly doesn't like her to do that. That girl needs to keep her money and get some savings together. She needs to use her head more, Freya, to keep her cards to herself and tuck her heart in safe. That's always the way with Freya; such a flighty, fragile little thing and everything pouring out of her – all her love and all her ideas just pouring out. *No safety valve to Freya* – that's what Dinny used to say.

Molly would like to buy her a little house – a little house for her and the boy. She will, only she needs to find a way to do it that doesn't make Freya feel beholden, that makes her feel she has done it herself. It's a shame she has to work like that, but Dinny thought they had made a mistake with their three. He said it was important to know the value of work, that with their girls they had forgotten that. So excited, maybe, that they could suddenly pay for things – all the things they never had – it was something Dinny and Molly hadn't considered. Then suddenly, it was all Dinny talked about, his big regret – *Do you realise, Molly,* he said, *the great mistake we made? Our girls have never worked a day in their lives.*

There is a new type of milk in the shops now – 'night milk' taken from the cows at dusk. It's the milk meant for the youngest calves, to help them sleep. Yellower than the normal milk, and a purple label on it with a pale crescent moon. She picked up a carton in the deli and took it to the till – it would be a lovely thing Freya could use for Jem's cocoa at night… but then she changed her mind and bought the usual milk, thinking of those silky newborn calves and the lowing cows, and what a terrible thing it was to steal a mother's milk. Stupid old girl, because of course the same could be said for any cow's milk, or goat's milk or anything. It's only that it seems less personal when it's white like that. Stupid old goose. She's getting soft in the head. She's getting sentimental. There's something isn't there? Something is bothering her. There's some way she's made a show of herself today… her knitting. The heel flap! Imagine forgetting to pick up the heel flap?

Molly purses her lips as she places her cup into its saucer. Shouldn't she be ashamed? The last time she did that she was six years old and Sister Celestine didn't just pull it back to the heel – she pulled the whole sock back, wound it into a tight little ball and made Molly begin again.

Some of the sisters used the stick but not Sister Celestine. Sister Celestine was the best of them. Decent.

But what a fright it was to realise what she'd done – knitting on, round and round like a silly eejit without turning the heel – and then she went and made a song and dance over it. Poor Cara looking at her in alarm. Those great earnest eyes she has. Cara must think she's going soft in the head. It's just that it hits Molly sometimes, how things are squeezing up now, and it's not that she minds so much the idea of growing old, or even the coolness of death coming in on her – it's the way time seems to be coiling in, winding smaller and smaller and faster and it makes her head tight sometimes, with the panic. Her granddaughters are women now – the creases around Cara's eyes (*Oh* she said, and her eyes made the O shape as well as her mouth, *Oh – you were just distracted Grandma*) – and her great-grandchildren are growing so suddenly it makes her dizzy. *Mimi, guess what number I am?* and she couldn't. She couldn't make a number of the years that had already gone into little Den… What a goose she has been. All down those years she's been handling her time like portions she could measure out and weigh – but that's not the nature of the thing at all. It moves in gushes, washing over her with its great crash and spill before she has a chance to draw breath and look at things and say goodbye to any of it. And all the different types of milk there are now. For goodness sake, people aren't right in the head. But new calves, well, such lovely things as could make you weep – a filmy sack of water, and pink on them, clunk of bones under the slick hide and white gunk in their folds. She saw one born in a barn once – at her uncle's farm – spindly legs and the straw sticking to its womb-wet skin and a blood smell so frightening and good, like turned earth.

There is a reassuring rumble and suck from the utility room – she has Cara's coloureds in the machine. Things are so easy now. It's no work at all, just to pop the clothes in with the powder and press the button. Mother help us, the things Cara dresses those little girls in – denim slacks, like boys', with the knees worn down, and gym suits and all. Even Cara's pyjama pants – nice, comfortable cotton – have a pattern on them like a man's dressing gown. Molly was satisfied to notice a glossy stiffness in the seat of them as she turned them inside out and tossed them into the drum. She worries, sometimes, that Cara is a negligent wife, and it is a comfort to know that they are close in the bedroom, she and Pat. When a couple lie close together, it does a lot for a marriage.

Tired. She should eat something – a slice of brown bread is always nice, with a bit of cheese maybe, or some of that ham. Maybe an egg, boiled. Then the sock. She'll feel better when she's put that heel flap right. Lunchtime already. Will they be having the soup now, the children, or will Cara hold onto it for the evening meal? Poor little Jem... he has a good appetite at home, because Freya and Molly know what he likes – chicken fillet fried in butter, potatoes mashed with a bit of nutmeg and a leek. He didn't want to go to his Aunt Cara's this morning in case she made that brown rice and beans thing again. Does Cara know to soak them well? Beans can be dangerous, you have to be careful with beans... No, Cara won't want the hassle. She'll serve the soup for lunch, probably. There are extra meatballs in it so the children won't have to squabble over them, and little discs of carrot, and Molly minced the celery so small they won't even see it. It was such good stock that it cooled to a jelly you could cut with a knife. Two chickens she put into it, gizzards and flesh and all, and she simmered it on a low heat until the kidneys bobbed and the spines loosened to strings of gritty beads – Oh!

The breath rushes back at Molly's throat and punches into her gut so that her gasp, when it comes, is a high, shrill thing like the whistle of an old kettle – those tiny bones! Did she strain the broth properly? Or could there be a nugget of spine in there, small enough to slip through unnoticed but hard enough and big enough to stop the breath of a little thing like Jem with his brown eyes big and his face so suddenly drained and – Oh oh oh! There's something not right. She can feel it in her waters that something is not right.

Molly stands quickly and makes for the cloakroom. Sore – her knees are sore, the shiver pain of bone scraping on bone. She has Cara on speed dial – number 2. She'll just tell her she's to check each bowl of soup as she ladles it out, and she's to remember that if there is something ever lodged in the breath of a child, you don't bang the back like she once thought. No, you thrust your palms into his belly to force it all back up—

Molly flicks on the cloakroom light and grabs for the phone but before she can lift the receiver, a short, clear ring comes sounding in at her from all three phones in the house, so that it feels like her home itself is bearing down on her. She keeps her hand there, letting several trills vibrate up through her grasp. The cloakroom is all shadow under the orange bulb – greased cotton, leather and an intimate, scalpish smell. Dinny. She never cleaned his Barbour jacket afterwards. She pushed it in at the back with the white flakes still speckling the shoulders and an oily, working smell off it. She takes a calm breath and picks up the phone.

'Yes, hello?'

'Mammy?'

Molly feels for something to hold. The glide of her fur coat. The chair.

'Yes.'

'Mammy? It's Eileen. It's your little Eileen, Mammy. It's Lily.'

'Oh.'

Molly runs her hand over the leather back of the cloakroom chair. Dinny put it there a long time ago, so she could sit and chatter to her sister as long as she liked without her legs tiring. She grips the cool leather, lowers herself sidelong onto the seat. She thought it was gone – the splintering of love that her youngest child could send through her.

'It's your little Eileen, Mammy.'

'Yes I know. Hello.'

'Hello, Mammy.'

'What do you want, d—' Molly can feel her voice trip onto the next word, and she tries to suck it back in but too late, ' darling?'

'I need you, Mammy.'

'Oh?'

She's keeping her voice even and flat. Dead to the sting of it. Buying herself time to think. *I haven't my glasses* – that's what she thinks – *I need my glasses*. The blurring feeling is wrapping her like a shadow and rushing right inside her now, like smoke filling up her nose and muffling her face. She lays her thick, dry fingers across her eyes. She is a practical woman and she will not swoon like this. *Your Eileen* like Molly is some eejit, like Molly will forget… Lily. Lily. Oh but it's a sharp thing, her child's voice bursting into her tired belly, her tired flesh. Tired today. Oh.

'I need you Mammy. I have a mission. Your Lily has a mission, Mammy, and I need you.'

'What do you want, darling?'

'I was in Canada, Mammy, did you know that? And I went to the ancient pools, and I was chosen, Mammy.'

Molly squeezes her lips and nods into the dimness of the cloakroom, her eyes dry, her voice sore and too big for her throat. 'I see,' she says.

'I was chosen by the spirit of the elders to bathe in the sacred waters.'

'I see.' Molly rubs at the rough patch of skin on her forehead. It has been there for some time, raised a little browner than the rest of her face, and she knows it is darkening into an age spot right there on her front for all to see.

'What I learned from the elders, Mammy, is that I need to make another exhibition. But this time it won't be painting Mammy. What I must do is a carpet of colour with the faces of the elders showing up through – transgenerational hauntings, Mammy, that's what it will be about, you know...'

Molly's eyes are closed now, a stinging heat rushing up from her stomach. She rubs at her forehead so hard it hurts. She can feel little rolls of it under her fingers, the bad old skin lifting up off her and the shock as her blood meets the stoic air of the cloakroom.

'So Mammy, I suppose you're wondering where you come in? Well, I need you to knit, Mammy. I am going to bring you the wool. It will be wool from the clothes people have died in, and I will pull it out and wash it and wind it back down. Don't you worry about that Mammy, I'll do all that. All I need you to do is to knit each ball of wool into a patch. I want big patches and small patches, okay? All different stitches, whatever stitches you want. Then I will arrange them, and the spirits will show up through. Oh Mammy, it's going to be spectacular! Daddy would be so proud of me. I'm going to exhibit in Soho, where Daddy began. Mammy, your little Lily is going to win the Turner Prize! I know it, Mammy, in my *heart*, I know...' She makes the word 'heart' heavy, like a big stamp of the foot, emptying her lungs entirely. She says it again, 'In my *heart*,' carefully and slowly, like a theatre actress, and then she says it again, 'In my *heart*, Mammy.'

'No, darling.'

'No?'

'No, darling, no.'

'No? What do you mean *no* Mammy? Why would you do that to me? No! That's all you ever gave me Mammy – no no no no no. After all these years, here I am working through all the pain of all your no-ing, forgiving you, asking nothing of you. You are my mother! Doesn't that mean anything to you? You are my *mother!*'

Egged on by her own performance, Eileen is screaming now, that way she does – each sentence rising to a great climax and breaking then, as though she is about to cry. But is she? You never know with Eileen. You never know where you are at all. Was she always like that and they just didn't notice?

'Goodbye, darling.'

Molly lays the receiver down slowly into its cradle. She sits in the cloakroom and rubs and rubs at the little patch of oldness on her forehead. The phone rings again, of course it does, the sound coming in at her from the landing upstairs and from Dinny's office, and from the little table beside her. It rings and rings – it rings and stops, and rings again, swelling up against the old coats and the furs, and Molly can only sit here on the chair that her husband once lifted in for her. She holds her face in both hands and she hears her own sounds – her wet sigh and her voice small, old and strained like an elastic band pulled too thin, 'Dinny' – and the telephone's relentless, rhythmic call, pushing at the walls and clamouring at the shut door.

5

THE CHILDREN CROWD ONTO the portico, their facepaint already smeared and fading, balloon swords and balloon flowers swishing frantically in farewell. Freya smiles and waves, smiles and smiles and waves and smiles as she manages the three-point turn and at last drives out of sight.

A few metres from the house, she pulls up on a squelch of muck and grass, and checks the next address – another posh one. She uses a crayon to write on the back of the envelope – *1pm Full Package €180: €80 Polly's Parties /€100 Genie Gilly* – and stows it in the door of the car.

She draws her hand down over her cheeks and jaw to ease out the cramp of all that smiling, scrapes a ridge of blue paint from under her thumbnail, and runs a wet wipe over the back of her neck. Chewing mechanically on an oat biscuit, she pulls down the car mirror to check her face, and rubs at the mascara that has made its way beneath her eyes. She sprays some of Cara's deodorant into her armpits – it smells like vanilla; Grandma's sponge cake.

Two more to go: another Southside now, and then a 5 pm

in Naas. She flicks through the details. The next one is a christening party for a baby, Reuben-Alexander – lots of puppets and bubbles.

She types in the address. After baby Reuben-Alexander there's a birthday party for a nine-year-old boy called Sweetness. The mother spoke in an accent that made the word 'Sweetness' sound hefty and regal and very earnest. She insisted on booking the standard package, even though Freya explained that there are way too many kids. Between painting twenty-six faces and making twenty-six balloons, there won't be time for much of a magic show… but it's the last party, no harm if she ends up going overtime a little, and they might tip. By the end of the day she'll have three hundred euro – one for tax and savings, the rest will cover petrol, groceries, new shoes for Jem. And phone credit. Fucking nut-job client ran down her phone credit.

Two more gigs and then back to Jem. Her Jem. He'll enjoy making the birdhouse, and he'll have Grandma's soup for supper so there won't be an issue about Cara's over-wholesome cooking. Two gigs to go and then she'll pick him up – his great, clear eyes, the impossible density of his lashes, his bony limbs folding into her warmth – *Mammy*, the way he says it; that faith that she can continue to make his world, though it keeps expanding beyond anything she can possibly keep hold of – new shoes, and that mean boy at Montessori, and the bedwetting that hasn't stopped. She needs to save more money.

Baby Reuben-Alexander will be an easy one and then Sweetness and all his cousins and his warm-voiced mother; that one will be fine. Then Cara will drop her home to Grandma with Jem; glasses of water by their beds; wool blankets and cool sheets. The smell of hyacinths from the landing, and Grandma waiting in the early dark, her girlish nightdress soft against the bony breast, and her night cream with a smell like crushed rose petals…

6

MOLLY HAS GROWN TEARLESS and cold, her behind fizzing into numbness on the chair. She will have to lift herself up. She will have to stand and walk out of the cloakroom into the warmth of her house.

Eileen. Lily. She was a funny child – cheeky – but they used to laugh at her. *Never backward about coming forward,* that's what Dinny said. She could make Dinny laugh.

Where did she go wrong with her? *You are my mother!* It's been such a long time since that child left her body, and still she has that claim. What does Molly owe, now? How much of this sore love does she still owe?

Until Dinny died, Molly never thought twice about being a mother; the give and the get of it. She knew it was a terrible thing in its own wordless way – quietening down bits of yourself, creating new flesh from your own. Of course, it took something out of you, but, oh, it was marvellous too. She wouldn't have chosen anything else. She wouldn't swap anything for that night with her first baby suckling at her breast.

But her youngest, Eileen – where did they go wrong? Full

up of struggle, always; such rage in her. Nowadays a woman could have it all, so why was their Lily so angry?

At least two years it must be, since Molly last laid eyes on her. It was late at night and she pressed on the doorbell without letting go. She'd come for Jem, she said, straining at the latch chain – *He is* my *grandson!* That time, Molly thought how fresh and young Eileen's skin looked, the cheeks all rosy, even though she was already a grandmother (How had that all happened already?). Freya ran upstairs and put a cartoon on for Jem in his bed. Then she helped Molly get the door shut, but Eileen stayed outside the house until light, shouting. It was Dinny she began to rage against, such strange things she shouted – *Daddy never respected my work, and you neither – just because I was a girl you thought I should spend my life just having babies! You promised you would pay me for my babies... you owe me for those babies!*

After that Molly spent a long time thinking about it and not sleeping at night. She was so glad when, in the encyclopaedia, she found a word that made some sense of it: 'mythomania'.

But why was that the way with Eileen? An anger in her of such force that she had to feed it with inventions? 'To elevate the ego' – that's what the encyclopedia said, but what did it mean? What had Eileen ever to be angry about? There was that great disappointment with the orchestra conductor – the girls' father – and a great hullabuloo when he died so suddenly and out of the woodwork appeared his wife; and his children no younger than Eileen was. Molly had heard of such things – two families and neither knowing – but was Eileen really such a fool? Surely, she knew. Of course she knew. He wore it like cologne. Afterwards, Molly went to great lengths to convince Dinny that Eileen had been duped; but Molly never believed that. It was the first thing Molly said after he came to tea that time, 'I don't trust him.' And he a well-known fellow, it wouldn't have taken any digging at all to find out he was married. No, Eileen liked the theatre of it; she liked to be the star, no matter how tragic the show. And she liked to feel sorry for herself, Eileen. Always did.

Throwing away the most precious parts of a life. Leaving those little girls on Molly's doorstep one by one like old playthings – what mother could do such a thing? God, and wasn't there a widow on Viking Street who left her eldest girl in a home because she couldn't feed her. Afterwards she came and wept with Molly's mam, and the next day the two of them went together to collect her. How that woman suffered to keep her four children with her – Dada gave her potatoes from the allotment whenever he could, and cabbage even. There was a shoe collection every year to get the boy some boots and the widow woman was so ashamed, but Molly heard her Mam say to her harsh, *Don't let pride separate you from the children God gave you.*

There are things she has almost forgotten – her mother in the kitchen, speaking close and hard like that, the smell off the pot, the housecoat she wore. They come to her unexpectedly, very suddenly, very fleetingly, and she tries to hold them now.

And Lily. The tiny baby she was. The gaunt little arms. The way you could see the veins running beneath, bright and mysteriously logical, like something from another world.

She has no shame, Eileen, no love, maybe. Maybe she has no

love. Didn't they give her all they could though? Was she born that way? A tiny baby, her Lily, so tiny when she arrived but such a long and hard labour, such work to bring her in – a tiny, bald thing, born with her fists clenched and all the rage of the world there in her first high scream.

Molly had wanted to paint once; she had aspirations, less grand than Eileen's, granted, (the Turner Prize how are you!) but too big, all the same. She had such ideas once, of all the things she would like to paint.

She drew Dinny with hard pencils on thin paper. It was cold, upstairs in his rented room. Those first touches, opening her blouse and unbuttoning his shirt, just to feel his skin on hers as he kissed her; the surprise of that. She couldn't feel ashamed of those things, even if she wanted to. To think how they posed for one another, laughing and making love and then sitting again to be sketched.

There is something to be said for religion; for the mysticism it makes. It had seemed supernatural – the pull of desire between them. All the rapture she knew was for God, and so their attraction had seemed to her a sacred thing; a spiritual thing. The idea of lust didn't occur to her, the idea that they were merely beasts; that the animal parts of human life could be the most beautiful. It was only when she felt her first child open out of her that she understood that.

Silly girl. But she is glad of that silliness. Oh, she had her times, beautiful times that not everybody gets in life.

Once they arrived in London, though, she stayed very quiet about the paintings she had in her. It would have humiliated him if anyone knew his wife had notions like that. He never said it to her; they both just knew suddenly that it wasn't on. As it was, he did not belong in Soho – the Irish there were all wealthy big-house fellows pretending to be poor, no place for a working man. Was he a laughing stock, her Dinny? In his clean, rough shirts and hardwearing boots? There was so much posturing had to go into it, and Dinny wasn't made for such things. Sometimes he came home at night and wept into her breasts, mewing like a kitten.

The art scene in Soho was ruled by a ham-faced fellow in a leather jacket and she's sure to this day that he used a compact on his face. She's never forgotten that man, his waxy skin and the way his eyes twinkled with something like friendliness while his mouth twisted a cruel sneer. There was a time when Dinny hungered for the approval of such men. That man made very ugly pieces; rendered human figures meat, but by then he was already growing very popular and he had influence; it was important to be liked by him.

Sometimes Dinny took her with him to those strange pubs they had there for artists to go and boast about themselves and drink with the right people. There was one called 'The Caves' but pronounced *calves*. There was an ash-frail figure always sitting at the bar – a Welsh woman who wet herself and slept with sailors. 'The wizened whore' is what Dinny called her, his beautiful lips hitching to a disgusted shape. Molly scolded him for speaking so crudely, but it was true that the woman smelled terrible and could be seen sometimes with her little breasts hanging out the side of her dress. She had skinny legs, stringy flesh, a mouth smeared so clumsily red. Someone told Molly – it was a gentle, quiet boy brought there by one of the queer fellows and ignored like a woman – that in Paris she had been lauded as some kind of painter. When she learned that, Molly had felt a trembling heat rise up her face and her scalp all a-scald; a feeling like anger that quickly settled to shame. One evening, when that woman stood and left, all who looked could see that she had dirtied herself right there on the barstool.

Stupid old woman, sitting there in the cold like that. Now her legs are stiff. A screeching feeling, like forcing the rusted lids off jam jars. Molly knows the importance of decent food. She puts an egg on to boil, but she turns it off before the water is warm, and sits at the kitchen table. She's cold. She should turn on the heating. No, she won't manage an egg. But the thought of the cheese and the thought of the ham send a terrible nausea going. She wishes Freya would come home – what time did she say she was finishing up? And the little boy.

There were no bones in the broth – of course not. She would never be so negligent.

Oh, she can't think now. She can't organise her evening now.

She could sit in her armchair and watch something on the television.

She should eat something. Even a little thing.

From the adjoining room, the carriage clock chimes the hour. She counts four but she started late and can't be sure. She likes that clock, the pleasant, steady dongs it gives out, anchoring the days. But what time is it? It's hard to see the time on the microwave. Depends where you're standing, like a watermark. She'll go in now to the TV room to have a look at the clock.

Oh, tired now. Let Freya and the little one come back and let all the hours of the day arrange themselves straight like a line of ants all marching towards the same home. Let today end.

Jam. She could manage jam on a slice of bread and butter. Old people die from not eating. They just stop eating and then they die. That's the way she'll do it, rather than go softheaded and stone-limbed, shrivelled up and bushy-chinned – but not yet. Even half a slice is something to keep the body ticking. That's the trick – just choose the task and carry it through, keep the time looping over.

Molly takes the bread from the cupboard and lays it on the table beside the butter. Then the jam.

Time is closing up now and there are things Molly will have to do – the letter.

She takes a knife from the drawer, a plate from the cupboard.

Molly has known for some time that she will have to open the letter. She will not be here forever, and she doesn't want to leave it after her for the children and the grandchildren to find.

It was in the days before his stroke that Dinny wrote it, and Molly knew he wasn't there in the head – the terrible sadness that came upon him, and the things he said about their children. What had happened to Eileen, he wanted to know, and for hours that morning he shook his head and said, *What happened with our Eileen?* But it was their eldest daughter, Aoife, he was trembling against. He wrote so slowly. Oh, his hands had started a terrible shaking, and it was the hardest thing age could have done to him. It made him throw his brushes at the canvas and slash at his work. Even as he moved his pencil so unsteadily across the page, he muttered to himself – Aoife was the greatest of his disappointments. She was an idiot, he said, she was a greedy, cultureless whore, and she had no business attaching herself to his name. She had no notion about art. He sealed the letter and wrote Aoife's married name on it. Molly was supposed to post it. She drove out to the post office right then, but she couldn't do it. It was the word 'whore' that froze her stiff at the wheel. She lied to him that time, when she came back in. That was one betrayal, but to open the letter was quite another. She kept it in the glove compartment for three days, wondering what to do, but then Dinny had his stroke and she forgot about it in the relief; and in the horror of the beaming imbecile face he had on him for those weeks, and the heaviness and stiffness of him lying there. Afterwards, she took it from her glove compartment and put it in the drawer in Dinny's office and she has left it there for six years.

She told Freya about it – she didn't plan to tell, she didn't even consider it, but she suddenly came out with it one day as they were sitting together. Freya said she was right not to post it. She will open it, or ask Freya to. She will do that soon, in the next days she will do it.

When she has them all out on the table – the butter and bread and jam; the knife and the wooden board in the shape of a leaf – she sits herself down and begins to butter a slice of bread.

She can go easy now. She can go gently with herself. If she takes her knitting to bed instead of sitting in her chair, well no one will know. She has that good sitting-up cushion that Sinéad bought for her. Freya and the little one will be back late, but they will be back. In the morning there'll be the little boy in his pyjamas at the table, waiting for his porridge and his orange juice.

Molly avoids her image in the bright hallway mirror. She doesn't like putting on the house alarm. She's always afraid she won't be quick enough or she'll put in the wrong number and there will be a great noise. That happened once, when it was first installed. There she was, flustering around for the number and then it was too late – she couldn't even think for the wail of the thing, or push the numbers or anything, and she had to scurry into the cloakroom to phone Freya like a helpless old biddy.

She puts the numbers in as quickly as she can.

Upstairs, she sits at her dressing-table, bends to help her feet find her slippers. She pulls her padded bed jacket on over her blouse and makes her way down the hall to the toilet. *I'm off to powder my nose* – that's what Dinny used to say whenever he needed to use the toilet, or *I must make my ablutions*...

In her bedroom she undresses slowly, laying her clothes on the chair – her decent brown skirt and her nice springtime blouse.

There's a chill in the evening, but oh what a day it was today – so bright and airy and all those daffodils have come out again to defy the prissy new neighbours and their irises with miserable streaks for faces. She puts her knickers and her vest in the laundry basket, and flings her stockings at the washbasin.

She gets them done quickly – rubbing the toes and the heels with her bar of Sunlight soap, rinses them one by one under the cold tap, and squeezes them out before laying them across the back of the chair to dry.

She puts her dentures in a glass with that cleaner they say you should use now, carefully brushes her four remaining teeth, washes her face.

That's the real meaning of that word 'ablutions' – she found it out only recently. It means to do your topping and tailing and your teeth and all that.

Dinny.

She got on with it after Dinny went. Her days go on, there are things to do. But night is the hard part. Sleeping alone; she hasn't got used to this part.

After she has only just counted eight chimes, they come. The growl of the car, the click at the door, the shuffle – there is nothing wrong with her hearing – she can hear it all – the yip of the alarm and Freya pressing the code in like a little tune 334 – a moment of hesitation while she finds the 8 – whispers. The little boy speaks, a high voice breaking the stifle. 'Shhhhhh' says his mother. She is winding the clock – that's what it is, or she is letting the little boy do it. Together they are winding up the clock so it keeps time. Molly slides her hand under the pillow and pulls it in under her chin. What a lovely big pillow. Time is winding up, yes, but it might be gentle as the rise and meld of warming pastry.

The little boy. Molly smiles and nestles down into the sheets. She's fixed the sock, pulling it right back to the turn and knitting all the way to the toe. She sewed it up so smoothly you'd never find the seam.

They are beginning up the stairs – great slow creaks. Some things are so nice. Sleep is so nice, when it comes.

Lips on her cheek. The blanket is tucked up over her shoulder.

'Night night, Grandma.'

Something brushes her hand. 'Night night, Mimi.'

7

FREYA WAKES TO THE shudder of the windowpane. Loosened by the wind, a clutch of ivy gropes at the glass. On the bedside table her phone is flashing red – a missed call, or a text message – and her first thought is of Jem – some emergency. Of course not. He's here, just the other side of the wall. She tucked him in herself.

It's a missed call and two texts. She recognises the number immediately.

Unless you want me to come to Granny's door, pick up when I call.

She was immensely stupid to ever have contacted Jem's father. Grandma hadn't pressed her about who the father was or any of that. It was Cara who convinced her that it was the right thing to do, to tell him about Jem, tell him he could 'be involved'. But Cara didn't know what he was like. All he kept saying was 'cunt' and 'bitch', and 'Why did you keep it?' Why did she? Was it sentimentality, or something more? She could have got the morning-after pill. There was a number of things she could have done. Sometimes she thinks she got pregnant on purpose; that she knew Jem was there, waiting to be born. That she wanted him. His birth felt like a kind of reunion.

The second message was sent only ten minutes ago:

Cunt call me back or I will take legal action.

A drowning sensation in her chest – she realises she has been holding her breath. It takes effort to exhale. She reaches for the glass of water beside the bed and forces herself to take a little of it into her mouth. Sometimes he can go six months without contacting her, and then there are a few weeks of texts and calls. She can tolerate that, so long as he doesn't go to the courts for access, or turn up here, or at Jem's school…

Jem is chatting to Grandma. She can catch the inflections of his voice, but not the words. Quietly, she crosses the hyacinth-perfumed landing and leans in the doorway of Grandma's bedroom. There they are – Jem sitting up in the bed beside Grandma, his legs sticking out straight and the blankets across his lap. Grandma is sucking her dentures into place as she bends to the nightstand for her glasses. She pushes them onto her nose, draws back a little and peers at the book.

'Oh yes!' she says. 'The lovely book with the owl family. You know your Aunty Cara drew these? Isn't she a clever aunty? And look what it says at the beginning, "For Jem"… you were just a tiny baby when she made those pictures.'

Jem smiles fondly at the idea of himself as a tiny baby – his smile and tilted brows imitating Grandma's – but Freya can tell he is impatient for the story to start.

'She was always an artist, you know, your Aunty Cara. Her granddad said she came from the Old Masters… but she has her own style. She always knew what she thought, never went in for nonsense. You know once, when your mammy was very little – not much older than you – we were all together in a lovely hotel called the Shelbourne Hotel, in the city centre…'

'Mammy!'

Jem has spotted her. He stands on the bed, arms stretched up, as though about to leap into the air.

'Good morning everybody,' says Freya. She sits on the bed, letting Jem wrap his arms around her neck and climb into her lap.

Grandma pulls off her glasses. 'Well, Freya. Did you have a good sleep, darling?'

'A great sleep.'

'Good. Nothing like a good sleep.'

Jem twists himself off Freya's lap and clutches one of her arms, pulling her up towards the headboard.

'Come in the bed Mammy. Mimi is doing a story.'

'I'll get the porridge on. You have your story and then come on down.'

Jem harrumphs, falling heavily on his bottom beside Grandma.

'Okay, but eggy bread okay? Not porridge.'

'No Jem, I'm working today.'

'Please, Mammy! Please, eggy bread. I can help!'

'No, baby, you had pancakes yesterday, and your Aunt Cara is collecting you at eleven…'

'Poor darling,' says Grandma, 'isn't your mammy a terrible meanie? Come on and we'll make you some eggy bread, it won't take long. We can have the story tonight… You put your wellies on for me, and your jacket, and we'll go and see if there are any eggs in the henhouse.'

While Grandma and Jem are making breakfast, Freya gets ready for her party. Just one today; a fairy princess party. She does her makeup in the hallway mirror – pale, sparkly eyelids and lots of blusher. The idea is to be as cartoonish as possible without becoming monstrous. She can hear Jem and Grandma in the kitchen…

'Sugar?' asks Grandma.

'Check!' shouts Jem.

'Eggs?'

'Check!'

'Four of them…?'

'Check!'

'Cinnamon?'

'Is this it?'

'That's the cinnamon, yes.'

'Check, check, check, check!'

Freya uses hairpins to fix a string of roses around her head. Then she hangs her fairy wings on the back of the front door so that she won't forget them on the way out.

'Well, Jem,' says Grandma, 'you are the best eggy-bread-maker I ever have known!'

Freya lifts the lid off her coffee – it hasn't all filtered down yet. 'Don't let Cara see that you're still buying these filters, Grandma. They aren't very good for the environment you know.'

'Well, it's Fairtrade it says.'

'But all the plastic, Grandma.'

'I'm allowed my one sin, Freya. I like my filter coffee.'

'I might buy a coffee press, you know, something like what Cara has? It's not good, throwing away a plastic cup every time we have a cup of coffee…'

Grandma turns to Jem. 'Isn't your Mammy a terrible saintly one? If a cup of coffee is my only vice, Miss Freya, I'm doing very well thank you.'

Freya checks the clock – nearly half ten. 'So, Cara will be here around eleven Grandma…'

'Yes, marvellous. That's perfect. You know, I told Aoife I might go over to her for Sunday lunch.'

'Oh well that will be nice Grandma.'

'My Fifi can be very cranky these days, you know.'

'She can…'

'Is it since the change, do you think? I could bring her some lady's mantle, maybe, or some sage. But I was never funny for the change. My monthlies just stopped, that's all, you know. But Mrs Brereton had a bad time. Oh, she suffered. Once she came to the door and her face red, you know – well, *red*! As red, Freya, as Jem's pyjamas there… "Oh Molly," she said, "get Gerry from school for me could you?" And then she nearly collapsed right there on the step…'

'Oh. I liked Mrs Brereton.'

'Yes. I didn't like how the son turned out. You know him, don't you? A big article. Big potato head on him?'

'I can't picture him.'

'Oh, Freya, yes you do – big long jaw and a bony forehead like he was about to sprout horns…'

'I really can't remember meeting him.'

'You did, Freya – you must have met him ten times at least. Isn't your mammy a silly goose, Jem?'

Jem shakes his head, his mouth shrinking to a bewildered shape. Freya rubs his back.

'I might not be up to it today, Freya. I might cancel, you know. Though that might make Aoife blow up. You know how she is… Freya, I want you to do something for me, will you?'

'Yep. It's only I do have to leave now in five minutes…'

'You remember that letter I told you about?'

'Which?'

'That your grandad wrote.'

'The letter to Aoife?'

'Yes. It's in Grandad's office, just sitting in the top drawer. Go and get it for me, will you? It's time I did something about it.'

'Are you going to read it?'

'I think, yes. Or you read it. We could read it together maybe.'

'Okay, but maybe this evening is better Grandma, because I need to get to work…'

'Well, go and get it for me anyway, darling, and then we'll see.'

'Yes, okay, Grandma but then I'll have to go, okay? Cara will be here soon.'

8

CARA RINGS THE BELL to the rhythm that tells Grandma it's her – *brrr-brrr-b-b-brrrrrrrrr* – before using her key to open the front door.

'It's just me!' She shuts the door behind her. 'Grandma? It's Cara. I brought you the paper!'

She can already hear the television going. 'Today,' says a bass voice with a British actor's accent, 'Peppa and her family are going on a picnic...'

Cara puts the paper on the kitchen table. 'Phew,' she calls, 'windy day!'

The little television room is separated from the kitchen by a low archway. It's a curtained and carpeted den with a fireplace and a green marble carriage clock on the mantelpiece. From her high-backed armchair, Grandma lifts her chin and puts a hand back over her shoulder, wiggling her fingers. 'Hello Aunty Cara!' Jem is hunched in the cave of her body, watching the screen.

A family of very bright pink pigs are sitting on a chequered picnic blanket. 'Peppa loves strawberries,' says the deep voice. 'George loves strawberries. Everybody loves strawberries!'

'Have you had your coffee?'

'Yes, but I'll have another.' Grandma nudges Jem off her lap. 'Oh Cara, did you not comb your hair?'

'The wind.' Cara smiles at Jem, her hands on her hips. 'Are you not dressed young man?'

He smiles and shakes his head. 'We made eggy bread!'

Grandma pushes herself up from her chair. She is wearing a summer blouse with straight-cut short sleeves, exposing big, rock-like wrists and elbows, the flesh caught between them like wet plastic bags. She is getting old. She *is* old – eighty-five last January. Eighty-five is old.

'Well, would you ever?' she says. 'The nonsense they have on the television!'

Jem's eyes grow round as though someone has slapped him. His mouth crumples inwards. 'It's *Peppa Pig*,' he says. Then he frowns and gives a brave nod. 'It's a bit for babies.'

Grandma flicks Cara's hair back behind her shoulders, 'You need to take more care of your appearance, darling.'

'What happened to your forehead Grandma?' There is a square plaster stuck right by her hairline.

'A scratch. Well, where are the girls? They'll melt in the car. Bring them in!'

'I left them at home with their daddy.'

'Well, what a man. And he's able for all that is he?'

Cara rolls her eyes, and stoops to push Jem's hair back off his forehead. 'Well, Mr McGoo are you going to get dressed or what? Your cousins are waiting for you. We're going to go and see some baby rabbits today, won't that be fun?'

Grandma bends, wincing a little with the strain of it, and touches Jem's head. 'Big boy,' she says, 'go on up and get dressed. Your mammy left clothes on the bed for you.'

'Well, Jem, I don't believe it! Can you get dressed all by yourself?'

Jem nods up at Cara – enormous dark eyes and that fine little squiggle of a smile.

'Oh yes,' says Grandma, 'he's a great big man... go on up now, darling, quick as a flash.'

'We'll time you,' says Cara.

As soon as Jem leaves the room, Grandma's face drops. There is a purplish tinge to her top lip.

'Well, Cara,' she says.

'I brought you the paper.'

'Well, Cara, I'm glad you're here...'

'Oh?'

On the screen, the pigs are lying on their backs on the grass, laughing, snorting and kicking their trotters in the air. She looks around for the remote control – there it is, on Grandad's footstool.

'Well your mammy rang me yesterday... don't tell Freya, now will you?'

'What did she want?'

'Oh nonsense, you know. You wouldn't believe the nonsense. "Mammy," she says, "your Lily is going to win the Turner Prize!" You know how she can be.'

'Oh, dear...' Cara reaches for the remote control, and kills the screen. 'What did you say to her?'

'Oh, I rang off. It doesn't bother me now, you know. I'm only glad your grandad never knew how really bad she became... What is it that's wrong with her, do you think, Cara?'

'We'll never know, Grandma. No point dwelling on it... Do you think she's in Dublin?' Can Grandma hear it in her voice? The cold, trickling dread.

'Oh, I don't know, darling. I don't know. She rented out The Morrigan, as far as I know. She might want it back now, I really don't know. Don't tell your sister now, will you? Poor Freya, you know how upset she gets.'

'Have you been taking your iron, Grandma? Will I get you a Ferrograd C?'

'You could darling, you could. Although Freya says not to take it with coffee... But there's another thing now and see what you think of this... Well I don't know, did Freya tell you about the letter?'

'The letter?'

'Dinny wrote a letter, you know about it, do you?'

'I don't think so...'

'A letter to Aoife. You do. He wrote a letter. One of the days when he was really very down, Cara. He could be very angry in those last weeks, do you remember? You know it was difficult when his hands began to shake like that, and he wasn't very happy about Aoife's taste in art... oh, you know how he could talk sometimes, "No culture". He could be very down about it at times. He asked me to post the letter, and "Oh yes," I said, and when I came back then he asked, "Did you post that?" and "Oh yes," but I hadn't posted it.'

'You didn't tell me, Grandma.'

'And I didn't open the letter either, you know, until this morning.'

Cara lifts the medicine box down from the shelf above the fridge. 'What did it say? Or do you want to tell me?'

'Well, you know, he was very angry, Cara, and he said some very hard things, you know. I've torn it up now so no one will ever read those ugly things he said… but the thing of it is Cara, I think he could have been right about something and I'm glad I opened it…'

Cara opens the box – a bitter, hygienic smell. She lifts out a bottle of alcohol, aspirin, a sheet of cotton wool rolled in blue paper. 'I can't find your iron tablets Grandma—'

'It was about our will, actually, you know.'

'You might not want to tell me, Grandma—'

'It was strange to read it, you know. It was hard, like. You know the way Dinny could talk? The way of his words, like. I could hear his voice, nearly. I remembered his hands. That was hard on him, wasn't it? "Look here Aoife, you three girls have had the best of everything, and you are wealthy women…" And, well, think about this now, Cara – your Aunty Sinéad has no children, does she? And what does she want for? And your Aunty Aoife, well, that girl, she never did a thing in school – not a thing, Cara! And I think the teachers thought she was stupid, but Dinny said no, just lazy and wanting for nothing. He got her a job, and she had his name, you know, and that was it. You know we bought her that house? Before she was married? Just bought it outright, no mortgage or any of that. And then with Daddy's name she got a lot of clients, you know. So, she is a very wealthy woman, Cara, though you wouldn't always know it by the way she can go on... and what's she going to do with it all?'

Grandma stands at the kitchen table, one hand making a trembling tepee on the waxed tablecloth, the other holding a letter, wobbly fountain pen covering both sides.

'You're out of iron tablets, Grandma.' Cara tries not to look at the letter. She replaces the bottles and boxes – a tight roll of muslin, a tin of bandages, iodine – and slides the medicine box up onto its shelf. 'I'll get you the liquid one from the health shop. It's easier on the tummy anyway. It's just water, really. You mix it with juice.'

'... so he made a very sensible suggestion. "Look here, Aoife, you three girls had the best of everything. Your mammy and I worked and worked for years, we had very little for a very long time" – that's true, you know, we really hadn't a penny – "and you never wanted for anything, Aoife, and you are a wealthy woman though you never did a day's work in your life... it is unjust that you should inherit my life's work after I go..." So, and now I think he's right, he said he wanted to leave everything to the grandchildren – to you and Freya and your cousin Valerie... and I think, you know, I think I will do that. I think it is a very sensible suggestion. Because well, you know your mammy – Eileen will spend whatever she is given, on gurus and fortune-tellers and what have you, and you and Freya won't see a penny of what she inherits...'

'Sit down, Grandma,' says Cara. Even as the nausea billows up into her throat, her belly gives a little leap. Her mortgage, summer camp fees, the overdraft... 'Will I make you some tea or some coffee?'

Grandma lowers herself into her chair, but her voice rushes on, 'And, now I have been thinking while I was sitting there with that little fellow, well, when Daddy died, well, Freya hadn't had Jem yet. Oh, he would have loved him. My God, wouldn't he have enjoyed that little fellow?'

'Sit down, Grandma.'

Cara goes into the TV room, and pulls the curtains open, letting the yellow heat fall over her face through the diamond-crossed window. The truth is, given Grandad's disgust for 'whores' and 'sluts', he would certainly not have approved of Freya coming home pregnant by a mystery father. It's a thing Grandma has always glossed elegantly over. The daylight fizzes in over the thick green carpet, Grandad's low, mustard-coloured armchair, the slump of his ghost still hollowing the worn seat, and all the different shades of foliage and florals upholstering the little TV room. Her grandma's wealthy, but she hasn't changed the decor since she moved in here. Every year she has the whole house repainted the same colours.

'It's a beautiful day, Grandma. Do you want to come to the petting zoo with us?'

'Cara, stop flying about the place and sit down will you? I need to speak to you. Now, when your grandad died you had no children, and Freya neither – our little Jem wasn't born – and I am sure that if he had known them, your grandad would have included them too. So, I'm going to call Davitt Dunlin on the telephone and ask him to come here to talk it over. He'll understand. I'm going to talk it over with him. I think I'm going to divide everything between the three grandchildren and the four great-grandchildren. I think that's the best thing to do. That's the thing to do.'

'Tea or coffee, Grandma, which?'

'Tea, darling, please, thank you. No – coffee. Twist my arm. But tell me now darling, am I doing the right thing?'

Cara fills the kettle, slots it slowly into its stand and flicks it on to boil. How much would it amount to? Hundreds of thousands. Many hundreds of thousands. She could paint all day if she wanted to. She could get Denise a really beautiful violin.

'Biscuit?'

'Cara, I have been waiting for a full hour to talk to you about this. Now what do you think, tell me?'

Cara stretches up for the biscuit tin and puts it on the table.

'Aren't you a tiny little thing, Cara, up on your tippy toes like that just to get at the biscuits? Give it here.'

Grandma's dentures grit as she tugs at the lid. She has thick fingernails, glossy like little beetle backs, tapered fingertips. She removes two jam rings and passes them to Cara, then takes a chocolate Bourbon for herself. She points a finger while she chews, swallows hurriedly. 'Did you hear what I said about the will?'

Cara puts a cup of coffee down in front of Grandma. In her mind's eye, she is separating the table scene into thin horizontals of light and larger blocks of shadow. 'I heard you.'

'Coffee. Lovely. It's my only sin. Well? Am I doing the right thing Cara, what do you think?'

'I think you should talk it over with Davitt Dunlin like you say. I don't think you should talk to anyone else about it, Grandma. It's your decision, you know? And you know yourself what's best. It's really not for anyone else to say.' Before Grandma can reply, she says, 'Grandma, could I borrow a picture of Grandad's? You know the hare? Is it still hanging in his office? I don't know why I thought I had a copy in my house.'

'Yes, darling. Yes, of course. It's still there, I'm sure. Go and get it. And keep it, will you? I never go in there anymore. I'd like if you hung it up or something. It's only gathering dust.'

Cara pushes the newspaper towards Grandma. 'I got you the paper.'

'Good, thank you, darling. Well done. Hang the print in your little attic room there will you? I'd like that.'

'There's a supplement in there about Stoneybatter – apparently it's gentrified now.'

'What does that mean – "gentrified"?'

'Well, posh, I suppose. It's posh now. Look, they have a picture of Ard Righ Street and all. That's where you grew up isn't it?'

'Ard Righ. Yes. Bring me my glasses, will you? By my armchair.'

Cara fetches the glasses for her, and passes her the property supplement. She watches Grandma slide her glasses on and draw her head back to look. With her eyes she traces Grandma's contours – the soft, fuzzed line of her head and the curve of her neck. She imagines a little woodworm-like creature pulling streams of light around the rim of Grandma's cup, the bubble curls of her hair, fixing all those shapes into pipes of white space against dark, hatched penmarks.

'Well did you ever!' says Grandma, and there is a stopping sound from the back of her throat, like a draining sink suddenly plugged. 'That's our house.'

'Is it?'

Grandma holds the paper firmly in both hands and looks at it unmoving – the blind glint of her glasses, the downturned mouth. Still Cara's eye is at work, translating her onto paper, the little light-bearing beetle running over her padded shoulder and the hill of her wrist joint, the craggy curtain of her cheek.

'Mam always kept it so nice,' says Grandma. 'You can't imagine how Mam kept the house. And fifteen children, imagine. The Cannons next door and the Doyles just over the road. Mrs Doyle had miserable luck with children – trouble getting them to take root and then two born dead, poor woman – but they had a little girl my sister Greta's age – a scamp of a girl, actually – and they lost her when she was only seven. Set herself on fire playing with matches. Imagine.'

She lays the paper flat on the table, spins it around so that Cara can see. The photo is of a very small, dull brown terraced house with a red door.

'And what Daddy grew there on that apron of earth we had… we had an allotment, you know, just around the corner.

That's what we called it, "our apron of earth". Mam could make a feast from a few potatoes and a fist of herbs – a "blind stew", we called it. My mother was an intelligent woman. An intelligent housewife. There's a lot to be said for intelligence in housekeeping. People forget that.'

'It looks so small, Grandma. How did you all fit?'

It makes sense, suddenly – how Grandma has made a smaller house within this big one – a tiny, hot kitchen and a burrow for a living room, while the big airy rooms remain unused.

Grandma takes her glasses off and puts them on the table. When she looks up her cheeks are alarmingly red. Her eyes sag in sudden exhaustion, showing the curve of her eyeballs, the strips of pale pink on the inner lids.

'Exactly,' says Grandma. 'How could we all fit? Exactly.'

'Are you alright, Grandma?'

'Well, Jem!' says Grandma, beaming. The child is standing in the doorway, arms poker straight by his sides and his chin lifted in pride. 'Don't you look very smart?'

9

MOLLY NEVER THOUGHT SHE'D want that back – the close rows of houses and the front doors always wide open and the streetload of children crowding like flies at the stew pot and not a moment alone to do a little thinking even, or a sketch or to be looking at things. Not an inch to shift around in the bed and if someone wanted to play the piano, well then, they went to the Cannons next door and played it and everyone went in to listen and sing and all; no deciding for yourself what to do, for there was always the whole street in it. Even if you stayed put the singing would be coming in at you through the walls and the banging of the piano shaking the cups. There was no such thing as alone. That was a thing she took for granted, maybe – that no one would ever be left alone with themselves.

It's not everyone had the white sheet and pillowcase that was needed, so when little Sheila across the road went and burned herself so bad she died, it was Molly's mam who brought over the white things to lay her out. Molly and her big sister Kat were told to make sandwiches – Mrs Keogh came up out of the shop with bread and ham and a lump of butter and told them to make lots and cut them small the way people would feel they could manage one – and the others were to mind the little ones and keep them all quiet on the street. There were candles fetched from the church for a loan, and a little bowl of holy water for her feet, and as it was a child's death there was no shame in the women and the men both crying through the wake like she was their own. Mam and the other women were upstairs with the mother all night long, but Kat came down and said, 'You don't want to go up there, Molly; it's not nice to see her poor neck and hands like that; no one will notice if you stay downstairs now and tend to the tea and sandwiches.'

The next day the coffin was carried out by all the men in the street; all those strong, hardworking men that there were then, backs cobbled and dirt tracks in their faces, their eyes crunched small with the sobbing and drinking that went on through the night. A terrifying thing for a child, to see big men weep like that.

There was a coming together at those times, but she gave no value to that at all. It could be such a stifling thing to be woven in, always accounting for yourself, that she didn't even mind much her mam's scorn or the cruel things her sisters said to her when she went off and married *at the drop of a hat*, Kat said, *to the first fellow to sniff at you*, for she felt like a great heavy thing had been lifted from her face and she could breathe light, cool air in a way she hadn't known before. It was only after burying her little boy that Molly remembered her mam running over the road with the white things that time, and her face all stricken, and then the men carrying the little coffin out. Grown men, crying for the mother and for the little girl, and for each other.

In Soho, there wasn't much in the way of neighbouring, so when she held her little boy then, and he lost right there in her arms, she didn't think to go to the door and howl out the way they would have done at home. She only sat there with him on the clean floor for how long she'll never know and the word she heard out of herself was just 'Mam' over and over. She heard herself say it so quiet and soft – 'Mam Mam, Mam Mam Mam MamMamMamMamMam.'

She should have gone up that time, to see the burned girl laid out; she should have wept with the mothers instead of hanging back like that.

10

FREYA HAS BEEN COMING here with Jem since he was a baby. It's quiet in the mornings, especially on a Monday, and if the red-haired manager is on, he usually clears her bill. He hated the college crèche, which smelled of cigarettes and nappies, so as soon as lectures finished, she would pick him up and come here to work. She used to sit for hours over one coffee and a glass of tap water, reading while Jem coloured.

Jem is sitting on his hands, looking at his orange juice and croissant, chin pocked with anxiety.

'You're not drinking your juice, Jem.'

His mouth shrinks into a frightened blank and he just looks up at her with those eyes, asking something of her; an assurance that isn't hers to give. The man on the helpline told her it was better to arrange access on her terms. Otherwise, when it goes to court she won't look reasonable. They could give Dermot overnights, every weekend even, 'but children are very resilient,' the man said, 'and fathers are important.' She thought Jem would feel more at home, meeting Dermot for the first time here. But it was a mistake. It will be an intrusion to have Dermot come in here. It will break something.

'What's my daddy like?'

'Well...' It's only been five years since she's seen him, but it's hard to picture his face. Their affair didn't last very long. Or at least it turned sour very quickly. She can remember the beginning – the thrill of being wanted. She was a virgin and it had seemed to her like a miracle, that someone would want her like that. She remembers trying to get to know him, to have conversations with him – the disappointment of that, the way he would veer off into monologues, the way he tried to talk in riddles, to make himself mysterious and complicated. It seems so stupid now. Her attraction to him was so ambivalent and their relationship so fraught that she thought this might be the intangible 'love' people talked about. She remembers the terror when he became angry, the hopelessness of trying to reason with him; how pathetic he was, stuttering and spitting, kicking the wall and pushing things over, and the strange relief then, when he hurt her or fucked her or both. She can remember his eyes when he was aroused or enraged. They gleamed and darted. But what is he like? How would he seem to a stranger, or to an anxious child?

'Well, he has brown eyes, Jem.'

'Like me?'

'Well, different eyes to you, baby, you have my grandad's eyes, but also brown. And he – well, he used to, work in a hotel, I don't know if he still does... A porter, it's called a night porter... guarding the doors at night.'

'Is he nice?'

'Yes, I think so, baby. He is very excited about meeting you. It'll be alright, little man. It's only for a few hours…'

But as soon as he walks in the door she remembers – a lean man with crisp clothing – and nothing fits right on him, she remembers that now, even tight-fitting clothes are too big and square on his shifty frame – long, bony hands; meticulously controlled movements. He stretches his neck like a hawk, surveying the tables, and she remembers his throat – the way he wagged his Adam's apple to itch his throat. She reaches across the table and touches Jem's shoulder, tugs him off his chair and up onto her knee and there must be some way out of this but now he's approaching, and he's touching the table with those long fingers, and she remembers now that W-shaped smile he made when trying to ingratiate himself, the upper lip too long and pronounced, like the beak of a parrot. Her coffee burns up into her throat. She should have stood up when she saw him, but now it's too late. He is standing over them, too close.

'Well, hello there!'

'Hi, Dermot.'

'Long time no see. So, this is Jem. Hey, Mister! This is my son, then.'

'Yes. This is Jem.'

Jem puts his arms behind his head. His fingers grip Freya's neck and he twists his face into her shoulder.

'Are you going to say hello?' says Dermot, crouching down beside the chair and squeezing the toe of Jem's new light-up runners. 'I don't bite.'

Jem pulls Freya's face towards him and whispers very quietly in her ear, 'Is that him?'

'Yes, baby.'

'Right,' says Dermot, standing up. At his hip, he is wearing a rectangular bag of black canvas, hanging on a long, thick strap across his chest. He tears open the Velcro flap and pulls out a thick wad of A4 pages. Freya expects him to sit across the table, but he slides into the chair next to them, and moves it close. He is heavily scented. Something with a urine tang; the cat-spray odour of a teenage boy.

'I have some paperwork for you, actually,' he says. 'No big deal, just…' He leafs through the pages until he finds a spot with a dotted line and an X in pencil. 'It's just two forms. It's just confirming I'm a single parent, you know, for a tax break, and a lone parent allowance. We can sort out the access arrangements in due course.' He taps the page, then pulls a pen from a special little pocket on his bag.

Jem has taken both of Freya's hands and folded them across himself.

'Right,' says Freya, 'I'll read through them and get back to you.'

He smirks and shakes his head. 'You haven't changed, do you know that?'

He says it like a real question and Freya has no answer, so she says, 'Okay.'

'Right,' says Dermot. He puts his hands under Jem's arms and pulls at him. 'Let's you and me get out of here, buddy.'

'Hang on,' says Freya, 'hang on a second. Jem, do you want to finish your orange juice?'

Jem is standing between them now. He leans against her, his body pressed to hers and his mouth by her ear. 'Where are we going?'

'He wants to know where you're going, Dermot.'

'Wherever you want, mister!' he says. 'I thought you might like to come and see my place. I have an Xbox. Do you like Minecraft?'

Jem shrugs.

'You can go on the back of my motorbike. I've got you a helmet and all. Have you ever been on a motorbike?'

Jem shakes his head.

'No,' says Freya. 'He's not going on a motorbike.'

Dermot rolls his eyes. 'I'm joking.' He winks at Jem, tousling his hair. 'Can your mother not take a joke, no?'

Jem looks up at him, then back at Freya.

'Well, I'll see you in three hours, Jem,' says Freya. Dermot is standing above her now, smiling that jagged smile. 'So,' she says, 'I'll see you back here at two?'

'Ohhh,' says Dermot, squeezing up his face in mock regret, 'that wasn't the plan now was it, Freya?'

'I thought that was the plan.'

'No. Sorreeee,' he says in a singsong voice, cocking his head to one side. 'You're picking him up at my place. Around seven is fine. Come on, Mister. We're going to have great fun, you and me.'

'Where's your place?'

'I'll text you.'

11

WHEN MOLLY OPENS THE front door, she is shocked to see how the years have wrung at Davitt Junior's face, how downy and ashen his hair has gone. He's her Aoife's age, isn't he? Not much older, anyway, for she remembers them playing together at ten or eleven – he red-nosed and fish-boned and dangly on the arms, and Aoife taller and stouter, the way girls can sprout up at that age quicker than boys.

'Well, Davitt!'

'Hello, Mrs Kearney, how are you?'

'You're very good to come, Davitt. You know I saw you through the window, standing on the step there, and I thought it could be your father.'

Molly's fingers rush to her lips – stupid old halfwit why did she say such a thing?

Davitt Senior was a decent man, but he could be very harsh on the young fellow. She can remember calling to his office in Dalkey one day, when Young Davitt had just joined the practice and she could see by the look of the boy that he was swallowing down the tears. Molly had smiled at him, *Well how are you getting on DJ?* and the father whipped around in his fancy spinning chair, eyes all aflash – *That boy is a bloody eejit Molly! I can tell you I don't know what they taught him in his high-and-mighty university at all. I'm sick of the sight of him.*

'It's not too much trouble for you, Davitt? Taking you out of the office...'

'No no, Mrs Kearney!' Davitt Junior shakes his head. There's a sorry look about him, standing there on the doorstep with big shades blanking out his eyes; the sun coming in from behind to light the shiny head he has now, the halo of duckling fluff on it. 'Delighted to get out to be honest!' he says.

The father had a lot of hair, if Molly remembers rightly. Any time she saw him it was with a great crop on top.

'You know you can always call me and I'll come out to you... Never a problem at all, Mrs Kearney.'

He smiles at her like a boy, but no, there is a gauntness to him now certainly, furrows like claw marks down his cheeks. He thrusts one fist into his pocket and with the other he gives a little jiggle of his briefcase. He is wearing a fine-quality shirt buttoned tight at his hairless white wrists, and no tie and no jacket with it.

'Well, come on in Davitt, I have the kettle on. Don't you look the part in your shades? Everyone wears them now in the summer, don't they? Used to be only crooks wore shades.'

'Is that right?'

He steps into the hallway, takes off the sunglasses and folds them, looking at them quizzically, as though they belong to someone else.

'They must be very useful, are they? That's what my Freya says, that they're very useful for driving on a bright day.'

'Oh they are, yes. They are.'

Molly leads him into the good sitting room. It's warm and smells fresh because she's had the windows open since seven this morning, and then an hour ago she shut them and drew the heavy curtains closed, and put the heating on.

'Sit down there, Davitt. Make yourself comfortable. Tea or coffee?'

'Oh, tea please, Mrs Kearney. Thank you...'

'I'll be back in a moment.'

To save time and fuss, Molly has already scalded the teapot, and set the tray with two Delph cups in their saucers, and the milk and the sugar bowl and a plate of generously buttered Rich Tea biscuits. She has even filled the kettle already, so it's only a matter of bringing it to the boil and pouring it into the pot. At the last moment, she adds some pink wafer-and-icing fingers to the biscuit plate.

When she enters the room, young Davitt is standing with his back to her, hands clasped at his flat bottom, looking at the snow scene that Dinny liked so much (they paid a lot for that, it seemed a lot at the time, anyway). After closing the curtains this morning, she switched on the little pipes of light that run along over each of the pieces in the room. It's rare that she does that, and it's nice to look at them all again, lit up like they deserve. Davitt turns away from the painting and hops to get the door for her. Still gangly in the legs, the way he was as a boy. 'Stay where you are, Davitt,' she says, nudging easily around the door with her hip and elbow and sliding herself in, still holding the tray steady. 'I'm not such a helpless old biddy just yet! Sit down there, Davitt.'

There are some large envelope files of salmon pink and dirty yellow stacked on the coffee table, and Davitt moves them aside to make room for the tray. The couch and the matching armchairs are very low-set, and his sharp knees push up higher than the little coffee table. Molly takes the straight-backed armchair, which feels a little unseemly, because it makes her sit higher than him, but if she was to sit in the low chair she'd have trouble getting herself up out of it again. Davitt leans forward between his legs, and begins to pour the tea out before it's had a chance to draw.

'Oh, leave it a minute I think, Davitt...'

He nods and puts it back down in one little movement. 'Pink wafers!' he says, lifting one up and smiling at it. 'It's years since I've had a pink wafer. I'd forgotten they existed!'

He doesn't take a bite, but holds the wafer like a cigar between two fingers. With the other hand, he pats the stack of files. 'So I brought all the files pertaining to the will, Mrs Kearney.'

'Did you? Lovely, thank you, Davitt.'

'How is the family, Mrs Kearney?'

'Wonderful Davitt – you've met my great-grandson, have you?'

'I don't think so.'

'Jem, such a character... a fine child. A really magnificent child. A little monkey. There he is on the cabinet there. That's about a year ago now. He's shot up since...'

'He's the eldest great-grandchild, is that right?'

'Freya's little one, yes. He'll be six soon. You know Freya, do you? Eileen's youngest.'

'Yes...' Davitt gives a queer little blink, as though something has splashed him in the eye. 'So, tell me, Mrs Kearney, how can I help?'

He takes a bite of the biscuit, and she can see he is enjoying the light sugariness of it. He could use a little building up, poor man. The wife is a nothing cook; she remembers Mrs Dunlin telling her that. They melt in the mouth, those biscuits. The children go mad for them.

'Well now, see what you think of this Davitt – you know Dinny and I worked very hard for a long time, before we really had a penny, and our three girls, well—'

'Is there someone at the door, Mrs Kearney?'

'Oh, well, there shouldn't be, Davitt. Freya said she'll be out all day with the little fellow, I don't know what it is she said they were doing...'

'I'm sure I heard something.'

'My Aoife comes at twelve on a Monday after her beautician, and what time is it now?' She glances at the big silent grandfather clock that Dinny put there to blunt the harshness of that corner. 'Only half ten, is it?'

'I thought I heard someone at the door. Would you like me to go and check just quickly?'

'There you are, Mammy!'

Her eldest daughter is leaning heavily on the open door, one fist tight on the handle, the other bent in on her hip, and a frown on her of such stormy fury that Molly almost gasps.

'Well, Fifi darling, you're early!'

'My ears were itching.' Aoifc purses her lips, all eyebrows and jowls. She is in one of her moods. She nods at Davitt. 'Hello, Davitt.'

Her hair has been coloured since last week. It's brushed neatly and the too-long fringe has been clipped up off her forehead, but the rest of it hangs down very straight either side of her face. It's a new shade, far too dark and reddish for her daughter's pale complexion. Best to allow the grey, sometimes. Her painted lips drag on her face.

Davitt lays the rest of his wafer on the tea-tray and puts his hands on the armrests to push himself up. 'Aoife.'

'Davitt. Sorry to disturb you, Mammy, my appointment was cancelled and I didn't know you'd have a visitor.'

'You forgot to ring the bell, darling.'

'The bell.' She rolls her eyes for Davitt's benefit. 'Yes, the bell, Mammy, the bell… Mammy likes us to announce ourselves, Davitt, she has a special ring she likes us to do. Isn't that right, Mammy?'

Davitt is standing now, rubbing his palms on the front of his thighs. 'How are you, Aoife? How is Brendan?'

'Oh, you know yourself, Davitt. Small-town solicitor – it's ten jobs in one.'

'Sure, I know only too well, Aoife, only too well... And the kids... or, just the one, isn't it?'

'Valerie. She's great. Doing very well in London... and how're your boys?'

'Oh great, yeah. Derek's just finished his finals...'

'Law, isn't it?'

'Yes. So now, hopefully now you know, he'll be keeping the family business alive!'

Aoife approaches, bends and kisses Molly's cheek, then squats at the low, soft chair beside her, as though to sit. But she changes her mind suddenly, and stands so close that Molly has to strain very much to look up at her. She nudges her chin at Davitt's papers.'Well, may I ask what this is all in aid of?'

'Oh, Davitt is helping me sort out some things, Aoife. You go on into the kitchen now, darling, will you? And make some coffee for yourself. I'll be in in a little while.'

'Mammy, I told you Brendan will handle the properties. You don't need to be bothering Davitt about those things.'

'No, of course you're right. Go on now, darling, we'll just finish up here and we'll be in now in a minute...'

'What's this about, Mammy?'

'I'll explain it all to you now in a few minutes, Aoife. Go on now, Fifi.'

Aoife shakes her head, her cheeks puffed out in a big sigh. 'See you in a minute Davitt,' she says, turning and swaggering from the room. It saddens Molly to watch the graceless cut of her as she goes. She has always been hefty, especially her bottom. Nothing wrong with a heavy girl, but Aoife never could accept her shape. Molly had hoped that she might grow into herself in her middle years, but she's only more awkward in her skin now, lugging her body about like an inconvenience. It is Molly's doing, perhaps; perhaps it is she who has given Aoife that wrong feeling about herself. She was a shock to Molly, when she came. The colour and the shape of her, and her face a stranger's.

Aoife leaves the door ajar. Molly looks at Davitt and raises her eyebrows.

'She who must be obeyed,' she says, grinning. Davitt nods, brushing crumbs from his lap.

Molly says, 'We can pour out the tea, I think,' her voice low and a wink to show him that she is in charge and he's not to worry.

'We might keep our voices down a bit, Davitt...'

12

AOIFE STABS ONCE WITH the paring knife. The blade is so worn that it only dents the thick foil. Stupid bloody things – why all the packaging? She pokes it again, harder this time, and twists until a coffee scent siphons out through the little piercing. She drops the knife onto the table and wriggles her fingers in, coaxing the hole wider.

What's Mammy like? Queeny in there on her throne, big hands bent over the armrests and her lips pursed, and Davitt crouching in the low armchair – *yes Mrs Kearney; no Mrs Kearney* – shuffling papers about and making her feel all important.

She'll have to phone Davitt later and make sure Mammy's not doing something silly; tampering with the will or whatever. Her mother is getting to an age now where they need to keep a bit of an eye on her.

The vacuum pack yields very suddenly, splitting down the seam and sending coffee filter cups clattering out over the table. They're a terrible waste of money, these things – individual plastic filters for each cup of coffee, only seven to a pack, but her mother insists on them.

When she's stacked the filters on the table, Aoife opens the dishwasher for the mugs; white with little blue flowers along the rims – one for herself, and one for her mother. She sets them side by side on the table and pops a filter cup on top of each. She'll have everything nice and ready when her mother comes in, and she won't let on she's wondering about Davitt. They'll sit and have their coffee, and she'll ask casually what it was all about. Her mother will be delighted with the chocolates she brought... Oh yes— the chocolates!

The living-room door is still ajar when she moves across the hall. Her handbag is on the console, beside a vase of tattered tulips. Where did Mammy even get those cheap tulips?

There's no sound from the two of them in there. Are they whispering? Or sitting, fingers on lips, waiting for her to retreat to the kitchen?

In the inside pocket of her handbag she has four of those chocolates collected from her coffees in town. All week she saves up her complimentary treats. Then she brings them with her on a Monday and shares them with Mammy after lunch. It's their little ritual.

Pulling the bag towards herself, she catches her face in the hall mirror, half concealed by the flowers – one baggy cheek, and one sombre eye and the blocky shadow of her newly coloured hair. *Miserable*. That's what her husband said last night, *Why do you have to be such a miserable cow all the time?*

But this morning she felt like a nice lady as she drove into the city with the chocolates in her handbag, no greys in her hair, heading in for her weekly pamper. She played Lyric FM in the car, and she drove calmly along, no rush, unperturbed by other drivers, only good will in her for the day ahead.

Now the sight of that vase brings a bright rage fluttering up to her skin and twitching in her fingertips. The state of the flowers! The petals lying splay, rotting shafts. It's shocking, how her niece Freya just takes and takes from Mammy.

Not a whisper from the living room.

Aoife can feel her upper lip thinning and tightening, that ugly way it has. The vase water is low and marshy, the pollen shedding all over the shiny wood and the strip of Brussels lace. It's the least Freya could do, to look after things like that; change the water in the vase, and wash the lace now and then.

The mirror needs a polish too.

She touches the skin beneath her eyes.

Davitt is pale-looking now. Old-looking.

She stands back a little – she has learned to do this. She has learned not to stand too long, to look too long or in the wrong light. This is closer than people come, she tells herself. No one notices those lines, no one is searching for them.

She turns her attention to the dark, silky interior of her handbag. It's a great handbag – grey suede on the outside and a lovely silky taupe inside. She bought it for less than half price in the January sales. A good handbag is important. She has explained that to her daughter. A good handbag and a good coat and you can hold your head up high... She only hopes the chocolates haven't melted into the lining from the heat. No, they're alright. One by one, she lifts them out and places them tenderly in her palm. Four lozenges, wrapped tightly in gold paper. They make her think of other small treasures – wild bird eggs, or the tangle of baby mice her husband found that time when he pulled out the skirting board…

Passing the door on her way back to the kitchen, she can hear nothing from the living room but the clink of a spoon on china. Not to worry – Davitt has more sense than to go behind Aoife's back.

They're taking their time. Aoife might as well empty the dishwasher. It's when she's putting away the glasses that she sees it – yet another photo of Freya's little bastard! When did that appear? It's a passport-sized thing, tucked in between the glass and the frame of the cabinet door. A school photo with a marble backdrop and he's wearing that ridiculous uniform. Aoife averts her eyes as she shuts the cupboard, turns to find that there's nothing left in the dishwasher. Well, she'll have her own coffee then. Might as well.

Waiting for the water to ease silently down through the coffee paper, she raps her glossy fingernails on the table, falling in with the tick of the carriage clock from the adjoining room. Her father used to take great pleasure in winding it up every night at seven.

Her father thought he had 'taste', and he had to sanction every item in the house – nothing could be allowed on the shelves or walls that did not meet with his aesthetic standards. No lollipop-stick picture frames, no lumpy sculptures… and yet there it was all those years, the centrepiece of their sitting room – that garish thing – lime-coloured marble and little gold-plated lion feet. It's so loud, that ticking, and dull, like a dripping tap. Sometimes, when dinner was tense – Daddy glowering at his plate, Mammy's cheeks simmering red, and Aoife's stomach tightening around her food – she used to imagine a sink filling up to the brim with all the ticks that Daddy wound into the house every evening.

It's Mammy who pays for that crèche – no doubt about it – a Montessori in Merrion Square because little Lady Muck can't be expected to send her child to the college creche like the other unmarried mothers. *Freya doesn't like it* – that's what Mammy said. Doesn't like it! Oh no, not content to take the usual precautions, Freya decides to go and have a baby. Not only that, but this child has to have only the best; no single mother's life for Freya. Ridiculous carry on anyway – five-year-olds in blazers and caps like Victorian dolls, and the shorts! Ridiculous nonsense – tartan shorts and knee-high socks. No doubt it was Freya who slipped that photo in there, her little message to the rest of them that she has her feet in under the table. The child looks like a gnome; a face on him like aren't-I-gorgeous-you-know-I-am and fat, dimpled cheeks and creepily round eyes that follow her around. Aoife's breath is growing sore in her throat. Despite herself, she glances again at the obnoxious photo. Well there's no reason she should have to feel like a stranger in her home; the home she grew up in. She stands quickly, plucks the picture out from the frame of the cupboard, flips it around and slides it back in. He can smirk in at the cups and saucers now instead of at her.

The coffee is taking so bloody long to filter that she goes

out to the hall. Someone has to change the water in that vase. Someone has to look after things. She slows as she passes the living room, taking careful, quiet steps.

'Lovely, Davitt,' says Mammy in her public voice, 'do that, will you? Thank you, Davitt, you're very good to come all the way out...'

She'll be accused of eavesdropping if she's caught in the hall, so Aoife grabs the flowers and returns as quickly as she can to the kitchen. She's swirling a cloth around the bottom of the vase by the time her mother calls, 'Aoife! Fifi darling, Davitt is leaving, he can't stay!'

Vase in hand, Aoife leans in the kitchen doorway, a nod and a smile. 'See you now Davitt, thanks for calling in on her.'

'Bye then, Aoife, give my best to Brendan now won't you?'

Mammy stands too long at the open door, waving and smiling while Davitt manoeuvres his car inch by inch out between the two others in the driveway.

'That's it!' shouts Mammy. 'Careful now, Davitt! Good man, you have it...'

'Leave the poor man alone, Mammy!' says Aoife. 'How can he concentrate on driving when you're there gawking and screeching at him?' Her mother ignores her, so she returns to the kitchen and finishes washing the vase.

When at last she's shut the front door, Mammy shuffles in, hands on the table to steady herself as she moves towards her chair.

'What are you doing to my tulips, Fifi?'

'I'm changing the water. It was disgusting, Mammy. It

smelled… the flowers are jaded anyway, you know, no more than a day left in them.' Aoife fills the vase with cold water, and pushes the flowers back in. Another petal drops.

Mammy knows she's in trouble. Her back ruffles up like a bird's in winter. She looks at the table and says, 'Tell me this, have you heard from Sinéad?'

'Not much. She's very busy, you know. The garden is tough going at this time of year…'

'I tried to phone her yesterday but she wasn't answering.'

'Probably in the garden,' says Aoife.

Her mother nods. 'She exaggerates a bit with all that gardening, I think.'

'Well, are you going to explain what that was all about, Mammy? You didn't tell me Davitt Dunlin was calling in?'

Her mother sits wearily at the head of the table, a big dramatic sigh. 'Oh my Feefs you are a nosy thing, aren't you?' There is a little quiver in her throat as she says that. Her top lip is a strip of purplish gristle. All that excitement has tired her out.

Davitt should have checked with Aoife before calling in. She could have told him Mammy wasn't able for it. 'What was that all about, Mammy?'

'He just called in, darling. He needed me to sign some things, you know.'

'Are you having your coffee or did you already have it with Davitt Dunlin?'

'Yes, please darling. No, I haven't had my coffee.'

Aoife pushes her own coffee towards her mother and pours

some hot water into the second filter for herself. Her life is full of these small unnoticed sacrifices.

'I brought you some chocolates.' She nods at the little huddle on the table. They look paltry now, their paper frayed.

'Oh, thank you, darling.'

'The Italian ones you like.'

'Aren't you a great girl, thank you, darling. We'll have them after our lunch.'

'So, what's this business with Davitt?'

Her mother's cheeks flush. She's hiding something – no doubt about it.

'Well, you know, darling I just wanted a little chat. It's been a long time since I've had a look over my affairs…'

Aoife rolls her eyes. What kind of an eejit does her mother think she is? 'So, am I going to have to ask Brendan to call Davitt, or are you going to tell me what's going on?'

Mammy looks into her coffee mug. 'You know Cara can be a serious girl sometimes – "Grandma, these are very bad for the environment you know…" And there's me sorting all the rubbish for the five different bins we have now, and switching off the lights after her, you know, she always forgets to switch off lights. Your daddy could get angry over that, do you remember?'

'The cheek of her, Mammy, telling you what kind of coffee to drink.'

'Well, aren't you a cranky one today?'

'How can you stand the sound of that clock, Mammy? Day in day out, I couldn't stand it. I'd just let it stop if I was you.'

'Well, isn't it lucky then that I don't mind it, and Freya neither?'

'Does it not drive you bonkers?'

'No, darling. I like that clock; you know that. Your daddy loved that clock.'

Aoife lifts the lid off her coffee, places it on the tablecloth, and peers in at the swill of water beneath the paper.

'You're making a fool of yourself, Mammy.'

'What?'

'Don't be getting Davitt Dunlin to come out to you like that. He has enough to be doing.'

'Yes, I'm sure you're right, darling.'

'So, what did you want with him anyway?'

'Oh, I just wanted to look at the will, you know, now that there are more children. There were no great-grandchildren, you know, when your daddy and I made our will.'

The indignation surges up into Aoife's throat. She closes her eyes and takes a deep breath in, then out, but it presses sore under her tongue.

'Mammy,' she says calmly, 'don't tell me you're going to reward Freya for getting herself pregnant outside marriage? Don't tell me my Valerie is going to be punished for keeping her legs shut like a decent girl...'

And this is what really gets Aoife, this is what makes her chest feel like a dam and her head clamour with brilliant, flapping rage – Mammy's frail-old-lady act. She can't bear to watch it – the face dappling red and white, eyes wild as though in fear, the way she clutches at her own hands. Then the voice, the warble like she's some crusty bat instead of Aoife's mother, some rickety old crow instead of her mammy. 'No, darling. No, of course you're right. I never thought of it like that.'

'Don't tell me you've gone and changed the will you made with Daddy, Mammy?'

'No darling, no you're quite right; you're quite sensible to say that. No, I only talked it over with Davitt. He advised me to think it over. I was going to talk it over with you darling…'

'I'll have Brendan call Davitt and sort it out. We'll sort it out, Mammy. No harm done… but you are a terrible eejit dragging poor Davitt out here on a silly whim. You're getting soft in the head.'

'I see.'

'I brought you your chocolates, Mammy, the ones you like.'

'Thank you, darling.'

'The Italian ones you like.'

'Yes, Aoife, you told me. Thank you, darling, you're a great girl.'

Bloodless lips pursed, Mammy rotates the coffee mug slowly with her fingertips, until the handle is at her right hand. It makes Aoife want to smash something. 'Well, Mammy, Brendan was very disappointed not to see you last week,' she says. 'I made roasted quails.'

Mammy runs the pad of a finger up and down the curve of the handle. 'Oh, was he? Well you tell him I'm sorry. You know, I was tired. I had a nap…'

'Drink your coffee, Mammy, before it gets cold.'

Mammy nods and brings two fingers to her brow in salute.

'She who must be obeyed,' she murmurs quickly, and takes a sip of her coffee.

Aoife won't rise to it.

'Honestly, Mammy,' she says, 'running around after that child all the time, at your age. That's what has you tired. Brendan would have picked you up, you know, if you were too tired to drive.'

'You're very good, darling. I'll come next time. Tell me what did you do with the quails? Did you stuff them or what? Or did you do that nice thing with the juniper berries – that was lovely you know. I was telling Cara about it...'

'Well come on Wednesday, Mammy, will you? Valerie will be home for a couple of days... she can't stay long though and she really would love to see you.'

'Yes, I'll try darling. I'll see if Freya can come. The little one finishes at twelve on a Wednesday.'

'Well I think Valerie would be disappointed, Mammy, not to see you on your own.'

'Oh.'

'It's impossible to talk, you know, with a child running around and chattering away all the time. I'm sure Valerie would like the chance to see you on your own for once... I wish you'd told me Davitt was coming this morning, Mammy. I could have done my shopping this morning instead of this afternoon.'

'Oh yes, that reminds me darling, I have a list. You're going to Brown Thomas isn't it?'

'A shopping list?'

'Yes, darling. You know those Sloggi?'

'The underwear?'

'Good cotton knickers – the ones that cover your bottom properly, and cover your kidneys. I want you to get me six extra small and six medium, can you do that?'

'Why?'

'Well, Aoife, you should see the little rags that Cara wears, and Freya, my goodness you couldn't trim a hat with the scraps she has for knickers!'

Aoife lifts the filter off her coffee. She pours a big dollop of milk in, drinks a deep, tepid gulp and wipes her lip.

'I don't mind helping you, Mammy,' she says, and breaths out to push this terrible soreness from her chest. She can see that her mammy is nervous though, knowing she has gone too far. She's clutching at her hands again like a big squirrel, her shoulders up and her bony chest heaped beneath her gullet. Aoife speaks low and calm. 'I'll get you as many knickers as you like, Mammy, if they're for you. You know I have no problem doing that. I won't even ask you for the money for them. But I will *not* run around buying knickers for the Ladies Muck. I will *not*, Mammy.'

'No. Alright then, darling. Well I want some knickers for myself then – six extra small and six medium, you know how my weight goes up and down…' Mammy tries to grin but she is nervous, flicker-eyed, like a daring child. She stands. 'I've written it out for you there and it's with the money under the chopping board.'

Aoife looks at her own hands – the perfect, smooth ovals for nails, and the incongruous chubbiness of her fingers – and breathes out. She can feel her mother move around the kitchen; slow and resolute. Two fifty-euro notes and a scrap of paper are placed ceremoniously on the table in front of her. Written in her mother's careful, knife-sharpened pencil marks:

Aoife Monday
In Brown Thomas please can you get:
Sloggi knickers, white (black or naked if no white) 100% cotton
6 × extra small
6 × medium
Thank you darling

Aoife raises her face to Mammy with her mouth open, a shout ripping at her chest, 'You mean *nude* Mammy. Not "naked", *nude.*'

But Mammy has turned already, her head in the open fridge now. 'Well I've made us a lovely salad for our lunch, darling, because I know you are slimming again. And I've made some nice mayonnaise too – one little spoon won't do you any harm. But tell me this, would you like a nice herb omelette as well with some scallions snipped into it? Chives would be better but Freya brought back a lovely little bundle of scallions from that market in the park. I've been waiting for a visit from Sinéad though, with those wonderful chives she has growing there out the front. I haven't had a word from her all week. Do you think I should call over?'

She closes the fridge and turns back around, four eggs cradled in her long, speckled hand. She looks Aoife right in the face, all conspiratorial smiles. 'It's not just you who should be slimming you know! Sinéad was always such a fine figure of a girl growing up and – well! Well, my God, when I saw her last time, well, I said, "Sinéad, what sort of a bottom have you grown?" and "Oh stop it, Mammy," she says, so I said no more. But she doesn't have the bones to hold all that size, you know! It's as if the fat can hardly hold onto the tiny frame of her. And the great thighs! Well, Aoife, I was shocked. Were you shocked? That happened very quickly. But what did you tell me there? When did you say you last saw Sinéad?'

13

MOLLY SETTLES INTO HER chair, massages the gnarl in her knee. It's the cartilage – worn down, or swollen, or both. Never mind. She will just sit for a while, get her rhythm back. Aoife can really take it out of her sometimes.

She pulls her knitting bag onto her knee. She's not going all the way upstairs for the sock. She'll start something new.

Baby Peig is always in hand-me-downs; neglected looking. It would be nice for her to have something of her own. Molly still has some of that fine merino 4-ply, a soft brown, like a wild baby rabbit, and so light to work with. She'll make one of those lovely little matinee coats. Perfect for a child of that age. Something Cara can throw around the baby to put her in the pram.

Molly opens her needle case and selects a round needle, size 3.25. The yarn is easy on her fingertips as she casts on rhythmically. She might have to look at the pattern in a bit, but she knows for certain it's fifty-three stitches for the back, then five rows of garter stitch. How many of those little coats has she made? Oh ten at least. At least. Didn't she make three of them for Aoife – pink, yellow, green?

Is it the change or what? Molly doesn't know, but she can really blow up these days, her Fifi. Doesn't like to be kept in the dark. Fuming. Fuming is the word. That's the word she'll use when she tells Freya about it. Aoife always had a temper. The great scenes she could make as a child – the jiggle of her cheeks and the fat boxer fists and the stamping of her sausage-roll legs. Dinny would be splitting his sides with the sight of her. *She who must be obeyed* – that's what he used to call her. Aoife used to make him laugh. He laughed a lot in those years. Everything was going well – Aoife was healthy; Dinny had friends; he was getting 'recognised' – that was the right expression. But the grief was still stuck into Molly. She hadn't the strength for it. Some days it hit her in the gut as soon as she opened her eyes. Some days, she couldn't breathe for it, she couldn't see—

Molly stops and straightens out the stitches. She's lost count now. Starting at the beginning, she marches her forefinger up along the needle, counting in twos, but, my God, she is weary after that visit.

She who must be obeyed. The way those cheeks huff and puff. Those dark, low brows that she got off of Dinny.

What is that, forty stitches?

She pushes the needle into the ball of wool, places it on the shelf. The cardigan will have to wait. She's too tired now.

God, her knee. Freya might make her a compress for it, when she gets in.

She could try to snooze, here in her chair. An afternoon snooze and by the time she wakes it will be evening. Freya. The little boy. They can have a light supper together, cosy at the table.

She had Aoife in Dublin, in the Coombe Hospital. Dinny was more stuck into all that Soho nonsense by then than ever before, so it was a great defiance when she said she was going home and that was the end of it. She was not a contrary woman; she was never a fussy wife. It was only that she knew – and she knew, she really did, and she told Dinny in no uncertain terms – that she couldn't let the child out of her otherwise. She went back to Ireland with four days to spare. She can remember on the boat, the enormous relief, rubbing her belly. 'We're alright little man, we're alright.'

When she first saw it, Molly thought there'd been a mistake – a girl. It was much bigger and much redder than the baby she had been expecting.

14

AT QUARTER TO SEVEN, Freya parks tilted on the pavement outside Dermot's house, and rings the doorbell. When there is no answer she gets back into her car and waits.

Dermot's house is near the river – a pocket of squat houses under a close, colourless skein of clouds. The street should be charming – the uneven rooftops and stone windowsills, the fat, smoking chimneys – but it's shadowed by a mirror-faced office block that smothers the milky sun. Even on sunny days, these houses must seem dark and mossy and cold.

At seven, she texts Dermot to say that she's here, and places the phone face down on the passenger seat beside a bunch of ailing daffodils.

Cars pass quickly on the wet road behind, and she can hear tense laughter from the off licence on the corner.

Every few minutes she checks her phone for a reply.

Twice she calls Cara, ready to tell her everything – how she sent Jem off with someone he's never met before, how Dermot's neck clenched when he spoke, how he is not where he said he'd be and has not answered the phone and it's nearly ten past seven. But she makes herself hang up before her sister answers. She often panics like this over nothing. She needs to control her anxiety. That's what Cara says. In any case, she's been so stupid. Cara will kill her.

The daffodils will have wilted by the time she gets them home. She should have bought the closed ones. Grandma loves daffodils. In springtime the house used to be filled with vases of them from Mrs Brereton's, but the new neighbour doesn't cut them.

At ten past seven she gets a reply from Dermot:

I suppose you expect people to answer your texts even though you never answer theirs? I hope you're not going to raise my son with that kind of hypocrisy.

He is trying to scare her. This is a game. She will wait. She will not panic and she will wait.

There is a little cul de sac off this street – a ring of five houses, and in the middle of the road, standing on a chunk of concrete with an illegible plaque, a queer little statue of the Virgin Mary serves as a kind of traffic circle. Her features have been smoothed by decades of cream gloss paint, and Freya watches the half-shut eyes and sad mouth fade as the evening closes over.

It's getting dark. She turns on her dipped headlights and for a flash there it is in front of her – the shape of a child, younger than Jem, a toddler standing there, arms limp by its sides.

Sometimes this happens when she's tired. Driving in the dark that figure sometimes leaps across the road, making her jam dangerously on the brakes. Often, it is more of a sensation than an image, nagging there just out of reach, a child about to fall off a high ledge, or get sucked under a wave. Sometimes, when she's leaving an empty room, she reaches down to take a little hand that isn't there.

She stares down at the daffodils – the cut stalks breaking through the damp newspaper – but still from the edge of vision she sees him. A little boy, just the shape of him; arms and legs and a pot belly, waiting in her headlights to be seen.

Shortly before eight the cool light of a car swings into the street, casting bleary shadows down the footpath and up the jagged rows of houses, unveiling for a moment the mournful, down-turned face of the Virgin and the narrow hands folded over her heart.

The car loops into the enclave and pulls up outside Dermot's house, facing Freya. She can hear the sorry lurch as the hand-brake is tugged and the engine stops, and after a moment the street is dark again. Her body warms with the impending relief of Jem's presence; that she will be near him soon – the heat from his skin, the smell of him. She closes herself up against her own softness and steps out of the car just as Dermot steps out of his. She can feel him watching her and it makes her skin keenly aware of itself – the cool air on her cheek, her ankles. The soles of her shoes feel thin as she walks the few steps towards his car.

Dermot is drunk. She knows that as soon as she hears the

too-forceful bang of the car door. He stands, swaying in the middle of the path, arms out, presenting himself as though expecting applause. She can't see Jem. Dermot moves to his doorway and turns, grinning sloppily at her. 'Ah,' he says, 'there you are.'

'Yes. Here I am.'

Dermot keeps smiling, his eyelids fat from drink, and Freya hears her own voice, the ridiculous, boring sounds she is making. 'I've been here since seven, Dermot, as we agreed. Where's Jem?'

She knows the panic must be showing in her face, and she knows this will please him. She is at a loss for anything to say, with him leering knowingly like that, as though what he is looking at is not her at all but something on her, or something past her, something she doesn't know about – lipstick on her teeth, a flake of snot… Her voice trails off and she looks past his eyes to the outline of his ear and wonders if it is the same as Jem's.

'It's late.'

'He had a great day.'

'Good. He needs to go to bed.'

'He is in bed.'

'Okay, Dermot, where is he? It's time to take him home.'

'He is home. Haven't you forgotten something, Freya?'

Freya looks dumbly at him.

'The forms?'

'Oh… They're not valid, Dermot. They're for primary or joint carers… The form is to confirm that you have Jem at least half of the time, and you don't, so…'

'We'll see about that.'

'Where is he?'

'He's asleep in my bed. I just went out for a few things.'

'Could you please wake him. It's time for me to collect him.'

'It's time for me to collect him.' He imitates her in a voice that reminds Freya of her mother. 'Is it now, Freya? Is it time for you to collect him? And who decides that?'

'Okay, Dermot, that's fine. I'll go to the Guards.'

He rolls his eyes. 'You love drama, Freya, don't you? I remember that about you, alright. Relax. Come in, he's in here.'

He unlocks his door and walks in. She takes a breath to call after him, then follows instead. Low ceilings. To her left, a shut door, and ahead of her, a short passage leading to a kitchen-sitting room. She pulls the front door, but doesn't let the latch close. The smell of the house is like the smell of the flat he used to live in – wood and mould and different colognes.

There is something contrived about the kitchen, like a set for a sitcom. There is garlic hanging from a butcher's hook; three framed album covers on the wall; and on the mantelpiece a row of about ten books. One of them says 'NERO' in very large, red lettering on a white spine. Dermot sits on a leather couch, arms spread high along the back; a performance of ease.

'So, this is my place,' he says, lifting his palms and looking around the room.

'Where's Jem?'

'He really likes it. Do you have that paperwork for me, Freya?'

'I told you I can't sign it, Dermot – that would be fraud.

We can talk about it another time, when we've sorted out your access.' There are stairs leading from the kitchen to a second floor. The banisters are of naked pine, the wood rough and incongruously new.

'Just got those put in,' says Dermot.

'Oh. Nice.'

'I locked the bedroom door when I left. If the kid woke up, I didn't want him wandering out and falling down the stairs.'

'He fell asleep?' It can't be true.

'Yes. Little kids sleep, Freya.'

'I'm going to take Jem now, as agreed. It's his bedtime – after his bedtime. We can meet face to face another time and discuss the forms and everything.'

'But that's not true is it, Freya? As soon as you leave here, you'll ignore me like you always do, won't you? And then I'll have to take you to court...' He rotates his hand limply from the wrist, 'and blah blah blah. More drama.'

'Dermot, bring Jem down here now please or I'll get the Guards.'

'Listen to yourself!' he says. 'Just listen to yourself! *I'll get the Guards* – and what? He's my son, according to you! Is he my son, Freya?'

Freya turns to leave, and maybe this is the wrong thing, for he is very drunk and Jem is in the house. Her mind reaches for better options and slips and can find none. Dermot blocks the exit with little effort. She is surprised at how much taller he is than her; she hadn't noticed that before. She moves towards the small gap that is left between him and the doorframe, but in a dipping motion Dermot fills the whole space and shakes his head, his hands up, as though he is defending himself against attack.

'It's a simple question, Freya.'

'Yes, he is. Please go and get him now or I will have to go to the Guards.'

Something rolls across the ceiling, and Freya looks up.

'Oh for fuck's sake, Freya. What is it with the drama? Always the drama with you.'

Short, weak knocks on a door. Dermot raises his chin and shouts, 'Hang on, Mister! I'll be up in a minute. Just have to deal with something here!'

Freya stops herself from calling out to Jem – it would frighten him to know she was here, trying to get to him. She can't trust herself to conceal the fear in her voice.

'Go and get him.'

'That's not a very polite way to ask, is it? Say please.'

'Please go and get him, Dermot.'

'In a minute,' he says. 'I just need to do something first.'

Hands spread across the doorframe, he leans down and plants a soft kiss on her mouth, and Freya can't move. Jem is upstairs. She should leave, get the Guards, but would they come? Can they? Dermot draws back to see what his kiss has done to her. He wraps his hand around her middle and her waist feels tiny to her, and pliable. She is a fraud for ever having thought more of herself. He kisses her neck now. His tongue moves on her skin, slowly and almost wet, like a slug. She shivers him off her. She can't help it.

'I'm getting the Guards, Dermot.'

'Don't be stupid, Freya.'

'Bye,' she says, and she wonders if she means it, because Jem is still banging on the door and what if the Guards won't interfere? What if she leaves now and can't get back in?

'I need to do a wee!' Jem calls.

'Just a minute!' calls Dermot. 'Sorry, Mister, this will only take a minute and then I'll be up to you!'

'Dermot, give me the key please?' Shit. There are tears breaking in her voice.

He smiles – his mouth reminds her of some animal, but which? 'Don't cry,' he says, 'I didn't mean to upset you. He'll be okay for five minutes, then I'll give you the key.'

And Freya stands there not looking at him; standing there while Jem bangs on the door. Eventually she says, 'He needs to go to the toilet.'

Dermot gives a breathy laugh. 'He'll live.' He takes her wrist and tugs it a little, moving past her. 'Come and sit with me for a minute.'

Freya should go to the door now, but instead she turns towards the stairs.

'It's locked, Freya, I told you. Don't make a drama. I'll give you the key now in a minute. I just want to talk to you for a bit, come here.'

And she does. She fucking does. She comes and sits on the couch beside him, and she lets him slide his hand around the back of her neck, and she lets him slide the gluey tongue between her lips and between her teeth. He takes her hand and he presses it to the swell in his jeans, holds it there a minute. 'Remember this?'

The quicker she does it the sooner it'll be over. Her mouth recognises the silky penis. She carries out the task from muscle memory, doing everything she can to hurry the thing to its conclusion – massaging his soft testicles until they tighten, rubbing at the little ridge behind, opening her throat so that the long, thin dick slides all the way down and her lips and nose crunch into the piss-and-laundry smell of his pubic hair. He holds her ponytail. 'Good girl,' he says. 'Now you get it. Good girl. I knew you wanted it.'

And she can hear Jem upstairs, the surprising calm in his voice. 'I had an accident. Hello? Is my mammy coming soon?'

She moves her tongue hard against Dermot's penis, circles it, slips her tongue-tip into the raw little opening at the top, and gives one last thrust with her throat, massaging the cum up out of his balls.

'That's it,' he says, 'drink it all up. Don't waste a drop.'

Dermot smirks as he tousles Jem's hair. 'Nice wheels. Granny's, is it?'

'It was, yeah.'

'What's the reg?' He bends his knees, leaning forward to look, hands in his pockets. 'Ha! 1989. Vintage. Vintage Mercedes.'

'Into the car, Jem, quick now, good boy. Let's shut the door. It's cold.'

Dermot stands smiling as the car pulls away. She goes slowly so that she doesn't go too quick. She stops and waits for a gap in the traffic. On the wheel, her hands are trembling. The figure of a child shoots across the road. She angles the rear-view mirror so that she can see Jem. 'Fold that over your knees,' she says, 'great boy.'

Jem sits bare-bottomed on her cardigan in the back of the car, his skinny thighs pale and his little penis hiding with cold.

'Jem, put the sides of the cardigan over yourself.'

'But the seatbelt.'

'Unstrap the seatbelt, put the cardigan around yourself and strap in again.'

'Like this?'

'Yes. Well done. Now strap in again. Well done.'

'Did you hear the click?'

'Yep. Well done. Best boy.'

'I like our car.'

'Me too, Jem. I like our car.'

She likes the way it is posh and scruffy at once; elegant and cumbersome with its beige leather seats and slabs of faux-marble plastic on the inner doors. She likes the outrageously unfashionable colour of it – school-jumper navy.

'Mammy?'

'Yes, Jem.'

'Is it night time?'

'Yes.'

'Is it the middle of the night?'

'It's the beginning of the night.'

'Is Mimi asleep now?'

'Oh, I'd say so.'

'Oh. Mammy?'

'Yes?'

'Em... we didn't get ice cream.'

'Did you not? Sorry, baby, I thought you would. I thought he said he'd take you for ice cream.'

'But we got crisps.'

'Did you?'

'Yes, and red lemonade – do you know what that is?'

'What is it?'

'It's like 7Up except orange colour.'

'Oh. And was it nice?'

'Yep. And he has a big television and you can play games on it. Racing cars games.'

'And was that fun?'

'Yes, but I was playing that for a long, long time. And then the accident.'

'Well, don't worry about that, little man. You can have a bath now when we get in. Put the cardigan over your lap, baby, it's cold.'

15

SINÉAD USED TO BE the type to refuse a paracetamol, clip her nails so short that her fingertips were tender, tug the brush impatiently through her hair, but these days pain frightens her. The sting of a paper cut, a knock on the elbow – the tiniest thing can send tremors through her.

She creeps her fingers up along her matted ponytail until she finds the elastic. Though she's careful unwinding it, some solitary strands snag and snap, making her wince. How long has it been since she's combed her hair? Or washed it?

There's a special brush her mother bought from someone at a promotion stand. It's a gimmicky thing – bright pink and yellow, like a child's toy, and the plastic bristles all different lengths. It's supposed to ease out the tangles. Her mother is always buying crap from people at those stands. She says she feels sorry for them.

She squeezes conditioner onto the spikes of the brush. She spreads the split ends across her palm, and crunches the bristles into them. Blobs of conditioner go sliding down her wrist, flecking the bowl of the sink, smattering her chin and neck. She's not even sure she hears the phone at first – a little beep under the sound of the hairbrush. But when she stops and listens, she is suddenly aware that it's been ringing for some time.

'Terence! Terence, can you get that?' Then she remembers – her husband is out by the woods, watching for the fox cubs.

On the landing, the cold sweeps over her arms and feet, slinks up around her bare knees and in under her nightie. Even the carpet feels cold. It is such an effort now, walking down the stairs. Her hips and pelvis still ache with loss. She is fat now – it took some time for her to realise that – she has become a fat woman. She takes the steps slowly, holding the banister, her breath high and loud, thighs easing past each other like great bags of liquid. The doctor didn't tell her she would grow so fat so quickly. It's to do with being bed-bound for so long, and something to do with hormones too. They explained all of this afterwards, when there was no going back. One of the nurses said she should try to eat sweet potatoes, for her hormones.

Sinéad stops on the turn of the stairs, places her forehead on her elbow and breathes. The ringing seems to grow shriller before cutting off mid-cry. There's a tug of pain pulling down into her groin. Could she be imagining that? They told her it would stop hurting after a few weeks.

The phone starts up again.

She moves quicker this time. The pain is probably normal. There is so much they didn't tell her. They didn't even mention the hysterectomy until they had already taken half the cervix. Then, before they discharged her, the doctor explained that he'd need to schedule her in. 'Nothing to be alarmed about,' he said, crinkling his eyes as though in kindness. 'Just a preemptive. A uterus isn't much use to you now, anyway, is it? At this stage of life.' She was still bleeding and bleeding and when the painkillers wore off it was too much and too deep– a shriek all through her, like her waters were boiling. They say childbirth is terrible, but it couldn't be worse than that; the sensation of wrongness, of having been looted.

She lifts the receiver just in time.

'Your mobile is off.'

In the dim hallway Sinéad lowers her head like a shamed child. 'Oh, is it? Sorry, Aoife… it must be out of battery.' She scans the hall for her slippers.

'Well. How are you?' There is an eye-roll in the tone, as though the idea of Sinéad being well or not well is a ridiculous notion that must be politely indulged.

'Okay. Still sore…'

'Oh, it's probably in your head at this stage Sinéad – it's been, what? Three months? More?'

'Em… let me think—'

'Well anyway I was with Mammy today – having lunch with her, getting her shopping for her and all that. She was asking about you. The place is a state, you know. I don't think Freya does a tap. She has these dying tulips on display in the hall, pollen everywhere…'

The band on Sinéad's wrist is tinselled with broken hair. She plucks at it with short, dirty fingernails, holding the phone with her shoulder.

'Mammy says she hasn't heard from you in a long time,

Sinéad. You'll have to get over this hysterectomy nonsense. It's only a little op, you know. Miriam Brennan had one last year and she was out for dinner the next evening. You're going to have to start thinking of others a bit now. I can't look after Mammy all by myself.'

'Oh,' says Sinéad, taking the phone in her hand now – her neck hurts. 'I'll call her tomorrow. Or this evening. I'll call her later—'

'It's nine o'clock Sinéad, what time do you think she goes to bed?'

'Oh, well, in the morning, then.'

'What time did you think it was Sinéad?'

'I didn't know.'

'Do you not have a clock?'

'I was about to have a bath.'

'No, Brendan is just off the phone to her. She'll be gone to bed now.'

'I'll call her in the morning.'

'Will you now?'

'Yes.'

'Anyway, she was asking if I'd heard from you and I said you were busy gardening. I didn't mention your little op. Still top secret is it?

'Yes, I – yes.'

'How is the garden?'

'Oh, well – hard work and all, but the tomatoes have been amazing Aoife – too many for me, I've lots in the freezer. I'll give you some – but then the other day they started to get this little grey patch on the bottom of them—'

'Well I'm glad you're enjoying it, but Mammy says she hasn't heard from you. She's looking for her chives.'

'Okay, well I'll ring her in the morning... I'll try to get over to her. They said I could drive now, but really it's sore...'

'Well, it's psychosomatic then, Sinéad. You'll have to overcome it.'

'How are you?'

'I'm fabulous thank you. Great. Valerie's coming back on Wednesday so I've just been getting everything ready for her. I got Daria to spruce up her room... There's something else I need to talk to you about. Brendan has sorted it out for now, but we need to keep a better eye on Mammy.'

'Why's that?' Sinéad's knees are starting to stiffen with the cold.

'Well, I was early to Mammy's today – my appointment was cancelled – she wasn't expecting me till later, but in I come, and who do I find drinking tea in the good room? Davitt Dunlin.'

'Oh?'

'He's aged a lot. Anyway, lucky I did because guess what I found out? The Ladies Muck are sniffing about, trying to wheedle money out of Mammy...'

'What do you mean?'

'Well, you know Mammy – completely evasive, talked in riddles, wouldn't disclose anything. She got passive aggressive when I asked her so I just let it go. But I called Davitt this evening and it turns out she summoned him to the house to talk about her will.'

'He told you that?'

'He told me without telling me, "sometimes elderly people want to take another look at their will..." that sort of thing. Anyway, she had some idea about providing for the grandchildren and *their* children – completely ridiculous – but I had Brendan call her and explain that it's com*plete*ly unjust...'

Sinéad examines her hands under the murky glow of the lampshade. Her hands are the only things that haven't fattened and fallen loose in the last months. The skin is weak though, and easily torn, the veins running too close beneath. She turns them slowly under the watery light; the hulking grace of big, sad sea creatures.

'Well, it's her choice, Aoife. It's her money.'

'No,' says Aoife sternly. Sinéad can see her now – poor Aoife, with her top lip pulling unpleasantly tight and her cheeks trembling – but she can't rise to her sister's outrage, she can't think beyond tomorrow, the orangery, the garden wall. All she can worry about is the tomatoes and how to save them. She planted them on a whim – three trays of 'Organic Medley Heirlooms' from the market. She didn't know what to expect, but when spring came, they tumbled out big meaty globes with yellow and pink mottled flesh; small sweet ones full like little capsules of fragrant blood that popped in the mouth; great crimson ones streaked with navy blue, pleating in on themselves, dew gathering in their folds, bending the whole plant over with their weight. Until those tomatoes ripened she didn't know such pigments could exist – a yellow that is also pink; a black that is also red and green at once. It defied what she knew of colour. They were the wordless stuff of matter.

'No, Sinéad,' says her sister, 'It's not actually. It's not her money – it's Daddy's money and our inheritance.'

'I'm not sure you should be putting pressure on her Aoife, I'm sure it will work itself out. I don't think Mammy would disinherit us... you might have the wrong end of the stick—'

Yesterday she noticed little patches of black blossoming just under the skin of the beef tomatoes, and she decided to order in some copper spray. But the invisible threads moved swiftly in the night; a ghostly breath that reached all the way down to the core of the fruit and rotted it in the dark. She went in this morning to find them all shrunken into rows of sticks, their spindly shadows thatching out the morning light. Armies of slugs had come in through the open door – was that a coincidence? While the green fruits rotted, the ripe ones were turned to mush by great orange slugs that sucked fast to the flesh – even against the force of her fingers – and left a layer of slime that she couldn't wash off. This afternoon she cut open one of her rosy little bell tomatoes to find it hollowed out; three pale, speckled slugs nestled like raindrops in the papery shell.

'Oh, Sinéad, don't be ridiculous! It's obvious what's happened here... it's what I've always told you but you won't listen. Obviously, it's Freya. She's a manipulative little bitch and always has been. She's always had Mammy wrapped around her little finger. Always. I tried speaking to Mammy myself but you know how she is. That's why I got Brendan to call her. She respects him...'

'But we can't change it, Aoife, if it's what Mammy wants...'

'What Mammy *wants*, Sinéad? What Mammy *wants*? So, we

should let Eileen's kids rob us of our birthright? Just because they have Mammy twisted around their little fingers, is that it?'

Our birthright – where did they get her from? Where does she even pick up these phrases? Sinéad lifts one foot up off the floor and reaches her hand back, making her shoulder creak. She squeezes the toes to warm them. Even at the height of summer, the nights are cold in this house.

'And you know, if she gives everything to the Ladies Muck, who's going to be left paying for Mammy's Shady Acre years?'

'What are Shady Acre years?'

'You know what I mean. She'll need to go to a home eventually, it could be years of costs. And who will pick up the tab? Me. Me and you. How much did you tell me it costs for Terence's Aunt Toots?'

'Oh... I can't remember now, Aoife. But, you know, his cousin helps.'

Poor Aoife. Even as a child she had that anger in her. She was competitive with everyone, a little bit begrudging, very quick to take people down a peg – but it was all because of the sickening feeling in her, the sense of never being quite right, or quite good enough. Daddy was difficult to please – was that why?

Perhaps as children they were close. There is so much that gets forgotten, but Sinéad and Aoife have been, for years, like strangers sharing a mother. Aoife has never had any interests, really, or any talents. She attends exhibitions because she thinks she should, reads books so that she can say she has read them... Maybe she is lonely now. She's started telephoning more and more often.

'Well,' Aoife lowers her voice, 'one thing's for sure. We have to sell the properties – the one in Monkstown and the one in France now and maybe even the house in Enniskerry. The warehouse too—'

Sinéad can hear the back door bang as a cool night wind rushes through the hall. Terence must be in. The blood is stagnating in her ankles. What has she done with the hall chair? It's in the orangery; the grapes. The grapes are a disaster – small and all pips. There's a reason no one grows them in Ireland. It was a silly idea. It's only that the leaves looked so beautiful and romantic, and the stalks with the little tendrils. And she thought that maybe, if they once grew oranges in there, then grapes might be possible too.

'There's four of them—' Terence is still in his garden boots. Sinéad frowns at them, and he looks down at his feet. She covers the mouthpiece and whispers, 'Aoife.' He grimaces, bearing his teeth, and whispers, 'There's four of them! I wish you'd seen them, they're beautiful!'

Sinéad uncovers the mouthpiece and makes listening noises for Aoife.

'… I mean, put it this way, Sinéad, it's not like she'll be going back there – and we can get her to divide the proceeds fairly and above board, because at least then it won't all go to the Ladies Muck!'

Terence stands there, waiting for her response, and Sinéad just rolls her eyes and shakes her head, pointing to the phone.

'Tell her you have to go!' whispers Terence.

'I know what you mean, Aoife, I do, but—'

If she tried, Sinéad could share in her sister's rage. Because it does hurt her, the way those girls soaked up her mother's love. Freya's son gives Mammy junk like ladybirds made from stones, with wobbly eyes glued on, and her mother displays them around the house proudly, something she never did with the things her own children used to make her. The daisy chains lying in the bin that evening after supper, and Mammy not even trying to conceal them, scraping the gravy-sodden gristle and bones in on top of them.

Terence is growing impatient. 'Bye bye, Aoife,' he mouths. Sinéad scowls at him and he mimes a glass, wobbling it in the air, whispers, 'Whiskey?'

Aoife is getting carried away now, her voice coming faster and louder down the phone. 'She owes a big sum to Valerie too – don't forget how she gave Cara a deposit for her house that time! They think we don't know about that. And I'm nearly sure she paid Freya's repeat fees for college! No, she owes Valerie a good sum of money to even that out…'

Their niece, Freya, always gets Aoife worked up. Freya, or Freya's child. Because Mammy is mad about that elfin creature, when he should really have been a source of shame.

'Oh, she thinks Freya's so different from Eileen, but actually the apple doesn't fall far…'

Sinéad pulls the elastic off her wrist and lays it on the hall table. Slug pellets and copper spray. Perhaps she can save the tomatoes.

Terence makes an exaggerated shrug and leaves, shaking his head and muttering.

Their father used to pay them a penny a slug, and they would go out in their wellies with buckets of salt water, pick them deftly off the strawberries and plop them into the killer bath. It used to make her feel sick, watching them curl into themselves and sink to the bottom. And there was one concoction their youngest sister Eileen made from things in the garden shed, which made the bigger slugs foam and judder and change shape. She remembers Aoife standing over the bucket, trying to conceal her horror, two hands on her portly belly and the serious, downturned mouth explaining to her little sisters that Lily's experimental mixture turned slugs inside out, that it was 'inside-outing potion', and must not be allowed to splash on humans.

She has no childhood memory of the slime they left on the fingers. The slug slime this morning was impervious to water. She scrubbed her palms with a nail brush but still the stickiness remained. It was impossible to shift. It sent a nausea right into her scooped-out pelvis and her shaky spine. Eventually she soaked her hands in the syrupy brown soap her mother uses for cleaning floors. It turns white when it's mixed with water. She has at least a dozen bottles of the stuff, left over from that phase Mammy had, of giving her cleaning products 'to help you get that house in order'. She sat looking at her hands in the basin of hot, cloudy water. She did nothing but sit and watch as the skin turned white and wrinkled and free from slug slime. Her nails frayed, layers peeling back in thin, transparent furls.

'Remember the library fine, Sinéad? Only that I found the receipt in Mammy's handbag I never would have known about that. Paying Freya's library fine! A fine, because she couldn't be bothered to bring her books back on time… Oh, I ate Mammy over that one, but she never learns.'

Sinéad knows how her mother must have trembled and nodded, saying as little as possible while Aoife 'ate her'. It's the same way she responded to Daddy when he would rant about one thing or another. She would nod, and look down or far away, and try to agree without agreeing. It gave Sinéad a pain in her throat, as though there was a wedge of cold porridge lodged there. She could never bear to see Mammy quiet and cowed and nodding like that; those sudden red patches under her eyes, and then her cheeks flushing so hot that as a child Sinéad would have to look away, or run to the bathroom to cool her own face with water. She could never speak to her mother the way Aoife does.

'Okay, Sinéad, I'm going to be completely honest with you here, but this is between us – you're not to tell a soul, because Davitt wasn't supposed to tell me all this…'

Maybe she never participated in her father's slug hunts after all. Maybe she refused. Because there was nothing familiar about the sensation of slugs on her fingers today, and she has no recollection of the slime they left. But she remembers him offering them a penny a slug, and she remembers little Eileen watching them die in the bucket – her boxy bobbed hair and gappy mouth and her eyes pale and round with the excitement of it; and Aoife's face too – the way she locked her jaw against pity, the way she had of looking sensible always, and respectable, plucking them swiftly and daintily, plopping them into the bucket, frowning.

'This new will, Sinéad, bypasses her own children! Davitt read it out to me Sinéad – "My children have had plenty of financial support over the years, they want for nothing..." all this jibber. Now don't tell me it's not Freya who's behind that – working on Mammy day and night to get what she wants. So, in this new will she wants everything divided in equal parts between the grandchildren – Freya and Cara and Valerie – *and* the great-grandchildren; so that's the little bastard as well as Cara's three...'

'You're being nasty now, Aoife. You can't call a five-year-old child a bastard.'

Oh, there's a deathly chill in the hallway. The ceiling stretches all the way up to the second floor, that's why. And the blind stuffed stag head hanging there, casting its dead gaze over the house. God, she has always hated Terence's family heirlooms – all of them; the stuffed things and the rust-bleeding knives and the once valuable tapestries and the handmade lampshades. Why has she never put her foot down and got rid of them? And where has he gone off to now? Trailing mud all over the house...

'Oh for goodness sake, I'm being accurate, Sinéad. He is a bastard. Or do you not know what a bastard is?'

'Whatever, Aoife. Go on.'

'She'll let us have a few of Daddy's paintings, but everything else is to be turned to money, and divided in seven parts, equally between them all...'

'Well, I suppose that seems fair to her...'

'Jesus, Sinéad, do you not get it? Instead of being divided in three between you and me and Eileen – it's divided every which way now. So, we are being punished Sinéad, do you see? We are being punished – basically you have been disinherited. Eileen's kids will get everything – you get nothing for having no children and the Ladies Muck take it all! Freya will, effectively, get twice as much as Valerie because she gets a share for the bastard – and Cara gets a cut for every brat she's popped out…!'

Her sister's voice hurts Sinéad, like something pecking, pecking, dragging her up like a worm from the earthy quiet she's been sheltering in.

'Tell me this, Sinéad, why should you be punished for being barren?'

Aoife knows full well how that word stings, carrying with it the image of a parched landscape, cracked earth, women with hairy lips and cheeks; their insides all wrong. But she can't help herself, sometimes. It's a kind of relief for her, to put people down, push them out of the way, feel better than them.

Aoife just never found her feet in the world – that's what Daddy used to say, that's how he explained her; *Our Feefs; she just hasn't found her place yet…* Perhaps that's true. Aoife seems always to be grappling; there's a kind of terror that lurks just beneath her chin.

Sinéad swallows quietly. 'That's not nice, Aoife.'

'Well, why should Eileen be rewarded for being a slut and having illegitimate children? And then Freya follows suit, knocked up in the first year of college, and Mammy acts like the Virgin Mary couldn't have done better.'

'It's upsetting, Aoife, but I don't see what we can do.'

'I've told you what we can do, Sinéad – if you were listening you would know exactly what we can do. Brendan has talked to her and she won't go ahead with it for now. He explained that it was unjust and she understands. But – now both Davitt and Brendan have suggested this so I really think it is sound advice – what we can do is distribute as much as possible now. It's better tax-wise anyway. What we do is we get her to sell the properties, and we sort out those proceeds first, and then we make sure she gives us the paintings now directly – I don't think that'll be a problem. They're just hanging in the studio anyway, she can't even bring herself to look at them…'

'Aoife, can I call you tomorrow? I'm sorry, I'm feeling very lightheaded.'

'Where is Terence? Is Terence there? Brendan wants a word with him.'

'He's out. He's watching for foxes. I just need to sit down for a bit. Look, I'll call you tomorrow. I promise.'

'Okay, well listen, we're having a lunch on Wednesday. Come to lunch on Wednesday…'

It is a relief to hang up, but the word is still here in the coolness of the hallway, settling on the mahogany console and the dusty pictures and the stag. *Barren.*

'At last!' Terence is standing at the entrance to the hall, the top of a big toe poking out of one of his nice lambswool socks. She'll have to ask Mammy to make him some more. He's holding two cut-crystal glasses with ice and generous portions of whiskey.

'Whiskey! Oh Terry sweetheart, thank you. Phew. Just the thing. Oh God, she's tough going.'

'She's a bitch. The Dragon of Dublin South.' He pads towards her, her soft-bellied, soft-chinned, gentle old badger of a husband. He hands her the whiskey. He kisses her temple. 'She always upsets you. I don't know why you answered the phone.'

'She's my sister.'

16

FREYA WAKES TO THE frantic light of an SMS alert:

> *Freya if u don't drop those papers back within 24 hrs u can expect a court summons if that is really my son like u claim then i want access half and half*

It's three in the morning. She pushes the power button until the phone dies, and places it screen down on the bedside table. She takes a mouthful of water from the glass by her bed, lies back, turns to face the velvet curtains – plush black in the dark. Her mouth is already dry again. She can hear the workings of herself; tongue unsticking from her palate, the even beat of her blood.

As she falls back asleep, she has the sensation of tripping forward, hurling into some unknown. Her foot gives a sudden twitch, and she turns onto her other side.

She is not going to vomit again. She is not going to take another shower. She is not going to give that skinny prick any more weight than he deserves.

But she notices she is hugging herself, stroking her own shoulder, her nose in her armpit. She'll need to cop on. She's a big girl now and she won't let a blowjob change her life.

Jem is fine. He's right there in the room next to her, just the other side of the wall. If she listens closely, she can hear him breathe – or is she imagining that? Did she check on him before she went to bed? No harm to peek in on him.

Seeping through the curtains, a haze of orange streetlight traces the shape of her boy. There he is – of course he is, bony limbs all heaped up at the pillow. There is always a scent of lavender in Jem's little room. She moves quietly to the bedside, feeling for the switch to his LED globe – a flimsy plastic sphere mapped with shapes of yellow and green and white-blue for the sea. When it lights up it sends a cool glow over Jem's nose and the sharp, moist peak of his upper lip. She turns it off quickly, letting the cosy darkness wrap him safe.

Across the landing, Grandma's door is standing open, and Freya can see a chair where her skirt and blouse and her sturdy beige bra have been laid out for the morning. There is a streak of white lamplight reflected in the mirror of the wardrobe.

'Grandma?'

A wire-frame bedside lamp with frayed golden tassels casts fuzzy curves over the ceiling and walls and turned-down sheets, and the head-shaped dip in the big pillow.

'Grandma?'

She's not in the toilet. She must be downstairs. Knitting

maybe, or cooking. That's what Grandma does when she can't sleep.

Wary of startling her, Freya whispers as she moves down the stairs – 'Grandma? Grandma?'

She knew Grandma wasn't right this evening; creases chewing her forehead, her voice quick and her eyes bleary with a kind of bewilderment.

It was nearly nine when Freya got in with Jem. Just as she was lifting him to the bell to herald their arrival, Grandma opened the door, her throat wobbly with panic, 'Oh, oh Freya, thanks be to God, I was worried!'

'I told you, Grandma. I told you we'd be late...' When she rubbed Grandma's shoulders the bones felt close and tight under the crunchy shoulder pads and straight-cut blouse.

There was a small pot of leek-and-potato soup on the stove, a leathery skin on its surface. Grandma ladled some into a bowl before realising it was cold. She looked like she might cry as she poured it back into the pot to reheat – 'Stupid old goose!' She had already buttered two stacks of bread: one brown, one white.

The hall is dark, but there's light coming from the good room.

'Grandma? Hello?'

The moment she opens the door Freya is hit by the metallic coldness of the room. Grandma is sitting at the big mahogany dining table, her back to the door.

'Grandma?'

The good room is huge and rarely used. It smells of furniture polish and chemical-cleaned upholstery. A big Turkish carpet covers one half of it, and the walls are furnished with matching pieces – a display cabinet and a big, tall unit with locked doors and a locked drawer. In the bay window, a sunken velvet couch and armchairs; a granite fireplace, and a tall grandfather clock. The family only uses this room when there's company, or for big gatherings, like Easter and Christmas dinner, when they light the fire and switch on the heaters, and Grandma covers the table with a lace tablecloth and silver trivets.

'Grandma?'

'Oh!' Grandma's hands flurry up to her mouth. She moves her whole body around stiffly, turning the chair with her, and the hands land on her chest. 'Oh Freya, it's you!' She taps her breast bone hard with hooked fingers, as though to dislodge her panic.

'What are you doing up, Grandma?'

Grandma is wearing only her faded floral nightdress, so thin that the straps of her thermal slip show through.

'Come and sit down, darling.'

'Grandma, are you not freezing? Let me get you your cardigan, it's just in the hall…'

Freya fetches the soft primrose cardigan from the newel and Grandma allows herself to be helped into it. 'Thanks darling. Aren't you very good. Great girl.'

'What's up, Grandma? Why aren't you asleep?'

'Sit down here, darling. Now look here at this.'

There's a big book on the table – thick chocolate-brown pages with sheets of parchment between them.

'Now look. Weren't we thrilled with ourselves?'

It's a picture of a couple, taken indoors. Freya recognises her grandad from his slender neck and straight gaze, but Grandma – Grandma looks so different, brazenly tall, and a closed, triumphant smile. She looks no more than a teenager, wearing a woman's tailored skirt and blazer, and a blouse with a lace collar. She's taller and broader than Grandad, who has hollowing cheeks and dark eyes.

'Weren't we two silly young things, really…' There's something girlish about the way Grandma pushes her hands into her lap, as though afraid to touch the picture. 'Delighted with ourselves so we were.' She nods at the picture: 'That was a wool suit I had my Aunty Dolly make. She was a spinster, Mam's big sister, but she had lots of friends, you know… She was a wonderful seamstress. And she could make pancakes. No one really made pancakes, but a French neighbour taught Aunty Dolly to make them like the way they do in Paris. That's how I learned to make pancakes – my Aunty Dolly. But I've told you that, haven't I? I've told you about my Aunty Dolly. I was her favourite…'

Then, as though it takes great daring, Grandma lifts a finger and touches one corner of the picture.

'It was a beautiful suit. Navy blue wool. A nice shade, like, not too dark. I changed into it in the hotel after work and the girls all came up from the kitchen to have a look at me and help me with a bit of powder for my face – your grandad never liked perfume or makeup, you know, so I only let them dab on a little rouge and some Vaseline on my mouth and lashes. Even the girls from reception came to see. And off I went, walking up the road on my own, to get married – wasn't I a little madam?'

There is something fragile about being here, and hearing this, and Freya is afraid of her own clumsiness. She doesn't know what to do with her face, or her hands, or what to say. But Grandma is looking at the book, asking nothing of her.

'They went berserk at home you know, when I said I was marrying Dinny. Well no, now that I say that, no – Dada was quiet, "Has he a house to take you to?" that's all, real quiet and worried like, "You're not going to those lodgings with him, are you?" But it was Mam who didn't approve at all – "And you who loves to dance and is asked everywhere," she said. She was suspicious of Dinny, you know, "And what's he been doing the last ten years child? He's not been waiting for you in a glass box I'll tell you that much." But they didn't know Dinny. You know what's funny, Freya? He *was*. He *was* waiting in a glass box. You know what I'm saying now don't you? You know what I mean? He hadn't a clue about women or the world – all he knew was books and pictures. He spent his time in the gallery, and he spent his money on postcards of paintings. He collected them in a photo album. I knew more than he did, and that wasn't much... He'd never been to Dublin before he came up for the CIE job.

'But Dada was right, we had no home to go to. Dinny's people had more than us like, but he was the youngest of eight boys... There was a bit of money left to Dinny by an uncle – a Protestant uncle, mind, but I didn't tell Mam that. A little tin of cash, but it came to a lot – it seemed a lot to us, anyway. Dinny got a piece shown in the annual RHA, and well – we thought that was it! We were made! Off we were to make our fortune by Dinny's paintings! Weren't we foolish little things? And selfish, really. That's what my sister Kat said, and we were. We were. I knew it then, even, but I didn't care. That's the truth of it. The bigger girls were sending money home from America, and passages for the younger ones and for cousins and everything, and I was off to London to be a painter's wife. I suppose, you know, I didn't think Mam needed me all that much by then… thought I'd done my time, maybe.'

She taps the page. 'Yeah. Well… and bold. Brave and bold little things, and selfish. Thought we were the first in the world to fall in love.'

She frowns at the picture. Then, after a few moments she says, 'You can turn the page, Freya. Turn over the page there now, good girl.' She places the sheet of parchment over her wedding photo, and waits.

'You know, we would have been married anyway, Freya. It was a foregone conclusion. But we were in a hurry for a reason. You know what I mean, do you Freya? My Aunty Dolly knew. I don't know how she knew, but she knew, and I think she went and talked to Mam because all of a sudden Mam fell very quiet on the subject. They came to the wedding in the end – Dada in his good coat and the lot, and there was a little party back at the house – but there were none of Dinny's people there. We never saw much of Dinny's people, really. His father was a cruel man. You can turn the page, Freya. Turn the page.'

They look older already on the next page, and very happy

– standing on a street outside a dingy-looking door. They are wearing winter coats and both of them are smiling, like they can't believe their luck. Grandad looks even skinnier, and Grandma's face is a little thinner too. On Grandad's arm, a round-faced baby of – what, four months? Six? Below, on a white strip of paper, someone has written in fountain pen 'Molly and Dinny and Dinny Óg. Soho, 1956'.

'That's him,' says Grandma slowly, and her eyes widen, as if something is just dawning on her. 'Our little boy. That's him exactly.'

She runs her finger around the edge of the picture, touching only the cream mount and not the photo itself. A gravel sound comes from her throat. She looks at Freya and nods, takes a breath, makes a smacking sound with her lips, and breathes out. 'Yeah,' she says, 'that was him. That was. Yes.' Her mouth stretches into a brave, wet smile that doesn't match her eyes, and she nods again, blinks slowly, takes a breath to speak, and swallows instead.

It was from her cousin Valerie that Freya had first learned about the little boy who died. They were down at the end of the garden, picking raspberries for Grandad. Valerie was a bully of a child, and she insisted on being the only one to pick the berries. Because she was younger, Freya had to hold the bucket; but she ate fistfuls every time Valerie turned her back, and told Grandad on her afterwards.

'Do you want to know a secret?' said Valerie.

'Okay.'

'There was another child, before our mammies. There was a little boy who died. He died when he was three. But we're not allowed to talk about it. Don't ever say it. Swear!'

She never said it, except to Cara, who knew already and warned her again never to mention it. But after Jem was born, Grandma sat by the hospital bed, 'Now you know, Freya. Now you know. You know now, don't you? What it was like when he was born, my first baby; our little boy; and why I would sit up all night beside the basket, knitting him booties and hats and more booties and waiting for him to wake again… Now you know, Freya. You know what that was…'

Grandma taps the page again, slides a finger in under the next one, as though to turn it. But she seems to change her mind suddenly, and she takes the rest of the book in her hand – all the thick pages and the parchment paper and the stiff back cover – and smacks it closed on its face. She rubs a hand up and down the faux leather on the back of the book, then takes it between both hands and turns it the right way around.

'I think probably that's the last time I will look at those pictures Freya. You know, I don't often look at them.'

She slides the book towards Freya. 'Put it with your private things, Freya, will you? Keep it. I don't want anybody else to touch the pages or that. Keep it safe, will you, and take it with you whenever you get your own house, okay? It's not for showing people, really. I don't want it mauled. Just keep it with you.'

Freya takes the album and puts it on her lap. 'Okay, Grandma.'

From the other side of the house, the carriage clock chimes gladly. Grandma looks to the far corner of the good room, at the tall, stern grandfather clock, its pendulum silently swinging. 'What time does it say, Freya?'

'It's four o'clock, Grandma. It's Tuesday morning already. You should try to sleep.'

'Well, what are you doing mooching around at this hour?'

'I was restless too. Couldn't sleep. Will I make some camomile, Grandma?'

'Well, you know. If you twist my arm, just this once I think I'll have a little cup of cocoa. I think I'll make us both some cocoa and then we'll go up to bed and have a good sleep. Maybe we should drop a bit of whiskey into it. I should have a sleep.'

She pushes herself up off the table. Freya straightens her cardigan for her, and fastens the top button, and the two women make their way to the good-room door. As they enter the hallway, Grandma reaches for Freya's shoulder, as though to steady herself, and Freya puts her hand around her grandmother's waist. Grandma still has a figure that curves into a crease at the waist, and Freya can feel the hard cleave; the density and sureness of the flesh there.

'But you weren't foolish Grandma, were you? You did make a life from Grandad's paintings.'

Grandma frowns for a moment. Freya has said the wrong thing.

'We'll lie in in the morning, darling, will we?' Grandma gives Freya a forgiving pat on the small of her back. 'For as long as the little fellow will let us.'

17

A FINE MESS SHE'S made.

Aoife scrapes out the gritty mush, tilting the bowl over the bin and shoving the mixture to the edge. Her new spatula is a tasteful shade of teal to match her mixing bowl, and made of silicone for easy grip and easy cleaning. It bounces cheerily as she bangs it on the edge of the bin; shakes and bangs, shakes and bangs.

A fine mess.

Slowly, impudently, the gunk turns on the soft blade-tip, drops. She scoops up another lump and flings it hard into the bin. It lands on the inside of the black liner and starts to tumble sluggishly down, a soft, sinister crackle as it goes.

She uses a wrist to push her fringe from her eyes, and brings the bowl over to the sink, squidges washing-up liquid, twists on the hot tap full blast and throws the spatula in.

She will start again, following the instructions more carefully this time. She has time; as long as the cleaner comes when she said she would, she has time to get this right. It's no big deal anyway; just a nice little lunch to welcome Valerie home. Sinéad couldn't be persuaded to come – perhaps that's a blessing, and her mother won't be here until one at the earliest. A casual little lunch, that's all.

Leaving the hot tap beating into the sink, she leans over the recipe booklet, and taps the page: 'Almond flour.'

The chirrup of her mobile phone. She rushes into the hall – she hates having to call back – unzips her handbag, fumbles to find thc right pouch. It's Valerie's name flashing on the screen. Aoife's sternum tightens. Her throat hurts. She slides right just in time. 'Hello.'

Her daughter speaks in a little-girl voice, 'Hiiii Muuum!'

'Hiya petal, are you near?'

'Mum, you'll never guess who was on my flight with me.'

'Who?'

'Guess?'

'Who, Val? Who was on the flight with you? I'm in a hurry… I made a dog's dinner of the starter, I have to begin all over—'

'Alex! Do you remember Alex?'

'No.'

'Alex? Alexia Sullivan? From school. Well, listen, do you mind, we thought we'd have lunch in Dublin and catch up a bit – the traffic will be terrible anyway, so I'll be in later tonight. Alex has a car so I'll get a lift….'

'Valerie, your grandma is coming and everything. She'll be very…'

'I'll call in to her during the week Mum – honestly, like the flight was delayed a bit too, you know, and I won't even be there by one, like even if I get the bus right now…?'

Aoife surveys the very clean tiles of the entrance hall; the

Moroccan carpet; the winding stairs and the magnolia-pale expanse of wall. She should hang another painting or two here in the hall. It seems terribly empty now with the half-full shoe rack and the antique boot-pull, the solitary shopping bag sitting there neatly beside it. In the end, she got the knickers for Eileen's kids. Why did she do that? *Aoife Monday, In Brown Thomas please can you get…* Just thinking about it now, Aoife feels the insult like a slap to the face. She shouldn't let herself be treated like that.

The fringe swings down over her eyes again. She thrusts out her lower jaw and blows at it. It's an impractical haircut, but her stylist is right; it takes years off.

'Grandma was so looking forward to seeing you, Valerie, she's driving all the way out to see you…'

Mammy never bought knickers for Valerie. Or pyjamas – that was the other thing she was always buying for those girls – brushed cotton pyjamas and flannel nighties.

'What am I supposed to tell her? She's really been looking forward—'

'Tell her I'll call into her during the week. Look Mum I better go, I'll see you tonight. It won't be a late one.'

Valerie has hung up before Aoife can respond. Her throat is raw with the silence; a taste like metal. She slides her phone back into her handbag and zips it closed. Then she stands for too long looking at the very empty wall. They used to have a series of photographs going up the stairs – Valerie as a baby, Valerie on her communion day, Valerie as a teenager – braces and lank hair. When did she take those down?

~

Back in the kitchen foam peaks are lathering up out of the sink. There's steam spilling over the worktop, fading across the kitchen in slow white whorls. Ninny. She twists the tap closed. She will have to wait for the water to cool before she empties the bowl. Does she have to wash the Wonder Whisk too? It doesn't go in the dishwasher – how does it come apart? Somehow, she didn't factor that in when she bought it. It's not like her to be so reckless.

On the floor of Aoife's stomach, a slow dread begins to gather. They're nice colours, these gadgets – all teal and buttercup and magenta. But look at them all! Was it a mistake buying so many? Has she made a goose of herself?

They saw you coming, Aoife, that's what her mother will say, *silly goose.*

She hadn't expected to buy anything at all when she went to the Tupperware party. It was hosted by one of the ladies from the village; Aoife knows her from Sunday mass. She didn't want them all to think she was too up herself to go – it is something she risks, she knows, living in the biggest house on the most prestigious road; wife of the town solicitor and daughter of a famous artist – So she made the effort to go, but she wasn't expecting much. All the kitchens in those semi-ds are the same – fitted units, formica worktops, parquet – common-looking. The women were friendly though, and the hostess mixed fruity cocktails; it isn't often Aoife drinks cocktails. She had brought a bottle of plonk with her; and she felt bad then when the kind-eyed hostess offered her a cosmopolitan – fresh lime juice and all. The Tupperware lady was the hostess's cousin, just moved home. She couldn't put an age on the woman. She coloured her hair, certainly. The skin around her eyes was taut.

The steam has settled in the kitchen like dusk. The window is misted and streaked with condensation. Aoife pushes the dying bubbles off the windowsill into the sink. That'll have damaged the paint.

She returns to the recipe booklet. She will go slowly and carefully. She will lay out all her ingredients first, and check as she goes, just as Mammy taught her.

'Okay,' she says aloud, 'almond flour.'

She lifts the almond flour – it's in one of her big rectangular storage jars; really handy things the size and shape of cereal boxes with airtight lids and easy-pour spouts – and places it firmly down at the other end of the counter. 'Check.'

'Wheatflour...' She slides the flour across – 'Check.'

'Parmesan' – has she got enough parmesan? Yes, plenty – 'Check.'

Parmesan is expensive; some people would replace it with the cheaper cheese displayed next to it in the supermarket – it looks the same and has a similar name, but it's not parmesan.

'One egg...' Stupid goose. The egg! She forgot to add the egg, that's what it was.

She opens the fridge and there they are – six eggs perched in their little holder in the fridge door. She forgot the egg, that's all.

That's what it was. She was all a-fluster, that's all. She'll start again.

At the Tupperware evening it looked so easy; the woman smiled and chatted as she did it. She had shiny blonde hair gathered elegantly at the back of her neck, not a strand out of place, and beautifully glossy red nails; really classy-looking. She didn't get a speck on those lovely nails the whole time. 'We just pop it all in here, and shake… you just drop it in here, and push the handle…*Voilà*! There was an exotic edge to her accent – she had just moved back from Canada, she said. A disastrous marriage, perhaps – no wedding ring. But she made it seem alright to be selling Tupperware for a living; she didn't seem in the least bit ashamed.

It really was impressive how quickly and easily she made the starters, but it is harder than it looks.

Perhaps Aoife should have stuck to a simple roast chicken, and smoked salmon for starter. Perhaps she is setting herself up with all this fuss. And Mammy might accuse her of putting on airs.

Aoife takes the Wonder Whisk apart – twisting the lid, removing the three twirly bits, getting the mixture on her fingers and the sleeve of her nice cashmere cardigan – and drops it into the hot bubbles. Best not to cut corners. She will start afresh and get it right.

She scrunches her sleeves up to her elbows – she'll have to soak the cardigan afterwards.

Last time Mammy came, Aoife really went to quite a lot of trouble. Mini quiches. She even made the pastry herself, because she knew Mammy would comment otherwise. But it didn't matter what she did. 'Quite nice, Aoife,' said Mammy, swallowing her mouthful and placing the rest of it delicately on the rim of her plate. 'You know – now you won't take it in bad part if I say this darling, but a bit of nutmeg makes all the difference. Well, last night Freya made the most beautiful omelette – well, beautiful Aoife, spinach and leeks in it, and I said, "Well, Freya, I know your secret – nutmeg and sugar"; just a pinch of sugar on the leeks, and a bit of nutmeg grated in at the end. Try it next time Aoife. You'll see it makes all the difference...' Then she made that gesture that sends the heat shooting up Aoife's back – the tips of her forefinger and her thumb pressed together like a parody of a chef, and repeated it like a mantra, 'All–The–Difference.'

Aoife lines up the measuring spoons before her on the worktop. She can feel her shoulders rise up, her lips tighten – she has always had a thin upper lip but these days, when she gets at all anxious, she can feel it narrow into a strip of sinew. That's how wrinkles spread. She needs to relax, but the whole thing with Daria is bothering her. She was supposed to come yesterday, and then she called with some excuse about her grandchild. She'll be here at eleven thirty, she said, but Mammy's arriving at one, and Daria won't have the cop-on to make herself scarce. Aoife will have to send her home at quarter to one, whether she's finished or not. There's the problem then, of cutting her €33 down to €14. It might be very awkward.

Never mind. She'll get her to start with the dining room and living room – Mammy doesn't need to see the rest of the house. She'll hand Daria an envelope and if she has the cheek to complain, Aoife will act insulted – *You don't expect me to pay you for work you haven't done do you, Daria?* She points the 10 ml spoon at an imaginary Daria, eyebrows raised, a little shake of the head, 'do you, Daria?' She hears herself mutter. Stupid goose. There's no need to get all worked up about it; it won't come to that.

When people know you have money, they try to take advantage of you. She's never been short, but it's the principle of the thing. Aoife won't be taken advantage of. She won't be made a fool of. The world is full of profiteers.

Right. The parmesan twists.

The important thing is to enjoy cooking – that's what the Tupperware lady said, and that's what Aoife intends to do.

When the landline sounds, Aoife grabs a microfibre cloth to wipe the egg from her fingertips.

'Hello?'

'Aoife, it's you.'

'Hi Mammy, are you not on the road?'

'Now listen here Feefs, you won't take it in bad part, will you? I'm just in from the hairdressers and there was a lot of traffic for coming back and – I can say it to you, can't I, darling? I didn't sleep very well. I'm tired. I would prefer just to stay at home now for my lunch. I only want an egg and I'll sit down then with my knitting... Aoife? Fifi, can you hear me, darling?'

'I can hear you, Mammy.'

Aoife has wandered absentmindedly into the hall again. She is standing before the bare wall. Her mother sighs down the phone, 'You don't take it in bad part, darling?'

'Well, Valerie will be very disappointed, Mammy.'

'Well, you tell her to call in one of these evenings and we'll have a nice chat, will you? Is she there now and I'll have a word with her?'

Aoife looks down at the neat shopping bag: cream and dark brown stripes.

'No. That's fine, Mammy. You suit yourself.'

'Well yes, that's what I thought. That's what Cara is always telling me – *Grandma, you need to just suit yourself,* she says… you know Aoife, I'm an old woman now!' – she says that like it's a joke; does she expect Aoife to contradict her? – 'Oh, there's the door, darling, I'll go. Now you don't take it in bad part, do you? You tell Valerie to come and see me? Oh goodbye, darling, there's someone at the door.'

'Who? Who's at the door, Mammy?'

'Well, Fifi, aren't you a funny one? I don't know yet, do I?'

'Yes, goodbye Mammy.'

Aoife kicks the shopping bag. It falls on its side and the contents spill cleanly onto the floor: twelve slim boxes of knickers, parcelled together in white tissue paper. Why the tissue paper? As if they were delicate or something… She kneels down and stuffs them back in.

When her parents first took those girls on, Aoife did her part to lighten the load, bringing them on days out to the cinema, or to the play centre with Valerie. Yes, she encouraged the three cousins to play together once. She thought long and hard about her nieces' Christmas presents and the best school to send them to. She was generous with gifts and generous with her time. It has been a slow souring, fuelled by the little one's red-faced whining and the way she clung to Mammy, and – oh God, when she thinks of it – the adenoidal arrogance of Cara; who quickly grew to have opinions – so many beliefs and opinions and hobbies, that were indulged by Mammy and admired by Daddy. Even then, Aoife continued to do her best. She forgave the vegetarianism and the sanctimonious little lectures the child would give; those offensive Christmas cards with a turkey on them saying, 'Get Stuffed Yourself' that Daddy found so funny and Mammy blushed about. When Aoife tried to speak to them about those cards, explained that they couldn't allow that carry on, Daddy just shook his head as if *she* was the troublemaker. *Vegetarians are like communists,* he said. *Anyone with a heart is a vegetarian when they're young…* He was right about one thing: it didn't last.

What a ridiculous child Cara was, and a ridiculous adolescent; an embarrassment to herself but too stupid to see it. From what Aoife knows of her she's still a smug little madam – anti-consumer and organic and all that. AKA grubby. Delighted with her silly children's books. Delighted to use Daddy's surname to get ahead, though she's no right to it.

This corkscrew is an amazing thing – she ordered it online, number one in that list of 'Top 20 Gadgets' in *Real Homes*. It pops the cork out in a moment, with no risk of splitting or crumbling. She opens a Mercurey from 2010 – a good year.

She'll leave the wine a while; let it breathe. Maybe she and Brendan will have a nice lunch together, and share the bottle. But he'll be disappointed about Valerie. He will feel he has come home from golf for nothing.

She was going to just hand Mammy the bag today as she left, *Of course I got the shopping like you asked me why wouldn't I?*

It's her mother's sigh that hurts – weary, as though Aoife is the problem, and not those girls. Just because Aoife thought her mother should look after herself instead of raising kids all over again. The three of them were sent to boarding school – she and Sinéad and Eileen – but not the Ladies Muck. Why? That dismissive shrug Mammy gives. *You're a funny one.* Her mammy, always just out of reach, disentangling herself from Aoife as though their relationship is an arbitrary misfortune. *Oh my Feefs. Where did I get you from?*

From her – that's where Aoife came from, the hot, bloody inside places of her Mammy's body. Does Mammy forget that?

Who was it at Mammy's door?

No, Davitt would call Aoife if there was something up. Brendan had a good talk with him. He'd know better than to go behind their backs again.

Brendan will be disappointed to come home to only her, and Daria still here doing the cleaning.

Aoife's not even hungry now.

She'll leave a note and an envelope for Daria and a sandwich for Brendan – he'll be late anyway; he's always late back from golf. She'll text him, tell him not to rush. Lunch is off.

She'll drive to Dublin now with the silly little knickers for the stupid little bitches and she'll catch Mammy minding the Golden Child, or whatever she's doing and she'll give her a piece of her mind about the terrible injustice of her trying to mess with Daddy's will – that's the word she will use, *injustice.* That will get Mammy thinking twice about interfering with her inheritance, giving everything to the young Ladies Muck while her daddy turns in his grave.

18

'CARA, I HAVE TO whisper, I'm in the library.'

'Go outside.'

'No, I am – I did – like, I'm in the toilet lobby place but I have to whisper. Listen, I'm way behind with this reading – any chance you'd collect Jem? I found a perfect book here, actually – remind me to tell you about it. You know my dissertation idea for next year?'

'No, but listen, Freya, I'm working. What time do you need him collected?'

'I told you about it, Cara – *Women who perpetuate patriarchy.* It's about patriarchal laws relying on women's participation. There's a book here on patriarchy and property... it's perfect but I'm not allowed to take it out. There's a huge queue for the photocopier, so I'm going to—'

'Freya, what time do you want him collected? I've literally just sat down to work. I've just made myself a coffee and I'm about to start...'

'Twelve.'

'Twelve?'

'It's twelve on a Wednesday.'

'Oh yeah. Fine. Okay. I've to get Megan too, I'll just get her early…'

'Thank you, thank you.'

Cara shouldn't have picked up. She leans back in her chair and cocks her head at her drawings. She hates them.

She plucks a sugar crystal out of the cork jug and drops it into her cup, careful not to cause a splash. She'll have her coffee at least. She runs her hand over the weird little jug. She puts it to her lips. The cork covering is uneven and warmish, like something alive.

Each piece is a wound – her grandfather told her that. Cork is made by slicing into the bark again and again, and harvesting the scab that the tree makes. He ran his fingers over the pocked swatches, tracing the seams with his thumb. *Do you understand why that is beautiful?* Cara didn't understand at all, but she nodded. She must have been only a teenager then, and it was frightening; the way he looked so hard at her, the slight tremble in his eyelids.

She pulls a sheet over her preparatory scribbles – she wasn't making much progress anyway, no character at all to Crafty the Rainy Day Duck. The park will do her good. She can study the ducks.

Jem sits in the back, his fine, dry hands neat in his lap, a dull-skinned yellow apple untouched on the seat beside him. 'Em, Aunty Cara, where's my mammy?'

'She's in college, Jem. She's doing some work. She'll come and get you soon. We'll collect Baby Peggy and Denise and we'll go to the park, won't that be fun?'

'What work is she doing?'

'I don't know – college work.'

'Where's Mimi?'

'I don't know, love, probably getting her hair done or something. No – lunch. She told me she might go to my Aunty Aoife's house for lunch. Come on now, eat your apple. Megan, are you eating your apple, Megan-my-baby?'

In the rear-view mirror, Megan nods, the apple covering her nose and mouth. Megan's eyes are eerily pale sometimes, like fog, or the air after rainfall. With effort, she pulls the apple away from her face, leaving a large, frothy chunk in her mouth. She chews and, her mouth still full, says, 'nice apple, Mammy.'

'That's good, my loveliness. Right, you two stay in the car – Jem you're a big boy so you're in charge, okay? Beep the horn if there's a problem – ONLY if there's a problem, okay? I won't be long, I'm just getting Baby Peig.'

Jem nods earnestly. 'I'll hold Megan's hand.' Megan lets out a shriek as he clutches her.

'No, it's okay, Jem, let go of Megan – you don't have to hold Megan's hand. You just sit nicely now and eat your apple and if there's a problem beep the horn, but there won't be a problem so just sit nicely, okay?'

'Okay.'

'Okay, Megan?'

'Otay.'

The new baby-room assistant opens the door only a crack.

'Peig's mum,' says Cara, 'sorry I'm late.' She rolls her eyes as though her lateness is a naughty child that they both know only too well and before she can stop herself, she has pushed into the hallway. 'Em... I've got the other kids in the car so...'

She has left them eating apples, of all things; apples that they could so easily choke on; apples proverbially used for killing pretty daughters...

The new assistant closes the door after her and they are left standing too close in the small space. Cara is too loud and big for the little porch and the thin girl in the pink gingham overalls. The assistant's face looks uncooked; vague features and very fair, blotched skin. Everything about her delicate body and her thin voice is so frail that Cara feels her own brashness like an insult. She takes a stray lock that has swung down in front of her face, twists it firmly and tucks it under the hair-slide above her ear. 'Poor baby, I meant to get her earlier. I got caught up... I had to collect my nephew.'

The baby-room assistant shrugs, yawns quietly into her shoulder, and gestures at the clock on the wall of the reception booth. 'It's not even half twelve...' She fetches a clipboard from the office and writes the time on Peig's sheet. Cara signs her name.

Cara takes the baby's tiny jacket and nappy bag from her

personalised hook (her name – Peig – with a penguin making the P). Baby Peig only goes to creche part-time – eight to twelve, usually – but because of Cara's new commission they registered for flexi-hours this month, just in case. That was a mistake. Cara never gets much work done during the day, flexi-hours or otherwise, but she still ends up leaving Peig for longer when there's a choice. *Wouldn't you be ashamed,* Grandma would say, and Cara not even bringing in minimum wage.

The baby room is cordoned off by a waist-high gate with a lock code. There's Peig! There, in the middle of the big bright play mat. She's as dark as Megan. Her short, silky hair sweeps in so many different directions that she looks like a frantically licked kitten. The mat is composed of different coloured squares arranged one after the other in maddening repetition. The tones are offensively primary; an abstract blue, a flat red, a crazy pure yellow – the colours of computer screens or laboratories; too eerily monotone to exist in nature. There are nine across; red, blue, yellow, red, blue, yellow... and twelve down. The next row starts with blue: blue, yellow, red; blue, yellow, red... and so on. This makes diagonals of each colour run across the mat, and they are so bright that they seem to lift away from one another and swagger in turn above the floor. Baby Peig is sitting on this mat and trying to thread the laces on a big pair of cardboard shoes. Cara watches her; wet baby lips too plump to purse, frown so low the brows meet her thick lashes – and she feels a sudden shot of outrage, as the minders fuss about helping other children with their tasks. Do they not notice the absurd beauty of little Peig? Sitting there with her earnest self-importance, the little paunch on her and the chubby hands trying to fiddle the laces into the holes.

There is a stuffed baby bear in the Natural History Museum. It sits like that with a round back and its legs curved around itself. In the morning, she will draw a little bear like that, a beautiful little Peig-bear, frowning at some task, a pink bear-tongue straining out of its muzzle with the effort of rooting honey from a hive. She won't worry about finding a book to put the bear in. It will be just a picture. She will make it a pen drawing with a light watercolour wash on the tongue and the pads of its feet. She will write 'Peig Bear' beneath it and put it in a little frame on the wall, and as Peig grows up she will look at the picture and she will always know how loved she is. Cara hopes she remembers to do that. She hopes she'll have the time.

The baby has seen her – her face shifts immediately into a grimace, and she begins a dry, comical cry, her whole mouth drawn down and open and her arms floppy in her lap, but she has been caught enjoying herself at creche and she knows it. She drops the shoes and, without leaving her spot on the floor, she stretches her paws up and grasps the air: 'Mam Mam Mam Mam...'

'Now Peig,' says one of the minders, 'we have to put the shoes away don't we?'

Peig wraps her arms loosely across her chest – her impression of arm-crossing. 'No,' she says, and points at Cara. 'Mam.'

She is a brat, her youngest little baby girl. She is a stubborn obstreperous little menace. *Fat despot* is what Pat calls her, fondly, as though pleased with himself for spawning such mayhem. *Our fat despot.* But Peig will be fine, she'll be fine out in the world. Oh, look at her, raising herself reluctantly off the play mat and her funny stride, shoulders dropped into an arrogant slouch, limbs swinging apelike as she waddles over to the shelves with the minder to put the shoes away. Afterwards she cannot accept that she has done as she was told, so she frowns and puts her lovely fat fists on her unformed hips, shakes her head and pouts. 'No.'

Cara laughs, but Lisa, the toddler-room leader, does not.

'Peig,' says Lisa, squatting down beside her, 'would you like to say bye-bye to your friends?'

'No.'

'Let's say bye-bye to your friends and then we will go and say hello to Mummy.'

After a pause, Peig nods, 'Yep,' and poddles over to a cluster of toddlers, 'Bay Bay!' and then her grin and that funny little fingery wave. Where did they get her from? She turns at last towards Cara, feet out-turned and her arms tucked up like wings. She is stealing something from the creche and trying to conceal it in one of her hands.

Cara will make it a duck in a mac for the *Rainy Day Book*; a little white duck in a yellow mac with a round, messy, feathery tummy. No, a red mac. Because the feet and the beak will be yellow. A blue mac, in fact, and red boots, and the duck will use its wings like hands and fiddle with pipe cleaners and craft tacks and get feathers stuck in the spilled glue. Yes, she can make the *Rainy Day Book* work.

There is a sign asking parents not to reach over the barrier for their children, to wait until a team member brings them out. Baby Peig is her lovely fat despot and Cara will pick her up when she wants to. She reaches over the barrier and then the child is clamped to her – all four of her limbs clinging fast and her head in Cara's neck. 'Mam Mam Mam,' says Peig, tapping her mother's back, 'Mam.' Cara breathes in the smell of the child; her coconutty sweat, her grubbiness. Though it's over a year since she gave birth, Cara's body still misses Peig; it is like breathing again to have her whole little body on her chest. She smells the back of her neck – dirt, the waft of teenage girl's perfume, but still the smell of Peig under it, and the milk drops in her breasts.

'Let's go get Den my little Peggy baby... Give the tractor back to Lisa. You can play with it tomorrow...'

Strapped into her car seat, Peig starts to complain that she is hungry, touching her mouth and saying, 'Am. Am.'

'Here, Megan, can you hold the bag of baby rice cakes? Give one to Baby Peig and when she's finished give her another if she wants it.'

'Can I give one, Aunty Cara?'

'Yes, Jem, sorry love, yes – let Jem give the next one, Megan...'

As she releases the handbrake, Cara sees a silver four-by-four swing into the spot opposite them and she lowers her head, pretending to search for something on the passenger seat. She is relieved to have collected her baby before the other mothers collect theirs.

'Dool' says Peig from the back, 'Doool'; by which she means 'Jolene', by which she means *Dolly Parton's Greatest Hits*. Cara obeys, nudging the cassette until the slot sucks it in and the thinning tape turns. She sings along – so does Megan and so does Baby Peig, her head back, the little fingers stretching taut in the effort and her voice open and as loud as she can make it, 'Dool… e, Dool… e, Dooleeeeeeeee,' and Cara loves her girls – she loves them loves them loves them, these lovely, ridiculous, weird little miracle creatures. A thread of guilt snags in her chest when she sees Jem in the mirror, his hands over his ears, big, sad eyes, and his mouth reduced to a little waver.

The traffic is bad, but Cara will take the other route – up the quays and out by Christ Church – and they should still be on time for Denise. Cara doesn't want her left waiting in the hall. At five, Denise is the youngest in the music class. The other kids are only a year or two older, but they have bracelets made with elastics up their arms and stickers on their violin cases and they play instrumental versions of pop songs and collect and swap some kind of round cards. Cara was never allowed to put stickers on her violin case. She tries to encourage Den to decorate it, but 'I just don't want to,' she says. 'Why would I Mammy? What if I change my mind and they won't come off?'

She is very good at the violin, her Denise, but Cara still isn't sure why she enrolled her in the first place. 'Well it seemed a waste not to use the violins' she told Freya, but was that why, really? She loves the violins; the smell of them, the warm, fruity wood, the *f* curls, the perfect weight of the scroll and the sticky dry summer smell of resin powder. And yet she remembers hating the violin, and that she was bad at it.

Her mother had an intercom between her bedroom and the music room, so that she could hear Cara playing while she sat in bed, and when Cara was not good, she used to scream and cry and then Cara could no longer hear whether it was in tune or not. She could hear only her own pulse and all other sounds took on a warped, faraway quality. So she should not cherish her violins like this, she should not want her daughter to play.

Cara should have been musical. When The Lily decided to make a child, she said, she didn't just grab anyone off the street. She was careful. She planned. She did her research and she selected Ireland's most gifted musician, because if she was going to do it, she was going to do it right. She told Cara over and over how she had spent each day of her pregnancy playing classical music to the bump, how Cara had been bounced and sung to at baby music classes from three months, 'The cost of it…' At one and a half, Cara was bought a tiny Chinese violin and began lessons, learning the formations before she was allowed to pluck the strings, tapping the beat on the triangle. One and a half. That's not much older than Peig. The lessons were held twice a week in a big wide hall and each child had a parent with them to help. How long did that go on? Long enough that she can remember it. Cara and her mother were always early and her mother talked to the teacher a lot and flipped her hair and threw her head back and laughed with her big jaw open.

It is one of Grandma's favourite stories, that Suzuki concert Cara did. She was only three – is it possible that she remembers it? But she does. The grotty guesthouse that they stayed in – Grandma and Mother and Cara. Cara remembers wetting the bed, and Grandma's brows fluffy in the night and her eyes small while she stripped off the sheets. Then in the morning, with a scoop of shiny jam in a metal bowl, her mother lifting food up on the fork and letting it drop onto the plate, muttering.

'What's the Ritz, Mother? What do you mean?'

'Shhh, Cara, your mammy was only joking.'

The special dress for the concert, the itchy matching tights, and the big stage full of children; the kaleidoscope shapes they made with their violins; rest position first, then holding the instruments up to face the audience, feet apart, their arms stretched straight for *Stop Sign*, and then up onto their shoulders until the teacher waved the stick to start. Could that have been real? Why had Grandma condoned it all? There's that story she tells – *One hundred and fifty little things on that big stage, and Mr Suzuki playing on the piano. And they all playing. And when it came time to take a bow, didn't they all take a bow to the audience, except that little thing. My little Cara, the smallest one of the lot, who turns to Mr Suzuki and gives a bow. Because she could see! She could see he was the one who played so well you know. Such a little thing and so pretty that they put her at the front, and all the little ones behind her, they followed suit, turned to that old fellow at the piano and bowed too. Well, we laughed! We laughed… and everyone clapped. And when I told Dinny he said, 'That wild little thing, I hope the world doesn't ruin her.'*

Some of Cara's classmates went on to become prodigies; thin adolescents playing solo at the National Concert Hall, or dressed in green for tours of America. It used to make Cara cringe with her failure, when Grandma pointed out their posters, their reviews, their names billed in the papers, and always that story about the big Suzuki concert.

It was the new teacher who saved her. When she was seven, she was sent to Mr Cooney, a kind old virtuoso who smelled like lentil soup. After three gruelling lessons during which he sweated and flinched while she played, he said they would try a new approach. For the rest of her time with him he made a pot of orange spice tea when she arrived, and let it draw while he tuned her violin. Then they sat in his cluttered lesson room eating biscuits and listening to recordings of Jascha Heifetz, Cara's violin lying at peace on its own armchair. After a year of this, he broke the news to Mother: Cara had no talent. The Lily raged and growled and said she could see it clearly now. Because she had been so sick through that pregnancy and she should have known. After that she could see everything that was bad in Cara – her gypsy hair and her big nose and the black sick heart she had. How long did Cara stay with her after that? She remembers being brought to healer after healer, her mother standing behind her and mouthing to them breathily, 'My daughter has *darkness* in her...' One man who took her up to a bedroom and put his fingers in her nose and ears. And a lady tried to teach her the piano but she would sit at the instrument and her breath would start flashing up into her head until she was dizzy.

Then she lived with Grandma and before long so did Freya.

Why was Freya dumped too? Cara should have been gifted, but what had been the plan for Freya? Her sex was a big disappointment; Cara remembers that. Their father's wife had only daughters. Perhaps The Lily believed that bearing him a son would increase her status, draw him away from his wrinkly old wife. He came on a Tuesday and a Friday evening, and Cara prepared him whiskey on ice when he arrived. That's what she remembers – the pleasant burn of whiskey in her nostrils, and the way he pulled his trousers up at the knee before sitting down, the way he jiggled his foot. But she can't remember his face. She called him Liam, not Dad. He called her Little Lady.

'Why is Denise allowed in the front? I'm bigger.'

'Because your mammy has to be with you if you sit in the front, Jem. Otherwise the police would take me away.'

It's a relief to open the car doors and let the children spill out onto the tarmac. As she lifts Peig into the buggy, Cara can see that she's ready to nod off, so she tucks an extra blanket around her to encourage sleep. Having been warned, no doubt, of the danger of car parks, Jem holds firmly to the bar of the buggy, but Cara's girls fling themselves around the place. They have lost a bouncy ball. Megan squats down, peering under the car, and Denise lies on her belly to retrieve the ball from behind the wheel, a spume of pale hair flung forward over the dirty ground. When she stands up, the ends of her hair are oil-black, like laces caught in a bike wheel.

'Say thank you to Denise, Megan.'

'Fank you DenDen.'

'Here, Denise, let me plait your hair before it gets all matted... Do you want to go see the ducks?'

'No,' says Denise, wincing bravely as her hair is plaited.

'No,' says Megan, still grateful to her sister for rescuing the bouncy ball.

'I want to see the ducks,' says Jem, hopelessly.

'Let's see what we see,' says Cara.

In a fit of optimism she slips a book out from under the driver's seat into the mesh beneath the buggy. She can't stand the caged-in playground, but thank goodness for the park. They walk onto the tarmacked paths towards the vast stretches of green, and Baby Peig's eyelids start to flutter on the brink of sleep. Jem is still clinging to the buggy, that serious good-boy look on his face. Denise skips along beside, humming something, tapping a tune on her right wrist with the fingers of her left hand.

'Oh Megan!' She is shocked by the anger in her own voice, but Megan is prancing around in front of the buggy, squatting to pick up stones or branches, using sticks to vault across the path. 'Stop it, Megan. I very nearly crashed into you...'

'Mammy?' Denise is still playing her wrist-violin.

'Yes, baby.'

'Do you know how I make sure each bit of the piece is different?'

'How, my baby?'

'I imagine a different animal for each one. There's a lion bit.'

Denise scowls and bares her teeth, still humming.

'Megan, stop it!'

Megan is running back and forth in front of the buggy, throwing a stick as high in the air as she can and watching it fall, the wheels of the buggy biting at her feet.

'Megan!'

Megan stops suddenly, and the buggy snags in her trouser leg. 'Owww!'

'I told you to stop, Megan.'

Megan drops her hands by her sides, tilts her head back and begins to wail with her mouth drawn down into a parody of tragedy. 'Iiiii stooooopped!'

A violent impulse twitches in Cara. 'Stop it, Megan!'

Megan pauses for a moment and fixes Cara with a stare, teeth bared, her hands in fists and her pale eyes narrow. 'YOU TELLED me to stop!' Then she throws her head back and begins another long wail.

Baby Peig startles, looks around and starts crying too.

'Megan, stop it! Look, now you've woken the baby.' Megan's voice lifts to a screech.

'Megan, SHUT UP!'

Jem has let go of the buggy and is pressing his hands over his ears.

'Look, Megan!' Denise points to a dead tree. 'Look at all the twisty sticks! There might be a nest in there, even. Will we go and look?'

Megan stops crying as quickly as she started, and rushes towards the dead tree to look for treasures.

'Hide and seek!' says Denise. 'Jem, let's play hide and seek – you seek and we'll hide!'

'Right – no one go beyond the grass,' says Cara.

Cara walks Peig up and down until she falls asleep. Then she settles herself down on the roots of a tree to read. It's Jem's turn to seek now. He squats beside her, his hands over his face, counting very slowly and loudly, and the girls scurry off.

'... twenty! Here I come!'

Then there is a little oasis of aloneness. Her book is called *The Queen of Bohemia*. It's about an underrated Welsh artist of the fifties. She bought it three years ago and has read the first page several times...

It's Megan's shriek she hears first, and the first thing she feels is only irritation at being disturbed, but then she hears Denise too, and Jem, and the shrillness of their voices; and when she looks up she can see the three of them at the other end of the green. She has to strain her eyes and guess at what's happening, but she can make out Jem slapping at the air, Megan shaking her head like a sneezing dog and Denise trying to pull her away from the hollow of a tree, and then she knows what it is and she's running towards them. And as she nears she can hear the electric charge of the wasps and she can see that they have made a big dark net over her children. The first sting is on her neck as she heaves Megan up by the waist and tucks her under her arm and pulls Denise by the wrist. 'Come on Jem!' but Jem just stands in the cloud of wasps, his mouth open, gagging for breath in the shock and pain of it. She can already see the stings swelling on his face. Grandma will kill her.

'Fuck.' She drops Megan onto her feet and hauls Jem under her arm, 'Hold Megan's hand Denise. Hold Megan.'

Then she's running away over the tarmac with the buggy in front of her and the children wailing, Denise tripping over her feet as they speed along, and the wasps stinging her wrists and cheek, and it's only now in the car park, after stripping Jem off, unplaiting Denise's hair to release a live wasp, rocking the crying baby, that Denise's face drops, washing red and white with the panic. Her lips pull down and open, all saliva and tears, brows glowing white in the bright face, and there is accusation in her voice as her cry rises up, 'Megan!'

19

UNDER THE CHAISE LONGUE, a fine-tipped paintbrush. Molly is glad she has seen it there, and she tries to hold it in her mind – the tapering bristles hardened in slow-dried paint, the smooth, fine wood of the handle, the thick swathe of dust – so that it will always exist. A thing that Dinny touched.

The lost bits of the world – a dead shrew in the gutter, the blade of a chicken bone, an envelope on the table. That was why she began to draw – the space she could make for those things, the weight she could give them, by delivering them into her sketch book or out onto a great canvas. But for Dinny, it was all about the possibilities of flesh; the worlds it could contain and the things it could mean. He was compared, later, to that thick-throated fellow they knew there in Soho with the muscular jowls like the shapes of his own paintings – peachy powder on his face (Dinny said no-of-course-not, but she'd bet her life on it) and black boot polish in his hair – but that fellow painted human shapes into pure matter. He hated the life in them. For Dinny it was the opposite – it was about showing what was human, what it meant to occupy a body.

‘You’re alright, love,’ says the ambulance man, ‘shush now love, we’ll sort you out now, you’re alright.’ He runs a hand lightly down each of Molly’s legs and handles her ankles in a way that she finds not-decent. My God, would you ever, that she could lie with her skirt so askew, and her slip, and pain so crippling that she has no shame, she who kept her dignity always – not a peep out of her through four labours. Her mind is okay though. That’s the main thing – that’s the big relief. She can remember all the different types of clouds there are – cumulus is one – so her mind is okay and that’s the main thing. The other one is where the clouds spray thinly across the sky and she has always had trouble remembering that one.

‘I slipped on my daughter’s handbag,’ she is telling the ambulance man. ‘My feet, my feet got tangled in the handbag but my head is alright you know nothing wrong there, nothing awry upstairs, sharp as a tack, oh the pain…’ but is he hearing anything that she says at all? Are the sounds leaving her at all?

A pain that clamps down over her and over all the words and welds all of her together into a hard and silent sensation.

Her mind is okay and that’s the main thing. Okay enough through the pain of it, that she can plot her story out so as to avoid a hullabaloo over a little fall. Sharp as a tack and fit as a fiddle. That’s the main thing. She is saying to the ambulance man that she slipped, lifting a painting down carefully; ‘Dinny’s paintings, Dinny’s—’ but it’s the pain that’s silencing her and someone says, ‘Rest easy, Mammy, it’s okay.’

There isn't one ambulance man, but two or three of them, all in blue and faceless but her glasses must be somewhere and she can hear her daughter saying, 'Mammy Mammy Mammy?' and it's a terrible tug on her, that voice, and her tongue is slipping on the name of her little girl, what is it, oh who is it saying *Mammy Mammy Mammy*?

She is coming out the door – their own door; hers and Dinny's, the studio they built, she is rising flat on her back over her own driveway and she's not on the floor now anymore and she can find no faces to look at her but she can hear a voice she knows and a deeper, calmer voice that she doesn't know and there is a touch on her hand but it feels far away and that is how she knows she is not right at all and not sharp as a tack at all because she can feel that someone is touching her hand but she can only half feel it and then a great sting somewhere in her but where?

Mr Brereton next door had a fall and next thing they knew there was a skip in the driveway and the house had the face of it torn off.

There is a loud sliding sound and a crunch and clank and the ambulance man is bossing: 'Sit down please ladies,' he says, 'or we can't move off.'

Has she sorted everything out? Where are things now with Davitt Dunlin? Where are things now with the will? What will hold that little brown-eyed boy up now if Molly loses her grip and everything she is making spills out into a tangled heap? Who will see him right?

Her daughter is speaking. 'You have a cheek,' she says and

then another voice answers – another daughter – Eileen; her little Lily. Dinny loved that little thing. He painted her naked once, in the garden. The scoop of her pelvis, and the white plum of her sexless groin.

That's better. She can sleep now; that's better. Oh a silent, steady pain. That's better, to be still and no sound and nothing.

Too bright the light, too bright and white, and the bump and roll beneath her too sore but she cannot lose her grip though her tongue can't make the words now for the pain. Dinny's affairs are not yet in order. The other clouds are the scraps of bog cotton speckled over a sucking bogland. Her uncle's farm. Sharp as a tack. No, she is alright; her mind is alright and that's the main thing. She is almost at the heel turn now on this second sock for her little man, the little brown-eyed boy, and she won't forget the turn ever again. It's only the pain making her eyes roll and the terrible shock of lying there shameless with her slip twisting.

She needs her glasses, for the faces are very unclear.

Dinny used to stare hard at people, and too close. He would begin a portrait at the centre – the space below the nose and above the lip – what's that called? She knows what it's called, or she knew… That was the focus, always – the rest of the person could be unearthed from there. Molly could see him watching people when they spoke, his eyes on that space, and that's how she knew he was killing people into paintings.

'Dinny's legacy' – the way her son-in-law said it, like he understood the whole thing in a man-to-man sort of way. Silly eejits, her sons-in-law, both of them silly eejits. Not a notion.

Not a notion what it took; how it took the two of them to bring any of that work about. The other painters in Soho were all rich, even without their patrons. They'd have it that art comes from nothing – that's what they would say – that they went hungry and made art from nothing. Such disgusting lies those were, and they knew it themselves, all the things that had to be so they could paint, all the things they needed to keep the work happening. Oh, the posturing that went into it all back then – everyone competing at hooliganism; men tipping their whiskey down the sink when they thought no one was looking. Those dinners they had where there was paint in the salad and gravy on the canvases and champagne chilling in the coal bucket – who did they think they were fooling? They knew as well as she did that the work came from having the time, the paint (all that Cremnitz White, oh, the cost of it; Dinny had to have it brought over and they went meatless for months over the five tubes he bought that time), the canvas, the broth for supper, the sleep and the tea in the morning. She would wait until Dinny had drunk his fill. Then she would top up the pot with boiling water for herself.

There are faces peering over her but she can't look back – her glasses must have gone somewhere when she fell.

Dinny had some dark times there in Soho. There were evenings when she could put his food down in front of him and he told her not to look at him while he ate so she didn't. She sat with her face turned to the side. But he looked at her those evenings. He looked and looked and there was a terrible violence in it.

It was around that time that his portraits changed – that stunned dusk after their little boy and before Aoife. There was one with her stretch marks showing and her face half in shadow, and she was holding a pencil like a scalpel and there was a little stream of blood running down her thickened thigh and her skin was water-pale and she looked boldly out from the canvas and she looked more like her than anything she had seen before. He destroyed it after he was finished and never painted her again, but that is when the brutal and beautiful shadows entered his work.

She was still in the hospital when he came for her, all his paints in a trunk and a roll of canvas. He sat beside the bed and looked at Aoife and smiled, 'Such a big one!' Then he wept. Molly was pleased – pleased that he had come after her, pleased that he was moved by the sight of the child. But then he said, 'Oh my daughter, your father is a failure.' He spoke real slow, as though what he was saying was more important than the whole life that had just come out of her. 'The RHA won't have me this year – not one piece. I'm a failure, Molly. She will be ashamed of me. My daughter will be ashamed.' And he laid his head on her ankles and he wept, 'I'm a failure.' She can remember it – because it is the only time it ever happened. She can remember that she hated him then, all of him, his beautiful hands and his poor sad mouth and the paint scabbing the cuff of his shirt. She couldn't sleep for a week after Aoife came, for fear the baby would drop dead, and because she couldn't stop remembering the night they laid out her little boy, just the two of them and their dead boy in their little flat in Soho. 'Oh Molly,' he said, 'this is the worst thing that ever happened to me.' It was a queer thing to say, but at the time everything was wrong anyway.

While he cried on her ankles, it came back to her – such a queer thing to say – and it made Molly hate him so much that for the first days of Aoife's life, her nerves tingled, her breasts were aflame with the milk that didn't come. She was sick with it.

In Dublin he rented a tiny bedsit with a carpet that stank, and for a while Molly didn't bother trying to keep things clean. She fed Aoife bottles with sugar and egg yolk in them. She still did her best in the kitchen, but how could she begin to clean? And the baby vomited a lot, and cried a lot. Molly is ashamed to think of it, how she allowed her failure and his to fester in that little place where everything was stained nicotine yellow. Perhaps he hated her too, then. But getting rejected from the RHA, coming back home – that was the best thing that could have happened. His luck changed, just like that. He was invited into the White Stag Group by one or other fellow and there he learned to keep his two cents to himself – his opinions about abstract art and all that. There he learned to work his way into his strangeness, not out of it. Things changed. Slowly at first, and then a decade later, with his hand around her waist at an opening, she realised suddenly, from the way the other women eyed her, that Dinny was the big man on the scene, the kind he had once envied. And they had money, suddenly. Suddenly they had money, though it took them a while to use it.

And what of it? *What of it*? That's what her mam would say and she'd be right. *Well for you* and *What of it*?

It is too bright here and above her there are strips of light the same colour as the ambulance men because where are her glasses and the lights are hissing above her like tubes of angry insects and who is squeezing her hand? 'Oh, Aoife' says Molly. The cord was knotted, and the milk didn't come for her, but here is her Aoife squeezing her hand, and little Lily, but isn't there her middle girl too? Sinéad with the bovine slowness, gentleness, candidness; never asked for much from life. Where is her Sinéad? Oh, they are old, her daughters, my God they are old now and her Sinéad; barren as a Connemara beach. She would have made a good mother. 'Oh, Lily,' says Molly, 'how old are you now?'

One of them rubs the hair back off her forehead. 'Rest easy, Mammy.' Her hair that is newly done.

Once, when they were in London (that was at the beginning, was it? Before her baby boy came and went) – a terrible flat in Soho – a dirty place though she worked day and night to keep it nice for him those first lonely months. Once – Dinny was out that night – she did a ridiculous thing, a foolish thing. (But she was very young. New married and giddy with herself and very young.) She painted a portrait of herself. She did it on the back of one of Dinny's used canvases, and the colour sank into the untreated fabric, so flat that she had to keep on painting and painting to pull her face up out of it with the brush, like dragging herself from the bottom of a bright lake. Hours and hours she sat with a mirror and a lamp. She was disgusted with herself even as she did it, and she made sure not to use the Cremnitz White or the Very Expensive Blue, but it was only the next day that the real foolishness of it settled into her.

He must have come in while she was sleeping – was she already carrying their little boy by then? She woke late to find Dinny's heat around her. She slipped out of bed to start the breakfast and there it was on the table – deep pencil lines cutting into the wet oil of her face and scrubbing out the line of her cheek. A thumb mark smeared away the creases she had so carefully tracked over her forehead (for she felt them there already, even if she was still a young woman then, new married and giddy with discovery and so young). Dinny had corrected her portrait.

Later, when he had sales and patrons, he could have left her behind and no one would have blamed him. He could have had a high life with one of the ladies of that circle – intellectual, high-society women. But that wasn't Dinny. Dinny wasn't that sort. Her Dinny.

'We're just waiting for them to come and get you Mammy – is the breeze too much?' says Aoife, then to someone else she says, in a much bigger and angrier voice, 'This is ridiculous! My mother needs care right now. In any case we are obstructing the entrance. If another ambulance arrives we will be obstructing.'

Oh, Aoife. Where did they get her from? Molly closes her eyes but she's alright. Not going anywhere yet.

Death was not a thing her little boy understood. They put him in a pauper's grave because that was before they had much money. There was just surprise for him and then nothing, but for her the moment stretched out – his mute shock and her banging his back and hoping she would hear him breathe now and cough but knowing she would not. Time could be a strange thing, overlapping and stretching out and pulling you back into what should be gone because the moment continued and she could not believe how long it stayed there under everything else. Even as her own body fell numb and her hands hung, there was a familiarity and calm and she felt she had known it already. She felt she was performing her shock, for the thing had already happened, long ago.

'Hello, Mrs Kearney,' says a big face over her, 'my name is Sheila. I'm a nurse and I'm just going to take a look at you and see what we can do for you while we wait for the doctor. We're very busy today...'

'Yes,' says Molly, and it is not a nice feeling when they wheel her down squeaky corridors into the belly of the hospital and behind her she can hear him – her little boy, though he didn't say anything when it happened, only his brown eyes opening big big with the shock but he didn't know did he, what was to come? That wasn't knowing on his face, was it? Only panic, only surprise, but why does she hear him now calling her like it's not too late already, like he could crawl his way back out of it, back up out of the flimsy pit they tossed him in because he was gone now anyway and no gravestone would bring him back and what with the cost of the Cremnitz White – drag him out of the catching, gagging moment and back to her if only she could reach for him because now she knows you heave the stomach of a choking child; you don't bang the back and that's what killed him and she knows it's him from the big wail of his voice and he's not choked but somewhere here in the hospital she knows it now for she can hear him wailing for her, she can taste it in the rot on her tongue and she can feel it in the pain ploughing through her; 'Mammy, Mammy, I want my mammy.'

20

HER LITTLE BOY IS crying for her. She can hear him in the background, his voice broken by big heaving breaths – 'I… want… my… ma… mmeee…'

'We're in the hospital now…' Her sister's voice is deliberately calm, almost scornful. 'He's fine, Freya, but he wants his mammy.'

'What the fuck, Cara? I'm coming now. Tell him I'm coming now. I'll get a taxi, I'll be there soon.'

A car honks as she cuts across the sun-sliced road at College Green. It is taking her so long, so long just to get across the road.

'He's alright, he's only got ten stings…'

'How did it happen? Why weren't you minding him?'

'Denise is fine, Freya, thanks very much for asking.'

'This isn't the time for sarkiness, Cara…'

'… but Megan's covered in them. She swole up really badly. They had to give her adrenalin…'

Freya doesn't give a fuck how many bites Cara's girls got. She trusted her sister with Jem. She trusted her to take care of him and now he's in the hospital and not even an apology.

'He's being a very brave boy, aren't you Jem? You're alright Jem… But Freya I think you should come. Call me when you get to the hospital and I'll come and find you…'

'I only have a tenner, do you have cash?'

PART 2

21

THERE IS A BUTCHER'S hook in the basement ceiling.

Using two hands, Sinéad hefts the bag up the stepladder. The tip of the hook is enamelled with dark stains. While she loops the slimy drawstring over it, she thinks of slaughtered pigs: dainty trotters tied with string; fresh slices of rasher with the nipples and bristles still on.

When Sinéad first moved here as a bride, there were four sows and a farrow of piglets every year. In spring they sold all but two, and last year's pigs were slaughtered noisily by someone her mother-in-law called 'my great little slaughtering man'. The killings left the air vibrant and reeling, as after a heavy rain. A smell like monthlies hung in the yard for days.

But after Terence's mother died, Sinéad left the sows celibate. They were too human; the big, dignified eyelids, white lashes, the terrible particularity of their ears. She fed them peelings and scraps in their sorry little pen and it was a relief when, one by one, huge and tough-fleshed, creaking like boulders, they toppled over, dead.

The bag drops with a decisive thunk, swaggers once, then hangs still, weighted by the fragrant squelch of boiled apples.

There is a kind of cold very particular to being beneath ground. It works into her muscles, tightens her jaw – she should go up to the warmth of the Aga. But she stands there staring, her knees stiffening, until at last the pectin begins to bead out through the muslin; tiny pinprick globules, like blood rising through a fresh graze. Drop by drop, the amber swell gathers into fine, slow rivulets, eking into the basin beneath.

She had no idea how much work apple jelly was. But when she saw the crates of apples on Mammy's back step, she was seized with a sudden hunger – is that what it was? Or greed? She felt desolate suddenly, bereft, as though everything she could touch and know herself by was pulling away from her. She was only calling in to check on the hens; Aoife told her they were being neglected. But it shocked her to be greeted at the door by her young blonde niece wearing Mammy's apron. Freya moved comfortably around the kitchen, filling the kettle, reaching for the biscuit tin, offering her tea-or-coffee. The house smelled different. The child was there at the table, sitting before a saucer of quartered apple, and he gave her a look like cold breath on her neck.

'Are you cold, Sinéad?'

'Someone just walked over my grave.'

Sinéad looked out the back window at the haggard apple tree. They had spent the morning gathering the windfalls, Freya said, smiling, and did Sinéad know how to make them into jelly?

'Easier if I just take them home, Freya, you've enough to be doing.'

'Oh. We were looking forward...'

Sinéad sighed in triumph when she had all the crates packed into her car. But then, halfway home, she was seized by regret, thinking of the cross face on the little boy, and the way Freya's skin turned very pink, her hair falling to catch the fluorescent sunset as she lifted them into the car for her.

It was more work than Sinéad had imagined – cutting out the worms and the rot, weighing them, timing them, taking their temperature as they simmered for hours.

No wonder Mammy used to go spare over the apple jelly. You knew autumn had set in when she was heard bellowing from the utility room, *There's apple jelly hanging. Nobody touch the bag! Girls? Girls do you hear me? No one is to go near the apple jelly!* Sinéad used to stand and watch, hypnotised by the steady slide and drip, battling the urge to feel the apple goo through her fingers. Squeezing the bag would let bits of mush into the jelly, making it cloudy and less disposed to set.

How could she have forgotten that smell? The clean, spicy applishness of the pips, the hidden sweetness opening in your lungs. It perfumed everything. She would smell it when she woke in the morning, on her clothes throughout the day. It reassured her.

Mammy worked so hard to make that kind of a home for them; a childhood that had the smell of baking bread on it, and cake, and the molten boil of jam. Some evenings, when she leaned over the bed to kiss Sinéad, there was a terrible weariness to her voice, as though the cords were fraying. *Goodnight, my darling.*

Her father's mood could change everything. He was the weather in which they basked, or against which they shored up their silence, their smallness. You could tell the minute you came downstairs in the morning – the temperature in the house would have shifted. Mammy's large fingers groped at her wrists. She wouldn't make things like jam or jelly during those periods, but spent all day mixing Daddy's paints and getting his dinner right. His rages could go on for weeks. The house was very quiet during those times, except for Daddy's mutterings and roars – he murmured to himself constantly, and then he would shout and bang the table because someone scraped their knife on the plate, someone said the wrong thing, or wore the wrong thing or entered the room at the wrong time. Sinéad was very good at becoming invisible, but it was easy to make mistakes.

What's that supposed to mean? An impossible question that instantly made Sinéad forget what she'd said.

Who do you think you are? Another impossible question.

At night they could hear him from their bedroom, *I'll kill myself, if he gets the prize! I'll kill myself Molly, I will!*

Shush darling, the girls…

Don't shush me, Molly! Don't attack me for speaking the truth! Shush shush – that's not the point. You're ashamed of me, Molly, I know it. You're right to be ashamed of me… Shit! It's shit. Look! Come and look. Look at the elbow it's wrong it's wrong it's wrong! It's not what I meant at all!

She and Aoife always shared a bedroom. There were plenty of rooms, but Mammy thought it was strange for children to sleep alone. On those nights, Sinéad was glad of her big sister. The astringent heat off Aoife's body when she lifted the duvet, the firm way she tucked it around Sinéad's shoulders, and the steadiness of her breath.

'Sinéad!' Terence is on the basement steps. He calls to her softly, almost a whisper, as though the gloam down here requires it. 'It's your sister on your mobile.'

'Which one?'

'The mad one.'

'Doesn't narrow it down.'

He picks his way towards her through decades of clutter – blackly oiled pieces for long-gone machines, boxes of fermented jam, a horse's foot topped with a gold disc, the animal's name and dates engraved on it. When Sinéad first moved here, that foot was a doorstop.

'Eileen,' he says

'Oh.'

'Will I tell her you'll call her back?'

'No. I'll come.'

He stops a small distance from her and picks up the horse's foot. 'It's cold down here,' he says. 'Do you need help? Need me to lift anything?'

'No. Thanks, sweetheart. I'll be up now in a minute.'

The yellow apple water has worked up a beautiful sweat in the muslin bag. She checks how much is in the basin. On the internet it said to leave the apples dripping for three hours, but

Mammy used to leave them overnight, so that's what Sinéad will do. In the morning she will have to measure it out. She might need to buy more sugar.

Her husband moves with an unobtrusive shuffle, making him look older than he is. He is still wearing that cashmere jumper. Even the elbow patches have holes in them. She has long given up buying clothes for Terence. He is more comfortable in old, worn things. He likes things with 'character'.

'I'm going out to the boathouse.' He manoeuvres around the dangerously sharp, rusted hinges of a tractor door, the horse's foot in his hand. 'I'm going to see if those corncrakes have left.'

'Okay.'

'Come out and join me for a whiskey if you feel like it.'

'Okay. I might.'

'You better come up then. See what Eileen wants.'

The boathouse is a rickety little structure that Terence built as a child. The windows are black with moss and there is water coming up through the floor. The wind splashes dark water against the windows. It has two chairs in it, and a little table covered in clammy newspaper. Terence spends hours there some days, drinking whiskey, watching the lake and listening for the corncrakes with a patience that makes Sinéad jittery. He might have made a very good father. He is interested in everything, but he has no desire to achieve or prove anything. Perhaps that's why she married him – to cure her of her own restlessness, to counter the exhausting demands her father wrung out of a lifetime. But sometimes it occurs to her that their whole life together has been spent simply passing the time, avoiding the grist. Perhaps that is as it should be.

Until she met Terence she had never known a person could be so self-contained. He inherited his wealth and is neither proud nor ashamed, hardly even glad of it. His family had hobbies, and they bought and sold horses and paintings, but none of them, as far as she understands it, had ever earned their living. For generations, they had been selling off chunks of their estate, until there was only this house and a handful of valuable possessions and connections.

She wipes her fingers on a tea towel before picking up her mobile.

'Hello.'

'Oh, Sinéad!'

'Hi, baby sister. Sorry, I was in the basement…'

'Sinéad!' Eileen's voice rises to a whine. Is she crying? Is she pretending to cry?

'What's wrong, Lily?'

'I'm so embarrassed asking you this, Sinéad. I'm so embarrassed. Oh God, imagine what Daddy would think if he saw me now, Sinéad!'

'What's going on, Eileen?'

'My tenants – those officious pieces of shit, they won't leave until their lease ends, that's in three months. So, I am destitute,

Sinéad. I am homeless. I'm fifty years old and homeless. Can you imagine what Daddy would have thought?'

'I thought you were staying with Aoife?'

'I can't live on her charity, Sinéad. I'm going to have to come to Stokerstown House for a while. Can I? Can I come to you for a while, just until I get myself sorted?'

'You can, Lily, but wc haven't done any repairs since last time. You remember you weren't too happy last time. Too damp you said, and you thought the peeling paint was making you sick, do you remember?'

'Has Terence not sorted that out yet, Sinéad? Protestants: tight. Daddy was right, they'd rather go shitty than waste a scrap of paper cleaning their arses… They take the lightbulbs with them when they leave a place, but I suppose you know that.'

'Why don't you just rent somewhere? Rent somewhere nice, or stay in a hotel for a little treat.' Lily was given her trust fund, the same as the rest of them. It hardly seems possible that she's lost it all.

'Rent somewhere, Sinéad? RENT somewhere? My own house occupied by scummy strangers and my sisters won't even afford me a spare room? I wanted to move into Mammy's for a while, but Freya wouldn't even let me in the door, Sinéad. She wouldn't even let me in the door of my own home, the home I grew up in—'

'I suppose, considering the way things are, Lily…'

'The WAY THINGS ARE, Sinéad? THE WAY THINGS ARE? What's that supposed to mean? The way things are.'

Sinéad isn't sure. The way things are is that both of her nieces have a sort of phobia of their mother. It has never been completely clear to Sinéad, what happened. First there was Cara, a lanky, morose seven-year-old living with Mammy and Daddy 'to give Lily a break'. Lily said she was a problem child, that she was violent, but Lily said a lot of things.

Then there was news that Freya was very ill – leukaemia. Mammy was beside herself with worry, on the phone to Lily day and night, driving back and forth to her house with chicken broth and bitters. There was even an article in the paper – *Mother of Leukaemia Victim Shaves Head in Solidarity with Brave Little Girl.* But there was no leukaemia, as it turned out, or chemo or any of it. Some kind of misunderstanding, that's what Mammy said. Suddenly Freya was living with Mammy and Daddy too, and Lily was gone – she had left the country. She sent a letter asking Sinéad to rent out that big ugly house Daddy bought her in Dalkey, and have the money sent straight to her bank account. Sinéad nearly jumped when she saw Freya that time – so skinny, the nimbus of stubble on her huge skull. What Sinéad remembers is her collar bone and the blades of her knees. Her eyes looking out of their deep sockets made Sinéad think of coins lost at the bottom of a well. She was a tiny child. So bony, and such white eyebrows. She said her mother had shaved her head; a misunderstanding.

'I don't know Eileen – I don't know. Of course, you're welcome here.'

'It's not her house, Sinéad! It's not for her to say who can and can't live there. What next? Is Mammy going to be allowed home after the hospital? Or will she be told to RENT somewhere?'

'Don't be silly, Eileen,' but she can't stop thinking of Freya yesterday, wearing that embroidered apron, pouring Sinéad's tea for her. *Do you know how Grandma makes the apple jelly, Sinéad? She showed me last time but I didn't pay attention…* Somehow, Sinéad has never grown as close to her nieces as she would have liked. There's only so near you can get to them. Despite all the smiles, the apparent warmth, they have a strange steeliness about their cores, both of them.

'It's up to Mammy, Eileen. But you know she's still not herself. I think I'd just wait out the three months if I were you. It's not worth upsetting Mammy, is it?'

'Mammy wants her out, Sinéad. She told me!'

'Did she? She doesn't seem to know what's going on at the minute, Lily, to be honest with you.'

'She wants her OUT, Sinéad. Only she's scared of saying it. I'm going to help her put it into writing…'

'You are welcome to stay here, Lily. Just stay here until your tenants are out. Or, you know, talk to Brendan about it but I think you have the right to tell them to leave, if you're moving back in yourself…'

'Well, Aoife's right, Sinéad. She said you'd be no help.'

Sinéad closes her eyes. She could do with that whiskey.

'Sinéad? Aren't you going to say anything?'

'What do you want me to say, Eileen? I think you're causing trouble for nothing now, to be perfectly honest.'

Sinéad looks out the kitchen window at the wet yellow field.

A loud rain has started, great fat drops coming slantwise at the windowpane.

'It's raining,' she says, 'can you hear it down the phone?'

'No,' says Eileen. 'It's not raining here.'

She leans against the draining board and watches the rain, allowing the crackling silence to tighten between them, until Eileen hangs up.

At the back door she pulls on her wellingtons and her Barbour jacket, and makes her way out across the field to the boathouse.

22

HIS MAMMY IS WEARING the grey knitted dress with the pink cherries on it, and the man at the till smiles with his eyes going up and down the dress, counting the cherries in his head while he beeps their shopping along. Jem has counted the cherries. There are thirty-six.

She frowns at the man and Jem puts his fingers between hers and kisses her hand and leans his cheek against the end of her dress, and he touches his lips to her silver nails – smooth and hard like the outside of a car – but then her phone beeps in her pocket and she pulls away from him to take it out. Then the man says how much money, and Jem's mammy drops the phone into her bag and looks quickly in her envelope-from-work and her teeth squash her bottom lip and her eyebrows fold and Jem's tummy feels like a fist squeezing. His mammy doesn't like when they have to put things back, and Jem doesn't like it either, especially because he knows it will be the chocolate spread or else the jellies. But it's okay. She gives lots of notes and the man says, 'That's great, love. Have a good evening now,' and he gives her some coins with the receipt and then he winks at Jem and says, 'See you now, buddy.'

When they get back to the car, they have to stuff the shopping in on top of all their things in the boot and it blocks out the back window. But it's only when he sees his 'Our Planet' light sitting beside his booster seat that he remembers what's happened and why he has that stingy sick popping up his throat.

His mammy bought milk, and Jem knows milk needs to go straight in the fridge, but his mammy doesn't start the car. They just stay there in the flat car park outside Aldi and she unfolds the piece of paper again and looks at it for a long time and he hears her breathe for a little while – in and out and in and out like she's sleeping – and then she says, 'I think it's going to rain, little man.' She gives him a biscuit to eat, and a carton of apple juice with a straw, and they listen to a CD of a sad man singing and Jem looks out at the cars wheeling into the carpark and rolling out and the people putting their shopping into their boots and thumping them closed. Everything is soapy grey out there, like cold bathwater, but there is no rain yet.

Jem and his mammy have a special speaker on the dashboard – Bluetooth; it works with the phone, and the music sounds big and clean, not like in his cousin Denise's car where they have tapes and you can hear the ribbon crinkling and pulling.

The two halves of Jem's 'Our Planet' lamp are back together again, but when he thinks of the little bulb in there, his nostrils get hot and wet.

While his mammy was packing everything into the car – his Lego and his slippers, her books and her costumes and the little bottles from her dressing table – he was sitting on the step holding the two halves of the lamp in his lap. His Great Aunty Aoife and the other lady came out of the house to watch his mammy putting their things in the car, and he saw his mammy's cheeks twitch, but the thing that made him really sad was the black thread waggling inside the bulb like a little bit of ash. He knows his lamp isn't going to work anymore.

The biscuit has chocolate on the top with a picture of an olden-days prince made out of bumps in the chocolate. Jem wants to keep it for later but then the chocolate starts to get sticky in his fingers so he sucks it off, and licks it, and then he eats the biscuit bit too even though the apple juice is burning his tummy.

He knew that Mimi was coming home from the hospital soon, so when he heard the front door he thought it was her. He wanted to go and give her a kiss but it was a very important part of the *Dalmatians* – the part when the mammy and daddy dalmatian are sneaking all of the puppies away from the bad guys – and he was just waiting until that bit was over before he pressed pause.

It was his Great Aunty Aoife, though. When he came into the hall, she was there with her arms crossed, talking in a slow and careful way, and his mammy was holding a piece of very clean paper, with fold marks across it. She said to keep watching the *Dalmatians* while she packed a few things. She said they were going to stay in Denise's house for a little while. The other lady was in the driveway, sitting in a silver car with no lid on it.

Jem clicked the *Dalmatians* back into the box as quickly as he could, careful not to touch the shiny part, but it was tricky because Aunty Aoife was standing very still in front of him with eyes like small torches and her tongue poking her cheek.

'Well, little man,' says Jem's mammy, and she turns around from the driver seat and smiles at him, but then she sighs a crying sort of sigh, 'your Aunty Cara is waiting for us. Best get you to bed,' and Jem says, 'Two more minutes,' and then he doesn't know why he said that.

'It's getting late.'

She puts on a new playlist before driving out of the car park and onto the road. One song says 'One day yooooou'll understand,' and usually Jem and his mammy sing loud with that one, but now she sings quietly. She turns her head back to look at him and her eyebrows go up in a way that makes Jem's middle so sore and frightened and her lips go into her mouth and she squeezes his ankle and as she says the words with the song there is a bad crinkle in her voice just like the tapes in Denise's car that are running out and then she says, 'Oh, your seatbelt Jem. Strap yourself in my little man. Best boy.'

Babies have lots of bones, more than children, and a child's got more bones than a grown-up's got. When he has strapped himself in, Jem asks his mammy how many bones he has in him and she says she doesn't know.

'Children have more bones than adults though,' she says. 'I know that. There was an ad on the TV when I was little, with a skeleton dancing around singing, "them bones them bones need calcium…" and the skeleton said, "A child's got more bones than a grown-up's got", so I know that much.'

'I know about that, Mammy. You told me that.'

'The calcium makes your bones grow together. It was an ad for milk I think.'

Jem smiles at his mammy because he wants her to smile back but it gives him a sick feeling, thinking of his mammy being a little child with lots of bones. There are things he has heard about when his mammy was little like him, and it sounds like a bad land she was in sometimes, and frightening, and it gives him a terrible feeling like slipping suddenly and being not able to get up. His mammy smiles at him and squeezes his ankle and says, 'My little man. You're a great boy, Jem, do you know that?' and Jem smiles but his tummy is twisting.

His mammy has fewer bones than him and that's okay; that's how come she can walk like that in the supermarket and smile at the man who fixes their car, and that's why his mammy can make things safe and still for him, and not slippery like that feeling of thinking that his mammy was a little child like him before, with lots of bendy bones not-joined-up.

'Mimi is older than you, isn't she, Mammy?'

'Just a minute, baby,' says his mammy, 'I have to concentrate here…' but she squeezes his ankle again with one hand while she turns the wheel with the other so he knows she is thinking about him and feeling him there behind her and she will turn to him soon and say, 'Sorry, Jem, what were you asking me?' He understands now and he is so happy that he understands now. Mimi is older than his mammy and older than his Aunty Cara, and older even than his mammy's Aunty Aoife. Mimi is old and so her bones are growing all together and that's why her knees don't bend so well and her neck doesn't move so well for turning around and looking when he goes to see her in the hospital. He thought Mimi was coming home. But there's the slipping feeling again – like that time on the ice skates that Jem didn't like very much at all – the heavy blades for feet and the cold hard ice and holding onto his mammy but his mammy slipping too and the two of them slipping and nothing steady to grab. Because he knows now, and there's nothing to ask his mammy now when she turns around in a minute to say what is it Jem because he knows for sure now and it will only make his mammy sad if he tells her, that Mimi's bones are all pulling together, and that she will grow tighter and tighter now until she is only one bone, only one hard, bumpy rock and not his soft Mimi anymore.

'Sorry, Jem, what were you asking me my little man?'

23

'IT'S A GOOD THING you're here, Freya. I totally forgot about it until I got her text…'

Cara is rooting in the cupboard, pulling out glass jars of grain and beans. She passes Freya a tall Kilner with a badly rusted clasp. 'What was I thinking, inviting them? I don't have time for this…'

Freya opens the jar: a sweet smell reminiscent of sweat. There's a dried apricot at the bottom, wizened and complexly wrinkled, like a shrunken head. 'I'd throw out this jar, Cara.'

'… I wanted to work tomorrow. I really wanted to get to bed and work in the morning – Aha! Duck confit! Is it in date though…? Don't tell them it's from a tin, will you?'

'Relax, Cara, it's fine. It'll be fine. Will I make devilled eggs for starter? You've loads of eggs. And then you make your main course. You have lentils – simple. Lentils and leek mash and duck. Do you want me to run out to the shops? Ice cream or something for dessert?'

'Thanks, Freya. I have ice cream. Homemade ice cream. I'll text Pat to get chocolate and wine. Peig's asleep, Megan's down;

will you just get the others to bed and I'll make a start here? What do I do? Just hard-boil the eggs?'

'Yeah, just boil them for three minutes, then put them in cold water and I'll deal with them. Make sure you leave me two eggs to make the mayonnaise with… Jem! Denise! Upstairs now it's time for bed! Jem?'

She finds them on the landing. Denise is on her knees, crunching tin foil around one of Jem's feet.

'Silver shoes, Mammy.'

'Magic shoes!' Denise leans back on her bum and kicks her legs. Her feet are covered in layers of aluminium.

'Don't let your mammy see that, Denise. She'll go spare. Come on you two, in your jammies quick. Put those shoes in your cupboard, Den.'

'Is it because of the waste, Mammy?'

'Is what because of the waste?'

'That Aunty Cara will go spare?'

'Yes.'

'Told you, Den. And is it because of 'Our Planet' too, Mammy?'

'Get into your pyjamas you two. I'm going to roll up the rest of the foil now so your mammy doesn't notice, Den. If you hurry we can have a story.'

'I want a story with just you, Mammy. No Den. And Grandma.'

'Not tonight, darling.'

'Mammmeee!' calls Den. 'Jem hurt my feelings!'

'Oh stop it, Denise, your mammy is busy. Get into your pyjamas or there'll be no story.'

When Jem is tucked in, he says, 'How much longer, Mammy, before we can go home to Mimi? I don't mind if her brain is tired. I don't mind.'

'In a little while, Jem. In a bit… another few weeks, baby, I think.'

'When can I see Mimi? I need to tell her something.'

Pat is just in when Freya comes downstairs. His shirt and his paint-scabbed trousers are dull with wood dust, and there are parings dangling from his hair. He drops his trousers onto the doormat and steps out of them, begins to unbutton his shirt.

'Hi Freya. What's the story, alright?'

'Hi Pat.'

Cara comes out of the kitchen with a tea towel over her shoulder. She kisses Pat's cheek and then his mouth. 'How was work?'

'It was work.' He has stripped down to a thick, sleeveless vest and long boxer shorts. He has strong arms, strong legs, two hairless patches at the tops of his thighs, long, frizzed underarm hair of glossy jet-black.

Cara picks up his clothes, opens the front door, and shakes them in the drizzle and wind, before rolling them into a ball.

'Did you get the chocolate?'

'Yes, what's it for?'

'We have dinner guests.'

'What? What dinner guests? You didn't tell me you invited people!'

Cara hugs the bundle of laundry. 'I know, I forgot, I'm sorry, baby. It's a pain, I know. It's a couple whose kid is in Denise's music school...'

'I was looking forward to... I wanted an early night. I've had a long day. A long and boring day.'

'I'm sorry, baby.'

'Are the girls in bed?'

'I just turned Denise's light out.' Freya moves towards them. 'Megan is asleep. I'll stick a wash on, Cara, will I?' She reaches for the clothes. There is an adult smell – clean wood, dust and wet, day-old sweat.

Cara nods, relinquishing the ball of dirty clothes. 'I'll run your bath, baby.'

'Oh, it's hard for men,' says Freya softly, a hint of Grandma in her intonation. Cara laughs, picking up the joke. She shakes her head the way Grandma does, 'Oh it's very hard for men.'

'She's dead right,' says Pat. 'Grandma knows a thing or two. You should take a leaf out of her book. Dinny wouldn't have put up with this, would he? Unexpected guests? Can you imagine?'

'Poor darling,' says Cara.

As she leaves for the utility room, Freya sees her sister take Pat's hands and kiss them. She puts her face into his palm, as though she wants to drink him.

~

The guests have brought a bottle of wine in an unbleached cotton wine bag. The woman pushes it at Cara: 'It's organic.'

The husband – soft-featured, a bald head peaked like the tip of an egg – rolls his eyes at Pat. 'Organic!' he says. 'Anything to up the price. Am I right?'

Freya stands in the hall, watching the two couples crowd inside the front door while the husband tells an anecdote about a friend who manages a sugar packaging plant: '... I'm telling you, literally the same mound of sugar and they bag it up: so many bags of organic, so many bags of own-brand. What a racket!'

'Well, I don't know,' says the wife. She is pale and pretty, with carefully done blonde hair, enough volumising spray and rouge as to suggest latent ill health. 'But I like this wine, I have to say.'

'This is my sister, Freya,' says Cara. Her voice has lifted a notch above her usual pitch. She is wearing heavy-looking earrings and a square silver pendant on a too-long silver chain, which she keeps touching. 'She's staying with us for a while...'

The woman's name is Gwen. Pat takes her by the elbow. As he turns her towards the lounge, he gives Cara a wink and Freya feels left out of some joke. Her sister's marriage is a puzzle. Most days, it looks like a work agreement. Until the children are asleep there are things to be done, and the couple bustle about the house, giving each other orders and discussing schedules like friendly colleagues. But sometimes they pass each other in the kitchen, or the hall, and they smile at each other – huge, goofy smiles just for no reason at all.

Pat makes them all very strong cocktails, which the woman refuses. 'I'm driving. I'll save myself for a glass of wine.'

At first, no one touches the devilled eggs, but then the husband takes one. 'Must be decades since I've seen a stuffed egg! My mother used to make them for parties.' They are all eaten up quickly after that.

Over the course of the meal, Pat stealthily tops up the glasses. The blonde lady's face grows ruddy and she starts to talk very earnestly about her child. She frames her anecdotes as concern, and it takes a few minutes for Freya to realise she is boasting: 'Some days I just wish she'd run outside and play like a normal little girl, you know? Can I ask you, what's Denise's reading speed?'

'I don't know,' says Cara.

'You should get it checked. Gifted kids need extra support too you know, as much as the slow ones. Well, Ellie reads and reads. She would read a dictionary, honestly. We had her assessed when she was five…'

When they ask what Pat and Cara do, Cara's body language changes. She begins to move her hand with flourishes, and she shakes her hair about. Freya has never seen her in this light before. 'We're artists,' she says, 'but you know, we do other things. I illustrate children's books. Pat does woodwork.'

'Ha! I finish furniture,' says Pat, 'Laura Ashley furniture. I'm a glorified assembly man!' and he hunches a little as he fills all the glasses.

'We met at the National College of Art and Design.' Cara says it like a question. 'My grandfather taught there for a while, actually. You might have heard of him?'

Pat knocks back glass after glass of wine and leans his head on his hand while Cara talks. His face is blank but for a childish thrust to his lower lip, and a question suddenly twists in Freya's throat – does he love her sister? Because it seems so clear to her now: some bitterness or resentment there in the clamp of his jaw.

'Oh, Kearney, Eugene, was that the exhibition we went to last summer…'

'No, Gwen. That was Bacon.'

'Oh, Bacon, yes…'

'Ellie does a sculpture class on a Wednesday, doesn't she, Gwen?'

'The woman is brilliant,' says Gwen, nodding eagerly, 'but I mean, the standard is mixed. They've had to move Ellie up a class already. Her fine motor skills have always been excellent. Sometimes I wonder if I overdid it on the quinoa when I was pregnant with her, you know! I read it was good for fine motor skills, so I ate buckets of quinoa the whole nine months…'

Covering his eyes and sighing as though speaking is a great effort, Pat says, 'Of course it's killing the Bolivians.'

For a moment, no one speaks, and it seems as though there might be some collusion to ignore the comment. Then Gwen says, 'It's killing the Bolivians? What do you mean? I – I thought it was good for you. That's what I read?'

'Well, not quinoa. Quinoa's not killing them, but aspirational westerners like ourselves, eating up all their staple food. It's driving the price up. Natives aren't able to afford it.'

'Sure. But you can get Fairtrade quinoa,' says Cara, 'and they grow it in France too...'

'Freya,' says the husband, 'you never told us what you do.'

'I'm a children's entertainer. I do magic shows for kids' parties.'

'Very good,' says the man.

'I'd say that's great fun,' says his wife.

'And she's in her last year of law,' says Cara, 'at Trinity.'

'Oh,' says Gwen, 'Eugene read law...'

Cara has made her 'go to' chocolate cake for dessert. It has melted chocolate on the inside, and they have homemade mint ice cream with it. They talk about the dessert all through its consumption and Cara writes the recipe down, assuring them that it's 'ridiculously easy'.

In the kitchen, Cara fizzes with busyness; opening the fridge, grinding the coffee beans. Freya matches some chipped little teacups with their saucers and arranges them on a tray. She can't seem to catch Cara's eye.

Watching the lovely curves of her sisters' shoulders, the knuckle where her spine begins, and the way the light catches the fine film of hair on the back of her neck, Freya is suddenly overwhelmed with a desperate love. She hugs her sister around the middle and kisses her cheek, resting her chin on the taut bridge between neck and shoulder, and she can smell her sweet maple-syrup smell. Cara's body, which usually feels sturdier and more maternal than her own, is stiff and bony under the rough muslin hippy blouse. There is something missing, and it occurs to Freya that her sister is usually pregnant or holding a child.

'So it was fine in the end,' says Freya.

'God, I'm sorry, I know this must be boring for you.'

'Don't be silly.'

'I'm not used to these people... other parents, you know? I'm not sure how to be.' There is a vein showing beneath one of Cara's eyes, a long, fine line curved like the crack of an egg. Cara isn't pretty anymore. Her eyes are different shapes. When did that happen? Is that how it goes? Will Freya's summer end just like that, with no warning, or will it wait for her to use it up on love and children?

'They're nice,' says Freya, 'they like you. It's fine.'

'The duck was too salty.'

'Cara, don't be silly. It was delicious. And the cake – the cake was SO delicious! The most delicious cake in the world. My favourite.'

'Okay. Anyway. Let's get the coffee going. I've left poor Pat in there on his own and he's knackered after work. He's only fit for bed.'

'Are you okay?'

'I – fuck, Freya. I spent the mortgage money. I spent a thousand euros in O'Sullivan's. I was out of pens and ink and I needed a new board...'

'It's easily done. It's only a grand, Cara, it's fine.'

'I'm due money in but my agent hasn't got it yet. Pat will kill me.'

'Do you want a loan?'

'I wasn't asking for a loan, Freya. I can't take a loan. You're my little sister. It's pathetic.'

'Don't be stupid. I have it. I have it in cash. I'll give you two grand, okay? I'll give it to you in the morning and you can pay me back whenever, okay? I don't need it. It's savings.'

'Okay.'

'Does that solve things?'

'Yes.'

'Okay, so it's fine. Nothing to worry about. Come on, we better get back out there...'

Pat comes into the kitchen, grinning with his mouth closed.

'Freya,' he says, 'I dare you to ask them if little Ellie is autistic.'

'Stop it!' says Cara, filling the cafetière, and 'someone go out there. We can't leave them on their own.'

Pat holds his wife by each shoulder. He rubs deep into her spine with his thumb, and plants a small kiss on the back of her neck. 'Okay?' he says. She nods, her features realign.

'Just reminding you we have cream in the fridge. For the coffee.'

'Go back out there,' she says. 'We can't leave them on their own.'

Things seem easier when they come back in. They are playing music: some underrated Mexican–American musician with an Irish cult following, who Pat and the nice woman both know all about, and they are chatting excitedly. Freya sets the tray down on the coffee table – three half beer barrels that Pat has sanded and varnished and bound in steamed wood. Cara smiles apologetically at them all. 'Now,' she says, 'coffee.'

'So, Freya, do you live here during term time too, or on campus or what?'

'Oh,' says Freya, 'it's complicated. I actually—I live with our grandmother. Or I did, until recently.'

'She had a fall,' says Cara, 'and she was in hospital for six weeks.'

'Your grandmother?' says Eugene.

His wife purses her lips and nods. 'That's always the way, isn't it?' she says. 'That's how it starts – a fall.'

'So, while she's there, our aunt gives Freya this typed letter, signed by our grandma, saying she wants her out of the house.'

'Oh.' The couple look at each other sidelong. 'That sounds complicated,' says Eugene.

Freya is already regretting the conversation. She shrugs, 'Well, it is and it isn't…'

'It's difficult,' says Cara. She tugs the big pendant from side to side, and the chain presses into her neck. 'Every time I visit she asks me where Freya is, she wants to know when she'll be home. And Jem – that's Freya's little boy. She wants to know where he is.'

'Oh.' Gwen is interested now. 'So she doesn't remember writing it or what?'

'You have a little boy?' says Eugene, a note of admiration or horror. Freya nods, 'Jem.'

'Oh no, she didn't write it,' says Cara. 'It was our aunt or our mother, we think. She signed it but she was on a lot of medication in hospital and she has no memory of signing it or knowing anything about it – I mean she really wasn't with it. Anyway, she's home now and she's getting better. Our mother is living there with her, but I'd say she'll be moving back to her own house soon – our mother will. There are tenants in her house but they'll be out soon. We're just waiting for her to move back to her house, and then Freya will move back in. It'll be fine.'

'We don't want to rock the boat,' says Freya. 'I don't want a big showdown in front of our grandma, you know… she's quite fragile, after her fall.'

'Always the way,' says Gwen. 'After a certain age a fall changes everything.'

'So you said your own mother made her sign this thing, you think?' says Eugene.

'Yes.' Cara's face turns red. 'It's complicated.'

'Our grandparents raised us,' explains Freya. 'Our mother is… she's a baddy. She has personality disorders and stuff.'

'Munchausen by proxy,' says Cara, and Gwen's face grows tight with discomfort.

'Narcissistic personality disorder,' says Freya. 'At least, that's what one analyst told her she had.'

'So she fired her!' adds Cara. She tries to laugh but no one joins her.

Pat rubs his face with the whole of his hand, takes a gulp from his cup and says, 'Lovely coffee, baby.' Cara smiles, a brittle, grateful little movement of her lips, and half nods. She turns to Eugene: 'So where did you do law?' Gwen's face lights up, and Eugene starts giving his credentials. Freya has an impulse to touch his head. It would be satisfying in a way she can't put her finger on, like holding a golf ball or a sea-smoothed pebble. She had a teddy bear as a child, with a silky label on it that she used to twiddle her finger in. That is what it would be like to touch the smooth, domed head. Now Cara is explaining how she finds the time to work.

'But I've found recently, you know – well, we read them a story every night, and then Den reads to herself in bed for a bit – I think books are so important, don't you? But I've found that when the kids are all in bed I run myself a bath and I always intend to read in it but I can't – I'm too tired. I don't read anymore, I've only just noticed it. We go to all this effort to get the kids into books and the result is there's no energy left to read ourselves! So, you know, I mean. I said to Pat, what are we preparing them for? What example are we setting?' Her voice rises, thinning, and a panic starts in Freya... She can't help her sister out of this, wind her back up and hold her tight.

'But parents are like teachers, I suppose!' Her shrillness makes Freya squirm. 'Those who can't do... we teach our kids to do the things we know are good for them, we dedicate our lives to it, but in doing so we...'

Pat puts his hand on Cara's knee. 'But you paint still, baby – what are you on about?'

'We don't read,' says Cara. 'We teach them to read so that they can have a richer life, but as a result of all this we no longer read ourselves... I mean, I don't even read the paper anymore.'

Freya looks at her knees. Cara never read the papers anyway. She can remember Grandad giving out to her about it.

Pat laughs. 'Well. We're only lousy humans!'

Then he unlocks a drawer that he's made in the beer barrels, and takes out a tin of tobacco and a little wooden box, and some cigarette papers. The couple look shocked but neither Pat nor Cara seem to notice. Licking the cigarette papers, he opens the tin.

'Do you smoke a bit?' he asks the man, and this time the entire head flushes. He nods like a teenager in the bike sheds. 'Yeah, not so much these days but...'

'I'll drive,' says Gwen, who seems to share her husband's alarm, but nods to him, sanctioning his participation. Pat's face has taken on an expression of mirth and mockery. When the joint is rolled, Cara gives an artificial sigh and says, 'This will be the one big perk of weaning Peig. No need to pump and dump.'

'Oh,' says the woman, nodding slowly and smiling and peeking at the weed out of the corner of her eye, as though the twists of grass were some irresistible sexual image that she doesn't want to be caught looking at. 'What does that mean?'

'Oh, you know, express and then dump the milk... It probably wouldn't do any harm... I mean the tobacco is Fairtrade organic and the weed is locally grown – I wouldn't buy it otherwise. I wouldn't support that industry, you know... But obviously if I'm feeding, I pump and dump four hours later. Just to be sure.'

Freya is relieved when Jem calls down the stairs for her. He says his cheek is too hot, so she opens the little window that faces out onto the silent drive, and she lies beside him long after he's fallen back to sleep. The couples' voices rise up through the house, settling like smoke in this little room. There is a short silence before the long goodbyes in the hallway, the click of the front door.

As the guests move outside, the sounds become suddenly crisper, as though they have emerged from a fog – the clip of Gwen's heels, the beep of their car unlocking.

'He's not as bad as *she* is…' says Eugene.

'Shush.'

'… he's alright. Poor bastard.'

24

'EILEEN IS FULL OF light,' that's what people could say of her, 'Eileen is full of wisdom and love and light, coming back to take care of her elderly mother...' At the funeral – well, she's getting ahead of herself, but it's something she just knows now – at the funeral people will nod their heads, and whisper to each other as she stands at the altar. She will wear an elegant black veil, and when she lifts it, people will see how big her eyes are, and how the tears are running steadily down her smooth cheeks. She was her Daddy's favourite, no one can deny that. And even if Mammy misunderstood her sometimes, Eileen's the one who is here now, when it most counts.

Sometimes Eileen explains her story to herself this way. It helps her to get a bit of a handle on things. Her life is such a scattering of experiences, such a mixture of blessings and horrors, that she needs to put it into words for herself sometimes, just so that she can look in the mirror and know who she is and what to wear and how to speak.

She picks the rubber stopper from the base of the salt cellar and shakes the salt into the bin, spilling some over the floor. The minder can clean it up, that's what she's paid for.

From her chair in the TV room, her mother makes an ugly lowing sound, trying to heave herself up.

'Mammy, stay where you are, give me a minute.'

But her mother strains her head back towards the kitchen, her features warped with pain. 'Oh Lily, what are you doing now?'

'It's for your own good, Mammy. Salt is one of the greatest toxins you can ingest. After wheat and sugar, it has a huge part to play in depression, cancer, heart disease...'

'Everybody has to die some way, darling.'

Eileen takes a slow breath in through her nose, pushing her rib cage wide, visualising the light filling her lungs and pushing the darkness out. She will not give in to anger. 'I'm making you some millet, Mammy.'

'Oh Lily, not your birdseed again, darling...'

'It's very good for you.'

'Freya says we are killing the Bolivians... they need all that birdseed over in Bolivia. They're starving for it...'

Nothing is ever good enough for her mother, but Eileen feels no resentment now; only forgiveness. Things are coming right at last, and just in time.

Her mother can't walk now without her frame. It's a pity, but in a way perhaps it's for the best, for now her mother can't bustle about, averting her eyes, avoiding the question, shutting her out. Now there are long afternoons where she sits by her mother's side, talking and talking, and she knows her mother has come to appreciate her at last.

'Where's Polina?'

'She's gone off for her lunch, Mammy. Don't worry, Lily is here. I'm making lunch for us.'

Eileen looks down at her blue gingham dress. It was Anton, the facilitator of the 'Awakening Your Truth' workshop, who told her she needed to get in touch with her feminine energy. He was right. She feels good in the gingham dress, the way it springs out at the waist, the way it swishes when she moves. It makes her feel like little Lily again. Daddy's little Lily. Pretty, cheeky, spunky little Lily.

Eileen used to sit by her Daddy's feet and lift them one by one out of the warm, soapy water, and clip his toenails and scrape the dirt out from under them.

'Ow.' Her mother is trying to raise herself out of her chair again. Eileen kneels by her, the big skirt lifting and settling in a lovely dome. She needs long hair to go with this new look. Her hair is still toffee-coloured, hardly a grey in sight – it's a sort of miracle, and she should appreciate it. Her sister Aoife went grey at thirty. If Eileen had long hair, she could plait it, or put it in bunches, but her hair is taking so long to grow past her ears…

'Are you hungry, Mammy?'

'Yes, darling – there wasn't a biscuit left in the house for elevenses; of course I am hungry.'

'They weren't good for you, Mammy. Processed wheat… You know I really think that, after sugar, wheat is the most toxic of carbohydrates. Anton says there'd be no war or rape if it wasn't for wheat.'

'Is that right, darling? Well I miss my elevenses…'

'Well, we'll sort a few things out now and then we can eat.'

'Yes, okay…' Her mother winces dramatically, her whole body suddenly tense and her hand lightly touching her knee and flinching away again, as though it burns. 'Fetch me some Paracetamol, darling, will you, it's very sore.'

'In a minute, Mammy; we need to sort this out now, Mammy, and no more evasion, okay?'

'What is it?'

'I found him. I told you this yesterday, Mammy.'

'Found who, darling?'

'Oh Mammy, no! I refuse to play this game with you. You know who! My brother. I found my brother and I want to bring him back here and have him buried beside Daddy and you.'

'Leave things alone, will you darling? Leave things alone.'

'He's my brother, Mammy.'

'Let him rest. Ow. My pill, Eileen.'

This is not the first time Mammy has taken extreme measures to avoid what Eileen needs to say. After she reached her dead brother that time – the medium's voice going high and sweet, her palms spreading and her eyes rolling back – Eileen had come straight to Mammy to tell her the message. He wanted to be buried beside Daddy. At first her mother didn't want to hear it – she wept and trembled and all that, but Eileen knew she'd thank her in the end. She was just beginning to get through to her, when in came Aoife, throwing a real spanner in the works. It was Aoife's fault, leaving that big Brown Thomas bag there for Mammy to trip on, but Eileen is certain Mammy did it on purpose – she didn't like it that Eileen was the one he came to.

'It's what he wants, Mammy.'

'No, darling.'

'No? NO?'

'No darling, leave him be, please.'

'Well I've gone to a lot of trouble Mammy, for you to just turn around and say no – you may be happy to leave my brother in a pauper's grave, but I'm not.'

'Please Lily, quieten down darling. Rest easy darling, please.'

'Do you want me to leave, Mammy, is that it? Do you want me to leave you here in your chair? You want me to leave so you can piss yourself again right here in your chair?'

'Don't Lily, don't go. What do you want, darling?'

'It costs me a lot you know, driving back and forth, getting your shopping – the price of petrol, for one thing.'

'Well take it from my purse then, darling, whatever you need.'

Her mother's handbag lies all day by her feet like a faithful dog. Eileen lifts it into her lap and feels around for the purse. It's not easy for family carers like herself – she heard a woman on Joe Duffy yesterday saying it. It's not easy because the state support for carers is minimal, and it is a full-time job. Perhaps she should call up Joe, and tell him about her brother. But people can be very close-minded about these things; very quick to dismiss anything they don't understand. Perhaps she should get long hair extensions while she's waiting for her hair to grow.

The notes are filed neatly – fifties at the back, then twenties, then tens, and one crumpled fiver at the front. She slips two fifties from the back row of notes, folds them and tucks them into the white, lace-edged socks she is wearing. Then she looks at Mammy sitting there mightily, like Mother Courage with her mouth drawn open, both hands on her knee. A sudden indignation flashes through Eileen – she will not give way to rage, but she will take what's due to her. 'And the milk, Mammy, and the millet… how do you think I buy those?' Ridiculous that she, the daughter of Dennis Kearney, that she should be there worrying about the cost of hair extensions, living off her tenants like some kind of a nobody.

'Take what you need, darling. Disgusting amounts of money I have now, you wouldn't believe the bank statements. And isn't it well for me.'

Eileen takes another two fifties before buttoning up her mother's purse. That will do.

'What do you want, darling?'

'I won't be treated like this, Mammy! I won't hang around here, waiting on you hand and foot to be treated like this! Who cleaned up your shit when the Solpadine made you shit everywhere? Who wiped the shit off your legs, Mammy? Who scrubbed your shit out of your skirt? That skirt you're wearing right now? Me! Me, that's who!'

Her mother needed to hear that – the sobering truth of it. Eileen has to be firm, as well as kind. After all she's been through in life, she has at last learned not to let herself be taken advantage of. Eileen was once an innocent, but she has learned to be tough. It took some trials and tribulations though; the married man who duped her, and the dark gremlin of a child she bore him. How she loved that child – for the first six weeks she even fed her from her own breasts. She should have known immediately, of course she should have. She was expecting a boy to carry on Liam's gifts – and then out came a girl who looked nothing like him, but Eileen persisted. She gave that child every opportunity but she was a bad one; dark-haired and dark-hearted and wrong. Some wrongness you can see straight off – by the shape of the skull or the width of the eyes or whatever – but there are other kinds of wrong that take some time to show. She thought the second one was the right one – white-blonde hair and great green eyes – but she was a useless idiot without a note in her head and so fat, my God, so fat. Never mind – the truth is that all Eileen ever really needed was the courage to access her own specialness, her own gifts.

She knows she's got through to her mother by the sudden gulp, the bright trail of red spreading like ivy up her neck to her cheeks. Her mother's mouth, once so sensual and womanly, has grown lean and masculine, little puckers of loose skin hanging down either side of it with a gravity that says she understands how much she owes Eileen. She's clutching her knee now, her eyes squeezed shut. 'Get me a painkiller, darling, will you?'

'Let's get this sorted first, Mammy. I have the form here, and the cheque book. I've done all the legwork that you couldn't be bothered doing – I have his birth cert, his death cert, your passport, all I need is your signature for the exhumation, and a cheque. When we've got you better, I'll bring you to see the new plot…'

'Darling. Get me my pill, will you please?'

'Let's just get this sorted now, Mammy, and then we'll do all that. And we might even change you into your nice blouse then after lunch, what do you think? Aoife is coming later to see you, Mammy. She's bringing Valerie. Won't that be nice?'

25

MOLLY HAS STRANGE DAUGHTERS. But there must be some sense to it. They were knitted into life in her private nooks; they are the culmination of it all.

Growing up, they escaped her. Always she was looking, looking and looking, trying to see them clearly like those magic pictures you have to stare at in the right way, but now she never will understand for her mind is full of snow – a blinding thing – and thinking is like wading through it. It is heavy. It stops her breath; cold in her mouth.

There are nightmares in her. She can hear them braying now in the silences left when words slide away. Now she knows they are coming for her, their hooves growing louder on the packed earth, the terrible muteness of them before they shriek.

There are things better left in the dark.

Did it happen after the birth of her little boy, or only with her daughters?

Her daughters' first years were haunted by the darkest possibilities. She would see it with every blink – the choking – and she would put her face close and her hand on the little chests to feel the breath. Walking down the stairs, she would have to stop and cling to the banister, for fear that with her next move the baby might slip from her arms. She could see how the head would be dashed on the steps – the blood congealing in the silky newborn hair. She knew the silence. The sense of waiting; waiting to believe the thing that has just happened, waiting for the mind to catch up; the lungs, the heart.

Dinny shrugged; the shadow side, he said.

It became worse with every birth, so that when the last one came – scrawny, fussy little Eileen – Molly had only to look at her to see every violence that could befall the child. She couldn't tell Dinny the gruesome things that went on in her mind's eye. As she knitted, she would fight the images of the needles stabbing her child through the eyeballs, in through the ears, the tiny anus. She could feel it; the resistance and give of that tender body. Everything Molly did was terrifying. She couldn't chop an onion or she thought of what that knife could do to her baby, the neat slices it could make, the way it could open her. If she boiled a pot of water, she could hear the screams of scalded girls.

She told Mrs Brereton a little of it. Mrs Brereton had something like that, she said, after her son was born. She said she used to dream about climbing up onto the roof and letting him drop. In the dream, she said, she had no remorse, but she was very frightened of what her husband would think.

The visions made Molly fearful for Lily, and she was given to panics over nothing. She couldn't bear to see her cry, and nor could Dinny. There was a feeling between them, a sense that she might be taken from them at any moment, that they didn't quite have her. People said she was too protective. They said she indulged Lily, spoiled her. Dinny's mother said it, and so did Molly's sister Kat and her Aunty Doll. They warned her.

That's why when that thing happened, she wasn't sure had she imagined it or what. She heard it, didn't she? But Lily was giggling so much, perhaps she had misunderstood?

'Mammy! Mr Edwards is putting his fingers into my knickers again! My front bottom Mammy...'

And when she rushed into the good room, Dinny wasn't there but off fetching something to show his friends, and the three men looked up from their whiskey, their faces bewildered. Lily was sitting on Edwards' knee, smiling, and Danny – a really decent fellow – said, 'Honestly Molly, I was right here the whole time. I don't know why she said that...'

Molly's face was numb with the shock of it. Her voice sounded like it was coming from outside her, and far away. 'Lily, stop pestering Daddy's friends. Come and help me in here in the kitchen.'

Edwards was Dinny's best friend. He was often about. They could sit for hours, chatting, drinking whiskey; sometimes when Molly came in with the messages, he was there. He was a very talented man and very knowledgeable about Irish folklore. He was what they called 'cultured', and sometimes she thought Dinny was flattered by his friendship. He drew books for Lily, lovely books full of pixies and fairies.

Was she wrong to say it to Dinny? He wrote Edwards one of his letters and they never spoke again after that. The other friends – Danny and Casey – they stopped coming so much.

Even back then you could never tell, with Eileen. You could never tell if she told the truth or a lie and you could never understand why she said the things she did. *For a reaction* that's what Dinny used to say, *Lily likes a reaction. Doesn't matter what it is…*

And when Molly asked her about it that evening, and even months later, all Lily did was laugh at her. She looked her in the eye and laughed and laughed, as though she was being tickled.

26

DAINTY WRISTS, TINY WAIST, the neat little chin of a cat – the girl just blinks back at her. Language barrier or no language barrier, Aoife knows insolence when she sees it.

'HERE,' she says, patting the hall console. 'The book is HERE. You have to WRITE' – she mimes writing in the air. She does it very close to the girl's face, but what of it? Aoife is the client, isn't she? This Mitzi or Kitty or whatever she calls herself – she'd do well to remember what her work visa is for.

'You have to WRITE the NAME of whoever visits my mother…'

The girl nods, blinking slowly. 'Yes.'

Many Christmases ago, Aoife bought a doll for Valerie. It had dark eyes like that, hardly any of the white showing.

'Write the TIME—' She taps her watch, then with two hands, she demonstrates something coming towards her, '—they COME, and the time they—' she shoos the imaginary person away, '—GO.'

'Yes.'

'Remind me what your name is?'

'Katie.' She's wearing a very cheap chiffon blouse, big doily collar on it. The buttons run down between her small breasts. *Petite* – that is how that sort of figure is described.

'Well, Katie. You write the time they come and the time they—' Aoife chops at her forearm with her other hand and lets it finger-march in the direction of the door '—LEAVE.'

'Yes, I understand.'

'Do you?'

'Mum…' Aoife turns to see her daughter standing in the door, big hands hanging by her sides, her face tilted, earnest as a child's.

'Mum. You're shouting…'

'Valerie, what are you doing in the hallway? Why aren't you with Grandma? I told you to stay with—'

'She's asking for Katie.'

Aoife's throat clogs. She can feel the redness of her cheeks. Her eyes water slightly.

'Okay.'

She heads back into the kitchen, the petite Katie hurrying behind.

Putting her handbag on the kitchen table, Aoife calls, 'I brought you some chocolates, Mammy.'

The carer rushes to Mammy. 'Did you want me, Molly?'

'Is that my Fifi giving out again?'

'Not giving out, Mammy. I brought chocolates… I'm just telling you I brought you chocolates, and you say I'm giving out…'

Mammy doesn't look up. She's speaking to Katie, who is

kneeling by the chair, smiling–Ha! Bright gums and a clutter of discoloured teeth. Not so pretty after all!

Valerie squeezes Aoife's elbow. 'What's wrong?'

'Stick the kettle on, Valerie.' She returns to her handbag, rooting out the chocolates. 'I'll tell you what's wrong. The Ladies Muck haven't been writing their names in the book when they visit. So, I told the carers to write it in. It should be no great challenge for them to log visits in the book, should it? I bought a log book. I showed it to them. I said "you write in the names. If they don't sign in, you write it in the book." What could be simpler? Yet here we are: no names are logged for today, but there's no doubt that someone has been here.'

'How do you know, Mum?'

'Mammy's ring is missing, and there's all this mess. Look. All you have to do is have a look around. Crayon under the armchair. Apple butt in the fireplace.'

'Oh. Well, you've explained now anyway. I'm sure they'll write it in from now on. Do you want coffee is it?'

The carer is standing at the threshold to the den, apparently delighted with herself.

'Your mother has been in good form this morning. Haven't you, Molly? You had a good appetite at lunch, didn't you? And you are wearing your nice cardigan, aren't you? That looks very cosy.'

Aoife smiles tightly. 'She prefers to be called Mrs Kearney. Please do not patronise my mother.'

'Okay.' Lips closing over those frightful teeth, the girl walks past her to the kitchen door. 'No problem. Well, I will leave you alone. I will be in my room if you need anything. See you later Molly.'

And off she shuffles, to snuggle down in Aoife's childhood bedroom. She is wearing the most unprofessional shoes Aoife has ever seen – plastic clogs with rubbery flowers stuck to them.

'Valerie, are you making the coffee or what?'

'Hang on…' Valerie is writing something into her phone, frowning. That's all she's been doing since she came back – tapping at her phone, grunting. The minute she arrived she got into bed with a hot water bottle, claiming period pain. Aoife dragged her out to brunch today – a nice little cafe in the village and she found herself worried that she might bump in to someone, that's how bedraggled her daughter looked. She tried to talk to her a bit about what she wants out of life. 'Don't you think about children?' she said. 'Wouldn't it be sad if Grandma never got to see your children?'

Valerie is still staring at the phone as she fills the kettle and flicks it on. Aoife can no longer deny it: her daughter is pasty and scrawny. Is she a failure already? She was so full of promise once, going off to acting school, then moving to their sweet little Baker Street flat. Aoife envisaged a lovely little life for her; not hugely glamourous, but respectable, at least. But since graduating seven years ago, Valerie's had no more success than a television ad for bathroom cleaner and a radio ad for a gym. Sometimes she tells them she is starring in plays, but they're not real plays. The last one was in the upstairs of a bar. 'Profit shares', is what she calls them. A few years ago, they gave her one of the Dublin apartments to look after. It had been in her name for years anyway. Aoife hoped it would encourage her to come home, but she's just stayed in London, not working, not acting, not dating, living off the rent money. Aoife wouldn't mind all that if she looked after herself, if she had parties to go to, friends to see; if she made herself attractive. Brendan thinks they spoiled her. He even suggested they make her pay rent on the London flat.

Valerie sighs, and slides her phone into her back pocket before pouring out the hot water.

'Are there any biscuits? Do you want a biscuit, Grandma?'

'Aoife, what is this now? What are we making?'

'Oh!'

In the adjoining room, Mammy is sitting in her big chair, running her fingers over the book of swatches – eight different shades and qualities of satin to choose from. 'Are you making a gown to dress me in?'

'No, Mammy we don't need that anymore… We'll have some coffee, Mammy. And I brought you some chocolates… Go and take that from Grandma, Valerie.'

'What is it?'

'Nothing we need. We thought Mammy might like to choose what lining to use… it's from the undertakers.'

Valerie's face drops. 'Mum, are you serious?'

'Not for *her* Valerie – what kind of a ninny are you? I'll explain later.'

Valerie frowns as she puts the samples on the table, but she keeps quiet. She fans some chocolate bourbons out on a saucer.

They make the shape of a flower. Her every gesture is lethargic, reluctant. She doesn't look well. She's not even thirty, but already, if she's not careful how she holds her face, her mouth turns down into a sloppy grimace.

'You having a biscuit, Mum?'

'No. None for me. Valerie, do you remember that doll you got from Santa? You called her Snowflake. She had a blue dress with snowflakes on it.'

'Doll? I don't remember ever being into dolls.'

'Don't you? Oh well. How quickly they forget... I'll do the coffee, Valerie, you'll only make a song and a dance of it. Put that samples thing out in the recycling will you?'

'Where's the recycling?'

'Oh forget it. Give it here, I'll put it in my handbag for now.'

Snowflake was beautiful, with a weighty, bean-stuffed body. She closed her eyes when she was on her back, and when she was moved upright the eyelids slid open with a gentle click. Valerie slept with her for years.

Valerie carries in the tray as though it's a great effort, and sets it down on Mammy's footstool. 'Will I milk your coffee for you Grandma?'

Mammy starts. 'Who's this now? Who is this now with the white face?'

'Valerie is back from London to see you, Mammy.'

'Where is Freya? Freya? Where is she?'

'Valerie is here to see you, isn't this a treat? Usually we only see her at Christmas but we've had two visits so far thanks to your clumsiness!' Aoife forces a tight laugh from her chest, adding, 'Thanks to you falling over my handbag like a ninny and worrying everybody...'

Valerie looks up sharply from her phone. 'Mum!'

'Let's get a photo, Valerie. Kneel down there beside Grandma and let's get a lovely photo of the two of you... Smile, Mammy!' A slow, silent flash. The photo is terrible.

'One more... Oh, I really wish you'd wear the right makeup for your skin-tone, Valerie, you look like a ghoul. No. Not enough light in here...'

'Freya? Where is the little fellow? Have you lost him?'

'No, Mammy. No. We have that all sorted out now, remember? You chose the light blue satin. We have a nice white box. We'll put him in beside Daddy very soon. Don't you worry. Valerie, why don't you tell Mammy about London?'

'I'm back from London for a bit, Grandma.'

'Oh yes. London is very busy these days, isn't it?'

'Drink your coffee, Valerie. We need to shake a leg. You start packing up the hens. I need to sort something out here with Grandma, then I'll come and help.'

'What? Mum! I have a really bad period, I told you.'

'Still?'

'Still. And I didn't bring any wellies.'

'Don't be such a whinger, Valerie. Just unpack the boxes at least, and close the henhouse. I'll be out to help you catch them in a bit.'

~

As soon as Valerie leaves, Aoife starts to unpack the clever little camera. She bought the set online – she hates the rigmarole of buying online, but how could she have explained it all to someone in a shop? All about her nieces and her half-mad sister and everything? Aoife is no specialist when it comes to these things, but it turned out to be quite simple to use. It is a discreet contraption, a 'nanny cam'. Certainly no one will ever notice it. Aoife has spent a long time studying the instructions. She printed them off so that she could read them properly, but really, they are very simple.

Mammy is snoring now. Big, comfortable snores. Aoife touches her hand,

'Mammy. My mammy.'

She plugs the camera in behind the TV and sets it on top of the DVD player. She sits on the couch and looks at it – it's so tiny there's no way a person would see it, except for the little flashing red light to show that it's on. Aoife has considered this ahead of time, and she has brought a lump of Blu-tack with her to stick over it; no one will ever notice. And such an ideal spot for it – the DVD player, facing the whole room. She is pleased to have thought of that. She can be wily too when she wants to be… And apparently all the footage will be recorded and sent to Aoife's computer, so Aoife can just fast-forward to when the young Ladies Muck are there.

There they will be, giving Mammy whatever sob story they give her to get themselves on her will and extract cash out of her, rifling through her handbag and trying on her jewellery, and all the while Aoife will be sitting at home in the study, watching them.

'Fifi,' says Mammy – it almost makes Aoife jump. 'Fifi, my poor Cara. What will she do with all those children and only her scribbles to rely on?... that beautiful little boy – so clever. You'll make sure Freya has enough will you? Will you sort out a cheque for her?'

Aoife's eyes water. 'What kind of an eejit are you, Mammy? Why should you pay for her mistakes? She has plenty of money anyway. She is using you, Mammy – how do you not see that? You think she visits because she likes it here? Ha! I cannot allow you to be used like this, Mammy, I cannot—'

Aoife can hear her pitch rising, but her mother is no longer listening.

'Yes,' says Mammy, 'yes, of course you are right, darling. My Fifi. Where did we get you from? But do that for me, darling. Make sure she is looked after.' Then she pretends to fall asleep, and then she is really asleep, the snore pushing wet through her lips.

If nothing else, this little speech of Mammy's has proven, as if there was ever a doubt, why Aoife is right to install the nanny cam. She kisses her mother's forehead.

Well, that took no time at all. A ruckus of clucking from the back of the garden. What has Valerie done now?

'Katie!' she calls up the stairs, 'Katie can you come down here please? We'll need you to pack up the hens for my mother...'

27

BLACK THREADS CHART THE veins like poison ink. Sinéad slivers off the top and bores out the core and uses the knife-tip to wheedle every streak of rot from the seeds and flesh. She puts the healthy green bits into a big stock pot and pours cider vinegar over them to kill any traces of mould. Fungus has invisible filaments that reach deep into tissue, breathing sickness into everything – fruit, meat, even flesh.

In July, she sprayed the tomatoes all over with a fungicide of startling turquoise and fed them with fertiliser. It was a stupid thing to do. The plants kept on going right through September, but she had created a little tragedy for herself out there. For weeks she watched the tired stalks push out more blossoms and fruit. She picked the tomatoes daily, and every single one was tainted with a soft, grey bottom before it grew ripe.

It was a relief to succumb to the autumn, ripping up the stalks by the cool light of dawn, laying the last of the fruit in a wooden crate and tossing the wiry plants into a big heap at the end of the garden – she will burn them, rather than risk infecting the compost heap.

Next year, she will steep the March nettles in hot water for a week, and then pour it into the prepared soil before planting her tomatoes. She found a blog that said rot could be prevented that way.

Rescuing the last of the tomatoes from decay has become an obsession. Sinéad hasn't stopped working for hours; not for breakfast or a cup of coffee. She is intent on her task but she works clumsily, slicing into her thumb and fingers with the sharp steel knife – an old, wooden-handled knife with a silver hilt and a crooked, wire-thin blade that rusts if it isn't dried well after washing. There's a bitter satisfaction in the way the vinegar and the tomato juice send a searing pain into her arm when they enter the fissures in her skin.

She'll try the nettle thing next year. Nettles are good for the kidneys – who told her that? When Sinéad was a child, her mother went out with her rubber gloves and gathered the first nettles of spring. She made meals with them – stuffed pillows of pasta, mud-coloured soup with nutmeg and black pepper and a swirl of milk. A long time ago now. They had less then; Mammy had to be careful what she bought. The nettles tasted like spinach, only spicier.

Only a few tomatoes to go. Tomorrow she'll start on the chutney. Chutney is the only thing that can be made from underripe tomatoes. And jam. Green tomato jam.

She'll have to finish up soon though; make herself presentable and prepare something for lunch. Her niece Valerie is arriving today with the hens.

Sinéad gave up on her own chickens three years ago, after the pine marten got the fat little black one, but she still has everything they need – a shed with nesting boxes and a run. She loved the little black one, and it really broke her heart to see it lying there with its speckled throat pulled open. This time she has nailed shut every tiny hole in the shed. She and Terence patched up the run themselves. It took two weeks to dig an extra barrier of chicken wire down deep into the soil, and her hips are still screeching from it. She will lock these hens up safely every night; she'll be vigilant. She'll keep them alive until Mammy is well again…

She has stale bread in the cupboard, does she? And chicken breasts in the fridge.

She'll dress now in a minute, and maybe prepare a quick lunch for Valerie; something tasty and simple and maybe she'll sit with her a bit and her niece can tell her things about being young in London. Sinéad does a great breaded chicken. It's a long time since she's made that. The secret is in the double dip – egg white, flour, egg white, breadcrumbs – and she puts a spoon of mustard and one of paprika into the egg, and a dollop of milk… that makes all the difference. That's what she'll make. Lovely.

Her mobile sounds. It's Aoife. Sinéad puts it face down on the kitchen table. Watching it ring out, it's a kind of heartbreak she feels. It is a kind of frustrated and hopeless and unworthy heartbreak; 'Aoife,' she says aloud. The word strains in her chest. She shakes her head, 'Aoife,' and sighs dramatically – a performance for no one. She has given up worrying about this new habit of talking to herself – she likes it; it feels like health to be able to make sounds and words that fit. 'Aoife!' – her throat is tender with the pain of it – her queasy regret for how her sister is now. For years at a time Sinéad could forget how she had laughed sometimes with her sister, how Aoife could be witty and light once. In those stretches of amnesia it was fine to listen to her sister's rants and think, 'Oh Aoife.' But – was it the shock of the operation, or Mammy's fall? But something has lifted her out of that kind of time, and the chubby nineteen-year-old Aoife, funny sometimes, warm even, rebellious and mischievous, is now palpably present, juxtaposed with the chronic bitterness and stiff rage of the woman at the end of the phone.

The ringing stops, and a text message comes in:

Mammy tired but fine. Ate a little.
Polish girl is stealing going to have to fire her
new girl available in a fortnight. Asian.

She stands on the stone steps, waving a tea towel at a shiny red Mercedes bus crunching up the gravel drive. She is surprised by a surge of affection when Valerie grins down at her from the driver's seat, as though after a great achievement. Oh, but all that makeup, all that hair dye; poor Valerie. She has one of those faces that has never been girlish – shapeless eyebrows like her father, a rubbery nose, and, no matter how thin her body gets, she has Aoife's heavy cheeks. When she was a toddler, Daddy painted a portrait of her called *The Little Washerwoman*, and he took to calling her that then, because of the dour, old face on her and the thick arms. The girl has little character to her face, no quirks; nothing that can tell a story. Perhaps that's why she spent those years dressing in black and painting her face like a corpse – to make herself special, give herself character. It was terrifying – the white, white skin, black lipstick, corsets and all that garb. She called herself a goth. She would drive to Dublin in that little car Aoife bought her, to hang around Temple Bar, smoking. Poor Aoife. It was mortifying for her.

There is a residual morbidity about Valerie. She still wears a lot of black. She still dyes her hair black and wears very pale foundation but she is too sloppy-featured to look like a dying Victorian.

Valerie kicks the door open and puts a careful foot on the step leading down from the driver's seat – Sinéad puts out a hand to help her and is struck by how feeble they both are: she middle-aged and bloated; Valerie limp-fingered, tiny on the waist and a nauseating whiff of sugary perfume off her.

'Were you okay driving that thing?'

'Not really.' Her niece leans close and places a kiss on Sinéad's cheek, touching her shoulder with a tenderness that makes a warm blush rise in her cheeks. That must be something she has picked up in London – Sinéad has never been on kissing terms with her nieces.

'It's Aunty Eileen's…'

'Why does she have a bus?'

Valerie shrugs and slides open the passenger door. The low,

panicked cackle and err of frightened hens and a warm, dirty smell; the tang of their feathers, the powdery faeces under their claws. They have been inexpertly packed in cardboard boxes, which have been duct taped closed and pierced on top with a knife.

'Six of them aren't there?'

'Yep. I have a big bag of grain and grit for you, too. Is Terence here?'

'No. He's visiting someone in England… the two of us will manage, Valerie!'

After their ordeal, the hens don't enter the henhouse, but hunker down on the sparse grass. 'They'll be grand,' says Sinéad. She throws a handful of grain through the wire and one of the hens stretches her scrawny neck in interest, then retracts it into her breast, puffing against the cold.

Sitting at the table in the dank back kitchen, Valerie looks painfully delicate – a large head wobbling on a little neck.

'Can I help, Sinéad?'

'No, no, stay where you are.'

As she moves back and forth, laying out plates and cutlery and condiments, Sinéad keeps sneaking glances at the girl, hoping to soothe the guilt of her earlier observation by finding something beautiful in her face. 'So why did Eileen buy a bus, do you think?'

'I don't know,' says Valerie, 'she drove to our house in it and she said we could use it to move the hens. I don't know why, I didn't ask...'

'You could have fit them in a car.'

'I suppose.'

'Well, a law unto herself is Eileen. Who knows why she does anything?'

Eileen came back into their lives dressed like a fifties teenager, full of intimate smiles as though the years of exile had never happened. Sinéad never hated her little sister the way Aoife did. She was only saddened by her parents' grief over the things she did, their shame. But it makes her almost squeamish, the sudden cosiness between Aoife and Eileen; and this exhumation thing fills her with a delicious kind of terror, not least because she can't resist her own pleasure in it. She is glad they tracked him down, glad they pulled him up and took charge; she can't help it. It feels like an exorcism. It's when she wakes in the night with her abdomen aching that she feels it most keenly – the exquisite satisfaction, the guilt, the genius of it; that her sisters could launch this irreproachable revenge on that little ghost. It never would have occurred to her that such a thing could be done.

Valerie picks at her nails. 'So did Mammy tell you she's fired the carer?'

'Has she? Well I would have thought she'd talk to me first...'

Then again, what has it to do with Sinéad? She offered to split the cost of the carer with Aoife, but she wouldn't hear of it. *Don't be a ninny, Sinéad,* she said, *Mammy will pay for it. She's already signed the cheque.* That made sense, of course, but something about it makes Sinéad uneasy.

'Apparently, she's been drinking Grandma's expensive coffees – you know, the filter ones she gets in the Superquinn delivery? She gets the delivery on Monday – Mum arranged it – and apparently by Thursday there was only one coffee left...'

'You'll like this chicken, Valerie. It's years since I've made it so I hope I have it right...'

'Oh. I'll have a half a one, Sinéad. I'm not feeling the best...'

'Okay. Well, taste it anyway.'

'Thank you. That's loads. Thank you. It looks lovely.'

'So how are you getting on in London, Valerie? How long are you home for?'

'Oh... well, I – I don't know. I don't know what I'm at really.' The skin on her niece's face is a green-white film of foundation, and very uniform in tone – but a terrible redness rises suddenly from her neck, making the makeup glow like a flimsy lampshade. 'I had an abortion last week, and I just... I just wanted a rest then, after.'

'Oh.' Sinéad looks at the ketchup bottle – the brown-red scab around the cap. Her niece's presence has exposed the filth in every nook of her kitchen, the grimy smells in it. She looks at the kitchen floor – in the dip of a cracked tile, a little triangle of dust and fluff and muck. She stopped trying to clean this house years ago.

She cannot look at the girl. Is it so normal now, that thing? Is it such a normal thing that people mention it over lunch?

Valerie makes it sound like something that just happened to her; there's self-pity in her voice but not a hint of culpability.

'What does your mammy think of that?'

'Oh, she doesn't know. Don't tell her will you please? She's a bit stressed at the moment, I don't think she'd really approve…'

'Is it because you're not married?'

One side of Valerie's mouth lifts in a grin and she gives a breathy little laugh. 'Not exactly, Aunty Sinéad… sort of, not exactly…'

Things have changed a lot. When her sister Eileen got pregnant – well, that was decades ago. The eighties, was it? The nineties? They are women now. Cara must be almost thirty, and the little one into her twenties… Eileen's pregnancies were terrible scandals but there was no talk of abortion. *Lily has been duped* is what Mammy said, but had she been? *Don't make a spectacle of yourself,* that's what Mammy said to them when, as children, they misbehaved: *You're making a spectacle of yourself,* or *You're making a show of me.* But Eileen always loved to make a show. When the musician fellow died, Eileen seemed almost to enjoy her grief and the great humiliation of the whole thing. *His ugly old bitch of a wife drove me from the funeral… those nasty little shits won't even acknowledge their half-sisters…* and so on. She must have known he was married. She must have. Oh, Daddy took that all very hard.

'I see, well… Are you okay?' says Sinéad. What does her niece want from her? Kissing her cheek, touching her shoulder like that, telling her this terrible, terrible thing.

'Oh yes, it was fine actually. It was really simple – I just took the tablets and then it was just like a bad period. They have to monitor you for a bit, you know, in case it doesn't work – if it doesn't work they have to go in and take it out. I was really afraid of that. But it worked. It was fine actually. I just feel a bit tired now. I feel like I need to take stock… I shouldn't have let it happen, of course. Stupid. Imagine being so stupid…'

'Well. That's good. Good that they didn't have to go in. What age are you now, Valerie?'

'Twenty-nine,' she says, running a fingertip over the tarnished tines of an old silver fork. 'Twenty-nine.'

Valerie isn't touching her food. The food that Sinéad planned and so carefully prepared. Instead, she's picking at a patch of thick polish on her thumbnail. She rips off a big flake and it takes a sheath of nail with it. Something sore and unkind is gathering in Sinéad's belly – it's her niece's presumptuousness, sitting there at her table, telling her this – the unfaltering voice, the – what is it, what is it that's making a terrible rage fill Sinéad's belly, her chest, her skull? – entitlement. Entitlement is what it is; as though all these choices are hers to make. 'So stupid,' repeats Valerie, inviting Sinéad to contradict her. What right has Valerie to tell her this? She is implicated now, in this terrible thing, because she cannot stop her compassion for the girl anymore than she can stop her rage. What is the girl doing? Living over there in London, having careless intercourse and disposing of the consequences? Choosing to tell her this terrible thing, and not eating the food that Sinéad took such care to make for her?

'... I was there crying away in the surgery, you know, looking at this tablet – you take one the day before, so like, there's no going back actually, and then you go in and take another two – one orally and the other up there, you know?'

'No,' says Sinéad, 'I don't know about those things. I didn't know that. This is – this is all stuff we knew nothing about, growing up.' No doubt Valerie will have children in the future, as soon as she wants to, no thought for the miracle of it at all.

'Well that's what it is, anyway, and she was really lovely, the lady. It's an Irish thing, I suppose, there's a bit of a stigma still, isn't there? The lady said it's normal. She said, like, it's not only Catholic and Muslim girls who find it hard, your body finds it hard too; your body has one idea, and you have another. "There's no great choice in this situation," she said, "only a better and a worse choice." And that made sense to me. I felt better then. That makes sense, doesn't it? Sometimes there are no nice choices, only less bad ones.'

Sinéad realises she's been holding her breath, afraid to break whatever spell is making Valerie talk like this. She exhales slowly, and touches her brow, dizzy with revulsion. What a world. What a world this is.

It was something she thought about a lot, after that last pregnancy. She could lie awake relishing the memory of those images she had seen on Grafton Street – for years there were a pair of unwashed old ladies to be seen shuffling up and down, holding pictures of aborted foetuses – and she wished she had seen her miscarriage when it came out; she wished they had shown it to her so she could have known what it looked like, how big it was, whether it had the right number of heads or finger nubs or whatever; why it had just stopped like that.

The hysterectomy was over twenty years after that last miscarriage, but it started her wondering again. The evening she got home without her womb, she went on the internet to find out what had happened back then, but there were no answers. She looked up 'nine-week-old foetus' on Google Images. The pictures she got were nothing like those posters – a nine-week-old foetus was a hard-looking little prawn of a thing, all gristly spine with seeds for eyes. She looked at picture after picture of the little globs. One of them was lying on a woman's palm – it was no bigger than her thumbnail but there was a tiny knitted hat on its head and a tiny knitted blanket around it. Sinéad couldn't believe that there were knitting needles so small. All that was visible of the foetus was a pinkish jelly bump with those blind black eyes in it.

Valerie finally eats her half chicken breast, and then accepts the second half, dipping each forkful in a little heap of ketchup. Then Sinéad makes a pot of tea and Valerie talks and talks. She tells her every detail – the pregnancy test and the first appointment at the abortion clinic, and the way the blood looked when it came out. Although Sinéad can do nothing but sit in bamboozled silence and pour tea, Valerie thanks her for listening.

'Why didn't you have children, Sinéad?'

'It never happened,' says Sinéad. 'Barren, I suppose. They can do things for you these days – things if you don't want it, and things if you do. Interventions. Back then it was the luck of the draw.'

'So, you would have liked children?'

'I thought I'd have them. I used to talk about it, before I got married. Three girls and a boy.'

After that last miscarriage she had bad days, when all she could do was drive to her mother's house and stand, weeping on the doorstep. *What if they got it wrong Mammy? What if the machine was broken?* The first few times, her mother held her, rubbed her back, wiped her cheeks, but then she grew impatient: *Pull yourself together,* she said, and; *You're not the first disappointed woman in the world! You think miscarriage is the worst thing that happens to women? Grow up child! Grow up my girl.* She behaved foolishly for those months; her mother was right.

Nowadays people start babies in their forties, but back then thirty-six was old enough to be called barren. After they had taken the last miscarriage out of her, the word clung; whispering in her skin and glaring out from the great sanitary napkins they sent her home with – huge long, fat things, sterile white. It was the word on her dry palms and tremble-tender belly: barren. She was barren now.

She had lost pregnancies before but that last time was different – no spotting, no cramps; and three periods missed. The morning of the appointment she had vomited four times. Everyone said that was a good sign; she had been so sure of herself that she had even told Aoife about it. Once, resting on her back in bed, she had felt it ripple under her skin – could that be true? Or was it a lie that had come into its own?

Truth or trick, she remembers how it felt – soft petals, tiny fleshlet skimming quick as light beneath her surface.

It was the first time she'd made it to the twelve-week mark, but at the hospital they said it had probably been dead for weeks. They said it was her head keeping it in. Now that she knew it was over, it would start to come out.

But a week later her belly was so swollen she couldn't wear trousers, and even on the way to the appointment Terence had to pull over three times so that she could vomit onto the road. She felt sure they had made a mistake. Mistakes happened. When they went in with their metal tools and scooped it out of her, one of the nurses would spot a tiny fairy-child, wriggling there in the bright bucket, and they would know they had made a mistake but it would be too late. That's not the kind of thing they'd ever tell you, of course; they would never say sorry.

They've made a mistake, she said. *Terence, they're wrong; they've made a mistake.*

That must have been hard on Terence. It must have frightened him to see her eyes wild like that, the frothy yellow bile coming up out her lips. He said it was just because she was fasting – she always felt sick when she fasted – and the hormones could be making her paranoid.

He was right, of course he was right. After listening with the trumpet and shaking her head, the nurse made her an appointment to see a man with an ultrasound machine. Then Sinéad had seen it herself there on the screen, a little black shadow, no bigger than the last one. The man pushed and pushed with the scanner on her belly, but the shadow was stubbornly still, stubbornly dark; ingrained like a stain into the fabric of her. The man switched on the sound, searching for a heartbeat. It sounded like being under water; the whoosh of her own body, nothing more.

Who did she think she was fooling? Inside her it sounded like an empty sea. There was nothing in her that could emerge to a new thing. *Me*, she thought. *I am full only of me.*

The man switched off the sound. Terence touched her hand but she flinched to a fist.

She'd had a dilation and curettage before – a 'D and C' is what it was called – and lots of women had them. It would give her the best chance, said the doctor, of conceiving again.

She had to bend into the foetal position, and an elderly nurse with a Donegal accent stroked her arm. 'Think of something nice, darlin.' All the nice she could think of, though, was the little baby booties she had allowed herself to crochet, the tiny tumble of creation; a whole flower-fish world unfurling inside her.

When her niece has left, Sinéad stands in the drizzle, fingers hooked in the wire fencing, watching the hens waggle their bottoms into the soil. She listens to the creaky sounds they make. They still haven't entered the henhouse.

She tries to call Terence, but he's not picking up. She realises very suddenly, with a mixture of relief and terror, that she is alone in the world. In her waterproofs and wellingtons, she makes her way down the sludgy field to the boathouse, where she places her mobile phone on the table and pours herself a whiskey.

There is a low wind starting, and the lake meets the windows in dark, mulchy sloshes. A small croak escapes from her throat, then a long, high whimper bouncing off the walls of the little boathouse, the low ceiling. She is alone out here. There's nothing alive in the water. Everything has gone south.

Even the eels are gone.

Terence says eels are mysterious. No one knows how they mate. They are all born somewhere in the sea, beneath impassable waters. They go there to mate and they go there to die in cool, deep privacy.

The dark lake tongues at the glass. Rain pecks at the roof.

Mammy is going. It has already started; she is ebbing out.

28

SOMETIMES DENISE OPENS THE violin case just to smell the caramel wood and the lump of rosin like a warm forest. That is what she's doing when her mammy says it's time to go. She loves when it's time to go to music because they sit in the car – just Den and Mammy – and they can listen to whatever tapes they want or no tapes at all.

But when Denise comes downstairs with her violin on her back, Mammy says, 'You need your musicianship folder too Denise; it's Saturday.' On Saturday, Denise has musicianship class before real violin class. Denise hates musicianship class because of the singing-all-together and the sore benches that hurt her bum. She likes real violin class which is just her and her teacher and their violins.

Denise plays best when her violin teacher, Mo, is listening. It's a kind of magic, being in that room with Mo. Mo casts a spell, like she's giving Denise all of her brain energy for playing. Practising at home is not the same. Her little sister Megan is three, and she doesn't like the violin. If she hears the sound of it, she puts her hands over her ears and screams. Daddy says that's just because the sound confuses her on account of her ears are glued and she needs grommets.

Just when she is about to say no to musicianship class, her mammy's phone rings and when she picks up she clutches the phone to one ear and puts a finger on her other ear and frowns, and says, 'Okay, okay Grandma, I'm coming. Yes. I'm coming now.'

Mammy runs upstairs herself for the musicianship folder, telling Denise to hurry into the car. Then she kisses Daddy and talks quickly and quietly to him, and she pulls Denise's jacket on her so quickly that the sleeves of her jumper stuff up at her elbows, and she rushes her into the car and starts driving without checking that Denise is strapped in and with no tapes playing and she says, 'We're in a hurry now, Den; we need to go to Mimi first.' Maybe she will be late for musicianship. That would be good.

In the back of the car there is the amazing-and-beautiful necklace that Denise made in school. It took her loads of days to make it, because she could only paint one side of the pasta at a time. When they were all dry, she put them on a ribbon. Some people in her class didn't do it right, even though Ms Dowling said about patterns and they all practised patterns on paper. Denise's one is amazing-and-beautiful and Ms Dowling said it was perfect and pretty. It is a three-pattern: blue pink yellow; blue pink yellow. Denise checks every piece again, to make sure that it really is amazing and beautiful and perfect and pretty, before stuffing it into the pocket of her tracksuit bottoms.

When they get to Mimi's house, there is a blue van in the drive, and they have to park outside the garden wall, with the car half on the pavement and half on the road. Mammy says, 'Wait in the car, I won't be long,' and Denise doesn't whinge to go in. Mammy shuts the door very hard and hurries towards the house. Denise watches her disappear around the gate, but very soon Mammy comes back and opens the back door and says, 'Actually you better come on in, Den – your Mimi would love to see you. Sorry, chicken, I'm not with it. Sorry, my darling. Everything is okay.'

Mammy knocks at the window and Mimi's minder comes to the door with her white-plate face and yellow hair and stands back to let Mammy and Denise into the hall. Denise holds Mammy's leg. There is a new smell in Mimi's house. It is a smell like opening a new toy – sweet and clean and a bit poisonous – and Denise knows there are strangers in the good room because she can hear them talking and banging things.

'They're replacing the carpet,' says the lady, and her face is serious.

'Did Grandma organise it?' asks Mammy.

'No, no of course not, Cara. She's very confused and frightened by all the traffic in the house. I've shut the doors and tried to keep it from her... It was Aoife. Aoife has organised a new carpet and new furniture... she had Mrs Kearney write the cheque.'

Denise doesn't want to let go of Mammy's leg, but she does want to see, so she creeps very quietly to the good-room door and looks in. There is a big ghost sheet over the dining-room table and the other big things and they are together at the end of the room, and all the walls are naked and the big friendly clock is gone from the corner, and there are men pulling up the carpet and under is just slices of dusty wood.

'Oh, it's a big job,' says her mammy behind her.

Denise pushes herself back into her mammy's legs, and she feels her mammy's hand on her chest and she clings onto her fingers. The nice lady is talking quietly. Denise loves the strange shapes of her words.

'... Cara, I am sorry but I need to talk to you; this is not the only thing. Aoife is coming with papers for her to sign – every few days there is something. I don't know what they are, but your grandmother doesn't know either and it's – it's not ethical. She becomes very anxious and distressed. She writes cheques for Eileen. All night she was talking about a trust fund? She has dementia, but your aunts refuse to get a diagnosis... I'm sorry, but I can't witness it all and not say anything. You have to do something to protect your grandmother. If it was my grandmother, I wouldn't stand by...'

Mimi looks very big in her chair. There is a fire going and the air is squiggly with the heat coming out of it. She looks a bit like a king, on account of how her hands are holding the arms of her chair, and no smile on her face, and the way she lifts her head very slowly. Her mouth is all tight and small, and her eyebrows curled and white; she looks different. Denise puts her hand into her pocket and feels for the amazing-and-beautiful necklace.

Mammy kisses Mimi, and kneels down beside the chair, petting Mimi's hand. 'Hello, Grandma,' she says.

'Have they guns?'

Mammy turns back and looks at Denise. In her pocket, Denise is passing each piece of pasta through her fingers, counting one-two-three, one-two-three, one-two-three, on account of that's the pattern she has made. Three/four time is harder than four/four, but once she played a waltz that went one-two-three, one-two-three, and she was very good at it and Mo said, 'Well done!' and, 'Great girl, Denise! You are a talented little girl!'

Mammy pushes Denise's hair back off her face and swallows, and when she speaks again there is a cheep-cheep sound behind her voice. 'Who, Grandma? No guns.'

'Kat's not here and Dada neither, but I've cleaned the gun very well with Vaseline; it's in the chimney.'

'No, no, Grandma. Just freshening up the good room. We're just… there's a new carpet going down, that's all. Nothing to worry about…'

'Are you sure, darling?'

'I'm sure, Grandma. Now what did you want me for?'

'Pass me my handbag, darling.'

Denise drops herself onto Mammy's back, her arms hanging over Mammy's shoulders, and cosies her head into the back of her neck.

'Get off me, Denise, good girl. You're too heavy.'

Mammy puts the handbag on Mimi's lap. Mimi slowly opens it and looks inside. She takes out her big purse that is all soft like the bellies of puppies.

'Look at this,' she says, and she pulls it open. 'Not a penny, Cara. I am so sorry my darling, I don't want you to be short, but could you give me something for my purse?'

'Of course, Grandma. Let's see what I have.'

Mammy takes some brown notes out from the back pocket of her jeans. She helps Mimi to straighten them out and slide them into the purse. 'Now,' says Mammy, 'is that better, Grandma?'

'Yes, thank you, darling. Did you ever? Wouldn't you be ashamed, asking for money like that?'

'No, Grandma, no shame. Now you mind your handbag, okay?'

'Yes, I'll do that, darling. Thank you, darling. I will pay you back, you know. I just need to speak to Eileen and tell her to get me some money. She has the card…'

'Don't worry, Grandma. It's no problem.'

'There's a letter in my handbag, darling. Take it out, will you?'

'This one?' says Mammy.

'Yes. Sort that out, will you, darling? Read it at home and sort it out. I am old, I think. The problem is I am old.'

'Okay. Grandma, I'm sorry, I have to drop Denise to music class. I'll come back, okay? I'll be back in an hour and a half, maybe two hours. No more than two hours…'

Denise takes the amazing-and-beautiful-and-perfect necklace from her pocket. She makes a bowl for it with her two hands and holds it up for Mimi to see. She opens her mouth to say 'Here, Mimi,' but then she can't speak on account of Mimi's face.

'Denise has made you a beautiful necklace, Grandma!' says Mammy. But Mimi still doesn't smile. Denise pushes the necklace a bit closer. Mimi looks down with her eyes and not her face. Denise can see into the holes in her nose: hair, and white snots.

'I see,' she says.

'What do you think, Grandma? What do you think of the beautiful necklace that Denise made for you?'

Then Mimi looks like she has had a big, big fright – like as if there was a big noise or something – and her head comes up and she stares at Denise's Mammy like she is frightened and in trouble, and she says, 'What do I think?'

'Yes, Grandma, what do you think of the lovely necklace that Denise made for you in school?'

'Well…' says Mimi, 'it's not mine. Is it that someone is trying to profit from me? Aoife says someone is trying to profit from me…'

'No, Grandma, no, no. Denise has made a beautiful necklace for you. What do you think?'

There is a big quiet and Mimi looks at the necklace for a long time, and then she looks all around her, and then at Mammy, but not at Denise. Mammy rubs her hand up and down Denise's back, and squeezes her shoulder, and there is a big balloon blowing bigger in Denise's chest and making her throat sore. Then, after a long time, Mimi turns to Mammy and says, 'I think you should find a bin somewhere and throw it in.' She flaps her hand for Denise to take the amazing-and-beautiful necklace away.

29

CRUMBS OF ANCIENT LEAVES thick on the polished concrete. A bright smell of mould coats her nostrils and tickles the back of her mouth. Valerie is too awkward for this space – her loose hair, her loud, dirty breath. The squeak of her shoes cuts into the mossy, hermit coldness.

As a child, she saw Grandad's studio only on rare and illicit occasions, and only with Freya there for courage. They snuck in during Grandad's tea break, or while he was entertaining guests. Even then, they stayed only briefly, never touching the canvases or paints, careful to leave no trace of themselves.

The first room, where Grandad used to work, comprises two walls of unpainted breezeblock, two walls of glass and a sloping roof with big skylights in it. To her memory it was always filled with very pale, surgical light. Now, the dim September bears in like a threat, and brown leaves suck hungrily at the glass overhead. She never liked it in here; the oily rags and the half-fleshed faces, the bare stool and the chaise longue for positioning models, bottles of turpentine and tattered drawings. There was something sinister and too functional about it, like a taxidermist's lair. Her mother has switched on the small lamp in Grandad's 'office' – which is really three plyboard walls erected around a big sink, with little square shelves built above it, a cupboard beneath, and a chair where Grandma sat to mix pigment powders for him and arrange his tubes of paint according to a system no one else understood. There were once many old, forensically detailed Renaissance prints hanging there, and newspaper clippings stuck on with tacks. Most of them are gone now.

Beyond the studio is a darker room with bars on the windows and a complex locking system on the door. That's where Valerie's mum emerges from now, struggling with a large, unframed canvas, her face flushing purple-red with the effort.

'The henhouse stinks,' says Valerie, though she didn't expect to say that, and her voice sounds big and contrived now in all the empty space, as on a theatre stage. 'It needs to be cleaned out…'

'Yes. Well we might just get someone in to dismantle it. No one keeps hens anymore, not so close to the city. I doubt Grandma even has planning permission…'

'She was wondering where you were.'

'There's a lovely fur coat in the cloakroom, Valerie. You should take it back with you to London for the winter… Grandma won't be wearing it again.'

Valerie grasps the upper edge of the painting. 'Oh for goodness sake, Valerie,' says her mum, jerking away from her, 'don't be a ninny-hammer. Get some gloves on before you handle the canvas.' As she says the word 'canvas', it slides from her latex grip and topples face down on the floor with an unceremonious pat. 'Shit Valerie! Now look what you've done! Go to the cupboard and get yourself some gloves.' She kneels suddenly and tilts her head.

Stretching a latex glove over one hand, Valerie squats beside her.

'Oh Daddy,' says her mum, looking dreamily at the underside of the canvas.

An eerie portrait of a girl. She looks far away, or under water, with enormous, searching eyes. Or is it two faces? A ghost face over a living one? Her features are a clash of delicate brushstrokes and thick valleys where a second, cleaner outline has been scraped into the paint, right down to the stained canvas.

The lips are lightly touching, the eyes too frank, trying to see out at them from another world.

Mum's voice catches at the back of her throat. 'Look at that!' she says, 'Oh Daddy…' Then, with a frown, 'Go on, Valerie – put on the other glove there and help me to wrap this…' And, as an afterthought, 'That will increase the value, I think. I think so… can't do any harm.'

When they have wrapped five paintings and packed them into the car, Valerie and Aoife return to find the carer sitting in the TV room with a book.

'Well, Aoife,' says Grandma. She nods politely at Valerie, her lips pursed. 'Hello.'

'We have some private business to arrange,' says Valerie's mum, 'so, Polina, maybe you'd like to give us a moment?'

'Of course,' says Polina. 'But Aoife, could I speak with you for a moment, in the hall...'

Mum rolls her eyes. With a sigh, she drops a large brown envelope on the kitchen table and marches out to the hallway saying, 'What is it then, Polina, I don't have much time...'

Valerie stands with her back to the TV. 'Would you like a cup of tea, Grandma?'

'I don't know, darling, what do you think?'

'Well, or coffee? I'll make us some coffee, will I?'

'You could. And make a cup for the nice girl as well, will you please?'

'Sure.'

'Lovely girl.'

While the kettle boils, Valerie sets four mugs on the table and puts one of her grandma's coffee filters on top of each. She glances at the door and, very quietly, she lifts the edge of the envelope and pulls out the contents – a small wad of white A4 pages with the letterhead 'Dunlin & Son Solicitors.'

The kettle lid shudders violently, the water spitting from the spout – she didn't close it properly. She whacks the lid down quickly; the switch flicks off and the boiling subsides.

Valerie slides the papers back into the envelope. She begins to pour the boiled water into the coffee filters, then stops when she hears her mum's voice rising from the hall: 'Do you not now? What are you – a doctor now too, is it?

The carer's voice is softer. 'Well, I am experienced. I think a doctor will say that she's not fit to make decisions…'

'What makes you think you know better than me? She is my mother, and this is my business.'

She comes into the room quickly, head down.

'Mum?'

Her face snaps up, lips tight, eyes small and fierce. 'Don't worry, Valerie. Just some busybody non-national got a bit big for her boots…'

Until Grandma's fall, Valerie had never seen her mother cry. She had never considered her fragile like this. She can't bear it.

The carer stands by the door, her hands clasped before her.

From the TV room, Grandma's voice carries like a caw, straining as loud as her breath will allow: 'Fifi, darling, stop it now. What do you want, darling?'

Valerie brings a mug into the TV room, sits on the footstool and takes her grandmother's hand. Grandma's face is squeezed up, her brow low and her mouth tense; two very red patches have emerged under her eyes, as though she might cry.

'Coffee is just filtering, Grandma…'

The carer's voice is very quiet, very steady. 'She is confused,' she says, 'and it's distressing for her. There are strategies that can help. I really don't understand why you won't get an assessment…'

Aoife is sitting at the table now, her back to the door and the envelope on her knee. She hulks around like a cornered animal, glaring up at the carer.

'How dare you?' she says, her voice a simmer. 'She is my

mother, and I refuse to treat her like an old woman. I refuse to tip-toe around her. She is my mother, and, and...'

Painful pity unfolds in Valerie's chest. Her mother looks old. She looks wretched.

'... and who are you? Do the agency know you carry on like this? I hired you to do your job, not to stick your nose into family affairs. She's my mother. *MY* mother, do you understand?'

30

BABY PEIG FEEDS WITH her mouth clamped over one teat, her hand over the other. If one of her sisters leans in to kiss or touch or speak to Mama, to take the goods that are everything that she wants, the good that is right around her and inside her and that is the opposite of gone, Baby Peig snaps her head around and growls, 'Mine. Mine Myum,' and feeds all the harder then, all the longer. *Mine*, is the first word, then *Mama*.

31

'SHE'S NOT UP TO it, Aoife. I'm going to leave her be. She's just not up to it.'

'Oh, for goodness sake, Sinéad. I knew there'd be some drama if I let you pick her up. It will do her good, Sinéad.'

'No, really, Aoife. She says no.'

'Well… I don't expect you to understand this, Sinéad, but take it from me – from a mother – it will do her good to see her child get a proper burial. I mean, is she dressed? I bought her an outfit and everything…'

'She's wearing a black blouse and skirt. She's sitting in there refusing to come. She's hardly even with it, Aoife, to be honest with you. She's staring into the fireplace. She's holding the carer's hand and staring into the fireplace and she doesn't want to come and I'm not going to push it. I'm sorry.'

'I should have asked Eileen to get her.'

Aoife hangs up feeling more foolish than angry. She shouldn't have trusted Sinéad to bring Mammy to the burial. She straightens the black skirt around her hips, quickly, before the undertaker comes back; it twists when she walks. She will have to remember to keep straightening it and never to wear it again. Without Mammy here, the whole thing seems like some morbid fancy.

The undertaker comes back – a thick-set woman with a greedy sort of glee about her. 'So there won't be many, is that right?'

'My mother won't be coming after all…'

'Oh.'

'I think we'll just meet at the cemetery. The priest said he'd do a few words there…'

It was for Mammy's sake that they got the white coffin. If they had known she wouldn't be coming, they would have saved the expense. And why did they get a lining? It's not as if any of them are going to look at sixty-year old remains. It was a silly extravagance having a lining at all. It was senseless. That's it though; people will go to any length to get money out of you.

It is a very sunny day. Eileen is wearing an extravagant mourning outfit – a pill-box hat with black mesh covering her forehead, and a very flattering knee-length bandage dress. Sinéad hasn't even bothered to wear black. It is just them, watching two teenagers in overalls lower the coffin in beside Daddy. Aoife stands quietly beside Sinéad. She thinks about taking Sinéad's hand, squeezing it, but Sinéad has her fingers knitted together.

Her face is unreadable. When Aoife lifts the first spade of earth, Eileen howls like a banshee, and puts her head on Sinéad's shoulder. Sinéad and Eileen each throw in a fist of dirt. Aoife tries to say a prayer.

Afterwards, she suggests that they go to the Shelbourne for lunch. Sinéad orders a whiskey with her soup. Eileen tells the waitress all about the exhumation and the burial and everything, and Aoife knows that when she thinks about it afterwards she will cringe, but for now all she feels is disappointed.

32

MOLLY WAKES WITH GRIT on her tongue and her guts full of scream and when she opens her mouth the whirl of sand rushing in and there he is with his eyes blank as buttons, his mouth tunnelling into dark and still maybe, maybe he will draw a breath now and maybe, maybe, maybe she should never have dropped to her knees that time and let herself think *gone* and her lungs pull for air but fail and fail for his nails are too short for clawing up to her; his fingers, his clean clipped nails, and under the baby skin and blubber the perfect arrangement of his bones and time is running out for she can hear the bells ringing…

'—Mrs Kearney? The phone, Mrs Kearney. It's your daughter.'

A neatly dressed stranger with a kind, open face. Wordlessly, she helps Molly to shift her shoulders and her neck, and position the big phone – a mobile phone, is it? But big. The girl helps her to hold it comfortably to her ear and puts a cushion under her elbow.

The phone says, 'Mammy.'

'Hello.'

'Mammy, it's Aoife.'

'Oh. Hello.'

'What day is it today, Mammy?'

'Yes, of course.'

'Mammy, do you know what day it is today?'

'Yes. No, darling.'

'Think, Mammy.'

'Tell me, darling.'

'Oh, Mammy, you ninny, do you really not know?'

'I've been sleeping, darling.'

'My birthday, Mammy!' Her daughter laughs – her grown-up daughter, Aoife – she laughs, but there is no mirth in it. 'Oh Mammy, you ninny-hammer! Imagine your own mother not remembering the day she gave birth to you...'

'Oh yes. I didn't forget. I was sleeping, you see. Happy birthday, darling.'

A year to the day, she came. A year to the day after Molly held him there and looked from the clean floor to his face and back again to the clean floor. 'Has your mammy been starving you?' That's what they said, for the cord was knotted tight as though to choke off the next life she tried. A year to the day. But the baby that came was red and with a hurt grimace and its cry said more more more and Molly's breasts grew shy and no milk came.

'How old are you now, darling?'

A year to the day, and oh, so many years to the day that it makes an ache in her to try to count them. While her daughter talks, Molly rubs at her cheek, her forehead, looks at her hands to find no clay beneath her fingernails.

The girl – sallow skin, a heart-shaped face, so pretty – crouches down before her, her eyebrows raised with concern. With fine lips she mouths the shape of 'Okay?' Molly frowns and nods. 'Yes, goodbye darling,' she says, and she hands the phone to the girl. She can hear the girl talking as she moves from the TV room away to the kitchen.

'Hello!' calls Molly. 'Hello, are you there?'

'Yes, Mrs Kearney,' says the girl. 'Yes, I am here. I am just saying goodbye to Aoife, your daughter. I said we will phone when you are more awake.'

'Is it Polina?'

'No, Sally. I am Sally, Mrs Kearney…'

'Yes. Do you like coffee, Katie? Stick on the kettle there, will you. Make us two cups of coffee, if you don't mind… Sit with me awhile?'

33

JEM STAGGERS BACK FROM the toilet bowl, the fright of it whooshing into his ears. It's there again – a bright blue wee glowing right there in the toilet. He holds his breath, afraid of its smell.

Someone in this Big School does blue wees and they leave it there for him to see. They want him to know. They want to see what he will do. The scariest part is, it might be a grown-up doing it. Last time Jem saw the blue wee, Sharon-the-class-helper had just been in here. Her hair is a wrong colour too – pink-orange like paints.

What will happen if he does a wee on it? Blue and yellow makes green. Green fizzing up out of the toilet like a can that's been shook.

Out in the yard, Jem stands by the wall. In Big School the children wear tracksuits instead of shorts, and runners that twinkle like Christmas lights when they run or stamp. When his mammy bought him light-up runners off the computer,

Jem thought she was the only one who knew about them, but when he started Big School he saw that the other mammies must know about them too. Some of the runners here are shinier than his, and some have lights at the front as well as the back.

His friend Lucy won't play with him today because of boy germs. She'll be out of the pink club if she gets boy germs. Most breaktimes the pink club makes him really sad, but today he is glad he has no one to play with. He needs to keep very still or the wee will come out.

After breaktime, Jem sits in his seat and he folds his legs together and he must be jiggling a bit because his teacher asks him three times does he need to go to the toilet. He holds it. He holds it all through the story about Jumping Jack. He holds it while he colours in the picture of Jumping Jack. He even holds it while he traces *J J J*.

At going-home time they have to find a partner and hold hands and make a line before the teacher opens the door. Lucy holds his hand and he wants to ask her what if Cliona sees but he is trying too hard to hold the wee. They are waiting so long for the door that their hands get slimy and they have to let go and wipe them on their tracksuits. When they go out Jem looks around for his mammy. The first thing he will tell her is that he has a wee and she'll bring him somewhere to do it. There are lots of other mammies waiting, but not his mammy. There are daddies as well. Dylan's daddy puts his hands out wide and when Dylan runs to him he snatches him up by the hands and twirls him around and around and then he throws him up and catches him and Jem can't see if Dylan is laughing or crying but he knows he would be crying if that happened to him.

It's only when he feels it go down into his shoe – warm and then cold, that Jem knows it's happened. He looks at his teacher but she hasn't seen. If his mammy comes soon, no one will see. It's in both shoes. His socks are wet. He looks down and he's happy that you can't really see any wee.

His daddy liked Jem's shoes. He knelt down and squeezed the toe. He sat down very close to Jem's mammy at their table and Jem wanted to cover his mammy with a blanket and cosy up with her.

His mammy is here and she's kneeling beside him and he's crying. He's crying and crying. His whole head is full of tears. There's tears coming out of his nose and his eyes and his ears and he can't stop but at least he's not making any sound. She keeps kissing him and saying what's wrong Jem what's wrong my little man I'm sorry I'm late my baby what's wrong.

34

IN ONE YEAR, AOIFE will be sixty.

It has been there on the horizon, something she had hoped to hide, to cover over. It has been there like an icecap beneath the crash and swirl, the hiss of the white seafoam. It is a year away. Who will throw her a party? And who will come? Already, she can feel the sense of failure that will settle on everything; the politeness of her guests, their quiet irritation, the dreary obligation to attend. They will be pulled from every brittle thread of her life – someone she knows from church, someone she used to share the school run with, someone she was friendly with when she did that accountancy course. None of them will know her very well, none of them will like her very much; and the fact of that will be undeniable amongst the pavlova roulade, the princess-warmed chicken fricassee, the balloons in tastefully muted shades – only two colours, three, at most. She knows this, because she has attended two sixtieth birthday parties already this year.

Valerie. It will have to be Valerie who throws the party. That will take the vanity out of it. That will excuse the tenuousness of the guestlist.

This year's birthday is slipping quietly by. This morning, she got a card from Valerie via email. It took a while to load – Valerie's face on the body of a tango dancer, the little tat-tat- tat of the music, the words 'Happy Birthday Mum' jangling on the screen. Valerie went back to London with no excuse. No audition or profit share. No boyfriend. Soon, Valerie will be thirty. Last night, Brendan took Aoife for dinner at a restaurant they used to frequent when they were first married. She realised how rarely they do that, these days. The restaurant has since changed hands – there's a new menu. The chips came in a wooden bucket with silver handles, like a miniature coal scuttle. Brendan drank three beers and a cocktail and ordered too much wine. He seemed bored, impatient for her to reach tipsiness. When her dessert arrived, it had a cocktail umbrella in it, and a single candle: red and white twirled together like a barber's pole. Two wait staff stood by while she blew it out. One of them clapped after; the other walked away. She understood, like a revelation, what the candles meant: another year snuffed out. The wax melted onto the icing and hardened there.

Afterwards, Brendan fell asleep lying diagonally across their bed in his shoes. She removed her earrings in the mirror, and she didn't look away from the bagginess of her face and the ugly dissatisfaction of her mouth. She kept looking as she undressed, and would not let herself pull in her stomach as she released it from the band of her tights.

~

She will be prepared for her sixtieth birthday. She has booked a Botox consultation, and joined the new gym. She bought the Canadian leggings Valerie recommended – very expensive, but worth it, with special elastic in them to flatten her tummy and lift her bum. The girl in the shop said she looked 'fab' in them. Today is her first Zumba class. She's left them in their trendy bag, wrapped in silver paper. She will enjoy opening them; a little birthday present to herself.

She is rolling up her special lightweight sports towel, trying to ignore the churn in her bowels, trying not to wonder who will be at the class – if they will be younger than her or thinner than her, if they will sneer at her efforts – when she hears her phone downstairs on the hall table.

It's Davitt Dunlin.

'Davitt.'

'Aoife, hi. How are you?'

'I'm fabulous, thanks. Really well.'

'I forwarded you an email there.'

'Oh?'

'Now, I don't want you to worry – it's your niece. I know you thought she was trying to interfere with things, and you're right, but I don't want you to worry.'

'Freya?'

'Oh, I'm not sure. No, I don't think it was Freya… let me see now… Cara. That's the elder one, is it?'

'Yeah. Hang on. I'm switching on the computer now. Bloody thing.'

'Aoife?'

'It's very slow. Hang on now…'

'Aoife, I've another call coming in. Let me know how you want me to reply, will you? Give me a call when you've read it.'

Aoife settles herself in her husband's swivel chair, logs into her account and waits with agitation for the emails to load. As she reads, she swallows again and again. Her mouth is stubbornly dry.

---------- Forwarded message ----------

To: davittd@dunlinson.com
From: carakearneyillustrations@gmail.com
Date: 20 October 2018 at 6:04 PM
Subject: RE: Molly Kearney

Dear Mr Dunlin,
I am Molly Kearney's eldest granddaughter, Cara Kearney. We have met on occasions when you called to my grandmother's house.

I know that my grandmother holds you in very high regard and trusts you completely. She still talks of the way you were as a young boy. I have no doubt that you practise your profession with the highest of ethical standards. Some days my grandmother tells me, 'I can trust Davitt Dunlin' a dozen times.

However, some recent events have led myself and my sister to believe that our grandmother's funds are being tampered with. She speaks of people telling her to sign things, and being unsure of what those things are.

Some days she is in utter panic about money and says over and over, 'I need to speak to Davitt Dunlin alone.'

She is sometimes very distressed because family members have, she says, been 'giving out' about the will, but that it will be sorted out.

What has kept me from acting so far is a fear that distress and humiliation might be caused to my grandmother were the issue to become an area of open dispute. Unfortunately, it has become too obvious a problem to ignore. While I understand that the measures we will need to take may not be your concern, I believe that the first step is to, at the very least, contact you to inform you that these concerns exist. An incident that my grandmother, in great distress, told me about some weeks ago, was one in which 'a very large sum' was transferred to a family member.

She said that you were involved in this transaction. This may or may not be the case, but it has occurred to me that you may not have been informed of my grandmother's mental state at this time, and that she may have seemed lucid to you. However, at time of writing, there are days when my grandmother does not know where she is. She also sees people who aren't there and is in a state of extreme confusion much of the time.

I feel it is necessary, at the very least, to make you aware that, while my grandmother is doing much better, she is often unaware of where she is, saying, 'When will they let me go home?' She speaks to my grandfather, who is not there, and some days believes that he is still alive. Sometimes she believes that she has just attended my five-year-old nephew's wedding, and speaks to him about it. In short, since she broke her hip she has been in no fit state to transfer money or alter her will, and, while I am still in the process of investigating the legalities, I am quite certain that altering a will is not something that can or should be done by other family members. I do not know whether this has happened, but I do know that she believes she has been 'told' to sign things changing the will.

I am hoping that I might meet with you to discuss these concerns.

I hope you are not offended by my correspondence. I wish only to make you aware of the complexity of the current situation, and that I am seeking legal advice. I wish also to have it on record that I have expressed these concerns.

I am, however, concerned that my grandmother would feel humiliated were she aware that I was stating that she has not been of sound mind since her fall. I would ask that you deal with it sensitively and that my letter remain confidential.

I can be contacted at this email address.

Regards,
Cara Kearney

35

'JEM.'

His mammy stands at the door. Her hands are on her hips and she is making a sad face. It hurts him: her squishy face.

'Jem.'

He is lying on the blow-up mattress and he looks up at the ceiling again. At home with Mimi there is a grey patch on his ceiling that sometimes looks like a dragon. But here the ceiling is very white and it has glow-in-the-dark stickers on it shaped like sheep. At night they are an evil jellyfish green. This room used to be Baby Peig's room but now Baby Peig sleeps in-with-Megan. It's not his room, really. It's only-for-now. There are bears on the curtains, as if he's a baby, and a strip of bears doing somersaults around the wall.

'What have you done with them, Jem?'

Her voice. When she says 'Jem', it's like she has no air left. His heart is broken. He can feel it under the bones, like something being ripped apart; like a big cry that's stuck. He did the bad thing and now nothing will ever be right again. The sad in his mammy's voice is new but it is like Jem has always been afraid of it. Like the worst bit of a nightmare, he knew it was there all along. He tries not to think of what he has done with his runners. If he thinks of them buried like that in leaves and muck, he might tell.

'Jem. What's the problem with your shoes, Jem? I thought you liked them. You wanted them. They were expensive. I can wash them, you know, and they'll be better than new. I can't just keep buying you new shoes, Jem.'

'Mammy, I know you can wash them. You washed them before.'

The shoes might blink out there in the dark, but no one will see them under the wet leaves. His daddy liked his shoes. They got wee in them that day too. His mammy is still standing there but he won't look at her. She sighs, and shifts about, and keeps standing there until his Aunty Cara says, a little crossly, 'Freya, can you help me please, with Peig. I can't be carrying her.'

He stays looking at the wall, pretending not to see Den as she comes in and crouches on the floor beside his mattress.

'Jem, do you want to do Lego with me?'

Den is his cousin and she is sometimes nice, but sometimes she is cheeky-and-bold.

Downstairs, her daddy, Uncle Pat, is trying to make his little cousin Megan eat her peas. Megan is making a fuss. Jem can hear her screaming and shouting and coughing: 'They make my froat itchy! I can't breave! They make my froat sore!' From the landing, Aunty Cara shouts down, 'Leave it, Pat. I haven't the energy, just leave it. She ate her carrots, it's fine.'

Denise taps him on the head. 'Do you want to do Lego with me, Jem?'

Jem should answer no if he wants her to go away but he can't say it.

'Jem, do you want to do Lego with me? Jem? Are you sad?'

Jem turns around so that Den can see his sad face. He wants to show her the ripping heart feeling he has. Den is holding a really good Lego boat in both hands.

'Don't be sad, Jem. Knock knock.'

Jem shakes his head.

'Jem! Knock knock… Come on, Jem! Say "who's there", Jem!'

'Who's there?'

'Dunap.'

Jem knows it's a trick. She's done this joke before and he knows it's rude-and-not-nice but he can't remember what happens.

'Come on, Jem, it's funny!'

'Dunap who?'

'Done a poo! Jem done a poo-hoo! Jem done a poo-hoo!'

'Go away! Go away go away go away!' Jem is screaming now. His heart hurts. His Uncle Pat is in the doorway.

'What's going on here, Den? Why is Jem crying? Why are you shouting, Jem?'

'I told him knock knock who's there Dunap.'

'Ruuude!' shouts Jem, as loudly as he can. He is a good boy. He is a good and well-behaved boy and it's not fair for

Den to be like this and for no one to mind. 'Ruuuuude! Ruuuude!'

'Dry up, Jem,' says Uncle Pat, and Jem's voice goes from him just like that, as though Uncle Pat has just snatched it away.

'Go on, Denise, leave Jem alone. He's not in the mood. Have you brushed your teeth?'

Out on the landing his mammy is using bad words. 'For fuck's sake, Cara, I know you're not *obliged* to collect him. I never said you were *obliged*, but you said you would and now you're not and I'm fucked for this tutorial now, that's all. You could have told me before, and now you're telling me I have to collect your kids, too.'

'It's not a lot to ask, Freya. It's not like I ask anything of you, it's not like you even contribute…'

Jem is not in his pyjamas and he knows he should be.

Den told that joke to Mimi one time before, and Mimi started play-acting – she made a sound like a scream, but happy, and then she smiled and sighed, and shook her head and said, 'Oh my DenDen you're a gurrier of a girl…' That time, Jem climbed onto Mimi's knee and he could see that Mimi knew Den was bold and Jem was the best boy. But now sometimes he is not sure anymore what his Mimi knows.

When she comes to tuck him in, his mammy has her own voice again but her face is a bit tired. One of her bottom teeth has got dark. It's ugly. She says he will have to wear his wellies into school tomorrow. Jem doesn't care. He lets her kiss him and he turns on his side and closes his eyes. His 'Our Planet' light is working again. At last his mammy got the right lightbulb. It took her ages. She kept saying, 'Sorry Jem, I forgot.'

His cheek is very hot, so he turns on his back but he hates this ceiling. The green of the sheep is like the eyes of bad guys.

It was Aunty Cara who put his pyjamas on him and no one has made him brush his teeth. He can hear his Aunty Cara downstairs and he doesn't know if it's his mammy or his Uncle Pat that she is giving out to. 'What are you talking about?' she says. 'We did not *agree* on a limit – you *told* me. You tell me how much I can spend. How much of my own money I can spend and you have no idea. You expect the girls to go around in rags. You think pyjamas are a waste of money – pyjamas! You have no idea, no idea…' There is quiet and then a shout. It's Uncle Pat. Uncle Pat is shouting at Aunty Cara. 'You STOLE! You stole from our family.'

'Shoes! I bought the girls shoes. How is that stealing from our family…?'

'It's not what we agreed! Fifty quid a month we said, on extras, no more.'

'Extras!'

Jem is not the number-one-fan of Uncle Pat.

Uncle Pat says in-this-house-we-eat-what's-on-our-plate and tonight that was little C-for-Cat slices of celery with bumpy backs like green caterpillars and a caterpillar taste. Den saw him putting them under the edge of the plate and gave him a tissue to wrap them in and hide them in his pocket.

He stuffed the tissue sack of celery in one of his shoes before he buried them.

That was nice of Den. He was badly behaved to Den tonight. But Den is badly behaved lots of times.

He can hear his aunty and uncle coming up the stairs. Their talk is quieter now, but he can hear the words on the landing.

'Your work,' Uncle Pat is saying. He says it like 'work' is a pretend word, or a funny word. 'It's a hobby, Cara. How much do you earn an hour? It's a hobby. You've never done a day's work in your life…'

At home, when he can't sleep, Mimi comes and turns his pillow so that his cheek is on the fresh side, and she puts a drop of oil on it from a tiny purple bottle that smells so nice and sleepy. His mammy doesn't know about those things. It's up to Jem now to turn his pillow when it gets all hot, and it's all up to him to get to sleep; to think of nice smells and nice songs and dragons moving like clouds across his sky.

36

IT RAINED DURING THE night. Cara could smell it when she opened the front door; the fecundity of worms and roots, the sliminess of the leaves. This car attracts bug life. Her wing mirrors were swathed in spider webs, each invisible thread jewelled in rainbeads. There were four garden snails suckered to the wheel-cap, their shells cool as marbles under the vague sun. Denise insisted on pulling them off before she would get in the car for school. *Poor snails.*

Cara's only just noticed the ladybird. It's clinging to the dashboard, trembling along with the vibrations of the car. Any moment now its shell will snap open, revealing the little frenzy of wings beneath. That's all it will take for the creature to be lost to some invisible nook of the car. Then it will turn up dead in the pocket of a door or the crease of a seat, compact and weightless as confetti, tossed in the dust with the copper coins. Thinking of that makes her feel weak and loose and sorry, like finding fragments of moth wing on the windowsill, or when her children tear open the buds of poppies, exposing the private twirling tissue of a flower that will never unfold.

The phone directs her calmly and clearly in a clipped English accent, but she keeps checking the screen with the same habitual glance she gives her mirrors, searching for the reassuring dot of her car pulsing along the roads.

While she drives, she plots the simple patterns of the ladybird – the blocky shapes for eyes and the funny little paddles of its feet. Poor mite must be drying out in here. She imagines it drinking a droplet of dew from a leaf or sliding down the side of the text in a big tear of rain, then pottering off onto the next page, two fat little domes of rain still on its back; and they splash off as it takes flight on the closing frame. She could work that into *The Rainy Day Book*...

The Rainy Day Book is a worry. 'Make it your own,' her agent said, but then they rejected the duck and asked for a boy and a girl instead. She was reluctant to accept the job in the first place, but she can't back out of a commission, not with Pat working all the time, saving and saving as though shoring up against some terrible disaster. It hurts Cara, and makes her ashamed of him and then ashamed of herself for that betrayal, to see him undo the rubber band and count rolls of money into envelopes before stashing them under the floorboards like a greedy criminal. 'It's fine. We've nearly saved our target for this year. It's fine...' He's started working weekends and evenings again – nixers here and there on the black to add to those envelopes.

'It's hard for men,' is what Grandma would say. 'Oh, it's hard for men. They think they must control everything. They feel great burdens. Try to understand it's hard for men.'

He opened her bank statement yesterday, and he went spare. But it only showed a bit of her overspending. He doesn't know what she took out of her savings account for Denise's violin. She isn't supposed to touch that account.

It will be fine. She can move money over. She can tell him she's getting a little less for this job, make it up that way...

She should get decent money for *The Rainy Day Book*. She hates it, though. It will involve illustrations of the various activities suggested for rainy days. They are stupid projects requiring double-sided sticky tape and craft tacks and pipe cleaners and all sorts of things that kids never have at their disposal. The editor emailed photographs of the finished products – characterless creations assembled by adult hands.

The GPS has led Cara into a little cul-de-sac beside a park and instructed her to drive through the house in front of her.

She will be late for this appointment, it seems, despite her best efforts. She is always late. Pat thinks it's a feature of her personality that she likes to cultivate, but he's wrong. She tries to be on time. She is ashamed of being late all the time, but still it happens. Parked in front of the angular new-build, she checks her emails to make sure she has put in the right address. She is left with no choice but to phone the woman and ask for directions. The thought of that makes her stomach flip and she rests her face on her palms and closes her eyes. The pregnancy sickness has started already. This time there seems no pattern to the waves of nausea. They come without warning, sweeping her into a useless heap when she least expects it.

She has been uneasy all day. This always happens to her if she doesn't work well in the morning. It is something she withholds from Pat guiltily; her inability to enjoy anything unless she's done some good work that morning. Pat – whose hands come back split clean to the tissue and angry with splinters, who works and works with his head bent until his neck aches, and then keeps working; who works only to support them all, to look after them – how would he feel, if he knew that she can't bear any of it; the cooking and cleaning and driving, the nonsense the kids talk in the back of the car, the ridiculous squabbles?

If she has rendered a detail perfectly, or planned her layout, or any achievement at all, she can appreciate it all, she can take pleasure in every little thing – reading to the kids, listening to their jokes; cooking elaborate meals and eating them together around the table.

But on days like today it is all a hassle, pulling her away from what she needs to do. Everything slides away from her; half real, half formed. If she hasn't been able to work, she thinks of nothing else. She sketches in her mind while her husband makes love to her; she pleasures him hurriedly, twitching with the need to put lines on paper.

Pushing her knuckles into her eyelids, she feels already as though she is in trouble for something – her own secret, wicked selfishness – thinking about nothing but silly scribblings.

A sensation like vomiting comes over her and she groans audibly, inhales as though this breath can suck her back together, and scrolls back to the email in her phone:

Dear Cara,

Thank you for getting in touch. I would like to meet with you to discuss your concerns. Please call me on the number below to arrange an appointment.

She almost hopes the woman won't pick up. She can leave a voicemail saying she's lost, then go home and put it all off until another day. It was the directness, perhaps, of the email, that made the whole thing seem so dramatic, and then the voice on the phone – dull, so very monotonous, as though weighed flat by the gravity of her job. But even as she wrote the enquiry, she felt the seriousness of what she was doing. A creeping fear set through her like something dropped into her blood. Once she has transgressed like this, there is no going back to the codes of family loyalty.

She hasn't had a chance to talk about it properly with Pat. Freya is always there, and Freya can't cope with what is happening with their aunts and their grandma and their mad mother.

Freya is like a child. She's let this thing with Jem's father get out of hand, and now she expects Cara to know what to do about it. She expects Cara to pick up all her broken pieces. Cara had to march her into the legal aid office and, as it turns out, ignoring him like that didn't 'do her any favours'. When it gets to court, they said, Freya will look unreasonable. She should have given him access as soon as he 'expressed an interest'. It's all Freya wants to talk about. She wants advice but she never takes it. It never occurs to her that Cara doesn't know what to do either, that she is barely holding her own life together.

The call rings out, and Cara feels she has willed it that way.

With her nail, she nudges the ladybird very gently. It tucks its legs under itself. Then she remembers something – the matchboxes in the glove compartment! Denise has been collecting them for school. Her class is making a matchbox town or something. Children used to come to the door in the summer, selling matchboxes full of ladybirds for ten pence. Grandma bought them for the roses and gave the children a handful of Fox's Glacier Mints as well as the money.

Cara slides open a matchbox and pushes it at the ladybird. The creature is still clamped up neatly, and it is easy to topple it into the box. She slides the cardboard closed and puts it in the door of the car.

Just as she is about to call and leave a voicemail, the phone rings. The woman sounds chirpier than she did last week. She says the GPS always gets them wrong, and they are back across the road, behind the church, that Cara will see the Health Service Executive sign on the gate of the car park. She is to ring the bell that says 'Protection of the Elderly'.

37

MAMMY IS SEEN FROM far away, as at the end of a deep cave. Her home is a muffle of floral upholstery, tasseled lampshades, rugs. She is handed a glass. She lifts it to her lips, sends it away again. She tilts her head one way, then another. She sleeps. She is helped to her feet, brought away, settled back into her chair. Slippers are pushed onto her feet. She plucks limply at a ball of tangled wool.

Aoife's eyes are growing weary. They struggle to pick out Mammy from the blocks of dark, the pixels of light. They slide away from the screen to the window, the filing cabinet, to the mousemat saying 'O'Carroll, Sheehan & Co. Solicitors'.

Is she imagining it, or are there dark spots emerging there on the back of her hand; only faint speckles now, but they promise frailty, ugliness. She had her nails done only yesterday – Antique Rose. At the time she thought the muted colour dignified, understated. No, it's an old lady colour.

Aoife skips forward: her mother fumbling with the remote control, her mother slumped to the side like a sack of sand.

She lifts her hand from the mouse, and the video slows to

real time: her mother sleeping in her chair, her head tilted back and her mouth a fuzzy nothing. Someone comes in dressed in pale colours, stoops to looks at her, leaves.

Aoife needs a cup of coffee.

At first, she made sure to watch the video feed every day, fast-forwarding to appearances of the Ladies Muck, but it's dreary work. The picture is not as good as she had hoped. The light is dim and the sound is useless – she can't make anything out. It takes hours to process a day of footage, fast-forwarding through her mother sitting there and, at the side of the screen, a carer ensconced in her father's chair, tapping at a smartphone.

They are paid to just sit there, basically.

But there'll be something in here, she knows there will. It's just a matter of persisting.

Aoife holds her breath. Someone is hunkering down beside Mammy – a bright mass of hair. Freya. She lifts her handbag and stands. Mammy looks up at her: what's she saying?

This is it; Aoife can feel it. Ha! She's caught her!

Her stomach lurches into her throat. Freya has put the handbag on Mammy's lap; she is kissing Mammy's cheek, and Mammy is saying something, leaning in, pointing – is she trying to defend herself?

Aoife pauses, rewinds. Yes. Of course, Freya is taking something from Mammy, but is it clear from the video? Not really. Using a biro, she notes down the date and time all the same. It might prove useful. She presses play. Freya leaves the room. Who is that off the side of the camera? A foot, maybe, a hand? The little boy. When did he come in? She must have skipped through his arrival. He approaches Mammy's chair; his hair aglow, his eyes dark. He stands beside Mammy, a hand on her armrest, but she doesn't seem to notice him. Freya returns to the room. She puts a cardboard box on the footstool, leaves again. Aoife might vomit with excitement – she has her! Ha! She has her!

Freya returns carrying something – a fat book. She places it in the box, right there in front of the camera, turns to Mammy, says something, and leaves. It goes on like that for seven whole minutes, Freya leaving the room and returning with more loot – a shoebox, a cylinder – slowly filling up the cardboard box.

Aoife pauses. She rewinds, watches it again to be sure. What a find! She is exhausted from it, exhilarated. Ha! She has her!

Leaning back against the kitchen worktop, the sunrise to her back, the kettle boiling, she dials.

'Sinéad! Did I wake you? Well, you should be up. Listen. I'm going to email you something. I don't think you'll have any more scruples once you've seen this!

38

THE SOCIAL WORKER IS there at the door already, raising a hand and nodding.

She watches from the door as Cara parks badly, and re-parks, and gets out of the car. Cara walks towards her, making a half-wave of recognition, then stops – she has forgotten her purse and phone. Too far away to explain, she makes a pantomime of remembering these things, smacking her brow and shaking her head at her own silliness so that the woman understands why she is turning around.

Her palms are moist when the social worker shakes her hand – 'Hi Cara. Bernie.' – and leads her along a short corridor. Cara thinks of lie-detector tests, the way they measure anxiety levels and perspiration. It can't be right, because telling the truth when nobody wants you to and no one might believe you – that is just as stressful, surely, as lying.

Bernie talks in a long, low monotone, like a background radio. She is only filling in the silence until they get to the office. Cara realises that she is barely aware of what the woman is saying.

'Everyone has trouble finding the place. Everyone... It should be better signposted.' She stops at an open door. 'It's an issue,' she says, and gestures for Cara to step in.

The room is tiny, with filing cabinets on all sides. It smells sickeningly like air freshener. Cara stands back while Bernie squeezes past her and in behind a desk covered in stacks of cardboard folders. Isolated in the centre of the table is a single envelope-folder of dusty blue. There are dents and swirls in the corner where drying biros have been forced back to life. Bernie perches her bottom on the window ledge at her back, nods at Cara. 'So...'

Cara takes a breath to speak, but exhales instead. Bernie doesn't seem fazed. 'Sit down,' she says. 'You can close the door if you like or – whatever you like.' She is younger than she looked in the car park, not quite forty, perhaps, though up close, it is clear that the crease between her eyebrows is a deep and permanent fixture. She has abnormally dark, hurt-looking eye sockets. It's as though someone has pressed a thumb under each eye until a groove has formed, bruising the flesh.

The door is being held open by a metal wastepaper basket. Cara shifts it with her foot, and the door falls slowly closed. She sits down on a swivel chair, too big and too luxurious for the little room, and too low. Her knees are higher than her hips. It will be an effort to get up.

That poor ladybird, tipped onto its back in the matchbox – has it managed to turn itself over yet? Has it even moved?

Cara heaves herself forward, so that she is sitting at the edge of the chair. It threatens to roll out from beneath her. She stands up again. 'Maybe not,' she says. 'Sorry. I'm clumsy at the moment. Baby brain already!' She rubs her abdomen and shrugs, as though it is not part of her at all, but a cumbersome attachment that she drags about reluctantly. She laughs and it sounds stupid.

'You're tiny!' says the lady, raising her pitch and her eyebrows both at once, and smiling, relaxed suddenly. 'I didn't even notice you were pregnant... how far gone?'

'Oh, nothing at all...' Cara knows she isn't showing. She doesn't know why she mentioned it like that. 'Like, eight weeks, I think... I just feel heavy,' she says. 'I'm starting to feel awkward.'

'Well, congratulations. Is it your first?' Cara loves this question. She laughs and tries to conceal her pride. 'No! My fourth!'

'Oh! Gosh, you don't look like someone who has three kids!'

'I started young. Youngish.'

'So, I have your email here,' says the lady, sliding open a drawer, as though the email is in there, and pushing it closed again, 'and it seems as though you have reason to be concerned about your grandmother.'

Her eyes stretch open, and she blinks frantically. Cara realises that the woman is exhausted, that it is pure effort for her to stay alert; her patience is wilful, her sensitivity professional.

Grandad used to have so many flesh tones on his palette at one time, steely blues and burgundy reds, drops of linseed oil to keep them soft. When he covered the palette with clingfilm, the paint flattened – each glob of colour turning ugly, private; like the underside of a snail. She imagines turning her brush in a lovely sandy tone, glossy with oil and the colours not quite blended so that she mixes them on the canvas, the pinks and yellows merging into skin. She would make the social worker rested and pretty – add layers beneath the eyes, phasing out the purplish blue. It is something Grandad never would have done. It would be a lie.

The social worker offers only her dogged patience to the silence. Then a tiny, suppressed yawn swells her throat. She brings the back of her fingers to her mouth. 'Excuse me,' she says, 'it's been a long day. Ohhh.' She allows an open-mouth yawn now, covering it with her hand. 'Sorry. So, it seems to me that you have cause for concern?'

Cara opens her mouth to speak and her voice comes out low and trembling.

'Does it? I don't know… I don't want to be, you know, dramatic. I just – I'm worried and I don't know what to do. I need advice.'

'Are you alright?'

'Yes, I just, I don't know if this is as serious as I'm making out, or if it's even something that I should be taking up your time over. I just want advice.'

'You said your grandmother has dementia?'

'I don't know if she's been… diagnosed or whatever. She doesn't know who we are a lot of the time. She tells me people have been asking her to sign things. She says she's signed things and she can't remember what… that's dementia, isn't it?'

'It certainly sounds like it. Has she been assessed?'

'I don't know. I mean, this is the thing. My aunts are in charge and they don't tell us anything. One of the carers said that the dementia wasn't on her file. She said she told my aunt that, but my aunt told her she'd lose her job if she didn't show a bit of respect.'

'In charge?'

'They say they are executors.'

'So they have taken power of attorney?'

'No. This is the thing. They are pretending my grandma is fine; they haven't taken power of attorney. And they are moving around her money, getting her to sign things, selling her property, having her house redecorated...'

'And they are selling her house?'

'No, her—' Here Cara falters for a moment, embarrassed, '—other properties. She is quite wealthy. My grandad was a painter. He was quite successful... they became quite wealthy.'

'Oh! Would I know him?'

'Dennis Kearney?'

'Rings a bell... I did art for my Leaving Cert...'

'The thing is – the thing that the carer said to me, is that my grandmother has no idea what's going on, but all these things are happening under her name, you know? Because she says they get her to sign things. You see, there are some family things... family issues.'

The lady nods and clicks her tongue. 'Oh I know!' she says gravely, nodding at the metal filing cabinet, as though there are dark, untellable stories running on in there in the drawers. 'I know only too well... you see the worst in people in this job. It's usually the mother who is the victim, it's usually the kids, they see it as their right, and it's usually about money.'

'It must be a hard job. It must be so tiring. I don't know how you do it. I couldn't.'

'Thank you. Yes, it's – it has its difficulties alright.'

'Well, you know, I don't want to take up your time. I don't know whether to be worried, or whether this is their right, you know? And in a way, my grandmother doesn't really know what's going on so she's not that upset about it so maybe it doesn't really affect her. She gets upset but then she forgets completely.'

The social worker has gained interest. She's leaning back on the windowsill, her hands knotted in her lap. She is looking hard at Cara and nodding.

'Oh, look, I don't know what's relevant. I just need advice. What say do I have in my grandma's care, for example? And is it illegal, what they're doing?'

'Yes, it is certainly illegal. Now who are we talking about here – just your aunt?'

'I have two aunts. I think they're both in on it, but one is sort of the ringleader… and my mother. My mother has taken Grandma's cheque book. Maybe for safe keeping, but I don't think so. I think she's using it. The carer said my mother got Grandma to sign them before she took it. She says she bought herself a bus, but I don't know.'

Cara cannot read the expression on Bernie's face now.

'And why are they doing it? Do they need money?'

'Oh, I don't think so. My aunts are extremely wealthy… my mother less so, maybe. But, you see, my Aunt Aoife, she doesn't think it's fair, that my grandmother looked after us more than my cousin, helping us out financially as well, I mean. We – see, myself and my sister – we grew up with our grandparents. Our mother is – she is strange. She joins cults and things. My little sister was taken away from her by social services, I think.'

'You think?'

'Well, they were involved. They were calling over and interviewing my mother and things so my mother just left my sister with my grandparents and left the country.'

'What's her name?'

'My sister?'

'Your mother. Your sister. Both.'

'My mother is Eileen Kearney. My sister is Freya Kearney.'

Bernie writes it down. 'I'll find out.'

'So, our grandparents, I think they paid for a lot of things for us growing up and certainly as adults. I mean, I couldn't have managed without Grandma, and my little sister is a single mother you know, and still in college and all. She lived with Grandma – my grandmother – and last summer my aunt kicked her out, and there was really nothing we could do because Grandma had broken her hip and she was fragile and couldn't walk or anything and there would have been a fight and, at the time, you know, we thought it would be too stressful for Grandma if we argued… but my aunt… she's settling the score, I suppose. According to my grandmother, you know, she made this… list. She worked out how much my grandma 'owes' her and her daughter, and she's organising it now that she has the chance. I suppose that's how she sees it. She's making it fair, as she sees it.'

'Well, that's not right.'

'Well, no. Because she's taking advantage, I suppose. But what I'm wondering is – is it really bad, what they're doing? And how I can address it without upsetting my grandmother.'

'And in your email you said there was a large cheque?'

'Yes, my grandmother gave me this letter.'

Cara has it folded in her back pocket – God, the social worker must think she's such a flake, carrying a thing like that around in her back pocket. She hands it over. Bernie frowns with a kind of glee as she reads.

'Who is Davitt Dunlin?'

'My grandmother's solicitor, she knew his father... so as you can see it's a letter confirming the cheque for €100,000 to my mother. He says, "You assured me you were of sound mind and were certain that you wished to transfer the money..." or something like that, doesn't he?'

'That's what he says, yes. He says Eileen – that's your mother, is it?'

Cara nods.

'He says she called him to the house, saying that your grandmother wished to change her will, but that "we agreed to leave the will as it is until you are feeling better". This is really strange. I've never seen a solicitor carry on like this before.'

'He's a family friend. He grew up with my mother, and aunts.'

'Well, I need to get in touch with this man.'

'Okay. I think he really believes it though, you know. I think he just doesn't know... but what I'm saying anyway is that I only know these things by fluke.'

'Mmmmm,' says Bernie, and suddenly Cara is afraid that the

social worker will misunderstand; she will think Aoife and The Lily are all Grandma's fault, that Grandma must be that way too, if her daughters are, that they are just a mad family doing mad things and that her grandmother deserves them.

'You were right to contact us.'

'Look, I don't want to be dramatic, I just—'

'I'll get you some water.'

Cara had no intention of crying. And now there is a wash of mascara on her hands, and her face must be a mess. Does she even feel the emotion running out of her? And now she is shaking and cold and for no reason she can understand.

While Bernie has gone to get water, it occurs to Cara that she may sound mad; that Bernie may think she has made it all up, that it is she who is after Grandma's money somehow. And then a cool terror trickles though her – this is exactly the kind of thing her mother would do. Her mother would come here, weeping like this, saying the first thing that came into her head, and believing it. What if Cara is doing the same? What if she has imagined it all? But no. There will be records. There is the letter from the solicitor.

When the social worker comes back Cara takes the water and sips, but it is too cold and her stomach seizes up.

'Sorry,' she says, 'I must seem mad to you.'

'Not at all.'

'I might be making a big deal out of nothing.'

'No. You're certainly not.'

'So, I suppose the question is then, as the grandchild, you know, where do I stand? What do I do?'

'Well, it's out of your hands now.'

'It is my responsibility. My grandmother looked after me all my life.'

'Yes, no I understand all that, but in terms of addressing this situation with your aunts and your mother. I will look into it.'

'Do you need anything from me? Proof of anything?'

'I will get all that. I just need you to fill in a statement for me.'

'But I'm not accusing them of anything, exactly, it's just what I told you – it's not so clear.'

'You just list everything you told me. Tick the boxes there for what your concerns are – emotional abuse? Financial abuse?'

'Both, I suppose.'

Again the reassuring, knowing nod, the heavy eyelids. 'Usually is. I'll leave you to fill that in at your own pace. Wait till I get back before you sign it. I need to witness it.'

'My grandmother would be heartbroken if they told her I'd said she was unfit. She would be humiliated. Do you see?'

'That's not what we would say to her. But you need to protect her, if people are taking advantage.'

'Will my aunts see this?'

'It's confidential. Don't worry. You're not implicating yourself in anything. You just list your concerns and then it's out of your hands. You owe it to your grandmother, you know.'

By the time she gets out of the HSE office, she only has twenty minutes to get to the music school. She should feel relieved after unloading all the shameful dealings of her family, but instead the meeting has left something pressing like a stone on her tongue, a queasy satisfaction tightening in her chest and a fear – as though she has exposed herself. What does she imagine they can do to her – the aunts? Money is all they have. Her grandad's money to fight her with, but they cannot hurt her babies and they cannot take Pat away, so why does she feel afraid? They could upset Grandma. They could tell her that Cara said she was unfit.

At the end of the road she has to pull up and get out.

It's just pregnancy sickness, perhaps, the nausea that has clenched her whole body suddenly, making her kneel by the car and retch at the tarmac. She is shaking. It's a thing she's never felt before, this sanctimonious dread that feels so like guilt; the loneliness of being right on her own terms.

There is a little garden on the corner of a street. A sign on the railings saying 'Community Garden'. It looks like an explosion of weeds, the green tangles tumbling out under the gate and coiling around the bars in a crazed celebration of vegetation. She wants to give the garden something, so she pulls up again, the little car almost toppling as the side of it mounts the kerb. She releases her seatbelt. She is late – late for her little girl; she is late and still she is stopping. She takes the matchbox out of the glove compartment, opens the car door and leans towards the garden. She will leave the little ladybird to feast on all the greenfly. Now that she is closer, she sees that the garden is growing parsley and rosemary and mint, and some strangled peas, with limp, frost-bitten pods. She slides open the little box and already she knows what has happened. She can feel the dry weightlessness of the box. The ladybird has died, its little legs clamped to itself, the flat black underside and the shell a frank crimson red, light as confetti.

39

MEGAN HATES DADDY.

Megan wants Mammy to be listening to her but Mammy bees closing together with Daddy on the Big Bed and does not be hearing her and as well does not be looking at her and just bees closing together with Daddy and kissing him and cuddling also.

Lots of the days Daddy has spikes on he's face. Megan does not like Daddy to be giving her kisses when there be spikes on he's face and Mammy should not kiss him when him has spikes or cuddle also acause the spikes can be hurting.

Daddy has telled Megan to go in her room and get in her jammies and Mammy has said, 'Yes, go and get your jammies on, Megan,' and Megan is hating Daddy so so so much she will cut off he's head maybe and maybe poo on it, maybe.

Megan is not be allowed in the Big Bed now acause she be a big girl now. When Megan beed two, Baby Peig has popped out and Megan has been wanting to lie aside the basket and watch when Baby Peig be sleeping, but Mammy has sayed no. Now she be sleeping aside Baby Peig and she can be watching her hands so squidgy soft and her breathing as well up and down, and Mammy sayed Megan bees such a big girl and a good girl for to be having Baby Peig in-with-her but that is a bit cheating acause actually Megan is happy to be getting Baby Peig in-with-her and even more when the little boy comes.

There be no goblins in Megan's whole town, but sometimes she splains to Baby Peig anyway, just for to be sure, so Baby Peig does not be being scared: 'I will mind you little baby,' she says, 'no goblins in this whole town and no bad fings in my woom.' And as well, when she gets a snail feeling on her neck, and on her feet, she remembers really really hard that there be no snakes in Ourland and she tells that to Baby Peig also.

Megan loves her doggie jammies but it is a hard jammies to put on, because it be having a bottom and a top stuck together and buttons on her front – so many of holes in for legs and arms and hard to know which one. Her daddy has comed to the door and he be saying something and Megan say, 'What you have sayed?' acause he be doing that talking again that is gloopy and far away and hard to listen out the words. Her daddy walk in her room with Baby Peig sleeping and put Baby Peig down in her crib and then him pick Megan up on he's so high arm and does a sloppy kiss on her cheek but otay cause he's face bees not spikey today. Then he plops her down on the bed and open her jammies – the hole for one foot and then the other foot.

Then she be buttoned up so cosy and she loves Daddy.

'Stowy Daddy.'

She does not so much hate Daddy when he not be spiking

her cheek and when he bees reading her story. Daddy says yes to story so Megan says, 'Two stowy?' and he laughs and says, 'Two quick stories then, but quick,' and Megan loves Daddy and Daddy be so cosy warm. 'Please will you lie with me, Daddy?'

Megan knows the little boy is be coming tonight – and she knows him is not be holding her hand and smiling and picking mushrooms with her together in the forest this night. Afore him come and pick mushrooms with Megan in the night, and they be having a basket for the mushrooms and a stick for pushing away the forest, but now when him comes him is just an open mouth like trying to make sounds and even like Megan is sometimes finding it tricky to pick out sounds she is knowing there be no sound in he's froat and that is making him sad and angry as well and he's eyes be very big and black and he's hands be fat and small and dirty and she does be frightened some of the times when him be reaching out to touch her froat.

PART 3

40

THE BIN BAG HAS fallen away from the window; a slow, clumsy rustle in the night. Freya tried to stick it back up but the tack has hardened. She'll get more tomorrow. Or maybe she'll use duct tape.

From the garden outside, a picket of solar lights, chillingly white, jumbles shadows across the bedroom wall: the slanted tower of the ironing board, the spindly forest of an old hamster cage.

The fold-out bed joggles and yelps when Freya turns on her side. She's clutching her phone in both hands. Sticking out from the cowl of her blanket, her fingers are cold, and her nose. She'll send the email. She'll read over it one last time, and then she'll send it.

From: Freya Kearney <kearneyfp@tcd.ie>
To: valerie.o.carroll32@gmail.com

Dear Valerie,
Hey Cos! I hope everything is going well over there? Grandma

tells me you have a job on *Love/Hate*, and that you are engaged to be married? This may or may not be the case – it is hard to know where she gets some of the things she comes out with these days – but anyway, I hope things are good. Did you hear that Cara and Pat are expecting a baby next summer? In the last scan they said it looked like it's another girl, but they couldn't be certain.

Anyway, I am really emailing about Grandma. I want to explain my recent actions, ask your thoughts and fill you in on stuff you might not be aware of.

About a month ago, I received a letter re power of attorney. You probably received the same letter? Basically, it says your mum and Aunt Sinéad are to take power of attorney, but you, myself and Cara each have a right to object to it.

I think I should let you know all of the following information:

As you may or may not know, before Christmas there was a HSE enquiry into elder abuse regarding Grandma. I think only your mum and Sinéad were investigated and they both refused to co-operate. I don't know why my mother wasn't. She should have been.

Freya deletes *She should have been.*

Your mum sent an email about it saying there had been false allegations, but I am not convinced that they were false and I'm not sure if the HSE are either.

You may or may not be aware that my mother extracted a

€100,000 cheque from Grandma very shortly after her fall. I am not sure if you saw much of Grandma after her fall, but I can assure you she was in no fit state to be making financial decisions. At a later date Grandma also told me that she thought they had sold her houses in Monkstown and Wicklow, and asked me to explain to her what was going on, adding 'they tell me I gave you money and they want to make it fair on Valerie.' Since Grandma moved out of her house, your mother has not let me in, even to collect boxes of my things from the attic.

When I received the letter re power of attorney last week, I sent an email enquiry to the Protection of the Elderly, outlining the situation and asking for advice. The woman who led the HSE investigation phoned me. She told me that there had been a HSE investigation already, and two GP reports which found that there was cause for concern regarding Grandma's mental state and the behaviour of her children regarding her estate. She strongly advised that I object to power of attorney, and highlighted that, with the HSE recommendation, Grandma would almost certainly be made a ward of court if one of the notified parties objected.

There is limited time within which we can put in an objection to power of attorney, so Cara and I put in the objection this morning. We can always withdraw it. I want to know what you think?

On the one hand, maybe the emotional abuse that Grandma suffered while her children needed to persuade or bully her into changing the will, or writing cheques, would no longer take place if they could simply make the decisions for her? There would be no more tearful phone calls from her about what so and so said about her favouritism, or reminding me not to mention to anyone that she paid for Jem's creche!

On the other, their behaviour so far has been disgusting and I see no reason why that would change. The HSE officer thinks it would offer Grandma more protection if she were to be made a ward of the court.

The HSE officer is Bernadette Murphy. Her email address is bernadette.murphy24@hse.ie

Freya

Freya reads it again from the beginning. The *Cos* thing is stupid, so she replaces it with *How are you?*

'Mammy?' Jem is hanging onto the door handle with both hands, his chin resting on them.

'What is it, darling?'

'Can't sleep.'

'What's wrong?'

'Mimi.'

'Okay, come in here then.'

Freya checks the time – after midnight. She presses 'send', and switches off her phone.

41

GRANDMA'S HANDS DANGLE OVER the arms of the chair. Cara lifts one in both of hers, runs her thumb between the bones that fan wicker-fine under the slip of loose skin, the heady blue push of her knuckles. She turns it over and kneads the palm where the flesh is full as a fish belly, lines smoothed plump by the sore swell of tissue, and presses her lips to the skin that doesn't smell like Grandma anymore, but like piss and perfume and the sediment of breath that settles in rooms like this one, with strangers in it, and storage heaters and closed windows.

The coolness of Grandma's body makes Cara think of frogs; the pulsing blisters of their throats.

One night, when Cara was little, she and Grandma sat and watched the mating frogs come out in their dozens to croak at the moon. Grandma sat Cara on her lap and wrapped a wool blanket around her shoulders and they listened to the flat, imploring calls, then the bald sloshing of cold-blooded sex. Afterwards, Grandma told her that some frogs can make their own hearts stop beating and it made Cara sick and frightened, as though she might slip on the muddy bank and become a grotesque and beautiful thing like them.

Megan stands close, patting Cara's cheeks relentlessly with her warm palms. Her face smells unhealthily like snot. She is not over this cold and Cara should get her home.

'Let's dow, Mammy. Mimi is tired. She tan't member us.'

Cara kisses her grandmother's cheek. 'We'll come back soon Grandma,' she says. Her voice is too public. 'I'll bring back your clean clothes. I'll make you that quiche you like, with the leeks. I'll bring it tomorrow...'

'Yes.' Grandma interlocks her bulky fingers with Cara's. 'But wait now, there's one thing—'

Cara's other hand is clamped in her daughter's sticky grip. Megan leans back and pulls with the weight of her whole body, making a performance of heaves and grunts. Cara shakes her off and waits to hear the one thing that Grandma wants to say.

'—Daddy hasn't been home in weeks and weeks.'

'Whose daddy?'

'Daddy... my husband.'

The colour is seeping out even there in her famously bright eyes – the blue is greying, the white is yellowing. She trembles a little these days. Every cell in her is faltering. She is blurring into death. Cara squeezes Grandma's shoulder firmly, as though the sensation might align her with this time and place and straighten out something between them.

'Daddy,' says Grandma, irritated. 'You're not stupid. You know who I mean.'

Her fingers tighten, and in a whoosh of panic Cara has a

sense of toppling down, of being weighted into Grandma's squeaky special chair, the stagnant feet, the muddled world she is sinking into. Cara lifts the hand to her mouth and kisses it again. Over the new smells there is a veil of scented lotion. It's something appropriately subtle – white musk or wild rose – something expensive that one of the aunts bought her, but still the fragrance is too robust for the dusty skin and the dusty hair and the flabby breath of a body closing down.

'You know who – Daddy. Who do you think?' says Grandma. 'Dinny! My husband, Dennis Kearney. Have none of you noticed he's been gone now for weeks and weeks?'

Then she raises an eyebrow into a sneering arch, and Cara doesn't recognise her. *She is testing my integrity,* thinks Cara, *she is challenging me to say it: he is dead.* After a pause, during which Megan gives a splutter of exasperation and plonks down cross-legged on the floor, Cara says, 'Don't worry.'

'Worry? Oh no. I don't worry. I never worry about that. We trust each other. But it is so strange, isn't it? Still you don't sleep. It is so hard to sleep alone. You don't get used to that, you know. Sleeping without them. I think you understand, don't you?'

She looks intently at Cara with a quivering stare, like the screen on an old television set that needs to be slapped into sense.

Cara tries to force Grandma's cuticles down a little. Despite all the hand lotion, they are grafted fast to the ridged nail and threaten to split.

'Will I paint your nails for you, Grandma?'

'Ha. So you can laugh at me?'

'No, Grandma.'

'Look at this stupid thing!'

She lifts her hand to show the plastic ring Aunt Aoife has furnished her with; a wad of mottled blue plastic set in sharp alloy, where her turquoise ring used to be.

'Stupid thing. Do they think I'm some sort of eejit?'

From across the room, a nurse who is administering tea smiles at her encouragingly, as at an act of charity. Cara kisses her grandma – her face and hands and shoulders. She strokes her hair like a lonely child with a much-loved pet. To the nurses all these grandmothers must look alike. They don't know what Grandma is; her harsh beauty, her dark eyebrows and sensual lips. All the life there was once in this dying body that has menstruated and sweated and given birth and howled with grief and tugged Cara's mane violently into a too-tight French plait. Someone removed the painting that Grandma brought here with her – a small oil portrait Grandad made of her when they were young and living in Soho. It was taken down off the wall of her little room and replaced with a clip-framed print. The nurses couldn't know, from that dull print, the life in that work, the sense of breath and sound, the disconcerting glossiness of her belly and the crimson shadows of her thigh.

Cara kisses the yellow-padded fingertips. She rubs the old palm vigorously as though to stimulate the tired waters and all the oily secretions of a living body.

'Mammy, tum *ooooon*!'

Cara swipes at Megan's nose with a tissue from a big box

on the coffee table, but there is no satisfaction in it – the snot is endless. Does she take proper care of Megan? Does she get enough iron? And B vitamins?

'That child's not healthy-looking. Blue mouth.'

'Megan's got a bit of a cold, haven't you, darling?'

Megan sits on the floor, glaring up at her. There is a purple tinge beneath her eyes, and her lips are pale.

'Well, she doesn't eat enough,' says Cara, 'and she can't eat eggs. You know I read you can use chickpea flour as an egg replacement. You can even make quiches with it. I bought chickpea flour and I'm going to try it. Megan might like them.'

'Is that right.'

'Yes. I'll bring you one to try. I have to go, Grandma. I'll see you tomorrow...' She kisses Grandma briskly, 'Bye bye.' But she is tugged back by the hand like a wayward puppy on a lead—

'What's that?' Grandma points.

'There's a baby in my tummy,' says Cara. 'A baby girl, they think – another one!' She laughs to try to make Grandma laugh at her for having lots of girls, but she gives a raspy sigh and raises her eyes to heaven.

'Oh. You think this is funny? I will not get one, you know.'

'One what?'

'One of those. I will get nothing in my belly now, will I? We had one once, our little boy, but I will never make anything now.'

'But you have three children, Grandma. Aoife and Sinéad and...'

'So you say. Did I tell you Daddy's been away, for weeks and weeks and not a word? Nothing. And nothing on the news. Not a word about him. Ah no. I'm not worried though.'

She taps her thick fingernails on the arm of the chair with a slow, muted panic that demands an audience.

'It doesn't matter,' she says, 'but… well, you know yourself, Cara. It's the night. It's the night. At night it's hard. It's hard to sleep without him.'

42

FREYA'S PHONE GIVES a little trill and vibrates three times against her thigh, but she resists the urge to pull it out while the woman speaks.

'Look, love,' the woman says, 'we aren't interested in the ins and outs of people's private lives.' She picks up a sheet of printed paper, and waves it. 'The bottom line is this – these are the documents you need. They won't process the application without these documents, it's that simple. That's just the way it is.'

Jem pulls at Freya's sleeve and says very quietly, 'Your phone, Mammy.'

'Thanks, little man, I'll look at it in a minute.'

'Listen I'm finishing up now,' says the woman. 'Sorry it hasn't worked out for you. You seem well-heeled enough. I'm sure you'll figure something out.'

The reception desk is very high. Freya has put the application form down flat on the marble top, and she can't look at it without going up on her tiptoes.

'But do you understand the situation? I have no contact with my mother…'

'Look, if you're fighting with your mother it's really not our concern... As far as we're concerned you've been in third-level education since leaving school – you're the financial responsibility of your parents. If your parents are under the threshold you can apply for funding by providing proof of their income. If they're not, you can't. They can write a letter saying they won't support you, but that's not usually very successful... that usually turns out to be a scam.'

'But there's no way my mother will write me a letter or give me her bank statements or anything like that... I have no way of getting any proof of anything. I was raised by my grandmother...'

'Is she your legal guardian?'

'I'm twenty-four!'

'I'm sure you get a single mother's allowance or whatever.'

'No, you can't get that if you're in full-time education...'

'Well, tell me this,' says the woman, 'you're in fourth year now, is that right?'

'I just started in fourth year, but I can't pay the registration fee or buy the books or anything. I'm supposed to be...'

'I find it very hard to believe you're hard up, love, to be honest, judging by the cut of you. Your blouse and your accent and all. And three years at Trinity. How did you live for the last three years if you'd no parents and no money?'

'My grandmother...'

'Right, so ask her to sort you out for fourth year.'

'No, she's in a home now, she's not—'

Her phone sounds again, and Jem yanks her cuff: 'Mammy, you got another message.'

'Yes, thank you, Jem, I'll get it in a minute.'

The woman lifts Freya's form between the tip of her thumb and her forefinger, and hands it down to her.

'Could I write a letter, explaining? I live with my sister, she could verify...'

The woman rolls her eyes and gives a growl of private despair. 'Look, they have criteria,' she says. 'They're not going to change the criteria because you write a letter. They won't read it, to be honest. I won't process it. I'd be shot for wasting time... we have too many applications as it is...'

Freya makes her way down the steps of the City Council office, Jem skipping along beside her.

'Are you going to read your messages, Mammy?'

'Shit' she says, 'it's nearly six, the parking must be up...'

Jem's lips pull small in panic. 'Oh no, Mammy,' he says, 'are they going to clamp us?'

'I don't know, Jem. Let's just hurry.'

'Don't worry, Mammy! Come on, Mammy, run.' He grabs her hand and pulls her down the steps, his bony fingers slippery on hers, his feet clacking like a tap-dancer's – and the guilt nicks her gut. She shouldn't have said that to him.

43

GRANDMA IS SNORING NOW, jaw open. Her dentures have dislodged, turning her face into a totemic mask with two mouths – one an open cavern, the other baring teeth. Her cheeks have dropped flat to the jaw; long, strained lines running down them.

In another five minutes, her sleep will deepen and Cara will be able to slip quietly away.

Megan, who has been wandering around the perimeter of the room, approaches with a pile of leaflets. She plops them onto Cara's lap, proud as a cat with its kill.

'Oh. Where did you get these, Megan?'

Megan points to a tall plastic display by the door. 'For tolouring,' she says, 'tan I?'

Cara nods and roots a biro out from her jacket pocket.

The leaflet is entitled 'New Cuisine for the Elderly'. It's about a pilot project – the rest home is going to be one of the first in the country to avail itself of 3D-printed food. On the cover, there are pictures of the dishes they will be serving – a plate of counterfeit sausages, an imitation chicken breast complete with gravy, and a platter of strawberry-shaped and strawberry-coloured foam fruits. The 3D-printed food will taste and look exactly like traditional meals, claims the leaflet, except that the texture is specially designed for those with mastication difficulties. 'No more mash for Grandma!' it says. 'Now the elderly can enjoy a Sunday roast with all the familiar tastes and presentation…' It will be coming soon to the home at no extra cost.

Kneeling at a low coffee table, her tongue wiping at her upper lip, Megan inks out the eyes of a distinguished old man in a lemon cardigan who is smiling at the camera, a spoon of spongey sausage about to enter his mouth.

There is a rogue leaflet a little taller than the others, and a darker shade of blue, sticking up from the pile. Cara pulls it out: a picture of an old lady sitting in a pool of dim light, her head in her hands.

'Don't stay silent,' it says. 'Elder abuse is real.'

It has been almost six months since she made that report. A few weeks later there was a 'family email' sent about by Aunt Aoife, saying that *someone has made false accusations of elder abuse,* and that *a woman came out and scared Grandma.* Bernie phoned Cara that evening. She said there was no doubt there was abuse going on. She said Aunt Aoife threatened to sue her, showed no concern whatsoever. 'All defence,' she said. 'Normally, if there is nothing going on, the family show concern; they want to know what's happening, they are worried about their relative…' She asked that any evidence be sent to her. 'It's not over. They won't get away with it… you will have to take action…'

'What action?' asked Cara.

'I'll be in touch,' Bernie said. 'I have to speak to my supervisor. Your aunt has threatened to sue and I understand she is very wealthy… it's not ideal.'

A week later, the new team of carers was fired, and Grandma was moved in here, and Bernie stopped returning her calls.

Beneath the words 'Elder abuse', is a list of all the things that qualify. 'If you, or someone you know is experiencing any of the above, it is your duty to contact us.' The list ranges from hitting and stealing to 'pressure' and 'threats of abandonment'.

She slips her hand carefully from her grandmother's. She needs to collect Denise from her rehearsal at six. She needs to get the dinner on and get the kids ready for bed. Touching Megan's dark, tangled hair (she needs a bath – when did Cara last wash Megan's hair?), she gestures with her head towards the exit. The child nods and places the biro softly on the carpet with the leaflet. Before she leaves though, she pats her great-grandmother's hand casually, as though greeting a good dog, and says softly, 'Bye-bye, Mimi.' Grandma's waking is hardly perceptible – a change in the rhythm of her breath – but then she opens her eyes, and her gums find her teeth, and her face opens in surprise and a look of imbecilic joy. 'Oh,' she says, 'oh Cara! You have come!'

'Yes, Grandma, we just popped in…'

'And the little one. Which one is this now? Not my little boy, is it?'

'No, Grandma, this is my little girl. My big girl: four soon. This is Megan.'

'Cara, here you are! Cara. My Cara. You have no idea how happy I am that you're here at last. I've been waiting for weeks. Now listen, they're telling me nothing about Daddy... and there's nothing on the news about him at all.' She pats her hair. 'Oh dear... Cara, can you help me? I can't find the hairdressers.'

'It's only open on Thursdays, Grandma. Not today.'

Aunt Aoife explained in her 'family update' email that they chose this home because there was a nail bar down the corridor and a hairdresser on Thursdays. 'Not like an old folks' home at all! And we all know how vain Grandma is!' She put an emoticon at the end of the email – a yellow face smiling mutely.

'They were just here you know. What was it they told me? Did I give you money once?'

'Yes,' says Cara, 'you helped us with a deposit for the house.'

'Aha. So they say...'

Grandma taps out the pace on the arm of the chair. This is a test of some sort, and Cara doesn't know the answer.

'That was years ago, Grandma.'

'Yes. And stupid goose you didn't know better than to tell them.'

'Tell who?'

Her grandmother continues to drop her fingers, slowly, one by one on the armrest.

'I thought you had the sense to keep that quiet. Fifi was put out. She is always like that, doing the sums, my Feefs. And Sinéad always following along like a stupid pup. Well, Aoife has all the bank records and there she is going through it with a red pen. Now they make me sign cheques here and cheques there. They say I was not fair – the things we bought to look after you. They want to make everything just. *Just*… My Fi – where did I get her? Has life been so unfair on her, after all? Did they sell my house?'

'I don't know, Grandma.'

'Don't lie to me, darling, you of all people.'

'I really don't know, Grandma.'

'I think they did you know. I think I signed. I think they sold that house we bought, me and Daddy. And the mews where he worked, I suppose that too… I think I signed just now. They were here just now. I think I signed. You will find out, will you? And tell me?'

Cara nods. Grandma sighs and shuts her eyes and the tapping reduces to an angry twitch of her knuckles. Her mouth makes a little twisting spasm and she says, 'Have they no shame?'

Cara holds the hand still. 'Relax, Grandma,' she says. 'It doesn't matter now. Relax.'

Grandma looks at her like a scolded child, eyes wide and wet. 'They have no shame,' she says. 'How is it that they have no shame?' and her head jiggles and falls back against the head-rest. Cara rubs the hand – the pasty palm and then the front, where the skin folds like clingfilm, too moist and too white, and blotched with soft brown spots like the ones that blister on pancakes.

'Oh dear, Cara. Can you help me? Is there a toilet somewhere?'

'Let's go back to your room, Grandma.'

Cara loves her grandmother's big white knickers. They are the same ones she has always bought for Cara – 'to protect your kidneys'. They cover the whole bum and reach the belly button. Cara leaves them scrunched in piss on the floor while she cleans Grandma's legs with wet wipes, and helps her into new ones. 'This foot now,' she says, rubbing the long, sinewy shin.

Cara pulls the big pants up over Grandma's groin, her hips, her navel. Cara's throat clogs. Her belly button; the place they tied before severing Grandma from her mother. Perhaps they taped cotton and a penny over it, the way Grandma did with Denise and Megan and Peig, to prevent a hernia or an 'outy'. The ripe little knot could be a toddler's, though the skin around it is puckered and dragging. It must have popped outwards with each of Grandma's pregnancies to become a sensitive little dome of a thing, the weakest point in the fortress of her great belly.

'Oh Cara, wouldn't you be ashamed?'

'No, Grandma,' says Cara, 'I wouldn't be ashamed. Didn't you change our nappies for years?'

That was the wrong thing to say. Cara meant to remind her that like her she is a woman, like her she is a mother, like her she is well equipped to deal with piss and blood and shit.

'But I know how you feel. Oh Grandma, they had to clean me up when Megan was being born. I was so embarrassed…'

But her grandmother cannot listen any more to stories like

this; stories of birth that might bind them as women, sweep disgrace into pride. Narrative doesn't fit into the new shapes of Grandma's mind.

Cara changes Grandma's skirt and puts her slippers on. She rolls up the wet clothes and pushes them into a plastic bag. When she comes out of the en suite, cupping Grandma's elbow, Megan is sitting on the bed, holding the remote control.

'Tan I make it go up and down?' she asks, and, picking up a piece of knitting – a stringy strip of acrylic yarn, hardly held together, all dropped stitches and uneven rows – 'What's Mimi making?'

'I don't know, baby. No, don't touch the control.'

Cara helps her grandma to move slowly towards the bed. She is going to be late for Denise; she really is going to be late now. The old lady pauses. Balancing carefully with one hand on Cara's shoulder, she touches her sparse hair, straightens her skirt and smoothes a hand over her bottom. She sighs and composes herself and suddenly her features rearrange and she has her own face again. Then she continues the slow journey to bed.

When she is lying on her back, she breathes out, and squeezes Cara's hand. 'Cara,' she says, 'I need to tell Daddy. Tell him – will you? He'll know what to do. I don't want to frighten you chicken, but I have dreams – our little boy… Tell Daddy, will you? I had a dream we lost him. He needs to watch him. You'll tell him, won't you?'

'It's okay.'

'Okay? Are you mad? No, Cara, it's not okay. You have to tell him. Did you never have that, Cara, where you dream a thing that's going to happen?'

'I'll tell him, Grandma.'

Then her grandmother looks distracted, as though she has just realised something. Her face grows harsh and masculine in a way that Cara has never seen before, some stiff resolve in her straight mouth. Her voice is low and certain.

'Send the child out,' she says.

Cara doesn't like leaving Megan alone. She sends a message quickly, asking Freya to get Denise, then hands Megan her phone and tells her to sit at the door and not to move, and that she can play the 'Acorn Maths' in the phone.

'I have to go soon, Grandma,' she says, 'but I'll be back… and maybe Freya will come in, if she can. Can you try to rest?'

'Cara,' she says, 'I changed the will, you know.'

'Don't worry about that, Grandma.'

'Do you hear what I'm telling you? You won't be short.'

'I have everything I need, Grandma. Don't worry… We all have everything we need.'

'Well, did you ever? Wouldn't you be ashamed?'

'No. I wouldn't be ashamed—'

'Will you get me something, Cara? Get me some pills?'

'I'll ask the nurses, but I don't think it's time for your tablets… are you in pain?'

'Stupid goose. You know what I mean. Something to finish it.'

Cara kisses her temple. 'Rest, Grandma.'

'I am counting on you, chicken. Get me some pills.'

'The nurses will give you your pills…'

'I see.' Grandma nods. She makes a clicking sound with her mouth, and it's that look again – nasty, sneering – but this time Cara recognises it. It's the face Grandma made once when Cara lied to her about smoking – a face that says, *You have crossed the line. You have disappointed me now and nothing will ever be the same…*

'Well I thought you were a brave girl. I thought you had guts, you of all people. You don't get used to this, you know. You don't understand, but you will. I don't usually ask things of you, do I darling? Do I ever ask things of you? Get me what I am asking, Cara. You're a good girl. I'm counting on you to do it.'

44

IT HAPPENED TO MOLLY once, on her first pregnancy. She was walking up to their little apartment. She still had a cough that had dragged on from winter into spring, and it caught her suddenly, there on the stairs. She stopped with her hand on the banister and the shopping basket over her other wrist. It was a high, tickly cough – nothing dramatic – and it happened, just like that. She only felt a little release – oh, but the relief – and she squeezed her thighs together but as she stood there she wet herself so completely that it pooled in the sole of one shoe. It wasn't the waters. She knew that. She continued up the stairs and into the flat, carrying the basket with onions and a very expensive cauliflower. She washed by the basin and put on her other skirt. Then she soaped and rinsed her soiled clothes, and then she went out and cleaned up the little trail on the steps and no one ever knew.

That was her little boy she was carrying. That didn't happen with the girls. The girls were different altogether. She was sicker with the girls, but she didn't wet herself.

She should feel relief, yes; she should allow the things her body is doing now. After her little boy was born, she enjoyed bleeding helplessly into the big brown cotton towels. She enjoyed every messy thing her body did – the milk staining the sheets, the syrup smell of her sweat.

But this fills her with panic instead, the piss creeping slowly into the bed, onto her thighs. She could enjoy being lazy, pissing into the big nappies like her own Grandma did; if it wasn't for the people who trick her and profit from her. The nurses who change their hair every day – sometimes candy-pink ribbons and sometimes blonde, trying to make a fool of her so that she doesn't know their names and they laugh at her; they chuckle at the things she says and it isn't kind.

And she has been a fool, because – Aoife explained it all – Cara, who she had loved, Cara wanted to profit from her. She had given things to Cara, things she doesn't even remember giving her, and now Cara is saying she is mad. Now Cara wants her chequebook removed. Cara wants her in a madhouse with the halfwits. Aoife explained it all and asked, 'Do you understand, Mammy?' And then the man too, Aoife's husband who is a solicitor and very respectable, he came and explained it all to her. She has been tricked, horribly tricked. She signed a thing that was not just. But she can correct it. They are sorting it out. Dinny would not have been so foolish, but he will not be angry when he gets here because he has been away for so long.

Her Aoife is old now, with a frown and hurt red daubed across her cheeks and nose; jaded from a life sitting pretty. More power to her to have all that money and that nice house and a husband you can rely on and nothing to do but enjoy it. Except that she is sad, her Fifi. Sad from nothing. And didn't they give her all she could need and she shouted today, whooping like an alien thing, telling off the nurses – poor little girls who try their best and they far from their mothers. One of them with a name like you never heard but Molly likes it – Precious – but she says she puts her name Paula on her curriculum vitae because, though they don't let on, the Irish have become a closed people where once they were welcoming. Precious has a grandmother back home in Nigeria who raised her and is old now and needs medicine and company. Imagine that she is looking after Molly instead of her own grandmother. Molly knows how that shame would feel, how it would make you squirm and bristle and how it could turn you sharp after time.

Her Aoife makes her ache; the way her looks betray something haggard and wrong in her. A bitter thread pulling through her, twisting her face and her high, tough shoulders, where she was soft and fatty and silly once, chubby wrists on her hips and buttery rolls on her legs and the fur up the back of her neck that Dinny could kiss and smile about. *Our little piggledy poo.*

How could that be her Fifi, who left in an angry flapping, all business, and her bag with many buckles? She needed to see her beautician about her skin, for she had a terrible case of red face that had finally been diagnosed.

Molly is glad to be left in peace here in her bed, but lonely too. Lonely is the word she has been searching for and she is glad she found it now. She will say it aloud, maybe, next time she has a visitor. She will say it to Cara. 'I am lonely, Cara.' Lonely without Dinny.

She needs them to close the curtains to make the night go away and she has pain but she cannot tell them where for it feels to be coming from inside all of her and from a great, deep place that was always there. She never liked pills. They were always pushed on her while she refused but now she wants them and no one will come. When she is at home she brews her own cures for things with plants and alcohol. The bitters take so long to ferment in the hot press and she has to turn the bottle clockwise every ten days. But now the garden is all dried up, so she needs some pills to blot out all this aching Aoife makes in her with her frown. And Lily. Lily with her far-apart eyes and shrieking and her ideas. What was that word she found for her?

Dinny can laugh at Molly sometimes, for being a queer one and spooky with her potions. Of course, her Granny Casey was a witch with tarot cards and a poison-yellow soup for a missed monthly and though those were dirty things to know it was because the motherline was dark. Tinkers once, with black hair. She was not like that with her clever head… Oh, her hands. Molly's hands are a fright – spots on them like toad-skin. Was it work made them that way? Washing up and that? And not wearing gloves for the cleaning on account of she can't stand the smell of rubber on her after. Sister Celestine's skin was always so silky and cool when she took your hands in hers and spoke gentle, and Mam was angry when Molly cried and said she would miss Sister Celestine's hands, for no one's touch was so soft: *Well wouldn't my hands be soft too, praying all day and never a cup to wash or a nappy to scrub, never an onion to chop…*

Cooking, Molly doesn't mind. Cooking is another thing altogether. She is never hungry for she tastes as she cooks and then she can sit and eat very little with Dinny and the children and it does not disturb her to go back and forth, serving. She could eat now, she thinks. That lovely quiche that Cara makes – such a clever little thing and how she finds the time Molly couldn't tell you – a sweet and salty buttery quiche she makes with tomatoes and cheese on the top like an Italian thing. Why didn't Cara come with the quiche? Too busy with the children, she would say; too busy looking after the children and here is Molly ringing and ringing on the bell that will make Cara come. Ringing and ringing and Cara must hear but she is too busy and it is hard not to be angry but she is a good girl thinking always of her children. Molly pulls the bell again. She will wait. If Cara does not come soon with the quiche and the tablets she will phone her.

She doesn't feel like today is the day that Dinny will come. It will not be today so she needn't worry about her hair and all that, and her fingernails are clean anyway, even if Freya has not painted them for her. She will ask Freya to do her eyebrows because that makes a big difference. She cannot greet Dinny with white eyebrows like a mad old witch and Freya does such a good job with a little bit of colour and sometimes a scissors to trim.

Dinny laughs at her because she could be spooky before, knowing things before they happened; knowing a letter would arrive before it did or that someone was expecting or dead or—

But it was not always nice to know things. That time the

little Reilly girl died and the father came to the pub, a face on him like a thing being dragged up a washboard and when Dada came to tell them, it was *she* told *him* – for she had seen it all. As she sat on the step making socks by the streetlight she had seen what her dada was seeing in the pub with the poor man's face and the other men looking at him and knowing it was too bad to ask.

A queer thing, that, the sort of thing her grandmother knew about but Molly did not want to learn it. So queer and out of order that she went to a priest – she who had such unsteady faith – and asked him to take it out of her and the priest looked frightened and he put his hands on her head and mumbled but still it kept on so that when she dreamed of their little boy stretched out on a table and she saw his lovely face thick like dough and his lips draining, she woke crying and could not drive it from her mind and she knew it would happen for she had felt for some time that it was too nice to be real; being together with enough to eat and loving each other and their beautiful little boy and Dinny kissing her back at night and putting his arms around her and everything nicer than she could have imagined. And Dinny had been frightened too, when she told him, and then when it happened how was it that he didn't blame her? Or is that it? Is that why she hasn't had a word from him now for weeks and weeks?

Her arm hurts. What has she been doing, clenching the bell like a mad old bat, her hand dead from hanging upright. What is she like? She should be ashamed to be this way. She cannot let Cara see her this way, though they have been summoned and will be here soon with the quiche and the nail polish, and what will they think of Molly whose bosom is not soft and welcoming the way they know it, but all tired now and knobbled under her nightie?

After he was born she fed him all night, sitting in a chair and savouring every moment of his living. So maybe she had known then too – in the first days after his birth – that he would not be long on this earth, for them who had lived had never kept her up like that with the miracle of themselves, drinking all of her into the rise and fall of his breathing and his lips like his father's and his fingers splaying like little blades of moon-light, and the nails so tiny and every detail of him complete so that she could not sleep for wonder—

People thought she might feel guilty for it but she could not, for it was she who had been wounded. He would never have thought he would die and there was no terror in his eyes, just confusion perhaps, and indignation, as he waited for her to help him for she did not scream – she did not want to scare him – but made soothing sounds and told him he was alright while she banged his back to bring it up but instead that banging must have knocked it down and made him die – that's what people thought – for you should punch the belly of a choking child, not bang the back and she should have known that but she didn't but she was puzzled too, while she did it, a little angry even, for he was a clever child and it was not like him to do a thing like he did – reaching into the bowl of soaking beans for he knew better. But had she told him not to? She hadn't told him not to and she had left it there and was it on purpose she had done that, to atone perhaps for things she half knew?

For just that morning as she rinsed the smalls she thought of her cousin May sent away and not spoken of and her Aunty Nora slow and steely after that and why had silly May – silly soft May, and so plain it was a shock to imagine how she had got that way – why had she not gone to Grandma for some yellow soup? And what did Grandma think of it all and why did nobody say about it, except with sighs and tears held in, and shaking heads and that look Mam had, that would send needles into you; that look like something too bad had happened and could not be unmade. The baby died anyway. She heard it from Kat many years later, and poor silly May had fallen mad in there washing other women's napkins. And they said then, after that, Cara or one of the children told her it was the nuns who sold those babies or killed them, though that would be a hard thing to believe with the soft hands they had and soft ways, and why had Molly never looked for May though she thought of her often? Stupid girl, May. But wouldn't you be ashamed, your own cousin, to never seek her out, to never help her out, even later when they had so much money. They could have helped her, certainly they could. She was afraid – was that it? Afraid of what she might find there, May an old halfwit… The baby died anyway, so for what, May? For what, May, did you go in like that, a martyr like that to waste away your life for a child who didn't want you either?

She had atoned hadn't she, for May's lost child and lost life, and for her sister Kat too and her mam, hadn't she? With her little boy. For nothing could be so bad as holding him there and knowing, suddenly, that the thing had happened. Her little boy.

Could that be how it was with her Lily too, with the thing that's not right about her and the fatherless grandchildren. But what of Jem then, with the eyes of the little boy they lost...

Was it for other things, maybe, that he had been taken from her? For she and Dinny, up in that little room. Unbuttoning his shirt like that.

Or is it just the way the world is? The Reilly girl, and her cousin May. A world full up of magnificently terrible things – the things you see on the news, the things people do to one another, people in uniforms, people with money. Is it that there are blameless little sadnesses in it too, that run right down into the guts of this earth and change everything?

They put him in a cardboard box because that was before they had much money and what with the cost of Cremnitz White... What a stupid girl she was, wasting money on that cauliflower that time; weeping about it that night with Dinny's arms around her and her little boy turning in her belly. Death was not a thing he understood. There was just surprise for him and then nothing, but for her the moment stretched out – his mute shock and her banging his back and hoping she would hear him breathe now and cough but knowing he would not, for the thing had already happened, long ago.

45

THERE'S NO CLAMP ON the wheel.

'Phew!' says Jem. 'They must have been nice clampers. They must have known we didn't mean to be late.'

Freya opens the driver's door and reaches around to unlock the back. 'Get in, little man,' she says. 'Strap yourself in. Good boy.'

In the car, she lifts her feet onto the seat, rests her head on her knees. Freya loves being in this car.

'Where are we going, Mammy?'

'Home, little man.'

'To DenDen's home?'

'Yes, Jem.'

'When are we going home to Mimi's?'

'We'll have to see…'

She needs to sort something else out for them; a flat for just the two of them. But so far, she can't even get it together to pay her college charges, let alone rent a flat. Will she have to drop out? Is she homeless? Could it be this easy to go from middle class to flat broke? The woman in the County Council office didn't seem to think so.

There is a trust fund – Grandma and Grandad set them up for her and Cara. Cara used hers towards her wedding and her house, but Freya has never touched hers. There should be more than enough in there, Cara said, to finish college, get a flat, keep her and Jem going until she's on her feet... but when she went to the bank to ask about it, they said she needed the trustees' signatures. 'My grandad's dead, though, she said, and Grandma's not well. I'm twenty-four...'

'They're not the trustees,' said the man in the bank. He lowered his voice, leaned in. 'It changed. The new trustees are Aoife O'Carroll and Eileen Kearney.' She emailed Aoife, who said Freya must have been misinformed. There's nothing left in that trust, she said, after deducting Jem's fees and 'all sorts of other things'.

At Cara's house, she hasn't been paying her way. She's been adding things to the shopping list on a Wednesday night – mandarins for Jem, fancy youghurts for her, and she never offers to pay for them. She will have to sort something out. Yet there is comfort in living with Cara, and the gentle, hardworking man she has married. When Freya falls asleep at night, she feels safe, the family bonds wrapping the house like a cloak.

Sometimes the three of them sort the laundry together, chatting, or watching the news on the laptop. On weekend nights they sit outside on the decking, tatty fleece blankets wrapped around themselves, and drink gin and tonics out of jam jars and chipped mugs.

For years Freya thought nothing of raising Jem alone – if anything, she thought, it was easier than all the bureaucracy co-parenting must entail. But she can see now why married parents say things like, 'Aren't you amazing, doing it all alone,' or 'Isn't he a credit to you – can't be easy doing it alone…' Cara and Pat are partners in a way Freya had never considered before. At night Freya hears moans and whispers and quiet, gentle chatter from their room, and she knows she is lonely.

'Your phone, Mammy. You got messages, remember?'

'Yes, thanks, darling. I'll look at them now.'

The first two are from Dermot:

You said I could be involved but you haven't exactly made an effort to keep in touch, have you? Well, you'll get what's coming to you. That kid is half mine you seem to forget that when it suits you. Oh well see you in court bitch.

Then, sent three minutes later:

ignoring me wont get you anywhere slut tomorrow we'll let a judge decide who's the psycho

A message from Unknown says:

Aoife wants to know how much you got for having Jem. She needs to know asap.

hugs and kisses xxx Mammy

Then a WhatsApp from Cara:

Wt Grandma can't leave can u pick up Den @ 6 @ music? U free 2 go 2 Grandma 2night she lonely?

'What are your messages, Mammy?'

Freya is dizzy. The air seems to tighten around her. Everything swaggers – the phone, the steering wheel, the pedals beneath her feet. They couldn't give him access, could they? They couldn't give him custody. To protect Jem – that is her only job. That is all that matters.

When she starts the engine, the radio comes on '… there were maybe fifty babies,' says a voice, 'all wrapped and placed on shelves, but the adult bodies were thrown into a pit, you know like very much without ritual…'

Freya switches it off. 'We've to go and get Den,' she says, 'then we'll go home. I just want to give Mimi a call, so keep very quiet while I have her on speaker okay? We don't want to confuse her.'

'Okay. Home to DenDen's?'

'Yes.'

'When can we go home to Mimi's?'

'We'll see, Jem. Stop asking all the time, Jem. I'll tell you when I know.'

Stopped at the lights, Freya calls the rest home. She slots the phone into the loudspeaker so that the sound of ringing fills the car.

'Okay, super quiet now, Jem, okay? Yes hello, I wonder if you could put me through to Molly Kearney please? Room twenty-six…'

46

'ONLY IF YOU LET me play.'

'No, Megan.' Cara pulls the phone off Megan. 'I need to call the music school. We're very late for Denise.'

She tries to get the seatbelt across Megan, but the child squirms away, snatching for the phone. 'LET ME PLAY!'

Cara opens the passenger door and shoves the phone into the glove compartment. Some tapes clatter onto the floor, some envelopes and scrunches of clean paper.

'Megan, sit down and let me strap you in. We're late. I don't have time for this.'

'No.' Megan crosses her arms and looks up at Cara, her lips drawn down into a parody of sadness; eyes pink under the low black brow and her whole face a blur of saliva and snot and tears. 'Not less you gib it to me. GIB ME VE PHONE!'

'Megan, if this is how you react when I let you play then I'm not going to let you go on the phone at all anymore. Ever again. Sit down.'

'No!'

'Sit!—' Cara grabs Megan by both shoulders, squeezing her

a little too hard, kneeing her lap – 'Down!' There's a hollow plastic bop as the child is plonked onto her booster seat. Megan won't allow herself to be folded in. She straightens her legs, twists off the seat, a flurry of elbows and squeals and whips of snotted hair, arms flailing for the glove compartment. She grabs a bill, scrunches it and throws it at Cara. It hits Cara's nose. 'Enough!'

She slaps Megan hard on the hip, and the child's face drops. Cara joggles her into the seat, holds her there with one hand and pulls the seatbelt with the other. Megan lets herself be strapped in. A silence of disbelief and her mouth shuts in indignation, but as the car starts she throws her head back and lets out a cry like a cartoon baby.

'Waaaaaaahhhh! You – hit-ted – meeeee!'

'You have to be strapped in. It's dangerous not to be strapped in. I'm sorry, Megan. I'm sorry I slapped you.'

'Sowy's NOT DOOD ENOUGH!'

'Quiet, Megan. I have to call the school and I have to call Daddy or Freya. Someone has to collect Denise.'

Megan fills the car with a long, metallic screech. Cara looks at the phone. No reply from Freya. Eight per cent battery.

'Shut up, Megan.'

She dials Pat. The phone rings on loudspeaker while she drives out the gates of the nursing home. He doesn't pick up. Stopped before the main road, she searches her contacts for the music school.

'Megan, be quiet while I make this call.'

'Noooo. I will NOT BE KVIET! YOU HIT-TED MEEEEEE!'

'Shut up, Megan. I need to hear them.'

She joins a line of traffic. The light is red. A wind whines in through a hole under her car. While she listens to the ringtone, she picks up the ball of paper, and smooths it out.

FINAL DEMAND

Re: Arrears of Tax

Dear Sir/Madam,

I hereby request payment of €4,094.31 in respect of arrears of tax. A schedule detailing the amount due is attached. Interest on the amounts due has been accruing from the due date shown, at the appropriate rate.

Failing payment within 7 days the amount in question may be the subject of court proceedings for recovery of the debt.

'Hello, Tawny Park?' Then the phone goes silent. A blue ring appears, turning for a second, and the screen goes black.

'Battery's gone. Fuck.'

'YOU HIT-TED MEEE.'

'Stop it, Megan, I need to think.'

'Mean Mammy! MEAN MAMMEEE! You Hit Ted Mee yee yee yee.'

Cara can feel it like something lashing loose from its peg, something heavy and leathery, something tight and dark and private, unfurling itself, opening its mouth, something angry at being forgotten. She hardly knows she's doing it and then she has turned around and she is screaming too, screaming at her daughter, her nails digging into the tired upholstery, her head banging against the headrest, her cheeks wet with tears and her throat raw with it, 'SHUT UP SHUT UP SHUT UP!'

47

MOLLY NODS INTO THE phone, speaking as loudly as she can, to be sure they hear her from wherever they are.

'Oh, Freya. Yes. Thank you for calling. It's very nice of you to think of me.'

She cannot find the person, but the name sends a surge of something through her – love and worry, love and worry. Freya, Freya, Freya. There is a snagging concern about Freya, something that makes her fret. It is not Cara but like Cara. Freya is love and worry, like Cara, but Molly can't find what Freya is – the face or the status of Freya. She must conceal this. She does not want to be found out. She does not want to be laughed at or fooled by them all. She must keep her cards close to her chest, under her chin, the backs facing out, showing only the purple clover pattern, the backs of the cards in the pack that they bought once in a newsagent, she and Dinny – and they were expensive – for a train journey to Galway, the cards they bought packed in a little felt pouch and each back the same. Rows and rows of slanted clovers, the pack piled on the rigid little table between them, and then her cards with the faces pressed into her neck and his cards with the faces pressed to his chest, bending his head low and smiling up like that while he bluffs, so that she loves him and she can't wait until he leans over to kiss her – though she has the feeling now that there are too many for her toad-wobbly hands to hold, that her bones are rigid as ancient megaliths and the cards are slipping through like water, cascading down her body into her lap, onto the floor, the faces exposed—

'How was your tea? Did you have something nice, Grandma?'

'... excellent. Oh, excellent. You have no idea. Beautiful... fresh ingredients. That's the thing. When the ingredients are fresh you can't go wrong.' Who is she speaking to?

'What did you have for supper?'

Her mind grasps for it. The voice is one she loves. Like her sister's voice. Kat has had great disappointments in life.

'You are disappointed.'

'What did you have though, Grandma? What did you have for supper?'

Trying to catch her out. Trying to rattle her with all these questions when she is so tired and they know she doesn't have the answer but they want to catch her and she will not be caught.

'Yes,' she says, 'oh you have no idea. Beautiful.'

'But what did you have, Grandma?'

'Oh... I think it was a kind of soup Ka–. Very nice.'

She over-salted the cauliflower. That was it, she knew there was something. Watching Dinny's face as he ate – and there was she, delighted with herself for getting that cauliflower, and then she saw him wince as he chewed and she knew. It was a beautiful little thing, ivory white and young tight leaves. She couldn't really afford it but she had to have it, and she had gone to too much effort, perhaps – she didn't want to scrimp on the salt and she had used a lot of mace too, and she had gone overboard. She should just have boiled it and tossed it in butter. Dinny ate it anyway, and that was the worst part – watching him suffer through it. She was really big by then, with their first baby, and she had heartburn and she couldn't swallow a mouthful.

'It's Freya. Cara was with you earlier. It's Freya, Grandma.'

'Oh, Freya. Yes.'

'Well I'm glad it's nice, Grandma. Is there anything I could bring you for lunch tomorrow? They might let us eat together in the refectory, if I brought something?'

She knows the refectory. Decked out like a toy restaurant. White light. Red paper napkins rolled into clouded plastic cups. People wheeled to the table. Negresses wheel them in – tall with regal cheeks and funny hair like ribbons, black fingers with coloured jewels for nails, and paler on the palms, like they are holding handfuls of clean, dark earth that has made valleys hidden in the folds, so it would be easier to read their palms than hers, and in the wheelchairs the pale, balding halfwits who eat baby food, pushing at it with their tongues and the black ones catch it from their chins and spoon it back in. A dirty job, poor girls. But she too has an unpleasant task. She is to sit with the dribblers and play the hostess. She is introduced to them. She is as polite as she can be, she nods at them and invites them to sit with her, but they drop food from their mouths. She conceals her disgust with a small smile but what can she say to them? The lady with the little hat on her, black netting over her eyes, her face powdered like a death-mask, balls of pink lipstick and gravy and mash beside her mouth. Why has she come like this into Molly's home? Molly does not remember inviting her but she is afraid to say as much, in case she has forgotten, in case the lady is a good friend, or her sister-in-law, and Molly has forgotten because she is so tired these days and she forgets.

'Well, I hired some very good girls to help the halfwits to eat. They can be very nice and just as efficient as you or me.'

There was a little restaurant she was in with her sister once and they had rabbit and then some very nice coffee with a plate of four fine biscuits, each one different, and there was a French name for what they were. Her sister was there and they laughed together.

When her own children were young there were black babies starving and they used to knit cardigans for them, though Molly thought that couldn't have done much for babies starving and parching under the crackling sun.

She paid.

Molly paid, because Cara is only young and has children and she worries about how she pays for things and she likes an excuse to buy things for her. She said to Cara, 'They can train them to do all sorts of things. Amazing how they can learn things so quickly. They have brains alright, same as you and me.' And Cara looked angry and ashamed of her, but then she laughed at Molly and kissed her, and then she told people afterwards beside the Christmas tree. She told everyone and they laughed at her and shook their heads and her face burned but she had a glass of champagne also and they said, 'Your nose is red, from the champagne!' They liked to tease her but it was not to be cruel. Molly is no racist. She thinks it is terrible what was done to the blacks. She likes Black Power. Malcolm X, when he calmed down at the end. Muhammad Ali. You can't blame them for their rage, sure who wouldn't be raging after what was done to them all, women and children and all? She liked Orson Welles being Othello that time. Very attractive. But don't talk to her about Americans. She wants nothing to do with Americans. Don't talk to her about Americans. They took babies from their mothers, sold people like cattle at the market, men to work to death and women to pleasure themselves with. Now they even buy their babies like dolls to make believe with. That was the worst. To take a child from its mother. The thought that her Sinéad could do such a thing… 'We might adopt,' she says. No. No, Molly wouldn't have it. There were rich ladies in France who took black babies from their mothers so that the milk could be used for their own babies instead. Dinny told her that. The corners of his eyes jittering back tears. Those ladies were disgusting. They weren't ashamed of giving another woman their babies to feed while they lay back on a chaise longue. They had a very ugly time of it, the black women, and the men too. They must have felt ashamed to see their women like that, suckling another's child while their own perished on a boat. But there was black like the girls she hired to wheel the halfwits – black that was on the skin and not black but up close really brown, brown skin like her skin, cocoa-brown to protect against the sun. Full lips too. Fuller lips, usually. Lips that would be beautiful to paint if you mixed the colours right.

That was negro people. That was people, dark-skinned people, darker than the Spanish gypsy skin. But then there is another dark in the night; not people at all – shadow people in the night and they are another kind of black; black that is no colour. Black like a space in the world, like a string of paper dolls cut out of the night, their skulls a hole where teeth and eyes glint like pebbles by the moon. They have no skin because they are made of something else. There is black in the night and strange words in the night. In the night figures cut out of the air come marching and they are made of no-matter. They come carrying sacks of sand to stack up against the walls and block out the day. They walk in lines like shadows on the walls outside her windows and she hears them stack the sand against the back door and they have guns and they plant bombs and they throw babies at the fireplace and let their little skulls crack. She is fortunate to have no such beliefs as the lady in the netting and hat with her rosary in her fingers, muttering like a mad woman, shrieking suddenly, 'fruit of thy womb.' Fruit is an apple, isn't it? Cut into wedges for the children. Womb is where they turn in the dark and emerge into life and are slashed in the face. It was all for nothing because all the love and all the joy cannot be reeled back in because he lay dead like that, laid out in a cardboard box because they hadn't the money for a white one – she washed him and laid him out like a gift for the earth and they asked her what words she would like and told her they had a priest who would do the funeral like charity as though they could give her anything after he was dead and as though she could give him anything now with words that the priest would say.

There were things she loved in mass, things she missed – the part with the shaking all the hands, and the part with the bread. When she heard the mass in English for the first time, she was already a grown woman and a heretic (though it was only Dinny knew it) but when she heard it that time – oh, oh, the poetry of it. The priest lifted up the holy bread in two hands, saying, 'He took the bread, broke it, gave the bread to his disciples and said, "Take this all of you and eat it. This is my body, which is given up, for you."'

This is my body – the way he said that made a little chink in her, and he cracked the bread in two, and she felt a sweet tearfulness sweep up over her face – *which is given up, for you.*

The lady on the phone wants to sell her something. They all want something now. They all want her to sign things.

'No. Thank you. I am very happy with the service. I am very happy with my belief I do not want your religion, thank you.'

Molly will go happily to dust and let that be the end of it.

'I have to put Jem to bed, Grandma, but I will come in the morning to see you.'

If Molly can only push her mind a little bit, she knows she can understand what the voice is saying, but she is so tired and she cannot do it.

'Yes, yes, we will make an appointment. Okay,' she says, and drops the phone.

She is supposed to hang it in its cradle. Stupid woman. Stupid old woman she is now. Did you ever? Shouldn't she be ashamed of herself? It is dangling somewhere beneath her. It should be beside her. She pulls the spiralled wire and she feels the receiver bounce on the end but she cannot find it.

Molly's granddaughters must be clever things – going to university like that; flying along. She saw the library once – Freya brought her in to see all the books there were there in Trinity College Dublin – a long room with high walls like a cathedral; balconies and books stretching to the ceiling. Was it a jealous feeling she had in there, or pride, or what, or just the beauty of the place, she didn't know but a tearfulness leapt up in her. There are so many things Molly is never going to know now, but what of it? We all know different thing, isn't that it? The smell of books in there too, of old pages, careful letters, crispy spines. And polish. Floor polish and wood polish. A fine place.

She uses her hands to heave her legs off the bed, but she cannot stand. Her body feels too heavy. Then she remembers – she needs to be helped to the bathroom now because she has broken her leg or something from hopping over fences with Dinny. Stupid goose. At her age to be hopping over fences. But such fun she wouldn't miss it. She pulls the cord with the red toggle, but they don't come.

There are kind negresses and small Oriental girls with heart-shaped faces and straight black fringes and sweet high voices. These are the women who wash her, and paint her nails, and she is glad to have these women with her at this time, not men or nuns who could be hard sometimes, and could be disgusted by things. She cannot wait much longer here for Dinny... but what else can she do? She cannot leave without him. She must warn him to look after their little boy because it would be terrible for anything to happen. She could not bear it if anything was to happen. She must ring Freya and tell her to sieve the child's food before she gives it to him – press it through a sieve and squash any lumps out.

Her neck is very sore, very stiff. She must lie down to sleep because her neck is sore from bending down into her chest. She pulls the red toggle and hopes they will come soon. She hopes Dinny will come soon before they start with the heavy sacks, blocking up the back door and the front gate so that he won't be able to get in, stacking them up one on top of the other like the bodies of soldiers until there is no light at the window anymore. Black and Tans black in the night and the inhuman things they could do... The boy who was touched forever after, walking up and down Manor Street, muttering to himself, because they threw him like that and his little skull cracked. And Kat with the great ugly scar down her cheek. She pulls and pulls and is becoming angry because she needs them to fetch Dinny and she must be clean before he comes. She is very, very tired and it is getting dark and she cannot sleep without him.

Molly presses on the button now because it's serious now and there are electric cries and beeps from the corridor and all the rooms full of drooling ladies in black mesh hats and on the wall Dinny's paintings are sinking out of colour and flattening and she knows that when she looks at her legs there in the painting there is not so much realness as once there was because she is blanching now the way photographs do when the light shines on them too long and the way asparagus does when you throw it in boiling water and she is limp now too, and white and wrinkled like an over-soaked thing, and she closes her eyes and she wants sleep to come soon, but not before the girl has come with her little boy so she can see that there has been a mistake, that's all *foolish old woman with your spooky dreams, here he is, smiling, here he is.* And Molly will see that he is alright, after all.

48

'I'M TOO TIRED. I'M sorry, Freya, I'm too tired to talk about it anymore.'

'I'm just saying, if they do give him custody, I can just leave the country, can't I? If they give him custody, I'll just pick up Jem and go straight to the airport. I'll just...'

Out of breath, Freya puts the back of her hand to her forehead. There's onion juice drying to salt on her fingertips.

In the pot, the butter has melted to a clear, fragrant pool. Cara lowers the flame and throws in a palmful of thyme. 'Don't be so dramatic, Freya. They won't give him custody. Guardianship, maybe. That's what the solicitor said.' The fat bubbles and fizzes. The tiny leaves jitter on its surface.

Freya picks up the knife again, presses it into an onion – the crackle of fine, dry skin, the crunch of the bulb. 'No, of course they won't. They won't, will they?'

'I've put in too much thyme. That's too much, I think... shit, will I try and spoon it out?'

'It's fine... But they couldn't, could they? Like that's just not something they would do...'

'Freya, I'm sick of listening to this. We don't know what will happen. Your guess is as good as mine.' Freya bites her lip, nodding. There are pools of mascara beneath her eyes. The onion is very fresh; white froth foams on the blade. She makes another slow incision.

'We don't know,' continues Cara. 'We'll have to see. We'll see how it goes and then we'll decide what to do.'

Freya stops slicing. She puts a hand on her hip, points the knife as she speaks. 'No, like it's not even a reasonable concern, is it?'

The butter sizzles – brown specks at the edges; a smell of caramel ripening to rancidity. Cara kills the flame, adds sunflower oil. A flap of smoke leaps from the pan. The fire alarm starts to yelp. Cara throws open the kitchen windows. She runs into the hall and waves a tea towel.

'Freya, please can you cut the onions? We need to get the dinner on. We need to eat and we need to get the kids to bed, okay? That's what we need to do now.'

At nine o'clock – an hour after bedtime, and it's a school night – they sit down to a thin risotto. Denise eats grimly, lips pulled back, scraping the fork with her teeth. Jem sits on his hands. He gives his mother a long, meaningful look.

'What is it, Jem?'

'Onions.'

'You like onions.'

'Not these onions.'

'Oh God, Jem, please?'

'If he's hungry he'll eat,' mutters Cara. 'Look, Jem, even baby Peggy is eating it.'

Sucking his lips, he shakes his head.

'Fine,' says Freya, sighing. 'What will you have then? Will you have cereal?'

'Not fair!' says Megan. 'I want cereal.'

'Oh Freya, why do you do this? It's hard enough to get Megan to eat well...'

'There's lots of cereal, Cara.'

'Fine. Fine, give them cereal...'

'It's fortified.'

'Oh, fortified, is it? Well then.'

Her own voice surprises her, the nasty inflection in it. She sees Freya flinch and her lip tremble.

Cara is bad.

There has always been something ugly in her, a steely core. It is when she should feel the most love, the most care, the hottest instinct to protect, that she knows it most keenly – the coolness in her; the bad, dead coolness right at the centre of her.

Her mother knew it, just as Cara knows her own children; Baby Peggy's ferocity, the kaleidoscopic world of Denise. Megan, my God, what a handful.

Peig has fallen asleep in her high chair. Just as Cara lowers her into her cot, she wakes and pulls at Cara's collar, making kisses with her lovely little mouth, 'mama ma'.

'Sleep, baby. Sleep, baby Peggy.'

But Peig hitches herself onto her mother with all four of her lovely limbs, the soft buttery fat on them, the strong fingers, the gravelly breath. Cara is tired. She pries the baby off, forcing her into her cot. The baby screams, pulls herself up, trips in the sleep-sack and hurts her shoulder and throws her toy dog out. 'Sleeping time,' says Cara, and she can hear the deadness in her own voice. 'It's sleeping time, baby.'

'No.' Slowly, and with great effort, baby Peig gathers the little baby-sized duvet and rolls it out over the bars.

'Sleeping now, baby...'

'No.' She cries and coughs and the cough becomes a bark and the colour leaves her face, and Cara picks her up. The baby nuzzles her neck, drooling, coughs.

Pat's lips are dry. There's dust on them. He stands in the door of the children's bedroom, and pulls a hand down his cheeks.

'I'll take her. Come here, baby girl.'

'Oh. I didn't hear you come in. How was work? There's risotto on the stove...'

As he reaches for Peig, Cara kisses his shoulder; a smell of wood and oil and sweat – his sweat. He is beautiful – the straight slope of his jaw, the big gentle lips, the square hands: hair on them, callouses, blunt nails, round fingertips. Peig screams and splutters, stretching for her mother, but Pat kisses Cara's mouth briskly.

'You go read to the girls. I told Megan she can sleep with Denise tonight. She says she's scared.'

His voice soothes her like a blanket, like stepping into warm water – how is he possible? But Cara is bad. Cara is cold. The way she shouted at Megan today – she recognised it.

It's a rhyming story: a dinosaur hatches all alone in a forest; he spends six pages looking for his mother; he meets a frog, a bird, a large tree, but so far, not his mother. Cara can hear her voice trip on itself, crackle and strain, and under it a hoarse roar, like grief. She stops reading, listens – Peig is still screaming. Her cough is like the bark of a seal; she's getting croup again. They'll have to leave her window open.

Denise taps her shoulder, touches her chin with both hands, directing her face towards the book. 'Yes, come on, Mammy, read.' But Megan wails, 'No Mammy, poow Baby Peig. Poow Baby Peggy.'

'Daddy's minding her. She's okay, Megan.'

When the story is finished, Denise smiles at her triumphantly – she has been chosen over the baby tonight.

'I love you, Mammy.'

'I love you too, little lady.'

'Are you going to go to Peggy now?' asks Megan.

'Yes, baby, I'll go into her now. But you know she's not really that sad. She just can't talk so she cries.'

Megan raises an eyebrow: 'I fink she is twite sad, Mammy.'

The baby stops crying as soon as Cara enters the room. She

stretches her arms out, opening and closing her fists, a big breath juddering into her chest. As Pat offloads her into Cara's arms, she gives a committed, congratulatory nod, as though they have all finally understood what she has been saying. 'Yep,' she says, 'yep. Up.'

Cara uses a muslin square to clean the dribble and tears off Peggy's face and neck, and lies her down in the cot. Her eyes stretch round as though she is drowning or choking, and she grapples for Cara, but Cara sits on the floor and holds her hand, and the baby sighs a rattly sigh and settles down onto her side, gazing through the bars at Cara's face, holding Cara's fingers – two to each of her hands.

'There, baby girl. We're okay, my baby. We're okay, you and me.'

She switches on Peig's mobile – Mozart – and sits cross-legged on the floor. It is peaceful in here, and very boring. She should read a book or something but she can't these days. It's always like this when she is pregnant. She thinks of food and warmth and drawing, and that is all.

She can hear Megan shouting at Pat: 'I want Mammy to kiss me doodnight. Not! Woo!'

Cara bought that chickpea flour. Why has she never thought of chickpeas before? They're not something Grandma ever made – she never used beans or pulses like that, perhaps that's why. Tomorrow she'll try that recipe. She'll make it in the morning and send it in Megan's lunch box. She might get some chickpeas into Megan that way. She might finally get something decent into her.

The baby's face breaks into a big smile: dimples, gums, eight very white teeth still jagged from cutting through. 'Hiya!' A rush of tears comes up through Cara; she has been forgiven.

Out on the landing, Pat is talking calmly and steadily to Megan. He looked tired earlier, rubbing his face like that. Pat. What does she offer him, except to assemble his sandwiches in the morning, a thing he allows only to make her feel useful. Pat, whose body makes the oils of labour and sex, whose physical proximity still makes her wet and aching for him, whose armpit smell clings to her hair like a blessing, whose children break his heart just by being out in the world and subject to all the little blows it will throw them.

What has parenthood done to them? And why won't she stop?

Every child takes Pat further from himself, from the things he used to want to make. 'I'm happy making furniture now,' he tells her. But the things he made – she remembers one sculpture, a woman's face shrouded and her fingernails tearing through the film over her face, like a birth. She remembers that piece, and the way she could not stop looking, and the feeling it gave her of frustration and hope at once, and the way it made her know some parts of Pat that could not be known any other way. The piece was sold to someone who thought Pat was the next best thing. And he was – Pat was the next best thing then. Some of their mediocre classmates, who had even themselves given up believing in their talent, have careers now. People buy their work. They stuck it out. They have become 'names'.

Peig blinks at her. She is a beautiful thing, all cheeks and eyelashes; the monkey darkness of her hair, impossibly plump lips, pudgy fingers that taper at the tips like the cartoon hands of a fat king. Cara realises she is crying. She is not right tonight; she is not right these days. Hormones, perhaps. Or is it just that she's a slave to these little girls? Hanging on the curve of their lips, their cries driving panic deep into her, their tiniest discomfort like a thing tapping at her bones.

She feels sick. She didn't say goodnight to Megan. Megan will be frowning in her sleep, her dreams sore with her sister's crying and the absence of her mother. These children own her.

And tomorrow Freya has this court hearing. Pat has to take the afternoon off to bring Denise to her recital, because Freya is insisting Cara goes with her. Apparently, she won't even be allowed into the hearing with her, but Freya wants her there anyway.

There is so much worry she could have. She has to quieten it all so that the day-to-day can go on; she has to ignore all the terrible beauty of her children and the quivering of her own heart, a fragile thing perched on every nuance of them, if she is to stay whole.

Peig is closing her eyes; another jagged little gasp. Her Peig, with the fat pout and tears beading her thick lashes. Peig, who wants only to hold Cara's hand while she drifts to sleep.

Nothing can hurt you as much as your children. No one could hurt her, if it wasn't for them. They are her weakness.

If there was – sometimes she can't help thinking of it – if there was a war and they did that thing where they made her choose which of her children would die, what would she do?

God, what would she do? The baby. She would let them take the baby. Because she would go stupidly, never for a moment believing she had been forsaken, all the while knowing that Cara was with her, that she would save her. Until she died, Peig would never know her mother had betrayed her, but the others would feel the hurt of her choice, so, yes, take the baby she would tell them.

The foetus turns – a thrill every time, the shape of it striving into being, striving to be a thing not her, and she puts her hand on the ripple it makes beneath her skin. Peig the already-baby opens her eyes, grasps for the hand, pushes her lips between the bars of the crib and kisses Cara's fingertips, a sweet wet little kiss that she has learned from all the kisses she has been given.

Pat snores. Before he fell asleep, he muttered, 'Your sister.'

'Freya?' Freya is beautiful. She really is. Cara was amazed she'd never thought of it before – that Pat might think about Freya that way.

'Your sister takes the piss.'

'Freya?'

'Never puts her hand in her pocket.'

Now he turns towards her in the bed. He worries in his sleep. His brow crinkles and his fist rises, the thumb lifting. He builds things in his dreams – a house for them, a roof, a crib for the new baby – he bangs her hip with his dream-hammer. Cara shifts away from him. If she wakes him, he will only be frustrated that he didn't finish. He will carry the unease with him all through tomorrow.

The landing light has been left on, but Cara is too tired to get up and turn it off. She can hear the fan whirring in the neighbour's en suite. She feels sick. It's the pregnancy, and all that burnt butter, and nostalgia for the long-haired, dark-eyed artist Pat was before, his hands running over the clay the way they ran over her shoulders and hips. Nostalgia for those shoulders and hips – how easy her body was then, how lean and singular.

She turns to face him; in his sleep he is scowling. He looks hurt. He looks bewildered. The nausea creeps into her throat. She turns onto her back. The baby shifts about, flipping Cara's stomach, creaking her ribs. She is sick with – what? Gratitude. Gratitude for having someone to love her children and look after them like that, and sick with guilt, because it is not the same for her – she has to work. She wouldn't love them if she didn't draw. Stupid. Such a stupid, vain thing.

Pat's arm twitches again. He lifts his hand, shakes his head, opens his mouth and makes a huge snore. His anxiety, his disappointment, is all her doing – her, and her pulsing, desiring uterus.

Pat puts his arm over her. She freezes.

She told Pat she had paid the tax bill, and she hasn't. She has spent the money for the tax. She was going to pay it out of her advance for this job – she told him she was getting less than she was, so that she'd have the extra money to pay herself back with. She was going to pay Freya back out of that money too. It's all her agent's fault. She was supposed to send it into

Cara's private account but she sent it through to the joint one instead. Pat was pleasantly surprised. 'Look at this,' he said. 'You thought you were only getting four grand for that job...'

She can't tell him that she lied like that. She can't tell him she overspent again. And on what? Pregnancy vitamins, omegas for the kids, Epsom salts, slippers for Megan – ridiculously expensive slippers made in Germany – the right one is a puppy, the left a kitten with a little pink tongue dangling from it. Megan hates them. She says they're itchy.

Her children are pulling her thin. Each of them, as they left her body, tugged a part of her with them out into another life. She is divided by each of them. She will die like the mint plant at the end of the garden. Last spring, its babies sprouted out from its roots, and all through the summer, the mother plant remained, a bunch of dry yellow twigs. She never dug it out. It's still there, gone black and slimy in the frost. It has divided and divided until it was gone. Is that what it's like for Grandma? Is she in her children and they in her?

She looks at the screen of the baby monitor – baby Peig lying on her back in her sleep sack, so still, like a big doll. It's a cheap, old monitor. The blue screen looks like something from a horror movie; the sound crackles like a wartime radio.

For now, Pat is bound to her. For now, they are surviving. But he has given up too much. When their children are grown there will be a reckoning.

49

NO! THERE'S BEEN A mistake. Molly knows where she is, she knows what it is that's happening. Worse than the dark, the blue light glowing here beside the bed, the insect fizz of it and the big dark window and the bad breath and gums and her voice creaky as a stranger's and the weight of herself. No, there's been a mistake; there's been a misunderstanding, she should not be here she should not be like this, this isn't how it goes; it's impossible. It's not her who is to die. It's not her who is to get old, break down, vanish from herself. It was never supposed to be her. She is not the one who dies.

She is the only one who knew his face.

Hers is the only body that bore him.

Without her there is no one in this world who ever heard him speak.

Have mercy. Have mercy, but she knows the things she has done but mercy have mercy. There is mercy, surely, at the end?

She knows what she has done. She knows it all the time; every moment since it happened it's been pulsing through her. It is in her blood, in her skin. It's in her every breath.

She said she only turned her back, but that wasn't it. She never told it to Dinny, she never told it even to herself – that she was hiding from him, from his lovely dry fingers, his chubby, spittle lips; that in the afternoon he had climbed all over her, *Wake up, Mammy, wake up*. He had pulled her eyelids open, put his thumb between her lips and – why? Why had she done it – why? It felt like she couldn't move, like she needed a moment inside herself. She had played dead – why? Only when he cried, she opened her eyes, smiled at him, kissed him, *Sorry, my little man, only joking. Not sleeping not dead, only a little tired…* she wasn't right that day. Hiding in the bedroom then, while he played with his spinning top there on the kitchen floor. Hiding like that just to sketch with a scrap of charcoal; a spider in its web. She had discovered it when she opened the window, and the big ugly egg sac it was wrapping. A quick, messy drawing – why? – while he climbed up onto a chair and reached for those new round beans she had soaking.

She will forget. Oh, mercy, let her forget. That bit at least. Let her forget.

50

Eventually, Cara must have slept, because she is woken by the discomfort of two children clambering into the bed, taking their usual positions with blunt entitlement. Denise is a round-bellied thing with the uncanny ability to cover the whole bed, diagonally, with her four stocky limbs. She sleeps face down with a determined little frown; her skin is very pink and her sleep is heavy and oblivious to all but her own comfort. Megan is restless. She has a different way of mastering the space. She takes Cara's arm and lifts it over herself and mutters, 'My mammy.' She shifts about, all elbows and knees and bony bum, and she snores and mumbles and throws the covers off her skinny torso and shivers. They both sleep with their plump lips a little open. They both drool. They are both too old to sleep with their parents, and too old to be satisfied the way a baby can be satisfied. They both feel things that Cara cannot know or heal, and they will both become people other than they are now. Life will do things to them that she cannot know.

She remembers her children's early days like whole eras. She remembers the fashions; the foods she cooked. When Denise was born, whale prints were in vogue: whale-print babygrows, whale-print bibs, a hat saying 'having a whale of a time'. Bunny rabbits and mice were the fashion when Megan was born; pink and white. Bunny ears on hoods, bunnies on her blankets. It was the same for Peig, or is it only that she didn't buy anything new for her? This year, it's unicorns and llamas. She has noticed llama-print baby grows, baby bags, baby blankets. A lot of indigo. The llamas are often wearing scarves and hats. This baby will be born into the year of the llama.

To think that they will love each other – that will help Cara to grow old without scraping the age spots off her thinning skin.

She remembers to lie on her left side – something she heard about only this pregnancy. You are supposed to sleep on the left. Something to do with the placenta.

Baby Peig is propped in Pat's armpit, her head slumped to the side, her face serious in sleep. Cara tilts her on a pillow, straightens her head, puts an ear to her chest. She's breathing. What did Cara expect?

She presses her lips to her husband's temple, kisses him in the warm space under his ear. He was too tired to shower. There are woodchips in his hair. She can't get near enough to the smell of his sweat and the oily, unwashed skin.

When Cara first met Pat, she felt the breath knock out of her, the way love is described in teen novels, or Grandma's stories. These days, when he puts his arm over her in his sleep, she feels the same discomfort she felt with her babies, when they were six months old and sat gazing at her with adoration, or kicked their arms and legs with sheer joy at the sight of her, and she was struck with an impulse to violence – to make an ugly face, or wipe the snots from their noses, to teach them not to love like that. It is too much; the children, the husband – she never expected so much love. She has too much to lose.

'Lift the girls,' she tells Pat. 'I can't sleep. Lift them back to bed.'

He tries to stay asleep. 'We're all asleep,' he says, 'go 'sleep.'

'Lift the girls. I can't sleep with them.'

He raises himself up in the bed, his face crumpled from deep sleep. He begins to slide his hand under Denise, lifts her foot from her sister's belly, her head from where it rests on Cara's hip. He begins to lift her. Then he looks through the dark at the puckered lips, the long, white eyelashes, and he sighs. He straightens her a little in the bed.

'You really want me to lift them? Poor girls. Let's leave them be. They're sleeping. They don't want to sleep alone.'

Denise suckers in a loud, nasally snore, and Cara turns her face into the pillow. The foetus has started to turn again – an elbow in the lung, spine moving snakelike along her ribs. Her new black maternity dress hangs on the doorframe, a triangle of pink morning light cutting across the ruffled belly. She needed something decent to wear to court, but what a waste it was, to buy a dress she will only wear once, maybe twice.

'They're asleep,' she says, 'just lift them.'

'Really?'

'Fine. I'll sleep in Den's bed.'

'Don't be silly. You won't sleep.' He pulls Cara to his chest, a hand caged loosely over her eyes, shielding her from the sunrise already creeping in through the curtains. It's uncomfortable. Her hips creak. She needs something between her knees. He kisses her hair; 'Just sleep here with us, baby. No one wants to sleep alone.'

'Pat?'

'Mmm.'

'Pat?'

'What is it, baby?'

'I'm bad. Pat, I'm not a very nice person.'

'Shush, baby, don't be silly. Sleep, baby. Sleep here with us. Sleep.'

51

SOME OF THE ORANGE chairs are broken or missing, leaving ugly metal fixtures like gums robbed of their teeth. Some have been replaced by ill-fitting grey ones of thinner, smoother plastic.

'Sit down there,' says her solicitor, and Freya sits.

The ceiling is very high. Currents of chilly air rush in through the big, open entrance doors. There is a sense of being outdoors, of being unsheltered, forgotten. From somewhere near above her, the occasional coo of a pigeon.

'Have you no one with you?'

'My sister. She's just dropping the kids to school, she'll be here soon. She'll be here any minute.'

Freya stands up again and tugs her skirt into place, smooths it down over her hips, sits.

Cara made her get the suit, but no one here seems to be dressed like this, except some of the solicitors.

Not everyone has a solicitor with them. A very young woman stands in the middle of the lobby, pushing a quiet baby back and forth in a buggy. She's wearing clean trainers with big soles, a velvet scrunchy with little diamante studs on it. Close to the walls, clusters of skinny men stoop together in urgent conversation; plastic bags saying *Spar* dangle from their elbows. The way the cans push dark through the plastic reminds Freya of girls in school who wore coloured bras to English class under the see-through blouses. Three seats up from her, a middle-aged woman is crying intermittently into her elbow.

Freya's solicitor is called Barbara. She has big eyes that slope a little at the edges, as though they are beginning to melt down the side of her face and is wearing a too-tight pinstripe blazer that seems to restrict her movement. She scans the room, looking for something.

'Right, let's go on up then,' she says. 'Let's see if we can find a consultation room.'

They take the lift up together. Barbara clutches some files to her chest. 'Don't be nervous,' she says, 'it'll be over before you know it.'

They get out on the next floor – a short corridor with a swing door each end and four pale doors arranged in a semicircle along the wall. One of the doors has an A4 sheet tacked to it, with two short columns of writing. A woman in a dark uniform is standing by it, staring grimly ahead.

'That's the courtroom,' says the solicitor. 'That's where you'll be going in.' She tries each of the other doors, giving a little knock before opening it. 'Sorry. Sorry. Oh, sorry.'

The next floor up is laid out identically, and the first room they try is free.

'So what happens—?'

She raises a finger to silence Freya – an announcement is coming over the speaker.

'That's the callover,' she says. 'Wait here. Don't leave the room. Text your sister, tell her to come up. Room 4A, second floor.'

The room smells like sausages and overused chip fat. There are four chairs at a square table. A small window faces onto a brick wall, painted white.

Cara arrives flushed, her scarf tangling her knees. She has a cup in each hand – those eco ones she's so proud of. They're made of bamboo or something; the colour of cardboard with 'for a greener tomorrow' written on them in sombre black print. She's got a coffee for herself and a hot chocolate for Freya.

'What a miserable place,' she says. 'All those people downstairs. Miserable.'

'Well, yes. Rag-and-bone shop of the heart.'

Her sister smiles and huffs a little laugh. Then she touches Freya's cheek with the back of her hand, rubs her arm. 'You're shaking, Freya. Drink your cocoa. Here, put on my cardigan.'

'I'm sweating,' says Freya. 'I'm cold but I'm sweating through my blouse. Look – you can see it. Sweat patches. Oh Jesus.'

'Take it off. There's a hand dryer in the ladies. I'll dry it and you can put it on right before you go in.'

But Cara is gone for a long time. When the solicitor comes back, Freya is sitting with her sister's big cardigan over her bra, examining the empty 'for a greener tomorrow' cup.

'My sister's gone to dry my blouse…'

'Right,' says the solicitor. 'There are five on before us, so who knows. We might not get seen until lunch. We got the judge we want. The judge has children, so that's good. That's good for you, I think. But I've spotted his solicitor. I'm going to go and talk to her, see where we are.'

Freya sits looking at all the notes she typed up for today – every text, every encounter with Jem's father. There is a sound like an extractor fan coming in through the little window. She scans her 'affidavit of means'. It is pathetic. Her solicitor laughed when she showed it to her. Is she poor? Is it that easy to become poor?

It never occurred to her that Cara would fail to pay her back, but it's been months now. Every time she tries to ask for it, Cara becomes agitated and flustered – some long-winded story about her money going into her joint account, Pat seeing it. She seems to lie to her husband a lot. Can't be healthy. But as Cara says, what would Freya know?

Eventually, Cara comes in with the dry blouse over her arm, and some bottles of water in a net bag.

'Sorry! There was a girl down there, her baby was screaming. She forgot to bring nappies so I had to pop out to the car and get her some. All on her own, poor girl. She's only seventeen; beautiful little thing. She's trying to get maintenance for the baby, but so far the father hasn't turned up… And I got us water. I forgot we'd need water. Here's your blouse.'

'Do you think I should have done that?'

'Done what?'

'Not turned up?'

'No. Oh, my coffee is cold.'

'Okay...' her solicitor is already talking when she enters the room, '... okay, you didn't tell me any of this. He has given me a lot of new information. Stuff you didn't put in your affidavit.'

'I put everything in the affidavit... But I don't want maintenance from him anyway, I told you that.'

'Well after listening to him now, I don't know. He has your mother here to witness for him?'

Freya looks at Cara. The solicitor seems to have only just noticed her. 'Hi,' she says.

'Hi.'

'You're Freya's sister?'

'Yes. Freya's big sister.'

Freya wraps the cardigan tight around herself. She can hear her solicitor's words but she finds it hard to grasp their meaning. She looks at Cara. She wants her sister to speak for her, to eclipse her.

'So, your mother will say you're unfit – that's what he says, and that she's trying to get custody...'

'That's bullshit,' says Cara, 'that's complete and utter – Our mother's not well. She's mental. That will be immediately obvious, when you meet her... We weren't even raised by her. She doesn't even know us... I mean, you can call me as a witness, if you want?'

'Alright, I'm going to need you to calm down. The judge might not allow her to be called; it might not be an issue. Hearsay.'

'Freya was removed by social services,' says Cara.

'Was I?'

'Well, I think so. Yes, you were.'

Barbara grimaces, as at a bad smell. 'Oh dear, this is complicated. Now let me just run through the other things. Freya?'

'Yes.'

'So, according to him he has some records from an aunt of yours? She has furnished him with proof that you have received eighty grand from your grandmother – is that right?'

'No.'

'Well, he says he has proof.'

'I don't see what that could be.'

'Is there a trust fund?'

'There's a trust fund, yes. There isn't that much in it though, I don't think. Although my aunt said there was nothing left...'

'That was nonsense,' says Cara, 'that was her hoping, or planning to use it or something. There could be forty...'

'... and I don't have access to it. My aunts are the trustees on it...'

'I see. This is complicated then... Oh, I have a headache just trying to straighten this out now... the judge won't like this. Now here's another thing they are saying, just to discredit you, I think. They want to settle, you see, so they're telling me everything they have on you.'

Cara looks furious. 'They *have* on her?'

'Yes, so they say you are taking a court case against your grandmother? For money?'

Freya is dizzy. 'What? What are they talking about?'

'The wardship,' says Cara. 'No, we're not taking a case against our grandmother. We're contesting the power of attorney. We're applying to make her a ward of the court. We probably won't go ahead with it, to be honest. We don't really have the money…'

'This – this doesn't look great, you know. This makes the family look dysfunctional.'

'Yeah, well, they are dysfunctional. That's why we have nothing to do with them… that's why we're contesting the power of attorney. It doesn't mean this little shit can blow in out of nowhere and take my nephew away from his mother—'

'You'll have to calm down. If I'm going to call you as a witness you will need to be calm and rational… reliable.'

'So what does he want?'

'Fifty–fifty.'

'Access?'

'Fifty–fifty access, yes. I mean he probably won't get that. He'll probably get weekends…'

Freya has a sensation of being thrust back and forth very fast. She closes her eyes. When she opens them, she sees her solicitor and she sees her sister but it's like looking at them through thick glass. She is going to faint. She thinks of the word 'swooning'. She is swooning.

'That's ridiculous,' says Cara. 'He has been through enough. He is five years old; he is not moving back and forth between two homes. That man is a piece of shit. He locked him in a room. Tell her, Freya – tell her what happened when you let him see Jem!'

'Hang on,' says Barbara, listening to a voice over the intercom. 'Sorry, I have another client here. He's up. Hang on. I'll be back. Get your blouse on. We might be soon.'

She closes the door, and for a moment all Freya can hear is the extractor fan. She feels very cold. 'I shouldn't have shown up.'

'Now listen, Freya, you need to cop on,' says Cara. 'Listen, you can't be coy about this, you need to tell the judge exactly what he's up to, okay?'

'I can't believe she has done this.'

'Well she has, so you need to get yourself together, Freya. Here, have some water.'

Freya drinks. The water is very cold: 'I'm cold.' She's sweating again.

'She's not taking Jem. I don't want her laying eyes on Jem. Neither of them are. Neither of them are getting their hands on him.'

'She won't, Freya. She hasn't a hope. Now come on, you need to hold it together for this.'

'I can't believe—'

'We'll get them to call me to witness, okay? I can witness. I can tell the judge she was abusive, I can tell the judge everything.'

'What proof do we have, Cara? And what is there even to tell? She was a bit of a bitch, that's all. And you were gone. You weren't there for it.'

'What?'

'You weren't there when she was being crazy. Oh, except the time you helped her.'

'What? Freya, what are you talking about? It was me she had it in for. I know she did that cancer stunt with you, but it was me she thought was evil. It was me she tried to exorcise. She tried to get me arrested for beating her, Freya, when I was seven. I was seven. She smashed her own arm in with a rolling pin to try to get me arrested! Bonkers stuff. What do you mean, I wasn't there?'

'Well, except when you were. Except when you helped her that time.'

Cara is looking into her coffee with irritation. She shakes her head.

'What time?'

'With the bath.'

Cara is drinking the cold coffee. She scowls as though to shake off Freya's voice, and Freya can feel herself blush.

'I don't understand, Freya.'

'When she had her friend over. That loud lady. They used to laugh really loudly together. They laughed at us. They watched us playing together and laughed. She said, "You'd want to see the rolls on Freya. You have to see her thighs." She wanted to show her. And I wouldn't take my clothes off, so she tricked me. She ran me a bath and then when I was in the bath you came in with her and pulled me out and she was laughing. You helped her. You helped her to pull me downstairs and she was saying, "Look at the rolls on her".'

'Freya. I don't remember that. I don't think that happened, Freya. When was this?'

'I was little. You were still living with us. I don't know. Look, whatever, anyway. I don't blame you or anything. It's not a big deal.'

'I – I can tell them about what I remember. I can tell them about her waking me up every hour to do my violin…'

'That's nothing, Cara. Jesus. It was so much worse. It was so much worse than you remember. She's not laying eyes on Jem.'

'I know. I agree with you…'

There is another announcement over the intercom. The solicitor comes in.

'We're up,' she says. 'I can tell them we want more time to try and settle, will I? Tell me quickly. Your mother didn't show, by the way. So maybe now is best.'

'I'll go. I'll go now.'

'Tell them everything,' says Cara. 'Tell them about the blow-job and everything.'

The courtroom is much smaller than Freya expected. It is like a classroom – cheap chairs, cheap table, blank walls. There are no windows. The judge enters through a door behind the stand, with an air of grandeur incongruous with the frigid decor. It's a woman. The judge is a woman.

Dermot makes a point of staring very hard at Freya the whole time, even when he is on the stand.

'Please address your answers to me, Mr McNally,' says the judge, 'and please speak up.'

He mentions her mother only once and when he does, Barbara stands up. 'Objection, your honour, my client was raised by her grandparents. My client has no relationship with her mother. She was removed by social services as a child.'

'Mr McNally, I fail to see the relevance of this,' says the judge wearily. 'Please get to the point.'

'I'm sorry if I'm chewing the ear off you, your honour,' says Dermot, 'but this is the only time I get to speak. She won't let me speak to her; she doesn't listen to me. She doesn't care how I feel.'

'Mr McNally, we are here to decide what's best for the child. Not to provide you with a listening service.'

'I've been speaking to her aunt,' he says, 'and she agrees that Freya is very manipulative… and Freya is rich. She's a spoiled child.'

'So, you've been speaking to the aunt now? Is there even a maintenance order here? Why is any of this relevant?'

When it's Freya's turn to speak she is surprised to find that she isn't shaking. She can feel Dermot looking at her but she keeps facing the judge. She tells the judge about the paper Dermot wanted her to sign, that he threatened to apply for custody if she didn't. The judge looks down the room at Dermot, who lifts his chin and tenses his cheeks. He cracks his knuckles, clears his throat. Freya fancies she sees the judge flinch. She says she tried access, and her son was upset. She says he was locked in a room. He's been wetting the bed since. Dermot wouldn't let him out unless she did what he wanted.

'And can you tell the court what that was, please?' says Barbara.

But Freya can't.

'I can't,' she says.

The judge raises an eyebrow.

'The papers,' says Freya, 'he wanted me to sign them, and...'

Barbara nods at her. 'Please tell the court.'

'... I can't.'

The judge says she wants to think about this. She says she wants a child psychiatrist's report on the child. She says she is not at all comfortable granting access just yet. The case is adjourned until June. She suggests to Barbara that her client puts in a maintenance order before then. She hasn't even given him guardianship.

Freya begins to shake again as soon as she leaves the courtroom. In the lift, Barbara says, 'I've never seen that before. No guardianship. The fathers' rights lot will be up in arms. You froze a bit there but you'll be better next time.'

'I have another client down here. Tell your sister it was nice to meet her.'

Freya presses the button and the lift closes before Dermot can see her. Cara will be pleased. Cara will be so proud of her. Grandma would be proud. Freya loves the judge. She loves her, she will always be grateful to her.

There is someone else in room 4A – a man and his solicitor, and they both look up silently when she opens the door, waiting for her to close it. The 'for a greener tomorrow' cups are still on the table, and the mesh bag-for-life, scrunched into a ball.

'Sorry,' says Freya, 'sorry, they're mine. I'll just take them.' The men don't speak. They watch her put the cups into the bag. They watch her close the door. Does she have her purse? Money for the car park?

She leans against the wall. There are three people in the corridor, speaking quietly and hurriedly. One of them, an older man in a tracksuit, eyes her suspiciously, as though she might be spying.

Where is Cara? What about all her passionate promises? What if they had tried to call her as a witness?

She takes her phone from the pocket of this silly blazer. She switches it on. Waits. Puts in her password. Waits. A text says:

> *SO SORRY have to go Megan in hospital st Vincents call you when no more call me when you get out can u get kids from school? hope it went okay?*

52

THE CORRIDOR IS SUDDENLY empty. In front of Denise there is a white-green wall with Winnie the Pooh painted on it, and a princess with birds flying around her head. There's something wrong with them though. Someone copied them from a picture, but they haven't worked out. The black lines are too thick, the colours are too simple. It's their faces. Their faces are a bit wonky, like they know they're not real; just a copy of someone else.

She looks all around the wall for a clock, but it must be too late by now. She must have missed it.

'Not to worry.' She strokes her violin case – it is covered in brown fabric, not plain black plastic like everyone else's. 'Not to worry.'

A rolling sound, and a nurse walks by pushing a trolley with a baby on it. At first the way the nurse looks past the baby makes Denise think it's just a doll or something. It's a bit smaller than Baby Peig. It has colourful wires in its nose, and blue knitted socks on. It lifts one of its feet, and turns its head, pulling the wires with it, and that's how Denise knows it's a real baby.

She taps her left-hand fingers on her violin case, the fingering for 'Animal Parade'. She can play it perfectly now, with all the feelings – the heavy elephants and the cheeky, chattery monkeys. Imagining the animals – a different one for each repetition – that's what makes it special. That's what Mo says. She hums the tune very quietly, inside her mouth. She taps the beat with her right foot.

Sometimes the music scoops her up and takes her with it. Even if she is just playing the scale of G; lovely dark honey at first and then up to the silver E and F and the sparkling golden G at the top, and down again. A tumbling water sound. The little stream that time when she went for a walk – just Den and Daddy – and saw it there, jumping out of the rock and the sun on it as it trickled down the stoniness and around the scraggly little bushes – even if it's just a scale it can take her with it and all the notes are right and the sound is good, like earth and wood and water and sun. That's since she got to use the bow. Before the bow, she always had to pluck and it sounded like raindrops and marbles.

Soon, Denise will learn vibrato. Sometimes, Mo does it when she is showing Denise how to play something, and Denise asks, 'How do you do the wobbling? I want to do the wobbling.' And Mo says, 'Don't worry about that yet, Denise,' but Denise wants to learn it. Mo says she can exercise her fingers by wobbling them on her hand, but not the finger board, and then, when she is six, and after she has played 'Animal Parade' really, really well at the Spring Show, where she will be the star, she will teach her how to do vibrato for real.

And the problem is, she's missed the Spring Show now.

Denise should be worried, but mostly she is bored. If Megan is dead she knows she'll feel really bad. But if she's okay then it's Megan who should feel bad because of Denise missing the Spring Show. And Daddy too, cause he's the one who didn't bring her. They were on the way there, just Den and Daddy, when the school called about Megan and Daddy started saying about allergies, really calm and then not at all calm and then he just forgot about her concert and went to the hospital.

So now the Spring Show is happening without her. She should be playing 'Animal Parade' right now, but she is sitting here instead looking at the wonky princess.

Her mammy was already here when Denise and her daddy arrived. She came rushing to them and her face looked weak. After her birthday party the balloons were left lying around and they got soft and weak.

'Oh, Pat,' Mammy said. 'She's all swollen. Don't get a fright...'

It was Mammy who sat Denise down here and told her to not move. Daddy went in. He took Baby Peig in with him, and left Denise here alone.

It is a pity about the concert. Daddy spent a long time getting all the bumps out of her hair. And Denise spent a long time practising.

She's very bored. Just when she is about to get up and start looking, Mammy is here with a frightening face saying, 'Sorry Denise, sorry, darling.' In a clap of anger Denise sees that her mammy has been crying, is maybe even still crying.

'Mammy...!'

'I'm okay my love. I just got a big big fright.'

'Where is Megan?'

'She's just in here, I'll bring you to her. Oh my goodness, Denise, that was a big fright, wasn't it?'

Denise shrugs.

'So it turns out Megan is very allergic to chickpeas.'

'Even more than egg?'

'Even more than to egg, yes. Her tongue swelled up and she couldn't breathe, but she's okay. They gave her an injection and she's okay now… we just have to be careful not to let her near chickpeas…'

Denise is afraid to see Megan with her mouth stuffed up with tongue.

'Will it go back to normal?'

'Will what go back to normal?'

'Her tongue.'

'Yes.'

'Is it your fault, Mammy?'

'I suppose it is, darling. Sort of.'

Megan's ears have been stuffed for ages. That's all Mammy's fault because Mammy said no to anti-bs and put castor oil in her ears instead and it was an infection. Denise knows that because she sits on the bottom step some nights after bedtime to hear Mammy and Daddy relaxing with a glass of wine, and one night, Daddy got angry about vaccinations and said about grommets and antibiotics. Denise thinks Mammy is scared about Megan's grommets, because she heard a little cheep cheep inside her mammy's voice then, like a frightened baby bird.

Grommets sounds like small people with wool for hair, and boots, and spanners for fixing ears, but that can't be it. Denise will ask someone what are grommets. She asked her cousin Jem, because Jem is a know-it-all-boaster, but Jem doesn't know either. Maybe Mo knows.

Megan is in a room with lots of other beds and they all have bath curtains hanging down beside them. Daddy is standing beside the bed holding Baby Peig, and Megan is there but her face is blurry.

53

CARA HAD FORGOTTEN THAT this happens. Breath clutching in her throat, ears fizzing, a muffling, like something being pushed over her face. She can see her hands on the wheel, but they are numbing and prickling the way they would when she was a child, sitting in the back of Grandma's car on the way to visit her mother.

She expected time to have diminished the house, but as she turns the corner it looms up bigger and sooner than expected. The clutter of red chimneys and slate peaks, that then seemed only sinister, look expensive now, with their bright window frames and the swathes of tied curtains. There is a rectangular, flat-roofed extension at the front of the house. That's new. Along the steep drive, the twiggy trees that once haunted this stretch have thickened into a wall of bark and branches. They bend in on her, shaking their leaves over her flimsy car as she tilts and bumps up the plush gravel.

There is a shiny red van in the driveway, two black cars – both sleek, expensive things with frowning headlights – and a pale blue convertible with its leather roof folded back. Cara tries to reverse the car, so that she can leave quickly if she needs to, but as she is inching it around, she sees them in the wing mirror, emerging one by one from the house – her mother and her Aunt Sinéad and her Aunt Aoife. They stand in a row, watching her. Her mother is wearing an exaggerated smile and clasping her hands together. The front of her hair is pinned up on either side, so that it flanks her face like spaniel's ears, and she is wearing a pink knee-length dress with a floppy lace collar.

'Chicken!' she cries, her eyes very round and her whole face strained with smiling. Even her hairline has lifted.

Cara pretends not to have heard her. She concentrates on parking, on steadying her breath, readying her voice. *Hello*, she will say. Just, *hello*. She will look her in the face. She will not squirm.

As she takes the key out of the ignition she notices the holes in her jeans – a loose hatch of thread across each knee. She had thought to change before coming here, but she didn't want them to think she had dressed up for them. She didn't realise quite how tatty she was though. She has worn these jeans through all of her pregnancies. This jumper too. It is frayed at the cuffs, stretched thin and bobbled over her belly.

She takes a deep breath, to try to pull herself back together, but her mother is approaching the car now – the driver seat with the duct-taped mirror. Cara hurries out of the car.

'Chicken!' Her mother touches her belly with both hands, giving a shriek that makes Cara flinch. 'Aaaa! You're so BIG!'

Her eyes stretch very round, showing the veiny whites. This

was a mistake. Cara can see that now. Her aunts are still standing by the house. They have both aged since the last time she saw them.

Aoife purses her lips. 'Hi, Cara.'

'Hi, Aoife. Hi, Sinéad.'

Sinéad, who has been looking everywhere but at Cara, nods apologetically. 'Hi, Cara.' Everything about her seems to have puffed up. Even her eyelids. Even her fingers, which hold each other in a kind of supplication.

The aunts file into the house, and her mother shoos her in after them.

Where did her mother get the money? Her cousin Valerie said it was a settlement from Cara's father's family, but that seemed farfetched. As a child, she did not appreciate the cost of a house like this. The huge marble hallway and the glass doors leading, on the right to the music room with its sponge-painted walls of manic yellow and orange, to the left the 'good room' where the curtains match the armchairs.

'Through here, Chicken, we're having tea in the sunroom.'

As she is ushered through to the far end of the hall, there are framed photos on the walls: portraits of each of Cara's children, black and white, a little bit pixelated. Peig as a newborn, her face still creased like poppy petals, a cotton hat on her head; Denise with her white hair piled up, her eyes a dark smudge; Megan with jam around her mouth. They have been enlarged from smaller prints. Her first thought is of spies photographing her family from far away – black cars with tinted windows – but then she spots a huge studio photo of her nephew. Jem is a few months old, sitting buddha-fat in his nappy, smiling gummily and grasping for some bubbles the photographer is blowing. She had forgotten how bald he was. A big bald head, and dimples. Grandma had that photo taken. She had a small print of it on the mantelpiece in the good room.

The kitchen has changed since she was last here. There are granite worktops, smooth white fittings, a giant butcher's block in the middle of the room. The Aga is still there – the big red Aga her mother never used.

'Cara, I don't think you've seen the sunroom since I had it built. Have you?'

'No.'

'W-Hell—' She spreads her arms to present a room off the kitchen – 'Isn't it JU-H-UST BE-HA-YUTiful?' She has a way of forcing all the air from her lungs when she wants to emphasise a word. The effect is a hoarse huffing sound that makes Cara feel like she is out of oxygen herself.

It's the extension that Cara saw from the front – a rectangle with high glass windows and a glass roof, a big farmhouse table and chairs. There is a jasmine plant trained up one of the walls.

'Don't you just love BEHATHING in sunlight?'

Cara's throat hurts. There are more photos in here – of Cara herself this time, and Freya.

'The SUHUN! Even in winter! Sit down, Cara, sit down.'

'Why have you got those photos?'

Her mother's lips pull tight to her teeth, her eyes bulge, but she keeps her voice sweet. 'Why shouldn't I have pictures of my children up, Cara?'

'But you weren't at my wedding. And the pictures of my children. Where did you—'

'Why wouldn't I have pictures of my grandchildren?' Her mother laughs incredulously, and so does Aunt Aoife. But Aunt Aoife knows she shouldn't have those photos – she must know.

'I made some brownies,' says Sinéad.

Arms wrapping her bump, Cara peers closely at the photos. They are small prints, but poor quality, as though they too have been enlarged. Facebook. That's what it is. They are all pictures that Cara uploaded onto Facebook. But how did her mother get on Cara's Facebook?

'Valerie sends her love,' says Aoife.

'Have some tea, Cara,' says Sinéad, 'and try a brownie. They're good. Well, I think they're good. These two won't eat sugar.'

'It's the wheat I won't eat, Sinéad. Poison. If you didn't eat wheat you never would have got cancer, you know. Get another cup from the kitchen, will you please, Sinéad? The white Villeroy Bosh.'

'Boch,' mutters Aoife, 'it's Villeroy *Boch*, Eileen, you ninny hammer.'

Aoife has settled herself at the end of the table, and she's fingering some A4 sheets grimly. There is text printed on them, streaks of yellow highlighter pen over some of the lines. She picks up a memory stick and puts it down again.

Cara sits. She takes a bite of the brownie and taps the crumbs onto a pink paper serviette. It's delicious – a sweet crust and then softer chocolate in the centre. 'Mmmm. These are lovely, Sinéad. Is there hazelnut in them?'

Sinéad is visibly pleased. 'Hazelnut flour. Yes, I think they're pretty good... lovely with a cup of tea.'

'Now,' says Aoife, 'we want to discuss Freya.'

'I thought you wanted to discuss Grandma?'

Her mother is sitting beside her, too close. She takes a loud breath in through her nose, and lays her hand over Cara's.

'Cara,' she says, 'your sister isn't well.'

'What do you mean?'

Aoife's eyes sharpen on her, quick as a pecking bird's. 'Did you know she has been bleeding Grandma dry? For years, she's been spending Grandma's money...'

Cara takes her hand back. She rubs her belly in circles. She closes her eyes. A limb sweeps under her hand – a leg or an arm?

'Right,' she says, 'I'm going to go now, I think. I don't think this is going to be productive.'

Her mother rolls her eyes. 'Oh for God's sake, Cara, don't be so dramatic!'

'Since we have taken over Grandma's affairs we've discovered all kinds of things,' says Aoife. 'Thousands and thousands Freya has got out of her, did you know that Cara?'

'I don't care.'

'What?'

'I don't care, Aoife.'

'What did you say? Speak up, Cara, what are you trying to say?'

'I'm not going to sit here listening to you bitch about my sister.'

Cara watches the jasmine plant over her mother's shoulder – its waxy flowers, the weave of its branches and the little green ringlets springing loose, searching for something to cling to.

'Well, believe you me, Cara, she has taken thousands and thousands from Grandma over the years,' says Aoife. She picks up the USB stick and waves it. 'We have evidence. Video footage. And we have stuff on you.'

'Well, that's neither here nor there anyway,' says Sinéad. Several times she has lifted her brownie to her mouth, and put it down again, as though embarrassed to eat. 'It's the power of attorney we wanted to discuss, isn't it?'

'We have you rifling through Grandma's purse,' says Aoife. 'We have Freya stealing from her.'

'She's sick, Cara,' says her mother. 'She has poor Davitt driven demented.'

'Davitt is very unwell, Cara,' says Aoife. 'He is dying of cancer and Freya is tormenting him. She set the HSE on him, hounding him for information about things – mad things. Mad ideas.'

Cara can feel the redness washing up from her neck. They think that was Freya.

Her mother squeezes her face up, shakes her head. 'She's never been right.'

'What kind of cancer?'

'It's the child I worry about,' says her mother. 'His poor father is very worried about him. He's desperately trying to get custody...'

'Jem's fine. I'm going to have to leave, I'm afraid.'

'This concerns you, Cara. She made Grandma change the will. She made Grandma give everything to her – to the child, you know, but he's a child, so actually, to her.'

'Well, not if his father gets custody...' says her mother.

'This is bullshit,' says Cara, standing. Her ankles hurt, her throat hurts. She needs to wee but the thought of pulling down her pants in this house makes her panic.

'She made some kind of bogus report to the HSE!' says Aoife. 'And she has some fantasy – some really crazy ideas. She sent some really crazy emails to Valerie. I have them here...' She looks at the paper in front of her, sneers, 'Listen to this.' In a sing-song voice, she reads: '*As you may or may not know, last summer there was a HSE enquiry into elder abuse regarding Grandma. I think only your mum and Sinéad were investigated and they both refused to co-operate. I don't know why my mother wasn't.* Who does she think she is? Valerie was disgusted. She rang me straight away. I told her not to reply. Just leave it, I said. I told her not to get involved. Listen to this, I mean it really is – who does she think she is? '*You may or may not be aware that my mother extracted a €100,000 cheque from Grandma very shortly after her fall...*' "Extracted"! Like I pureed her or something! Made a little reduction here in my cauldron! Essence of Mammy!'

'No, hang on now, this is from the latest one. She sent this only a few days ago. *As I have made clear to both your mother and mine, I find certain behaviours in relation to Grandma's money and property revolting...*'

'Behaviours!' says Aoife. 'She thinks we're bold girls and

she's going to put us in our places! She finds it revolting! Of course she does! She's not getting her way paid anymore… it makes her sick. *I replied by saying that I find their behaviour around Grandma's affairs really sickening and want no part in it.* And hang on here is where she lets her colours show: *I did not, by the way, "get" anything for having Jem! She did pay for childcare fees as she wanted me to finish university.* Did she now, Lady Muck?'

'Aoife,' says Cara's mother, 'read her the bit about me. About how she is being horribly harassed by her own mother, and poor her, her child's father wanting to see him…'

'Wait now, so here's where she threatens us. *While I do find the behaviour deeply unethical, I do not wish to proceed with an objection at this time as long as Grandma's direct welfare is not at stake.* Well, isn't that very good of her altogether?'

'Where's the mad bit, Aoife, about the father and me and all that?'

'I'm going now.'

'Wait, you need to know this, Cara. You need to know what she's up to. Okay, here it is. I mean, she doesn't even know what an affidavit is, clearly. Brendan nearly fell off his chair laughing at this bit: *Jem's father has gone into the district court with the following sworn affidavit,*and then in brackets she says, *(not very relevant to access, but extremely odd)* – I love the brackets, the brackets are my favourite – *He has told my solicitors that the following "information" has been provided by an elderly aunt.* Extremely odd indeed – just amazing levels of paranoia! *Elderly aunt* – she thought she'd insult me with that one… Oh hang on, here it is – the drama!' Aoife flings her arms out, gesticulating hammily as she reads:

'There seems to be some bogus record of Grandma's finances in circulation, and this has resulted in what is verging on harassment from my mother and an ex-boyfriend.'

'She's always had a persecution complex,' says The Lily. She pronounces the word 'persecution' very carefully, as though she's just learnt it. Rolling her eyes she says, 'Everyone is out to get her. We're all spending our lives trying to wreck hers... Like none of us has anything better to do.'

'Oh, this is where it gets really dramatic though, listen to this: *I do not wish to involve anyone unnecessarily in this sordid affair* – Sordid affair! – *the whole thing makes my skin crawl – but if you know what is going on please tell me as I need this to stop.*'

'*This sordid affair*!' says Sinéad.

'*I need this to stop*,' says Cara's mother. 'It's the little boy I worry about. It's the child I worry about, really. Am I going to have to go through the courts to get to see him, Cara? That's what I want to know. That's what I'm going to ask her.'

'Right, goodbye, Aoife,' says Cara. 'Goodbye, Sinéad, thank you for the brownie.'

Then she looks at her mother. She wants to say goodbye but she doesn't know what to call her.

'Look, this is serious, Cara,' says Sinéad. 'Speaking of sordid, Freya has done something really disgusting here.'

'She could have had me dragged up in front of the courts like a common criminal!' There's a tremble at the corner of Aoife's eyes.

'She caused Davitt to get critically ill,' says her mother.

Sinéad is picking the edges off her square of brownie. 'It's very upsetting for the whole family, Cara. Freya made Grandma change her will to something crazy. She took thousands and thousands from Grandma. Brendan shut that investigation down, but we were lucky. Imagine us all dragged up before the courts? Imagine Grandma dragged up? You can't possibly think that's right, can you? We're a respectable family. We are Dennis Kearney's children!'

'What do you expect me to say, Sinéad?'

'The power of attorney thing, Cara. We're going to have to fix this and you have put in an objection to power of attorney. There'll be nothing left, you know. Most of the money is going on Grandma's care.'

'We need to talk to you like an adult now, Cara,' says Aoife, her mouth set in a thin line. 'We have worked out how much money Freya took from Grandma and it's not fair. It's not *just*. And Grandma wouldn't have wanted that. It comes to eighty grand altogether you know, between one thing and another, and that's only in the last few years. And – now Grandma is in agreement with this – we are going to have to access some of Grandma's funds anyway, for her care. We're going to sell some shares she has, and we propose, well, to make everything fair, we propose we distribute it as Grandma wants – you included now, you and Valerie included – we propose we give you each eighty thousand and that way it doesn't all go to Freya.'

'You have no right to do that.'

'We do,' says Aoife. 'Grandma has signed off on it. We haven't taken power of attorney yet. You've put in an objection, so we got Grandma to sign off on it herself.'

Sinéad cocks her head; her eyes look so little now in her swollen face. 'Is it some nonsense Freya said to you, that made you do that?'

'I put that in because of some things Grandma said. And the way my mother got her to write a cheque for a hundred thousand.'

'A – what, Cara?' Aoife squints. 'You're muttering, we can't hear you.'

'Mammy got her to write a cheque for a hundred thousand to her…'

'How dare you!' says her mother. Something glistens in her eyes; a ferocity, a kind of pleasure.

'Oh yes, Cara, we know. You were bothering Davitt about that, weren't you? Well, don't worry about that,' says Aoife.

'She is *my* mother,' says The Lily.

'We've sorted that out, Cara. There was no need for you to go meddling in that. That was just a loan. Your mammy has paid us back our thirds. We'd be getting that in the will anyway…'

'If Grandma was made a ward of the court,' says Sinéad, 'it would be a disaster. Everything would go on tax and legal fees and Grandma would be dragged up in front of the courts.'

'Did Davitt not tell you? I have pulled the objection. I can't afford it.'

Aoife nods tightly. 'Well, Grandma wants everything to be fair. We'll send you a cheque will we? Or do you want us to transfer it to a bank account?'

'Bank account,' says Cara, 'I'll email my bank details…'

54

FREYA SHAKES OUT ONE of Baby Peggy's vests, smooths the ridge made by the clothes horse, shapes it slowly into a neat square. Her sister has not inherited their grandma's knack for housekeeping. The laundry is pilled and stiff – too weakly wrung and too slowly dried. The whites are grey or yellowish; the coloured things are faded. None of it has ever been ironed. There's a sour, brackish smell off it.

Freya puts the folded vest in the stack by her elbow. She pulls Jem's pyjama top from the clothes horse – little blue robots on a faded crimson background. She puts her face into it. She can smell him through the detergent and mildew. These pyjamas are getting too small for him. The cuffs are frayed; buttons are missing.

She shakes it out, folds it neatly and lays it on his pile.

That's it. There's nothing left to fold.

She leans back against the wall, legs crossed, not yet ready to face the empty house downstairs. Being up here amongst her sister's clutter makes her feel safe and like a child again, too small for the vast, curious jumble of Cara's mind.

Cara is a hoarder – that's the word for it. There are little hills of leaves and shells on the floor, unwashed coffee mugs, Grandad's encyclopaedias, loosely fastened papers stacked up against the walls.

She feels bold approaching the desk – transgressive.

Cara's sketches are covered with an old, paint-stained rag with faded pictures on it, of a girl and a boy walking. The girl has a wicker basket over her arm, and an oversized ribbon in her hair. The desk is big enough to hold a trove of inks and pencils and junk: a heap of unremarkable stones, the fragile shell of a snail, a dead ladybird, mute red. At the far corner, filled with roughly hewn cubes of sugar, is the little cork jug that belonged to their grandad. Freya lifts it by the handle, cups her hand around the pale, perforated cork. The cork has a living quality, always warm to the touch, as though it breathes through the holes. It has always given Freya the creeps; a suggestion of human skin in the swatches of cork, the inside glazed cool and smooth as a worn bone. Grandma loved it. Freya remembers her giving it to Cara, touching the cork, turning it over and tracing the rough signature at the bottom. 'It's cork, you know. Handmade. A beautiful object.'

It gives Freya a little rush, to be up here alone with Cara's work. She could pull the cloth off her sketches; she could look.

Cara's illustrations are busy compositions that fill up the whole page with tiny, hidden details. She gave Jem a hand-painted book about a donkey once. Every second page has a full-page illustration, and opposite it, on the text page, there's always a little grasshopper or a dandelion or something in one of the corners, or crawling along the letters. One page has a hatching cocoon dangling from the end of the letter Y. That's what Freya loves about Cara's books; the tiny, beautiful things you almost miss. She can spend hours flicking through them, swallowed in by the vast world of small things that her sister can make.

She lifts the corner of the sheet. The page is disappointing – nothing but ghostly shapes plotted around the page; vague human figures. Cara rarely draws humans.

Cara. Her faulty sister. It's some little madness that makes her draw with such earnest intensity. She has worked the same way since she was a teenager – first with light HB pencils, before pulling those fine black architect's pens from her dressing-gown pockets, or one of the jars she keeps on her desk, and rendering the final lines slowly, lovingly, her hand trembling, lips almost touching the paper, dribbling sometimes, in concentration; drawing every scale of a fish, every whisker of a mouse. As a child, Freya was mesmerised by it, and she would beg to be allowed to watch Cara. She would sit cross-legged at the end of her bed, as silently as she could, while her sister sat at their dressing table and drew friendly and anatomically perfect little snails, or smiling toads in top hats and bow ties, or pointy-eared pixies with 'Cara's special pens', which Freya was not allowed to touch. Cara used to snap at her for breathing too loudly behind her, and Grandad used to send her away. 'Leave Cara be, Freya. She can't concentrate with you there. Go help Grandma.'

Freya thought Cara-at-work was something magical and magnificent then; something she was grateful to be near.

Is it over now, the magic? Is Cara too tired now, too thwarted and disappointed? There is a hardness along her jaw. There are long, violent creases around her eyes.

Every morning, from the spare room, Freya hears her mount the stairs at five o'clock. She hears the wheels of her chair on the floor, the crossing and recrossing of her feet. She stays up here until eight, when it's time to wake the children. Sometimes she works at night too, if she has a deadline. So, she is always tired. And now that she is pregnant again, her face seems rubbed and smudged all the time, as though she cannot muster the energy to hold her features solid, as though there is no room for stillness in all the actions she needs to perform and all the worlds she needs to create.

Freya sits at the desk. She does a spin on the chair. It's only that she hits it with her foot, or she wouldn't have noticed it – the big hatbox that she took from Grandma's.

It was during those few days after they'd got rid of all the carers and before they put Grandma in the home. Freya had been sitting by Grandma's chair, telling her about Jem – a topic that used to make her beam and rattle on, repeating the same anecdotes and chuckling at them. Grandma began to list all the things she wanted Freya to take – nice glass jars she had kept for jam, a milk jug, her 'zoom zoom' for making soup. Freya brought a cardboard box in from the utility room and put it on Grandma's footstool. She placed in it everything Grandma told her to.

When the box was full, Grandma looked past her. 'Go upstairs,' she said, 'to my bedroom. Go to the wardrobe and up high – pull a chair over to stand on – and there is a box there full of the most beautiful cotton yarn. Bring it to Cara will you? She can knit them some warm vests from it. I will never use it now, my wrists hurt if I knit, and who knows what will happen to all my things. People passing through. People rifling through everything, dividing it up. That beautiful cotton will be wasted – who appreciates good cotton anymore? They will throw it out. I think sometimes that we might have spoiled our children. That's the problem. Give it to Cara, tell her to make something useful with it.'

There were two boxes. She took down the botched hatbox first, thinking that the yarn was in there. When she lifted the lid, it let off a dry, kittenish smell. There was a mixture of objects she vaguely recognised: a child's sampler with a hard vein in it where some dropped stitches had been retrieved by an adult and tightly picked up; a pair of white lace socks; a birthday card with shiny hearts stuck on the front. She put the lid back on, and rushed out to the car with it. She stole it. Why did she do that?

She put it in Cara's attic storage without even looking in it again. Cara must have taken it out when she took out the Christmas decorations.

She kneels on the floor and pulls out the box. She opens the card. There's a pop-up chicken in the centre fold, a speech bubble saying *Happy Birthday Grandma You are a Spring Chicken ha ha*. Under the card is a school project she once did on Irish bridges, and one Cara did on butterflies. She lifts them out one by one and lays them on the floor. She got five stars for the bridge project – she remembers that – and she felt like a fraud because Cara had helped her to draw the bridges. She takes out a flimsy cardboard creation; some sort of rabbit or mouse made from the inner tube of toilet paper rolls, with a coiling tail and a pompom nose and the eyes and whiskers drawn in great detail. Along the tail, tiny letters spell *for grandma love Cara and Freya*. There is a small, brown-skinned baby doll with a tiny hand-knitted dress, and an O in its mouth where it must have had a dummy once. There are two books – the first is a big book, *The Three Little Kittens*, with pictures instead of certain words, like a pair of mittens for 'mittens' or an S-shaped scarf for 'scarf'. The pages feel waxy, and there are strings running through it, like raw silk. The binding is loose and some pages are missing. The only thing Freya recognises is a copy of *Charlotte's Web*. The pages are frayed and soft and fragrant. On the inner cover Cara has written her name in pencil, the joined-up letters pressed carefully and with deliberate neatness onto the paper so that the lead shines dense like magnetite. Beneath Cara's name, her own is written in a lighter, shakier hand, *FREYA*.

Freya holds the book in both hands. She puts her lips to it. She wants it; those parts of her life with Grandma and Grandad and her sister that have been pried quietly away.

At the bottom of a box there's an envelope of very thin paper. A Polaroid photo of her mother with Cara and a white-haired baby – the baby must be her. They are outside. There are yellow flowers in the background. Cara has a pink nose and slightly pink eyes and her dark hair is in two ponytails. She is a little too close, reaching for something behind the camera.

Their mother's cheek is pressed to the baby's. She is smiling broadly, beautifully. She loves them.

Something painful moves up like vomit from Freya's stomach.

The things she knows – are they the fabrications of a sick mind? Have she and Cara made it all up, about their mother? And even if they haven't, what did she really do that was so bad? In a court of law, with her hand on her heart, what would she say?

Their mother was frightened of Cara. She thought there was something bad in her. Freya can remember that; she can remember how her mother lied to the police woman that time; how she dragged Freya into the lie, how it tasted in her mouth – like blood. But she can remember other times too, when Cara's wrongness seemed very real to her. When it was she and her mother battling the darkness, and she can remember how good that felt, how strong and happy she felt, the togetherness of that.

Strangely, she remembers very little of what happened after that – when Cara was gone and it was just Freya and her mother. There is a different colour to those memories, as though the lights were lower, as though they are submerged in dark water. She believed in her own illness; and she believed in her mother's cures. Her mother used to make her drink glasses of oil mixed with grapefruit juice, held the bucket under her chin while it came back up. 'Good girl… poor Freya.'

Freya rubs at the photograph with her thumb. She is crying but it feels like the crying is forced; like she is performing.

She knew The Lily once – she really knew her, and she knows her mother believed her own stories, her own lies, even as she covered them up. Perhaps she really believed it would do Freya good to vomit three times a day. Freya can remember the diarrhoea all through those months, and big green globs that came out of her, like things belonging to mysterious oceans, or nuclear experiments. They were toxins, her mother said; they were negative entities she had absorbed from Cara.

Was it abuse, the way the social worker said? Or some quirky alternative health fads? There is no unpicking the past – knots form, the yarn crimps and frays – there is no way of reconciling it all, of pulling out the stitches and weaving things back together.

She knows it is dangerous to pity her mother; it is dangerous to second-guess herself. Freya will need to do away with this photo; that's all. With difficulty, she folds it twice and stuffs it into the pocket of her jeans. She will get rid of it in some thorough and final way.

She can feel the photograph, sharp in her pocket when the doorbell rings. She is thinking about it as she opens the door; about how to destroy it, about what would be the least creepy way to destroy it. If she leaves it in bright sunlight, the image will simply grow whiter and whiter until it is gone.

On the doorstep there's a man with a clipboard. He's dressed in very clean blue overalls. Behind him, a van, another man in the same overalls opening the back of it.

'Hi,' says the man. 'Am I at the right house? Cara Kearney?'

'Oh. Yes. I mean, I'm not her but this is the right house.'

'I have three dishwashers here for her.'

'Three?'

'Three Bosch dishwashers here for her. Is that right?'

'She didn't say anything.'

'They're new models. They were pre-ordered. They were ordered a good few months ago. A delay… She might have forgotten. They would have sent an email, but she might have forgotten…'

55

THIS MORNING, LILY AND her sisters had prepared giddily for Cara's visit, laughing, reassuring one another. Aoife licked her thumb and wiped some mascara from beneath Eileen's eye; Sinéad made her some lemon balm tea.

But after Cara left, there was a disappointing quiet. The fervour had passed. For a few minutes, Aoife sat at the table. Then she said, 'Right, well I'm off.'

Sinéad finished her tea, and helped Eileen to clear up. She left the brownies wrapped in parchment on the butcher's block.

She'd love that. She'd love if Eileen ate the brownies and got as fat and diseased as she is.

Eileen wraps them tightly, squeezing them to mush in their soggy paper, and pushes them down into the bin.

She phones the gardener and tells him he needs to come urgently to weed the rockery, but he says, 'No, I'm sorry, Miss Kearney.'

'Oh, call me Lily, please Hugh...'

'I'm sorry, Lily, I'm not available until next week.'

'This is urgent,' she says. 'I'll pay you double. There are weeds choking my rock plants...'

But he is stubborn. She phones the electrician – she's going to have the living-room lights changed to dimmers – but he's not picking up. She rings him again, and again, and then she leaves a voicemail telling him to phone her back as soon as possible or she will have to find another electrician.

It's getting dark already. She pulls the curtains closed around the big bay window of her bedroom. She switches on all the salt lamps and turns up the daylight bulb very slightly, making a little twilight here in her room.

She sits at her vanity table and combs out her hair. She begins to count silently – she has to do a hundred strokes every evening or the spell might break.

This room is her sanctuary. The walls are bare, but in every corner there is a paper model of her house, the symbols for money and love placed in their appropriate rooms. All you have to do is wait. You make the models, you plant the messages, you ask the universe, and then you wait. Under the glass protecting the boxwood of her vanity table, she has put a hundred-euro note, a lock of hair, a laurel leaf. She kisses her fingertips, touches the glass.

In this lovely glow she can look closely at her face – she is very pretty. You can tell she is somebody's little sister, her daddy's favourite, the envy of her peers. Aoife licked her thumb earlier, and tidied her mascara, and everything was right again. Aoife remembered that Lily is her little sister. Pretty little, cheeky little, feisty little Lily.

Her hair – her hair is still toffee gold. She sighs and a kind of joy lights in her. It is good to take a moment sometimes, to appreciate the miracle of herself.

But it's made her uneasy, the way Aoife upped and left so abruptly like that. They forget – they all forget who Lily is.

Daddy shaved Aoife's underarms, more than once. Lily saw. It was no secret. Aoife would ask him to shave her underarms, and he did it using his shaving brush and razor. That was strange, wasn't it? That was not something Aoife would like to be reminded of. There was nothing more to it, but does Aoife forget what Lily knows? They shared a home for decades; they came from the same body. Does she think she can erase that, getting up like that, nodding farewell like a stranger, her lips tight with all their secrets?

Lily is a little shaken after seeing her daughter. Cara is so old. In the sunroom she took a worn bobbin from her wrist, held it in her wine-stained teeth while she scraped all that unruly hair into a ponytail, and Lily noticed a few crazed greys zig-zagging out from her temples. Her own daughter is grey before she is. Everything is out of time. Mammy is alive and Daddy is dead.

Her daughter is a wreck of a woman, bitter. *Why have you got those photos* – the cheek!

Who do those girls think they are?

She is their mother, for God's sake. She knows them better than anyone could. She knows them from before language, before who said this or who did that or what really happened or any of it.

Ridiculous, to think they can cut themselves off from her; keep that little boy from her. Her own grandson.

Eileen won't be denied.

The truth is dirtier, murkier than anyone can understand. Sometimes a lie is the only way to bring it into the light.

She has lost count, so she starts at the beginning again. Counting aloud this time: 'One, two, three…'

You get the child you are able for – she heard someone say that in a supermarket once. Two older mothers talking. One of the children had Down's Syndrome, and the other was running into the trolley repeating, *bash bang, bash bang, bash bang.*

There was always something off about the children she had. And she wasn't able for them; that's the truth of it. She tried, but she wasn't up to either of them. She was too innocent, too giving.

She did her best to cure Cara. There was always something dark and dead in her, something that sucked the good out.

The night after Cara's birth, Lily couldn't sleep. She couldn't get warm. The crumpled creature folded into her like a clam, pulling any heat it could from Lily's body. It was of a place beyond, a place utterly alien – how could it have come from inside her? Short, very black hair swirled on its forehead, merging with its eyebrows, fuzzing down its arms and over its back like soot. It seemed so foreign; it seemed full of dangerous knowledge.

Liam never asked her to get rid of it or any of that. And even if his visits became no more frequent, he was tender to her all through the pregnancy. Some evenings they didn't even have intercourse – just held each other, or played chess – and she felt sure that she had him; that once the baby came, she'd have him. It was only a matter of time, she thought, before he left his wife. She believed that.

He was there for the birth. He watched her in pain and at the time she was glad of that. There was nothing now, no currency of suffering that his wife could hold over her.

But then – she saw it as it happened, there in that moment, when the baby left her body, as his gaze moved from her face to the child – she saw his love shift from her. She felt it. The heat, the light, the love pulled off her face and shining onto that tiny thing. She remembers how cold she felt, suddenly, without his eyes on her, how she began to tremble, and when they handed the baby to him, how he rocked it, bending his head, never looking back at her. She lay trembling, the big cord still snaking out of her, and it was only when the afterbirth began that anyone even noticed her.

He kissed her as they took her to the ward. He put the baby in its glass box. 'I love you. I love you both,' he said, looking only at the box as they wheeled her off to the ward. And then he was gone. He didn't come back to the hospital and it would be months before she saw him again. He would say the baby had spooked him, and by then she would understand what he meant.

And those three days in the hospital, she learned about Cara – the long, sharp nails she had, the furred back. Sometimes, when she slept on Lily's chest, she seemed like a little accomplice; a witch's familiar. But the baby had a terrible power. She could melt Lily's faculties, she could draw her into liquid and flesh with her sucking and mewling, the flexing of her tiny fingers. Time collapsed in her. Lily could look for a moment at the wrinkled feet, and the whole day might have passed. She thought she would have to re-understand time and space now. She thought her world had changed.

She half expected Liam to be waiting when she got home, so when they discharged her, she put on her lipstick and her nice wool coat and hailed a taxi.

But she couldn't bear the emptiness in this house, the way the baby's cries rang against the walls. Cara was never satisfied. She used to pummel Lily's chest with her fists. She used to vomit up all the milk she had taken, and then feed again. Lily was frightened to be alone with the baby, because it was as though her very lifeblood was being taken from her when it suckled – her head spun, her hands were weak. She could see herself drained to a papery shell, there in the bed, limp with exhaustion, too frail to cry out for help, while the hairy little thing sucked and sucked.

She phoned her parents. Daddy came in the car for her.

It was in her mother's house that she saw, with horror, the real weirdness of Baby Cara. She was a disappointingly ugly little goblin of a thing, even Lily could see that. But just as she had drawn Liam's love away, she snaffled all of Lily's mammy for herself. *Such a beautiful child,* that's what Mammy kept saying, *such an easy baby.*

But Eileen loved her. She must have. Because she took her back with her six weeks later, when she went home. And she spent a long time pumping her milk into a little bottle – so long that her wrist ached – before she left her for the first time.

She gave the bottle to Sinéad. She was to look after Cara while Lily had her hair done – Liam would be back soon, she knew it. She must have loved it, because she was edgy that time in the hairdressers. She talked only about the baby. Milk stains blossomed on her T-shirt. The hairdresser was embarrassed. She gave her a stack of blue paper towels which she folded into her bra. They chafed her nipples and dissolved, sodden with milk. But when her hair was set, Lily walked the wrong way, away from the car park and through the streets.

She found a restaurant she had not been in before. She ordered a pot of tea and sat there for hours. She read a chapter in a book about Cuba and decided that she would go there. She thought she might do some shopping now, or see something at the cinema. She thought she might never go back.

Mammy was at her house when she returned. Baby Cara was sucking at a sugared rag, her little chest heaving in the aftermath of tears. 'I didn't know what to do,' said her sister, 'she just kept crying, so I phoned Mammy…'

'I could hit you,' Mammy said, her lips pale with rage as she stirred two sugars into Lily's cup of tea. 'I could hit you. I never thought I would feel like I could hit you, Lily. Have you no shame? You are a mother now. Your child is all that matters. Have you no shame?'

Cara cut her teeth early, and bit her until she bled. She was only a few months old when she started to beat Eileen while she fed. She had a small wooden rattle. She hit Eileen's breast bone harder and harder until she was bruised.

And why did Lily think the next child would be different? It was Liam called her Freya – 'flower' – because she came out so pretty. He didn't run away like he did when Cara was born. But Freya took more than love from Lily. After the birth, Lily's hair came out. It fell away in her hand. And she couldn't shake the weight. She was fat for years after, and her hair wasn't right for months. Freya tried to sap the youth from Lily. She tried to take her beauty. They were hard, those years. And then when Liam died, there seemed no point to the children at all.

56

'BUT AOIFE, WHY DO you need me here?'

'So that you're up to speed, Sinéad. Mammy made us *both* executors you know, we both have to take power of attorney.' Aoife can feel her lips thinning to her teeth. 'Why should I have to handle all of this all on my own?'

She rings the square bell with 'Dunlin Solicitors' written in faded blue fountain pen behind a strip of plastic. As they stand there looking at the varnished door, Aoife feels the moment shift a little and settle over itself; a déjà vu.

The young man who opens it doesn't resemble Davitt. He is fat in the way that makes men look like giant schoolboys. Expensive clothing and an unruly crop of russet hair.

'Hi!' he says, leaning forward to shake Aoife's hand. 'You are...?'

'Aoife.' The hand is clammy, and Aoife has to resist the urge to take out a handwipe and clean his touch off her.

'Aoife. Hi. I'm Derek. You must be Sinéad, is it? Come on up.'

As he mounts the stairs he twists his head back, talking to them. 'Dad couldn't be here, I'm afraid—' Aoife hears something clog behind his nose and for a horrifying moment she thinks he's going to cry. She looks back at Sinéad, who is struggling red-faced up the steps.

'Yes, how is he?' says Aoife in a manner cool enough, she hopes, to deter any intimacy.

'He's... We'll see. He's very tired. He said to tell you sorry he couldn't come but he has all the information for you. I have everything you need to know. It's strictly confidential, now. I'm the only one handling it. Hang on now till we sit down and we can go through it.'

At the top of the stairs, there are three glass-panelled doors, all with 'Dunlin & Son' in white appliqué. He pulls a key from his pocket and unlocks one of the doors.

The room is extremely bare. A new-looking green carpet, a big, cheap table and two sixties-style wooden chairs with tweed seats and dainty legs. They are standing far away from the table, facing each other. There is a small, slightly contracted water bottle on the table, its plastic fogged white.

'Hang on now 'til I get the files. I'll be back in a second.'

Sinéad pulls a chair up to the table, drapes her coat over it, and sits with her gloves on her lap and her hands folded neatly over them. Alone in the room with her, Aoife feels the need to say something, but what? She stands by the window looking down at the cold street, the rush of cars going by.

Soon Derek struggles in with another chair and two big box files. He is sweating. She saw from his email that he's only a legal secretary. Didn't make the Bar, so. Poor Davitt must be terribly embarrassed.

'Right,' he says, sitting down and locking his fingers together. 'So, Dad asked me to explain to you that your mother made yet another will…'

'She *what*?' Aoife looks at Sinéad for support, but Sinéad just blinks back at her.

'He says he had to witness it, you know, because she asked him to, but listen, he wants me to tell you it makes no difference anyway. He knows you're worried about your nieces being irresponsible and all that, so he made sure there was provision there for you to work with. And that money arrived through just this morning, so I'm going to distribute it the way you arranged with him and there are no immediate tax implications but you might want to get a good accountant on it for the next lot.'

'What's this new will?'

'He says there's something left to her grandson. Does that make sense?'

'Great-grandson, maybe,' says Sinéad.

'That's right. But listen, you are still the executors and – he explained this to me – it's left to the child himself, not to the custodian. He was careful to do that, so actually, you can sort of entrust it to anyone you like, within reason…'

'Ha!' A little chirrup runs up Aoife's back.

'But they'd have to keep it for him, wouldn't they?' Sinéad says.

'Not really. I mean, they could spend it once they could justify it. You'd want them to keep it, is that it?'

Aoife shrugs. 'Not necessarily.'

He takes a sheet of paper with tiny writing on it, and turns it around so that Aoife and Sinéad can read it. 'So here is a list of all the things it could be used for. They could buy a house with it, for example, if the child was to stay there sometimes. They could take a holiday if they brought the child with them. They could use it for legal fees… There's a whole load of provisions in there. In any case there won't be much left, will there?'

'No,' says Sinéad, and she chews the inside of her cheek.

'Not with the cost of care,' says Aoife, 'and, you know, the money Mammy owes people. She wants things to be fair. You're sending that through today did you say?'

'Yes, I just wanted to double-check with you…'

'And then we can take power of attorney?'

'Yes – Dad says once Mrs Kearney has signed all those papers, and those funds are in order, we can make power of attorney effective then, and after that it's officially in your hands what you do with the rest of it, but you know, a paper trail has to show it was used for her benefit… within reason, you know.'

'Well, I know who we will entrust it to, do you Sinéad?'

'Us?'

'The father. The boy's father and Eileen together. Ha.'

57

POINTED BUDS, GLASSY AS boiled sugar, scratch weakly at the bedroom window. Sinéad wakes to the shriek of the wind, like the cry of a banshee.

Was she asleep? It's hardly even a dream she's been having. It's only a vague memory – the smells and the tastes of Mrs Brereton's house: boiling potatoes, that big drooling dog, the oily, scalpish dust of the cloakroom, salted porridge.

When Mammy was in hospital having Lily, she and Aoife were sent next door to Mrs Brereton's for a few days. Mrs Brereton made her porridge with milk and salt and it had a flabby skin on the top. It so shocked Sinéad's palate that she gagged. Aoife spoke at her through her teeth, 'Eat it.' She raised the spoon again to her lips; it tasted like phlegm. In a moment of pure mercy, Aoife took Sinéad's bowl, swapping it for her own empty one, and ate the disgusting porridge for her.

There isn't much she remembers about those days. The garden, yes – picking peas and raspberries, planting bulbs. Her sister Aoife, that time by the shed, the pain in her face as she watched the slugs suffering in Lily's potion.

~

Sinéad folds the blanket under her feet. Where is that cold air coming from? And how can Terence sleep through it?

She wants to wake Terence – she wants him to know about the porridge that time, about the good things in Aoife.

She wants her big sister, suddenly – her certainty, her pragmatism. But it's the Aoife of their girlhood that she wants, not this new, cold woman, all quiet rage. The morning after Sinéad's hysterectomy, Aoife arrived to the hospital room, ears red and her eyes watering. They wouldn't let her in with flowers, she said. They had made her leave them at the nurses' station.

Sinéad is fond of flowers, but only in the earth. As a child, she loved the daffodils in the Breretons' next door; how they spread silently in the dark of winter, re-emerging higgledy-piggledy spring after spring, and the way they withered in the autumn, the slimy brown stems bending willingly to earth.

'I didn't scrimp on them either,' Aoife said, 'only to be ordered by some little madam to leave them outside!'

This was because of the pollen, of course, but at the time Sinéad, in the haze of anaesthetic and painkillers and the possibility, however vague and sanitised, of death, assumed that flowers were banned out of a kind of discretion. A bunch of cut flowers seemed an insensitive thing to place beside people like her, struggling to stave off their own decline, having bits of themselves removed and supplemented, bandaged and consoled. Flowers, with their inevitable wilting, sitting by the beds in plastic paper and plastic vases, fed by water and chemical food sucked up through the wounds in their stems, would make a mockery of all these efforts at health.

'Really, Aoife, I'm just glad you're here. I don't need flowers…'

Aoife's rage was too much for Sinéad. 'I'm very tired, Aoife. I need to sleep now…' And yet she had been filled with loneliness and disappointment when her sister finally left her bedside. They had agreed not to tell Mammy about the procedure – it might worry her. But Sinéad was not ready to be this grown up. Her sister's presence had made her crave the intimacy of her own flesh, and as that night in the hospital wore on, the absence deepened it into an raw ache.

The part they had pulled out was a place in herself that she had never seen. But the surgeon had looked at it, touched it, snipped it loose and – what? Passed it to a nurse, probably. And what did they do with her womb then? She saw a film once about the Magdalene laundries, where the nuns fed afterbirth to the pigs. But that's different, of course.

She hasn't really slept for days now. There's a natter in her head, something tapping at her, on and on – something that won't let her rest.

Terence came home yesterday. As he came through arrivals he looked so like his father – a crusty old man with nostril hair and ear hair and tufts of facial hair on his cheekbones, 'buggers' handles', he calls them. He kissed her beside her mouth, his breath slightly bad.

'Every morning she writes "do not resuscitate" on her chest,' he said. 'Poor Aunt Toots. I think that's it. I don't think I'll ever see her alive again.'

His body in the bed disturbs her – he sucks up the air, he snores, his skin secretes a grimy substance into the sheets. He was handsome once. Now that he is like this, who would choose him as a lover? In sleep he tries to reach for her – to reach for someone – and his touch only makes her feel more keenly the big lonely shape of herself.

She shifts away from him and lies on her back at the edge of the bed, looking up through the dark at the ceiling, a huge flake of paint sagging loose like a discarded chrysalis.

No, it's not Terence that's bothering her.

Davitt Dunlin is dead.

It was Aoife who rang her with the news. Is it since then she's had this feeling like a clock in her bones, bubbles in her veins, butterflies in her fingers? Perhaps it's her thyroid acting up.

The funeral is on Saturday.

Mammy always liked the Dunlins; she liked that they were family friends. And she liked it when Aoife married a solicitor. It used to make Sinéad bristle to hear her refrain, 'It's good to have a solicitor in the family.' But she was right. When the HSE woman came snooping, it was very lucky there was Brendan to know what to do, and it was a blessing that Davitt had their backs.

Now the HSE lady will have to give up. If she rings again, Sinéad will say, 'Davitt Dunlin is dead. Leave us alone.'

When she got the call from that Bernie woman, back in the autumn, Sinéad stayed on the phone to her longer than she should have. Sinéad thought she was lying at first. Aoife hadn't told her about the nanny cam. Davitt put it in perspective: 'Forget about the camera business,' he said. 'Don't put another one in but don't try to defend it and if they ask, say it's gone. Say as little as possible. About the house sale, tell them you don't know what they're talking about. Freya has made it up, tell them. They'll need all kinds of paperwork before they can actually insist you furnish them with any proof. Keep refusing and they won't have the funding to keep at you.'

Davitt was alive then, saying that, and now he is dead. His liver was already cancerous then, and chemo had reduced his hair to fluff, and he was trying to stay alive. Did he know, then, that he'd be dead before Mammy?

Sinéad is not used to lying, but by the time they met with the HSE woman she was prepared. The words ran out as easy as a rhyme, and it made her feel loosened from some foolish thing, soaring in a space where her words made the world. 'Property? A house, where?' she said, her heart rustling up her throat like something startled. 'I can't help you there... ah, it's my niece who said all this, no doubt. She's never been right. She was a teen mother, had my mother's heart broken...' And her big sister had another tactic; a stroke of genius and the kind of thing Sinéad would never have thought of – she threatened to sue. It made Sinéad grin with solidarity as Aoife played the woman at her own game. She said her mother was terribly upset at being visited by a stranger and asked all sorts of stressful questions. She said her mother hadn't been the same since; they were worried that the stress would kill her. If it happened again, they were going to sue the HSE, she said, the social worker would lose her job. *You are mistaken if you think you can walk all over us…* and Sinéad rejoiced when Aoife came out with the one that used to make them all cringe and laugh at her. *My husband is a solicitor.*

No, it's not just Davitt's death and the encroaching death of Terence's Aunt Toots, of Mammy, of them all, that makes her rush around all day, avoiding silences, flinching from her face in the mirror. When she wakes at night it's with a terrible thought.

Sinéad pulls the cover off herself. Her belly looks so foolish – a wonky mound under this nightdress. There's a bitter cold rushing up from the floorboards. The walls are damp, bleeding dirty water like a cold sweat. She pulls on her socks and a big itchy jumper. She'll go and sit in the morning room with her daddy's paintings. She'll take a whiskey in and sit with them.

Twenty-two of her father's paintings are down here, leaning against the mouldy walls and the dust-sheeted furniture. They should be somewhere drier, but at least they are safe from the grubby paws of her nieces. She and Aoife will split them. Perhaps she should feel guilt about that?

Sinéad pulls the oilcloth off the couch. She folds her feet under herself, pulls her arms into her jumper, takes a sip of her drink. It is warming. It is a relief.

The day Cara came to Eileen's, rubbing her big belly, sprigs of black hair escaping from her ponytail, Sinéad felt the real badness of herself. She was jealous. That was it. How is it that her niece has gone on having children? How is it that her skin glowed that day with all the life it had, and her hair so wild it couldn't be tied up? And she sat there so pleased with herself, so self-serious, so high-and-mighty it made Sinéad feel nauseous. 'I'm leaving,' she kept saying. Boundaries. That generation are all about their boundaries.

She couldn't have wanted to punch her niece, could she? Right in the belly. She wanted to pull her hair, slap her. She took delight in the way her face turned red and she muttered as Aoife spoke to her, the way she shrank when Eileen touched her hand.

The memory of that soothes her. If she's wrong, it's only a little crime. That girl has more than she deserves in life. So what if she and Aoife are taking matters into their own hands? So what? Those two have taken more than their share of Mammy.

It's only at night, only in the silence, that the thought comes creeping into her – they have done the wrong thing.

She has done a wrong thing, yes; a little wrong thing, but she can't regret it. Those girls will be fine; they might even find it a blessing, a kind of tonic, to be released from the shadow of inheritance. The tapping will go away, the nagging feeling like something caught in her tooth, the shriek of the wind coming in through all the crevices of this old house.

58

A WIDE-SET GIRL, NOT much older than Freya, moves in behind the nurse's desk. She puts both hands flat on the desk. A thick, llama-long neck slings low between the shoulders as she raises her face to Freya's.

'Sorry. Were you waiting long?'

'A while. Half an hour.'

Freya left Grandma sitting alone in the Recreation Room, slowly patting her hair, repeating, 'The state of me,' and, 'Wouldn't you be ashamed'. Beside her, a tiny, very white woman in a black pillbox hat was muttering the Rosary, moving pink plastic beads fervently through her fingers.

The girl nods. Her tongue moves over her teeth. 'What can I do for you?' Freya isn't sure whether the disapproval is meant for her, or whoever should have been at the desk.

'I'm Molly Kearney's granddaughter – room twenty-six. She was hoping to get her hair done. Could you tell me when the hairdressers will be open?'

Grandma used to have her hair washed and set weekly in big, soft bubble curls and a blue rinse. But so far, Freya has never seen the 'in-house salon' open. It's a room off the entrance lobby, with a glass front. Inside, it looks like a playset a child might have; all bright plastic chairs and lightbulbs around the mirrors.

'The girl comes in on a Tuesday. She'll have to make an appointment.'

'Can I make it for her?'

'Room twenty-six, is it?'

'Yes. Molly Kearney.'

The nurse turns slowly, pulls open a filing cabinet and marches her fingers along the files. She pulls out a clear plastic folder and opens it on the desk.

'Here we are,' she says. 'Molly Kearney. Now, let me see… right, what's your name?'

'Freya. Kearney.'

'I have the executors down here as Aoife O'Carroll and Sinéad Sheriden. They are also the billing names… so you'll need to ask them to make an appointment for her, I'm afraid.'

'I can pay for her now, maybe? I could just pay now and make the appointment…'

'It doesn't work that way, I'm afraid.'

Grandma is still sitting in that chair. She is slowly knitting an uneven strip from acrylic yarn, tomato-red. It makes tiny teeth-screeching squeaks with every stitch. Where did Grandma get that? She always said she hated knitting with acrylic. She chose spun cotton for jumpers, lambswool for socks. She used to take Freya with her to Clery's to root through the bargain barrels.

'Well, Grandma,' says Freya, pulling up a plastic stool and sitting close beside her, 'we'll have to wait for Aoife or Sinéad to make the appointment, but I'm sure they can sort it out.'

Grandma looks up at her, open bewilderment on her face. Then her mouth closes sharply and she greets her as though they are strangers, or have had a falling out.

'Hello.' She nods, pursing her lips.

'Hi, Grandma. It's Freya.'

'Oh, Freya. It is very nice of you to come and see me here.'

'How are you, Grandma?'

She sighs, 'Well, they tell me nothing. I have given up asking because they tell me nothing. I have to wait now. It's all I can do.' Then her face softens, and for a moment she recognises her granddaughter. 'Freya. My Freyalín! Do you have a baby yet, Freya?'

'Yes Grandma. A little boy, Jem...'

'Do you have a mirror?'

'No, Grandma.'

Grandma drops the knitting needles into her lap, brings both hands up to her head and lightly touches her hair. 'The state of me, Freya. Did you ever?'

The state of her, yes. Unpermed, Grandma's hair stands up straight off her head – each fine hair an electric filament of steel-cold grey. Beneath it, the scalp glows pink and hurt like the skin beneath a scab. The skull-shape that this reveals makes Grandma's death easy to conceive of – the eye sockets, the cranium; all the hard and calcium parts becoming more apparent as the flesh retires.

'You look lovely, Grandma.'

The woman in the hat shouts, 'HAIL Mary,' before trailing off into mutters again. She has two perfect circles of blusher on her cheeks.

Freya turns back to Grandma, who is still patting her head with the look of a shamed puppy.

Can this really be the place where all these stuttering lives should slow to a close?

In the space of three days, Grandma is visibly smaller. She seems paranoid, or dishonest, like an addict or an anorexic covering something up. Her face holds a harsh, ambiguous expression – a straight mouth and a frown and a vague jerk of the head that is neither a shake nor a nod.

She has let the knitting needles fall, and the ball of acrylic has rolled off the armchair, trailing a thin red line along the floor.

Freya bends to pick it up, winds it back and places the ball on Grandma's lap with the needles and the knitting.

'Will I put this away, Grandma?' But Grandma is staring into the distance, clucking and shaking her head.

'Okay, Grandma?'

'How could you lose him?'

'I… No, Grandma. He's fine. He's at school…'

'Stupid girl. Well, now what?'

'It's alright, Grandma…'

'That's all you can say… Ha.' She is smiling now, suddenly gleeful, as though she has scored a point. 'You weren't top of the class, were you? Until I left and then you came first and no one mentioned why it was and now you are going to university... Yes.'

Grandma begins to nod and smile and Freya doesn't know if the smile is bitter, or pleased.

'Yes. Well. Congratulations. Now listen, my granddaughter went to university. She brought me to see the library.' Grandma puts her thumb and forefinger together like someone tasting a good meal: 'Well,' she says, 'well, you have no idea – beautiful!' and she parts them like a kiss.

Grandma sighs now, a blubbery sigh because things are going all wrong in the workings of her body. Everything is swollen and shrivelling at the same time; everything is obstructed and untempered. She starts to drum her fingers slowly on the padded arm of the chair.

'Is it true what they tell me, that you have one man after another and none you can keep?'

'Who says that, Grandma?'

'Oh you know, Aoife was here. She says such funny things. But I don't listen. You know they are selling our house? I told you that, didn't I? I just hope Daddy doesn't go there to find me, and I am gone, that's all I hope. That's all.'

'Who sold it Grandma?'

'Well, I owe a big sum, you know. I have been a foolish old woman. People have been taking advantage of me.'

'Who?'

'That's what they said. Such a stupid old woman I have been. But there is time to put it right. Well, Freya, you should see all the papers I have to sign, but then it will all be done. They are very efficient at that, you know. It is a good thing to have a solicitor in the family...'

She looks suddenly at her palms, turns the hands over and studies the other side. She touches her face very lightly, then pats her hair, mouth lax. She rubs her forehead hard, and sighs.

'But you have a husband, Freya? It's not true what she says, that you have man after man and none you can keep?'

'No, Grandma, that's not true. Who said that?'

'Oh, you know, she can be a funny one, my Fifi. She can be jealous. But you know I had no milk for her. There was a knot in the cord. You should have seen her back when she was born, roundy like a little pink piggy, and the nurse – oh, big as a tank – she says, "Has your mammy been starving you?" and she meant to be kind but I still remember her voice Freya, a voice can get you like a punch, and the other nurse put her fist in my belly, in a hurry like, to push the afterbirth out, and her face a sort of revenge in it, but why? And the kinder one, colossal yoke of a woman, telling her "I'm watching you – easy, Nan!," and then looking again at the baby – well, Cara, a squeal out of it like I'd never heard. "Poor little thing," said the nurse, "has your mammy been starving you?" The cord was knotted and the milk didn't come then because I knew he was gone and I was cold. "A beautiful baby girl," said the nurse, "and you crying there over a child that's lost," and the other one nodded and gave me a look I'll never forget, ready to spit, like, and she says, "Sinful." I wasn't the first mother in the whole world to lose a child. But where did I get her from? So you are married, Freya? And you will have children? And you are happy, darling, are you?'

'Yes, Grandma.'

'You can't leave where you're needed and expect life to go rosy.'

'Leave where, Grandma?'

'Mam's chest was bad, and we would boil the linseeds up in a big pot. We would boil it and boil it and then we would dip cloths in the stuff – a very dirty black syrup it made, you know the stuff – very dirty… My sister sent me a cold letter then, when Mam died. Very cold. And she was right, she was right… my sister Kat, after all she did for us all and for Ireland.'

Grandma rubs her forehead too hard, so hard Freya flinches, worried that she will scrape away the thin sheen of skin protecting her skull. She takes Grandma's hand away from her head. The fingers are tense and hooked into their task, but she concedes. Freya puts her palm to Grandma's palm, but she can't make the hand unbend. There is a blackish-green stain peeping from under Grandma's ring. She scratches her finger and pulls weakly at the band. 'This stupid thing!'

'Maybe we should take that off, Grandma?'

'But we are too tough on my Fee, you know,' she says. 'Daddy always says. He says there is something in that girl that is hard to see. You know they were walking back from school. Raining and raining. Cats and dogs. And suddenly doesn't Daddy notice he is walking alone. He looks back and there he sees Fifi, facing the rain with her mouth open, and when she looked at him she was smiling. "Come on now, Aoife, we're getting wet," he says.'

Freya checks her phone. She has been here for two hours. That must be enough time. Grandma is drifting in and out of sleep with a rumbling, unsteady snore that sounds like she is drowning. Her head is cocked back and her mouth is open. She must be comfortable enough if she can sleep. But just as Freya rises to go, Grandma snorts and winces, frowns and shakes her head as though there is a pain somewhere she can't locate. Her eyes snap open, round with knowledge, then narrow with shame.

'I'm sorry,' she says. 'Sorry, darling. Am I a terrible old woman? Tell me, chicken. Am I tootle-loo-loola?'

'No,' says Freya, and laughs heartily for no reason at all except that she thinks it might make Grandma happy. 'No, Grandma, you're not tootle-loo-loola!'

'You are kind. Wouldn't you be ashamed?'

'Grandma, do you know I saw some snowdrops this morning? I thought it was early for snowdrops. They're beautiful, snowdrops, aren't they...'

'You know what Mrs Breteton said, when I told her about him? She said there's more to that, Molly. A child doesn't choke so easy. He had walking pneumonia, or something. When Aoife came I couldn't speak to her. I couldn't speak. It was like that choking on and on, like it was there all the time, happening. Still happening and there was nothing I could do. Too late. Daddy was in his studio all day, and I was in that little house with her and when the lodgers went out I was silent. Not a word. Not a smile – could it be I didn't even smile?'

'That must have been a very hard time, Grandma. I'm sure you were better than you think.'

'No.'

'Well, I'm sure Aunty Aoife doesn't even remember...'

'Children know.'

Grandma jerks her hand away from Freya. She plucks at the ball of crunchy, tangled acrylic.

'You know we buried him, but there was a feeling that went on, like everything was a dream; nothing was real and nothing mattered. Not really.'

'Well... it can be very tiring, can't it? And on your own. Do you remember how you minded me, after Jem was born? Bone broth, you used to make me bone broth all the time.'

'And it wasn't that I wanted to frighten little Lily. It's only that I wanted to see if I cared. She was screaming crying, you know how a baby can, wanting to be picked up. And I had the other two in the bath and Daddy's dinner on the stove. It was only for a moment, long enough to know I would never do such a thing. Did I really do that?'

'I think you are better than you remember, Grandma.'

'I took the pillow away, you know, as soon as I heard the silence from her. Her eyes were like his. Panic. But still, did I feel anything, I wonder? Would I have cared?'

'Oh.'

'My handbag.' Grandma pats around herself – the armrest, the seat – and roots her handbag out from under her hip.

'There it is, Grandma. Will we go back to your room? Will you let me help you?'

'That's it now. That's it now.'

She pulls the handbag onto her lap, strokes it like a pet and unzips it with her lips pursed. She pulls out a folded sheet of paper. 'Now read this for me, Freya, will you? And keep it safe for me then.'

'Okay.'

Freya unfolds the paper.

This is the last will and testament of Molly Kearney of Belarmine Assisted Living in the City of Dublin. I hereby revoke all previous wills and testamentary dispositions made by me. I appoint my daughters Aoife and Sinéad as executors of this will and direct them to pay my just debts, funeral and testamentary expenses.

To my granddaughter Cara, I leave all the paintings remaining in my husband's studio.

All the residue and remainder of my property of any nature and description and wherever situated, I leave to my great-great grandson, Jem.

Dated 20th December 2018

Signed

Molly Kearney

Signed by the testator as and for her last will and testament in the presence of us, both present at the same time, and signed by us in the presence of the testator

Davitt Dunlin

Leanne Keough

'Now,' says Grandma, and she nods, winks, nods again, 'you keep that safe.'

'Do you want to go to your room, Grandma?'

Grandma lifts her hands. She brings her thumbs towards her fingers, pinching the air. 'I can't hold anything, Freya. I can't hold anything anymore.'

Freya takes the hands, draws them together, kisses them.

'Tell me this,' says Grandma, tugging her hands free, 'tell me this now… did I do that? Did I really?'

But she has fallen back asleep, each hand landing on an arm-rest, head back, mouth open. Freya kisses her cheek and rubs her hand uselessly. She picks up the rough woollen blanket from where it has slumped at her feet, puts it over her knees and tucks it snugly around her. It is already warm in here – too warm – but what other gesture of love can she offer?

59

FRUIT OF THY… FRUIT *of thy… pray for us now and in the hour…* That's all you could hear, all the way to the street; the murmur of private rosaries, the clean slide and clack of the beads. As soon as the word flew out that old Mags Breen was dying, the wake was started right there in her front room just like that. Everyone from the street was in, filling up the little house. Sometimes the whisper-prayers all fell in together, and then it was the hissing parts you heard, the *trespasses, trespass, trespass against,* like steam over the bowed heads. The women took turns sitting with her, and old Mags sent down for anyone she wanted to talk to.

Molly and her friend Jackie hung about the feet and got given bits of bread with jam. They weren't expected to say the Rosary. Someone tied a rope up for them on the lamppost outside Mag's front door, and they took turns swinging on it.

Probably no one sent word up about two little Ard Rhí girls wanting to see Mags, and if they had, maybe Mags wouldn't have known them from any of the other Cow Town children. But the thing is, they had something important to tell Mags, some message she needed to bring into death for them... Molly can't remember what it was now. But old Mags sent down for Molly's sister, Kat, who had to be fetched from Viking Road, where she was helping the seamstress sisters. She was called up and sat a long time with old Mags. It was a great thing to be called up to the bedside, for old Mags was the grande dame of the whole of Cow Town. Everyone thought Kat was a great girl, and their brother Mick too, and Molly's dada. A Black and Tan threw Kat against the wall when she was only three years old and everyone thought she was a great girl on account of she got back up, her hand to her bleeding head, and said, 'Bad man.' But Molly was born after, so she missed all that terrible business. For a time, Dada kept a gun up the chimney, which Molly was allowed to clean with Vaseline, but he got rid of that after Mam cried about it one night.

'Tell me this and tell me no more...'

'Yes, Grandma? Tell you what?'

'What was that message, tell me?'

PART 4

60

WHEN MEGAN IN THE hospital choking with her tongue it beed not like this. It beed fast and blinking bright.

This hospital is no colours. School assembly hall. Strangers' farts. There a secret going on here. She can feel it in her neck.

'Cawy me, Daddy.'

Megan know it be a tonne weight for daddy to be carrying her and also baby Peggy but she does whinge and whinge acause she needs to be carried this day.

They be going to say bye bye to Mimi.

That meaned Daddy won the discussing, acause in the night Den did be crying and saying she want to see Mimi. Mammy say, 'No, Den. You don't want to see her like that…' but then Mammy and Daddy were discussing.

Megan sayed it very whispering: 'I have to tell somefing to Mimi' but they didn't be hearing her.

Mammy think Megan don't be knowing how it is. Den telled her and anyway she knowed already. All the bits of Mimi do be flying off like she be maked of birds. All her words be going and all her pictures and she be nearly all gone now but Megan haves to tell her.

When they be getting out of the car she thinked maybe Mimi is not being here. She be all flewn away maybe. Den has a face like she think so too.

They find the room in the hospital and that take a long time. When Daddy open the door, Megan bees very sleepy, so sleepy like she can't even see and she can't walk, and she put her face in Daddy's shirt.

Aunty Freya be there and Jem and they not saying Hi.

It is Mimi in the bed. That's what Daddy say, and DenDen say no and holds Daddy's leg and he can't walk anymore so Megan lets him put her on the floor and now she can stand and she can walk.

There bees a lie here. Some of Mimi be flewn away and in the bed is bits of her left. She know DenDen be scared even if she be a big girl and Megan not be scared at all. It be not very Mimi in the bed, but she go up quickly aside Freya and Jem and she stretch up at the hand that Aunty Freya be holding and there bees a smell like Mimi's house and very quickly, on the big big thumb, she tells a kiss.

61

ON THE WALL A flimsy clock ticks audibly and too slowly; a red hand trembling with the effort of each second. There is a dead, deep-bellied television fixed to the wall, but no sign anywhere of a remote control to switch it on with.

All windy night the roof of Aoife's well-built house whimpered like grieving puppies, and this morning there were long, deep scratches like claw marks on the Audi. She's not superstitious. It's not that. But she knows it will be today. It can't go on.

Cara is sitting there opening an avocado. She raises her head, breathes, 'Hi,' as Sinéad nods, dipping as though to hide herself in the greyness of the room. She sits a few seats up from their niece, rubs her palms slowly on her thighs. The gesture enrages Aoife. There are things she'd like to say to Sinéad, *buck up, cop on…*

Their niece is using a white disposable knife with a serrated blade, an ineffectual looking thing, so it surprises Sinéad to see the avocado shell split into two papery bowls of lurid flesh.

She places one half – the half with the stone in it – on the empty seat beside her. Sinéad notices a straggle of root starting at the base of the stone. You have to stick toothpicks in them, or something, and tripod them over water, to make them grow. Something like that. Sinéad has tried growing things from fruit pits. Once an apple seed sprouted a frail white shoot, but it rotted before it came to much.

The room they are sitting in comprises many shades of brown-grey plastics. A strip of tinted glass looks out onto the breezeblock wall outside. It reminds Sinéad of another room – the same kind of cold and the same ruthless hygiene – yes, somewhere buried in her memory she has been here before, in a room like this one with odourless air and seats that make a knot on each knuckle of her bottom, waiting with the sanitised surfaces for something to be given or taken away.

They are only waiting now. There is nothing else left to happen. Mammy's every breath could be the last. It's been this way for days, so by now time is stretched out; every beat another painful distance to be crossed.

How can Cara sit so easy like that, with Mammy dying in the next room? So easy that she can chew and swallow, her knees parted like a man's, rubbing her swollen womb proudly over and over with one hand, spooning the interior of the fruit into herself with the other, and around her face the unruly hair dark and wiry as a pubic mound.

Can't she feel Sinéad watching her? She pulls a hair out through her lips – a long, kinked thing wet with her mouth's contents. She lays it on her knee, and continues to eat. Then she inserts the next half of the avocado into the empty shell of its twin, and picks at the slimy stone to loosen it. She takes it out and places it in an empty paper coffee cup by her feet, parting her legs even more in the effort of bending herself.

Across the room, Aoife's face is twisting the way it does when she is angry or self-conscious; her tongue thrusting a lump in her jaw, as though searching food out from between her lower teeth. She is clutching her phone, glancing impatiently at the screen.

Aoife can't look directly at her niece, but there is something satisfying about Cara sitting there alone without her children, or her man, or her willowy little sister to bolster her up. She is exposed now amongst empty seats, nothing to conceal the awkward shape of her pregnant body; nipples and navel pushing shamelessly through the pilled cotton jumper like silly buttons. Her movements are deliberate, as though she knows she is being watched.

Ha! Aoife can see it from here – a little patch of horrid brown rot in the concave where the avocado stone was. Ha! Serves her right; sitting there, brazen as you like, scoffing her avocado. Organic or Fairtrade or whatever.

Cara folds the skins, squishing the remaining brown paste, and pushes them into the empty coffee cup. She raises herself up off the chair and slides it back, making the lino floor yelp. She moves with obvious effort to be quiet and subtle, but the clumsy bulk of her makes her ridiculous. She carries the paper cup with the discarded avocado bits to a bin outside the door.

It saddens Sinéad to see Aoife like this, her face ugly with fear and rage: pale eyes; sharp, quick pupils swivelling like the eyes of chickens. Her sister is staring at the door as though sheer outrage might pull Cara back into the waiting room, away from Mammy.

Aoife's phone beeps discreetly and she pulls herself tall, chin in her neck, and peers down her nose at the screen. Then she says victoriously, 'Valerie will be here soon!'

'Oh, good,' says Sinéad. 'Terence is on his way too.'

'Oh, good.' Aoife nods. Then, as an afterthought, 'It will be nice for Mammy to hear his voice.'

That's nonsense, of course. But it will be a comfort, perhaps, to have him here. He will be calm and appropriate and he will not feel too much. They have become that for one another; a comfort, a steady mooring.

Aoife is clutching the phone with both hands, waving it firmly like evidence.

'Valerie will be here in five,' she says, something like threat in her voice. 'She will bring us some coffee.'

Aoife removes her compact mirror slowly from her handbag – a great handbag with lots of compartments so that things don't get lost. Her father used to nod proudly at her fastidiousness,

'A place for everything and everything in its place...' She powders her nose to take the shine off. Her lipstick has disappeared, but the good-quality lipliner has stayed in place, framing the pale pleat of flesh as though in mockery. She takes her lipstick out of the special pouch, remembering how Mammy can be saddened by her blueish lips. 'My Fifi, look at your lips. Are you getting enough iron...?'

Aoife applies a thick layer of deep red paste and pats her lips with blotting paper. Then she applies another layer and blots it again, lightly this time. The blotting sheets don't really work, but she likes the smell of them – like talc and vanilla – and she likes the ritual. She replaces the compact in the inner zip and the lipstick in its pocket, lays her handbag on the seat and stands, stiff with the sterile cold of the room and the flimsy plastic seats. She wants to be near her sister. Sinéad is sitting with her hands on her lap, mouth closed and eyes flickering bewildered around the room. Aoife walks to the window and stands next to the chair where Sinéad is sitting.

She wants an excuse to go close to her sister. Things are fragmenting without her mother's ordering gaze. Things are sliding too quickly and they need to slow it down. Aoife is about to turn to Sinéad, to make some gesture – a hug perhaps, or just her wide hand over her sister's chubby one, a squeeze, or a pat on the arm – when at last Valerie enters with a gust of cool air, her scarf hanging long and her nose red with the outdoors. She is balancing a cardboard tray containing two takeaway cups.

Aoife clasps her hands together, dizzy with relief.

'There you are,' she says.

62

GRANDMA'S BODY IS FULL of liquid, the life forced into it through a glucose drip. She is propped at an angle but still there is a terrible flatness and weight, as though gravity has a special claim on her. Every slow breath shudders her ribs and sends sounds of drowning out through her lips. Her face is still, the skin drawn taut over her forehead and down her cheeks. One deep crinkle by her mouth bends and flutters and deepens when she inhales, betraying a great effort to heave up out of death and hold herself here.

Cara kisses Grandma's heavy hand. There's a purple hue under the overgrown cuticles, as though the pigments have lodged under her skin, soaked into her from all the years spent mixing colours like potions for Grandad's work. Her nails are glossy and thick. But Grandma is dying so there is no use in nails. And her eyelashes – why are they still there frilling her eyes? Why are they still dark and curled, and her brows still arched in a nod to beauty? Her skin smells like her, a smell like opening petals and browning butter, though there is no reason why that should be; it is so long since the hands have done the things that could fragrance them like that. It seems all wrong, this growing and scenting for nothing. Then it occurs to Cara that Grandma still has four of her teeth and that seems absurd, now. It seems like an insult.

She lays her head against Grandma's, and kisses her temple. Her hair smells like her pillow used to when Cara and Freya were allowed to sleep in her bed as children; a smell like soap and warm, new sweat. How? After months of nappies and disinfectant, how does she smell so suddenly like herself? There is no room on the bed to climb in with her. The metal bars press into Cara's keen belly and the foetus shifts – a foot under her rib, buttocks and thigh pushing up against her liquid-and-acid stomach where the avocado is curdling. Cara shuts her eyes into her grandmother's hair, and forces hot quiet tears to no relief.

'Grandma,' she says quietly, feeling stupid and phony and too tired for her own grief, 'Grandma...'

Grandma's head turns slightly and the eyelids flutter for a moment, showing a flash of white and overwhelming effort. Her mouth opens for a moment before she sinks back down on the bed and pulls a big breath in.

It feels foolish to speak, but it is the nearest they will ever be again to talking. What does Grandma want to hear from her? If sounds can be shaped to words in her mind – what is needed now, at this time?

'Grandma, everything is fine now,' Cara says, so quietly, in case the aunts come to the door and hear her, and sneer. 'Aoife and Sinéad and Mammy... they are all fine now. Mammy is better now. We all love each other…' and she is embarrassed before death and before Grandma; that her imagination stretches no further than this. That she can think of nothing else that could concern Grandma now but herself: 'And I am so happy. I have a wonderful husband and I will look after my little girls, Grandma. I have three little girls and another coming any day now and they are beautiful and I promise I will look after them. I cook them that soup you taught me – when we were little we called it Grandma's soup – do you remember? And Jem, Jem is a lovely boy and he is growing big and strong and he loves Grandma's soup. And I sieve it every time. Everything is fine now, Grandma. You have nothing to worry about. We are all fine now. We will all be fine now.'

Perhaps worry is the hook suspending Grandma here in life.

'Thank you for looking after us, Grandma.' Cara dismisses the cringing in her chest, the curling thing writhing and shrinking like a slug in salt.

'Grandma,' says Cara.

A nurse enters, irreverent in her busyness, followed by Aunt Sinéad, whose high brows and long forehead express a forlornness belonging to young mammals left alone. She is unsteady on her feet, clutching her side, and around her the space yawns as though unwilling to cradle the wobbly form of her. Then come Aoife and cousin Valerie, shuffling in unison.

Cara stands up and backs away from the bed a little.

'Hi, Valerie.'

'Hi, Cara.'

Aunt Aoife turns to the nurse. 'So you see,' she says, her voice deep, her words bending along strange vowels like a child trying to sound grown up, 'you see she seems to have a lot of liquid...'

'She seems a bit bubbly alright,' says the nurse. 'Too much water. That's all that is.' She marches efficiently towards the bag and locates a little tap beneath it. 'I'll turn it off.'

Aunt Sinéad flinches. 'But won't that... Doesn't she need it?' Then she glances at Aoife and puts her hand to her mouth as though trying to prevent herself from speaking

The nurse lowers her voice. 'We're not – we're not *letting her go* by turning off the water. You can always have it on again in a bit. There, you see. She's already more comfortable.'

Cara makes a weak gesture with the chair she was sitting on. 'Do you want to sit down, Sinéad?'

'No. I'm alright.'

'Aoife?'

'No.'

'She can probably hear you,' says the nurse, 'if you want to talk to her.'

The nurse's eyes flicker away from them, and Cara feels a fool suddenly, and she knows that Grandma cannot hear them. It is professional kindness to say such a thing, that's all. Aoife and Sinéad stand and look at Grandma, whose ageing has turned their faces into the same middle-aged lady – sagging cheeks, long neck, heavy, square chin. Aunt Sinéad clutches a bit of pink blanket at the end of the bed. Her eyes widen as though she is falling.

Grandma's breath comes drier now, no spittle at her lips, no drowning sounds.

'I have to get on,' says the nurse, looking at them softly each in turn and then, head to the side and the clipboard tight against her chest, she takes a moment to look at Grandma with an expression of bemused respect, as though gazing at a celebrated painting that she cannot draw meaning from.

Newborn babies, thinks Cara, all look the same to everyone but their mothers. It is the same with the old, the nearly-dead, only their mothers are long gone. It is up to their children to tell them apart, or to stop holding them apart – to let them die.

They stand around the bed. They wait in the silence between Grandma's exhalations and her next breath. Each one sounds like the last.

Aoife reapplies her lipstick, avoiding her own eyes in a small pocket mirror. Then she moves up towards Grandma's face, opposite Cara, and strokes Grandma's forehead firmly. 'It's Fee, Mammy, and Valerie is here too, Mammy. Valerie is here Mammy… Go over, Mammy.'

Then Valerie makes a sound like a muffled bark. There are grey mascara tracks down her whitened cheeks. Cara notices tears trickling on her own chin.

'You come over here, Valerie,' whispers Aunt Aoife. 'You come and sit by her head. Why should she be the one…?'

'Oh Mammy,' says Valerie, wiping her cheeks with the back of her hand: 'stop, Mammy.'

They grow bored of crying and tired of thinking of things to say. At last they all sit quietly in the room and listen to the difficult breath, the feet rushing past the door, the shrill throb of hospital machines in all the hospital rooms. They need a ritual, thinks Cara, a chant or something – a death song, or a death dance, something to release her.

Aunt Sinéad clutches hard at her side as though to trap a pain in her palm. 'Will we say a Rosary?'

'Do you want to sit down, Sinéad?'

'No thank you.'

The women begin to recite Hail Mary under their breath:

'Our Lady, full of grace, the Lord is with thee. Blessed art thou amongst women, and blessed is the fruit of thy womb…' The Rosary trails off.

Sinéad looks at the stubborn life grappling uselessly in her mother's old body. All of her parts seem cumbersome suddenly, bigger than they need to be, and sadly foolish. Soon she will be only those parts; she will be only matter. Sinéad will be next. Most likely she will be next. Then her sisters, then her nieces and then their children. Their children can't protect them from it. Even the foetus swelling up her niece's belly like a declaration against death – it will grow, perhaps, but it will die.

Valerie begins to smile. 'Grandma hasn't said the Rosary for over sixty years...'

Her grandmother's body, so heavy there under the covers, it could be putty all the way through. The arms lying on the sheet, the hands, the ears are all too dumb, like stage costumes up close, without the right light or the right set. Off stage and with no one there to play along, they are exposed for their composite parts – like nylon stitching, like cardboard corsets.

'Well,' says Valerie's mum. The rouge is sitting frankly on her cheeks, like a snide joke. Her hands clutch the bedrail. 'We might get her the last rites all the same... they say it helps people over all the same.'

There is a rap at the door but no one speaks. Then another timid rap and Sinéad reaches for the handle. A man dressed in an awkward navy suit enters in a dipping tip-toe. He says he is a Minister of the Eucharist. He apologises that there is no priest around.

'That's okay,' says Aoife, 'she wasn't very religious... isn't.'

The minister is long-necked with a carefully shaven gullet and glossy acne running down under his collar. He wears a lustrous blue tie. 'Ah, the poor dear,' he says. 'So you think it's the end, do you?'

'We don't know,' Cara says.

He looks at Cara's belly, where the baby is pressing down on her bladder, twisting a foot against her lungs.

'Ah.' The Minister of the Eucharist makes a circle in the air with two hands. 'The great circle of life here in this room… isn't that lovely?'

Aunt Aoife scoffs audibly. Valerie's cheeks flush.

'We don't know,' says Valerie. 'Mum called the whole family because they thought… but we don't know.'

'So you're all here with her. Well, isn't that lovely now?' The Minister of the Eucharist rolls his hands over one another.

'Well – most of us,' says Cara.

'Where's Freya?' asks Valerie. 'Is Eileen coming?'

'Freya's at work. I haven't been able to reach her. I messaged…'

The minister cocks his head the way the nurse did, and sighs.

'Ah the poor dear… Well, only The Lord God Our Father knows when he will receive us in his arms. I've given up guessing. For every one I get right, I get one wrong!'

Grandma exhales again, a big emptying from deep in her papery lungs. They wait for the next breath. The minister clasps his hands. 'But it seems like it, doesn't it?'

'We're okay now,' says Aunt Sinéad. 'I think we are okay now. We don't need the Eucharist…'

'Well, I can stay and just be with you so; there's no pressure.'

The next breath comes, pulling audibly into Grandma.

The minister stays. He makes small talk about economic recovery and the weather, lifting the intimacy with his intrusion. But then the women stop responding. He sighs loudly.

'So was she born in Dublin?'

'Yes,' says Aoife, 'she grew up in Stoneybatter. But my father was an artist – Dennis Kearney, the painter?'

'Oh yes. I know that name.'

'And they spent some time in London and in Paris, too.'

'Did they?' Cara never heard about Paris.

'Quite a life so.'

'Yes.'

'A full life so… Stoneybatter. What age is she now?'

'Nearly eighty-six.'

'My grandfather grew up in Stoneybatter. They had a lot of bother from the Black and Tans.'

'I think Mammy missed all that.'

'Terrible business… yip,' he says, more a suck of breath than an utterance. 'Ah dear. The poor old dear.' And as he sighs again, he takes Grandma's toe that is sticking out from under the sheets and wiggles it gently.

Cara glances at her cousin. Two little red poppies flower just under Valerie's eyes. She is biting her lip hard to keep from laughing. Cara smiles at her, and they both begin to giggle like girls.

'Valerie,' says Aoife, 'let's go down to the canteen for a cup of tea…'

Valerie looks at her mother. A shaft of light cuts across Aunt Aoife's face, catching the powder-thickened fur along her jaw.

'Okay,' says Valerie.

Aunt Sinéad looks up in alarm.

'I'll go with you…'

'I'll wait for the others then,' Cara says.

Aunt Aoife ignores her and waves her phone. 'I'll text the others,' she says, 'and tell them where to find us…' She picks up her handbag – a designer thing with a stiff handle and a clatter of flaps and zips – puts the phone carefully back in it and takes out her compact again. Just like Grandma, Aunt Aoife over-powders her nose, as though to blot it out of sight.

'Sometimes,' says the man, sleeking his tie with both hands, 'you know they say sometimes that we need to let them go.' Nobody responds. He sways back and forth on his heels.

63

SHAPELESS ACHE ONLY LIGHT and dark and sounds all a-jumble.

Things reveal themselves slowly, ringing clear like mystery unfolding but they are things she always knew; like Dinny's dimples, or the comfort of her mother's heavy housecoat at her cheek. Perching like restless butterflies; real for an instant and in a quiver gone. Her mother. Her mother's rough reassuring hands. The straight nails.

Yes, that's them; that's Mammy's hands. Dry, cracked hands and soft ones are real things, yes. The fullness of them there but passing now like smells.

A light silvery thimble.

A tadpole once with legs like a beautiful monster and a tin bucket with rust and a special clang.

The cigarette smoke of the woman giving birth in a bed beside, smoking and sweating and smiling as she introduced herself and Molly not afraid then but knowing the joy of the child that was to be delivered back to her from the grief in her own dark and bloody insides.

Yes.

Yes that happened. Yes. The whole moment is here. She has it; a whiff of them, the whole of it here and then not anymore.

The going is a feat impossible for going where and to what.

The stopping.

But it is painful, staying alive here pulling each breath in and letting it siphon out. It is a swollen and numbish thing and everywhere pain and an impossible effort like birth only she is the only one in it. An effort she cannot manage, to hold the things that are not anymore now, to hold here and not to stop but the stopping too is a feat that is heavy and sore and too new and there is nothing to distinguish the edges of herself for the pain is a blurring thing and the real things are passing over; such real and beautiful things without pictures.

Yes.

Yes that's it. That's it. That is a real thing the tadpole a real fat-bodied thing alive and real moving legs. Yes. Yes that happened. And the bucket. And the water.

A thimble to protect.

A charm, she can feel it in her mouth, the cool smooth pebble from the beach.

The painless space around her edges. A feeling like needing to vomit but without relief for it is needing to die.

Still more things to do and it is a joyish surprise too, and a disappointment to find with every breath that she has not stopped under the weight of it.

There is a man being pious. She can hear him, foolish. And a sister saying the Rosary, poor dear thing, such soft hands.

Dinny must be laughing at them but Molly cannot feel irritation now or anger. Dinny should be kind for they mean well and she should tell him that she doesn't mind. Let them at it; she doesn't mind. 'Let them to their comfort.' She wants to see Dinny for it has been so long since she has seen his face shaven so beautifully and his smile with dimples and that fine neck but he will understand that it is all this effort just to catch the sounds; that it is too much to look and see. Just to understand and catch the sound of them all here; that is enough. He will understand. And then the girls laughing – such a happy thing their young chuckles, her lovely girls who are good girls after all. Stubborn foolish little things that can stamp their feet and be cruel and jealous but good girls really.

There are others too.

They are telling her all is well.

Go on, Grandma, all is well.

A face by the bed, white fizzing around it and the eyes huge, black, melting down her face and – it couldn't be, could it? A gold crown and great pink wings rearing up over the shoulders. A clinking, jangling sound. The face comes close, so close to kiss her and it is too much effort.

The little one with the white hair.

The little boy.

Learning things Molly never could, all white and downy lovely little baby did your mammy not feed you? That's the little one. All is well they are telling her.

Dinny?

She is not making the words, is she?

Dinny?

Is she speaking? *Where is he, Dinny?*

Oh Dinny, you will mind him, won't you? For terrible things can happen no matter how beautiful he is, our baby, and no matter how we want him terrible things have happened in the world and can happen again. You will watch him and sieve the soup, Dinny?

Not a job for a man.

She cannot hear him now and she cannot make herself look. A sister with soft hands is murmuring prayers, '... blessed art thou amongst women, and blessed is the fruit of thy womb...' Bless the fruit, yes. Kind old thing with soft hands and a trembling behind her voice, a simmering in her for a life not lived, blessing the fruit oh yes yes that's it. Blessing the fruit for it can be a rotten thing too, needing to be dipped in vinegar and that is the thing to do is bless the fruit if you can. That is the loving thing. Thanks be to God in the highest and peace to his people on earth. Go on, Grandma, everything is okay now. Angel wings but very pink and tinselly a jingling jangling Christmas pony and cart.

Thanks be to God or the thing she knew when she prayed as a girl and felt the great pulse of the world with all the rot there is in it, and all the life that keeps coming on again and again from all the things that are burnt up and die and all the joy that comes again and again in spite of all the breaking, painful things there are, or out of them, like seedlings from the sore earth. All that is there.

The voices around her now in her little deathbed upstairs in her little house, the mothers muttering her on her way with the great love there is in them all, and the great sorrow. Another breath. Up here in her little deathbed. And down below her, down at the muck and the earth and stones and moving water, there are children playing by a stream. Three little girls and one of them only a baby, leaning in on the water like that and calling to her 'Come and look, Mammy! Come and look!' Oh her little boy is there too. What is it they are doing there by the water? Leaning too close. He is leaning in too close. They are making things sail – leaves and sticks and twine – and then shrieking with the miracle of weight and space and time as the things they make go spinning and twirling and sinking and bobbing and they are crying to her, 'Come and look, Mammy, come and look!' They need her to look, that's all. They need her to look and see it there and say Oh yes and say Janey Mack and say I see you, I see you my darlings, I see you. There you are.

It is only a case of releasing it. It is only a case of allowing it, of trusting that thing she knew once. The great whoop of the world going on.

64

GRANDMA'S HAND GROWS A fraction heavier. Freya waits for a last breath. She waits with something like dread or excitement or fear. She waits, and she is not sure when she will know it hasn't come. She puts two fingers to the too-weighty wrist. Jem looks at her as though it is up to her to decide whether it's true. She winces a nod; yes. It has happened. The silence is terrible.

Full of purpose, full of air and colour and the bustle of the world outside this room, The Lily is at the door.

Startled, Jem moves to the other side of Freya, away from the strange lady with the glossy mane. Freya pulls him onto her lap, but she is not afraid of her mother. She suddenly remembers that she's still in her fairy princess costume, and she wonders should she feel embarrassed. The Lily just nods at them both, a kind of resignation as she approaches the bed.

'Hello, Mammy.'

Freya's voice is stuck. It takes effort to speak. 'I think…' but her mother's face snaps up, a quick silencing glare. In a little-girl voice she says, 'It's me, Mammy. It's Lily. I've come…'

She bends and kisses Grandma's head, then takes a step back: a look of confusion, and then anger, indignation. A little trickle of terror begins in Freya's back. She hugs Jem, rocks him against her chest. But The Lily doesn't shriek or reach for her. 'She was waiting for me. She was waiting for her little Lily.'

Then she stands, looking down at Grandma, her hands dangling forlorn by her sides. Freya has never seen her so silent and still. She has never seen her face so lean.

A low, manly groan; long, steady, insistent; a sound like a night animal, a gravelly drain – it takes Freya a moment to realise it's coming from Grandma. There is judder in her chest and something yellow foams from her mouth. Freya can't move. She pulls Jem's face into her neck and he allows it.

The Lily's eyes are a little pink. She pulls some paper towelling from a dispenser and cleans up the bile with grim efficiency. Then she kisses Grandma's forehead, touches her shoulder.

'That's it,' she says. 'Don't people look so small when they are dead?'

Acknowledgements

My partner, Seán, has been tirelessly reading and editing this book for years. I can only say thank you – I know it is a better book for your irritating questions, tenacious criticisms, praise, suggestions and scrupulous readership, and for the courage and confidence you give me to go on and on, even during the times when I hate every word.

Thank you, Neil Belton, my publisher and editor, for your patience, encouragement and faith, for taking all my hesitations seriously and indulging my cold-feet moments. Christian Duck, Eleanor Rees, Florence Hare, Jessie Price – thank you for bearing with me and going above-and-beyond in last minute work and rework for this book!

Thank you, Lucy Luck, my agent, for the attention you have given this – not only for your advice, but for your uncompromising insistence on putting the book first and demanding that its needs are met.

About the author

ELSKE RAHILL grew up in Dublin and lives in Burgundy, France, with her partner and four children. She is the author of *Between Dog and Wolf* and the collection of short stories *In White Ink*, published by Head of Zeus and The Lilliput Press in 2017.